THE LAZARUS FACTOR

NICK CROW

COREY PRESS INC.

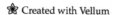

This book is dedicated to Dr. Sarah Tishkoff.

STAY UP TO DATE

Join the email list at:
https://www.nickcrowauthor.com/email-list

ABOUT THE LAZARUS FACTOR

A secret hidden in our genetic code will rewrite history as we know it...

Sara Morin, a brilliant computational biologist, makes a discovery that will fundamentally change our understanding of human evolution. But when she publishes her results, she ignites a firestorm she never expected.

Hunted by a ruthless assassin, Sara finds herself partnered with *New York Times* reporter Marcus Byron. Together they race across Europe, through Cathar castles, Aegean islands, and beyond. On the run, Sara must decipher a mysterious set of genome sequences.

As they begin to uncover answers, powerful forces turn their sights on Sara. If she can't decode the sequences in time, she'll end up dead—and the world will never know the shocking truth about the people who rule it.

CHAPTER 1
HARVARD UNIVERSITY

Cambridge, Massachusetts
12:05 PM, June 8th

———

With a click, the monk locked himself in the bathroom stall. He unslung his backpack and dropped it on the lid of the toilet. Leaning against the door, he closed his eyes, drew in a breath, and began to chant.

"Om mani padme hum…om mani padme hum…"

Words of generosity, wisdom, ethics, and perfection—Buddhism's eightfold path distilled into the fewest syllables.

Slowly, his muscles relaxed, and peace filled his mind. Only then did he open his eyes and unzip the backpack.

Inside glistened the upper and lower receivers of a Bushmaster XM-15 semi-automatic rifle. Carefully, he removed the two halves of the gun, connected them, and retrieved a thirty-round magazine. It snapped easily into the Bushmaster's magazine well.

He lifted the rifle to his shoulder and sighted down the

length of the barrel. He'd trained as a soldier before he became a monk, and he found the rifle simultaneously alien and familiar. While the materials and the mechanism were new to him, the method was the same: point and shoot. He knew he'd have no trouble using it effectively.

He centered himself again. "Om mani padme hum…om mani padme hum…"

He was here for a single purpose, and he needed to be focused. Yet a tiny part of him still hesitated. What he was about to do was not in any sutra or shastra. In fact, it was antithetical to nearly everything Buddha taught. But he was bound by duty, by obligation, by a deeply rooted sense of responsibility. This mission had received the abbot's blessing, and his brothers depended on him.

The monk slipped two additional magazines into his jacket pockets, then completed his preparation by pulling a black ski mask over his head. Leaving the backpack behind, he crossed from the restroom into the hallway. He walked quickly. He should have been raging with adrenaline, but he remained relaxed, steady.

His eyes locked on a sign above a doorway. He couldn't read the words, but he'd memorized their shape: *Fitzpatrick Lab*. Lifting the rifle to his shoulder, he burst through the door. Screams erupted as he scanned the room, but he tuned them out and muttered the mantra under his breath.

"Om mani padme hum…om mani padme hum…"

His gaze flicked to a group of young people a few feet away. Two men and a girl. Brown hair.

There she is. He aimed the rifle at the girl and pulled the trigger.

But even as she fell, he saw he'd erred. She wasn't the one. Her wrist was unblemished. His target had a small bird tattooed just above her right hand.

He continued to breathe slowly, his heart rate steady as he made his way deeper into the laboratory.

"Om mani padme hum…om mani padme hum…"

Then he saw her—frozen with terror by a lab bench, her hands raised in submission.

His finger flexed, and he fired three rounds into the center of her chest.

CHAPTER 2
HARVARD UNIVERSITY

Cambridge, Massachusetts
12 PM, May 27th

12 days earlier...

———

D r. Topher Fitzpatrick leaned back in his brand-new Herman-Miller Cosm chair. He couldn't decide if the chair was better than his old Aeron, but he'd charged it to the lab account, so either way, it wasn't as though he'd had to pay with his own money.

Did they have chairs like this in the Schröder Lab? He doubted it; Walter Schröder was a philistine. It was a wonder that the man had ever been admitted into the National Academy of Sciences as a foreign associate in the first place. He didn't belong there. *Topher* belonged there. This would be the year he finally got the letter of invitation. He was certain of it.

Topher closed his eyes and crossed his ankles, trying to relax, but his mind refused to cooperate. On his way into the office, he'd received a call from Sara, one of his graduate students, and she'd been in a tizzy about something she kept calling "genomic artifacts." Her agitation had, apparently, been contagious. Sara was brilliant, but he was going to have to temper her enthusiasm with the cool balm of rational thought. He would demonstrate how mature scientists operated.

He straightened his legs and leaned farther back in his fancy new chair. It was seriously comfortable. It was hard not to feel a little smug when he thought of his old classmates at Watford. They'd called him a "swot," pelted him with spitballs, wiped dog droppings on the back of his blazer. But then he'd been accepted to Oxford, went on to do his PhD at Stanford, and now, at the age of fifty-eight, he was a fully endowed professor at Harvard with a million-dollar house in walking distance from campus.

Most of his old schoolmates were probably on the dole.

A knock at his office door interrupted his thoughts. He sat up, quickly adjusting his glasses.

"Come in," he said brusquely.

Sara pushed through, gripping a laptop under her arm. Apart from her intensity, she reminded him of himself: brilliant, hardworking, and a wizard with computers. Petite with blue eyes, she wasn't bad to look at, either. Granted, it wouldn't kill her to tidy up her brown hair a bit and wear something other than black. For an instant, he imagined what she might look like naked, and he nearly smiled.

Behind her lumbered Arthur, one of his senior postdocs. "You asked to speak with us?" he said, interrupting Topher's thoughts.

"I have something important—" Sara cut in.

Topher lifted his hand, silencing her. She needed to learn her place. Professors dictated meeting agendas. "We'll get there, Sara."

He turned his attention to Arthur, who loomed over Sara.

He was at least six foot four, with a long face and blond hair, and looked like a cross between Fabio and a Viking warrior.

Of course he did. Every member of the Fitzpatrick Lab was required to have their entire genome sequenced and analyzed—an important step in identifying contamination in the lab's DNA sequencing pipeline—and Arthur, it turned out, had 81% Scandinavian ancestry. Nearly pure Viking, that one.

Unfortunately, he had been a disappointment as a postdoc. He'd accomplished almost nothing. No papers, no grants. The man had needed his hand held nearly every step of the way. Topher was desperate to move him out and make room for someone competent.

Topher leaned forward so his forearms rested on his desk. As he had no other chairs in his office, Sara and Arthur remained standing. The arrangement was intentional. It reminded everyone who was in charge. Sara was practically bouncing from one foot to another, clearly desperate to tell him about her discovery. That only made Topher more determined to delay her.

"Arthur. Let's begin with you," he said. "How is your work on the genetics of height in the Asian hunter-gather populations going?"

Sara's face fell.

Arthur straightened his shoulders. "Well, morphologically, they're really interesting. Some of the populations are extraordinarily small. The Jarawa people from the Andaman Islands off the coast of India have an average height of about four foot ten inches." He grinned, obviously pleased with himself.

Topher had to restrain himself to keep from yelling at his postdoc. That was all that Arthur had to say about the data? That the Jarawa were *small*? The Jarawa had been discovered more than two hundred years ago. There were hundreds of papers describing their short stature. You hardly needed a

PhD to break out a roll of measuring tape and work that one out.

Sara leaned forward. "Professor, if I could—"

"I'll get to your project in a moment," said Topher sharply, holding up a finger. "And the genetic analyses, Arthur? Have you identified any genes associated with height?"

Identifying genes was, after all, the entire point of being a geneticist.

Arthur's grin faded. "Sorry. I haven't turned up any significant hits."

"Did you try correcting for genetic relatedness?"

"Yes, but that just made everything less significant."

"Well, I suppose a null result was always a possibility for this study," Topher said, making his disappointment plain.

As Arthur looked at his hands, Topher finally turned to Sara. Her face had gone completely red, and she looked like she was ready to hurl her laptop at his head. He sighed inwardly. Women could be so emotional.

"Sara, how are the demographic analyses looking?" He made sure to speak slowly, still controlling the conversation. "Did you run a principal components analysis for the Andaman Island populations, as I asked?"

Sara flipped open her laptop and slid it sideways onto the desk so that both Arthur and Topher could see the screen. She clicked a few windows until it displayed a scatter plot. Topher was about to inspect the data when his gaze fell on her right hand. A week ago it had been unblemished, but now, on the underside of her wrist, was a small tattoo. Some sort of bird, by the look of it.

"What is that?"

Sara looked up, confused. "What?"

He pointed at the tattoo. "That."

"It's a tattoo."

"I know perfectly well it's a tattoo," said Topher, not bothering to hide his disapproval. "I want to know why you have one."

Sara's hand clenched into a fist. "I got it to honor my mom. She loved birdwatching."

He wanted to tell her that tattoos were unprofessional, that scientists didn't get frivolous remembrances, that hiring committees rejected candidates for far less, but he held back. HR hadn't been happy with him when he'd forgotten it was university policy to offer her bereavement leave. He didn't want the administration meddling with his lab again.

Gritting his teeth, he turned back to the laptop. "Show me what you've found."

Sara's fingers unclenched. She pointed to a cluster of points entirely separate from the others. "Okay, these are the Jarawa and Onge individuals of the Andaman Islands. The two populations share significant ancestry. However, I was hoping to tell you—"

Topher cut her off. "Can you at least show me the results for each individual's admixture proportions?"

Sara shook her head. "The algorithm is really slow. I don't think it will finish before next week. But—"

"So that's not complete, either," Topher said under his breath, but loudly enough that both Sara and Arthur could hear. "Well, assuming this PCA is correct, I'm not seeing any major red flags. Let me know when you have the analysis—"

"But that's not everything I found," Sara interrupted. She was speaking quickly now, apparently desperate to get this out. "I had some free time while the admixture analysis was running, so I decided to try to identify archaic regions in the genomes of these Andaman populations."

Topher tapped his pencil on the desk. "Why would you do that?" He hadn't asked her to look for ancient regions of the genome.

"Because some studies have shown that Asian hunter-gatherer populations have Denisovan ancestry."

Topher frowned. The Denisovans were an enigmatic group of extinct humans known from only a few tiny bone fragments. Nevertheless, scientists had extracted enough DNA from their remains to sequence a couple of Denisovan genomes, and, though he hated to admit it, there was evidence that they might have evolved in Asia.

"Go on," he said slowly.

"What's interesting about my analysis is how I did it," Sara continued. "I was able to identify the ancient genomic regions left by the Denisovans in the Andaman Island populations without the use of a Denisovan reference genome."

Topher's mind raced. A reference genome was one that had already been sequenced, and you needed it as a point of comparison when studying genomes. This was certainly unorthodox.

"And how, exactly, did you conduct this analysis?" he asked.

"Well, it's a bit complicated, but basically, I simulated a bunch of genomic data under a demographic model of Denisovan geneflow into the Andaman island populations. I used this data to train a neural network. Then I used the neural network to predict which bits of our genetic data were most likely of Denisovan origin."

"And with this approach, you were able to identify fragments of Denisovan genomes within the Andaman populations?"

"Yup," said Sara, grinning. "And then to verify that it worked, I matched the regions I identified with known Denisovan regions. They're 99% identical."

Topher smiled. This was actually brilliant. Already, he was envisioning a nice publication in *Nature Genetics* or maybe *PNAS*.

Next to Sara, Arthur crossed his arms. "What's so impressive about that? It's an interesting method, but it doesn't yield new data. There's already a sequenced Denisovan genome. This is just a different way of doing it."

"It's not the results that are interesting," said Sara. She was speaking *really* quickly now. "It's the methodology. I've shown that it's possible to characterize archaic genomes from a population of modern humans. And it gets weirder. I ran my software against the Rampasasa hunter-gatherer population from Indonesia. And do you know what I found?"

She waited, but neither Topher nor Arthur spoke, Topher because he didn't want to give her the satisfaction, and Arthur because he'd most likely completely lost the thread of the conversation.

Sara beamed as she delivered the kicker. "The Rampasasa genome contains fragments of another archaic hominid genome. Something new. Something no one has ever seen before."

CHAPTER 3
IBRAHIMI MOSQUE

Hebron, Palestine
7:15 PM, May 27th

———

The air conditioning in the security checkpoint was broken, and a droplet of sweat dripped from Ravid's eyebrow as he watched the elderly man ahead of him lift a small suitcase onto the steel examination table.

"Open your bag!" shouted the IDF officer in heavily accented Arabic. She wore a crisp olive green uniform, her hair was pulled back tightly, and she gripped an IWI X95 Tavor assault rifle. Her voice was as severe as her appearance.

Just on the other side of the checkpoint stood the Ibrahimi Mosque, a medieval building from the days of Saladin. Within the mosque rested the tombs of the founders of his people: Isaac, Rebecca, Sarah, even Abraham—the patriarch of Judaism, Islam, and Christianity. This was one of the most sacred places in the world.

As Ravid waited his turn to be berated by the IDF officer, he couldn't help but wonder exactly why he'd been sent on this mission. To steal something, of course—but what? What could be worth so much money? The mystery bothered him. Still, it wasn't his job to know everything.

He glanced back over his shoulder. Behind a pane of bulletproof glass, Hebron shimmered in the desert heat. This entire city was hot and dusty, much like Ramot. The difference was that Ramot was home, whereas this was enemy territory.

Hebron was in Palestine, the West Bank. Ravid was an Israeli.

"Next!" shouted the IDF officer.

Ravid drew in a short breath, steadying himself, but as he started forward, he nearly tripped. He cursed himself inwardly. IDF officers were trained to identify stress and anxiety. If he wasn't careful, he might be mistaken for a terrorist.

He was never this tense on a mission, but that just illustrated how much this operation had gotten into his head. In the twenty years he'd served as a Mossad agent, he'd seen a lot of crazy stuff. Had done some crazy stuff, too. But he'd never let emotion affect his performance. He'd always kept his shit together, all the way to retirement.

Accepting this assignment had been a mistake, that much was now clear. He should have stayed at home. If he'd simply said no, he could be relaxing in his garden, drinking a scotch and admiring his wife's perfect legs. But the job, strange as it was, had been too good to turn down. He'd been offered eighteen million shekels, a bit more than five million U.S. dollars, for a single day's work. At fifty-three, that kind of money would set him up for the rest of his life. He could buy a nice car, vacation in Corfu, visit his relatives in the USA.

But most of all, he could afford to pay for his mother's cancer treatments.

The doctors at the Sheba Medical Center in Tel HaShomer had told him she was too old for chemo. They'd suggested hospice. Heartless jerks. It was cheaper to let her die. But with this money, he could pay for custom immunotherapy. His Ima would spend a few more years with her family.

He inhaled again, and his muscles felt looser. This was just another mission. Everything was going to be fine. Assuming he could get through this checkpoint without acting as jumpy as a suicide bomber.

"Next!" shouted the officer again, her eyes turning to him.

Keep it together, he thought desperately as he unzipped his bag.

It was a gray duffle emblazoned with a faded Adidas logo. It didn't contain any contraband, only a dog-eared copy of the Koran and a prayer rug he'd acquired specifically for this assignment. He wore a simple blazer and a secondhand button-down shirt, hoping to blend in. Still, he worried he'd attract attention. Surely this officer would sniff him out as the imposter he was.

The officer finished searching his bag, then set it aside.

"Your papers."

Ravid handed her his passport. Like the rest of the men at the checkpoint, he'd been clutching it tightly, prepared in advance for this directive. But unlike the other men, the passport he held wasn't his. It was a counterfeit, mailed to him a week earlier, stashed in the bottom of a case of Malbec.

The officer flipped through the pages. "What's your business this evening?"

"To pray at the mosque," he replied in Arabic. Unlike her, Ravid spoke Arabic fluently. Languages came naturally to him, which was almost certainly why Mossad had recruited him so many years ago.

The officer studied his face for a long moment, then handed back the passport.

"Shukran," he said softly, thanking her.

Inwardly, he smiled. Everything was going to be okay. He'd complete the mission, save his Ima, then retire for good.

He zipped up his duffle and walked toward the gate that

led to the mosque. As he crossed through the turnstile, he passed three more IDF officers. Like the one who'd searched his bag, each held an IWI X95 Tavor assault rifle. They were shorter than the M16s Ravid had trained on, and were ideal for close-quarters combat. They'd begun issuing them just as Ravid was retiring.

Of course, when he traveled to the West Bank, the weapons he carried were considerably more discreet.

When he finally stepped outside the checkpoint and into Hebron's warm evening air, he stopped to gather himself and allow the cortisol in his blood to dissipate a bit.

In front of him loomed the massive structure of the mosque. It was ancient and monolithic, built more than two thousand years ago of giant blocks of limestone. The construction was so much like the Western Wall in Jerusalem as to be nearly identical. Not surprising, he reminded himself; both had been built by King Herod. Two of the most sacred buildings in the world.

A soft cough sounded behind him. He turned quickly. A speck of a man stood before him.

This was his partner?

Ravid had expected that the man would be petite—people with his particular skill set usually were—but this man was so tiny, he could be mistaken for a child of twelve or thirteen. Only a thin mustache hinted at his true age.

"It is sown in dishonor. It is raised in glory," said the man in a quiet voice.

"It is sown in weakness. It is raised in power," answered Ravid, completing the passphrase. He didn't know the man's name, and it would stay that way. His employer had given him only the information that he needed.

"I am to follow your lead," said the little man. He spoke English, but with an accent. Ravid guessed it was Italian, but he couldn't be sure. He wondered what the man had told the guards at the checkpoint. He'd probably played the tourist angle. The mosque was only off-limits to Israelis.

"Correct," said Ravid. He looked toward the entrance to the mosque. The rock glowed in the light of the setting sun, but more importantly, the evening worshippers had begun to file in. "The men will begin to pray when the sun falls below the horizon. We slip inside then. Stay close to me."

The little man nodded.

They loitered by the entrance until the last of the worshippers had entered. Then, with Ravid leading the way, they stepped into a small antechamber where the scent of incense hung in the air. The view through a set of painted wrought-iron bars made Ravid's breath catch in his throat. There was no mistaking what he was looking at. Draped in green silk embroidered with gold thread was the tomb of Sarah, wife of Abraham.

Why have I been sent here, of all places?

He must have stood a beat too long because the little man tugged at his jacket. "They've started to pray."

Ravid turned from the tomb. With his companion just behind him, he entered the main prayer hall.

Its vast walls, painted green, reached toward a beige ceiling at least four stories above them. Towering arches were an architectural reminder that the mosque had once been an eleventh-century church. But it was the tombs in the middle of the floor that demanded Ravid's attention. He didn't need to read their names to know who they were dedicated to: Isaac and Rebecca. In Hebrew, they called this place Me'arat ha-Makhpela: the Cave of the Patriarchs.

Between the pair of tombs, worshippers knelt as they incanted and performed the ritual movements of the Maghrib prayer. They were turned to the southeast, toward Mecca, with their backs to Ravid and his companion.

A wave of relief passed over Ravid as he looked to his right. The scaffolding was exactly where it should be. Draped with canvas and painter's cloths, it would provide the perfect cover for their work.

"This way," he said.

He and his partner ducked under the scaffolding, making their way into the sheltering darkness. The scaffolding had been his idea. At first, his employer had suggested that he kill the worshippers, but he'd pushed back. In 1994, an American-Israeli member of the terrorist Kach movement had gunned down twenty-nine Muslims on these very stones. That was not a legacy to which he wanted to contribute.

Instead, he'd suggested a simple subterfuge. His employer would donate two hundred thousand shekels to the mosque with instructions that it be used toward restoring the columns near the southwestern wall. With a few bribes to the right people, construction was underway two weeks later. The scaffolding now provided near-perfect concealment.

Ravid and his partner moved quietly, close to the wall of the temple, until they reached four stone columns that surrounded a feature known as the lamp aperture. It was a strange-looking shrine, a low, ivory-colored marble plinth carved in the shape of a lotus flower. To Ravid, it looked a bit like a fancy toilet seat, except that the hole was covered by a silver grate, with a padlock on one side and a hinge on the other.

He inhaled sharply as his pent-up anxiety returned in a flash. If he were caught robbing the Cave of the Patriarchs, his life would fall apart. Few would forgive him for desecrating a holy site. He closed his eyes, trying to steady himself. He couldn't afford to make a mistake like he'd nearly done back at the checkpoint. He reminded himself that this was how he would save his Ima. Even if the world shunned him, surely God would understand. After all, it was one of His commandments to honor one's parents.

"Is this it?" whispered his tiny partner.

"Yes."

Ravid opened his eyes, knelt, and slipped off his right shoe. From beneath the insole, he withdrew a small set of lockpicks. Made of pure titanium, they were specially designed not to set off metal detectors.

He was just bending down to pick the lock on the grate when a voice spoke behind them in Arabic.

"What are you doing here? This area is restricted."

Ravid's pulse raced, but he stood slowly, quietly palming the lockpicks. He turned, and he recognized the man who now stood before him. This was the head caretaker of the mosque, responsible for both the general upkeep and security. Fortunately, the documents had explained exactly what Ravid should do if the caretaker discovered them.

"I'm Umar el-Kader, from Palestinian National Authority," said Ravid, replying in Arabic. "I'm here to inspect the repairs."

"At this hour?"

"It was the only time I had in my schedule."

"What about you?" said the security guard, turning to Ravid's companion.

The tiny man didn't answer; he just looked from Ravid to the security guard, panic spreading over his diminutive features. Apparently, *his* briefing documents hadn't covered this particular contingency.

But perhaps his confusion could be useful.

"I don't know who he is," said Ravid dismissively, still speaking in Arabic. "I think he may be a tourist. I asked him to leave, but he refused."

The security guard frowned. "What are you doing here?" he asked again, this time in broken English.

While his partner spluttered, Ravid shifted his position until he stood slightly behind the guard. As soon as he was out of the man's line of sight, he slipped his right hand into his jacket pocket and felt along the bottom of the fabric until his fingers brushed the ceramic knife he'd sewn into the lining. Silently, he withdrew it.

It was funny: after all the unexpected jitters at the checkpoint, it wasn't until now that he felt perfectly at ease. Even so, he would only get one chance at this. Failure meant discovery.

The security guard reached for his colleague's arm, clearly aiming to detain him. Ravid lunged. In a single, practiced motion, and with the full force of his body weight behind the blow, he drove the knife into the back of the caretaker's neck. The man spasmed once as the blade plunged between his cervical vertebrae and instantly severed the connection between his brain and spinal cord.

As the caretaker started to fall forward, Ravid caught him by the back of the shirt and lowered him softly to the floor. The only sound was a soft gurgle as the air left the man's lungs.

Ravid's partner stared at him with eyes the size of dinner plates.

"Is he—" he started to say.

Ravid raised a finger to his lips. "We don't have much time before someone comes along looking for him."

CHAPTER 4
HARVARD UNIVERSITY

Cambridge, Massachusetts
12:15 PM, May 27th

———

cratch that, thought Topher as the news of the unknown hominid species sank in. They wouldn't be publishing in *Nature Genetics* or *PNAS*. This finding was a slam dunk in *Science* or *Nature*, the world's two most prestigious scientific journals. They were going to be interviewed by *The Wall Street Journal*, *The Washington Post*, *The New York Times*. Crikey, *National Geographic* might even film a special about this discovery. And best of all, NSF and NIH would be throwing grant money at him. His lab would be well funded for years to come.

"You're one hundred percent sure it isn't Denisovan?" Topher asked. "This is a new species related to modern humans?"

Sara beamed. "Definitely new. It's highly diverged from the Denisovan genome. The Rampasasa are the population that has the largest percentage of this mysterious ancient ancestor."

He was going to be famous. They'd just sequenced a new branch on the hominid tree. A third ancestor to the ancestral genome to go along with Neanderthals and Denisovans.

Not that Walter Schröder would ever congratulate him. Still, Topher could perfectly imagine the furious look on Schröder's face when he read the paper that described this work. The image made Topher feel warm and fuzzy inside.

"This is bloody brilliant," said Topher, smiling so hard his face hurt. "This is going to be absolutely enormous."

Arthur frowned. "I don't understand what the big deal is."

Topher didn't even try to hide his frustration. "Arthur, you should know this. The Rampasasa are from the Island of Flores. Do you remember the 'Hobbit' bones discovered in a cave in Indonesia a few years ago?"

Arthur nodded—slowly. Topher felt fairly certain that the postdoc still had no idea what was going on.

"Well, no one has been able to sequence their genome because the bones are fossilized. They're solid rock; you can't extract DNA from a stone. But Sara has *inferred* their genomic sequence with a neural network. It's an absolute paradigm shift in the study of human evolution. What other extinct genomes are hiding within our own? What other ancient species have been lost in the sands of time? Are there species we don't even know about yet? We may have found a way to identify the secrets of our most ancient and enigmatic relatives."

Topher had completely forgotten about teaching Sara a lesson in academic hierarchy, so caught up was he in the excitement of the discovery.

"But we have no way to *prove* that this genome Sara found is *Homo floresiensis*," Arthur protested. "Correlation is not causation."

Now Topher had to give Arthur credit. That was actually an astute point. He turned to Sara, waiting for her to respond.

"It's more than just a correlation," said Sara calmly. "Like *Homo floresiensis*, the Rampasasa are also tiny. Adults have an average height of about five feet. When I looked at the genomic regions that appear to be from *Homo floresiensis*, they're all centered on the HMGA2 gene. Mice with mutations in this gene are 75% smaller than average. *Homo floresiensis* genes almost certainly cause short stature in the Rampasasa." Sara narrowed her eyes at Arthur. "I *know* what I'm talking about."

Wheels turned in Topher's head. Not only would he be giving plenary talks at every scientific conference for the next ten years, but he could also use this discovery to finally move Arthur out of his lab. A finding like this should be enough to get any idiot a job.

He rapped on his desk. "Arthur, begin writing this up immediately. Coordinate with Sara. I want a draft on my desk by the end of the week."

For a long moment, both Arthur and Sara stared at him. Shocked. Speechless.

Finally Sara spoke, her face red and pinched. "It's my discovery. I was working on the paper about demographic analysis. Shouldn't I be the one to write this up?"

"You made the discovery under Arthur's guidance," said Topher firmly. "Isn't that right?" Never mind that Arthur hadn't even understood the significance of Sara's findings.

Arthur nodded. "She *was* working with me."

"So you will write the paper. Sara will be a co-author."

Sara looked like she was about to crawl over Topher's desk and choke him, a thought that Topher found oddly exciting.

"I'm sorry," he said before she could object again. "This is how science works in my lab. Arthur is your mentor. You're working on his dataset—"

Sara exploded. "But it doesn't have anything to do with Arthur's project! It was *my* idea! *I* made the discovery. *I* did the simulations, *I* found the ancient genome, *I* noticed the enrichment for height genes, the mouse mutant—"

"And it is brilliant work. Absolutely brilliant work," Topher repeated for emphasis. "This will alter how scientists all over the world study evolution, and it will open the door to discoveries we can't even dream of. It will make both you *and* Arthur famous." *And most importantly, it will make* me *famous.* "But you are only a graduate student, Sara. I pay your salary. And as the head of the lab, it's my call who writes the papers." He leaned forward, looking straight into her blue eyes. "Remember, I will be writing you letters of recommendation someday."

Sara's fists were clenched so tightly, her knuckles had gone white. "But—"

Topher looked pointedly at the door. "This discussion is over. You both have a lot of work to do."

Sara opened her mouth, then closed it. Fortunately, she was smart enough to realize she'd lost. Arthur crossed to the door, and Sara clenched her jaw and followed him.

Topher smiled as the door closed behind them. Every one of his graduate students had a showdown with him at some point. It was important for them to lose, to learn their place in the academic hierarchy. Certainly, Sara had gotten a raw deal, but she would get some credit for her discovery, just as Arthur would get the publication he needed to land a tenure-track job.

And he, Topher Fitzpatrick, would add a brilliant paper to his CV.

He closed his eyes and leaned back in his chair. This was the work that would finally elicit an invitation to the National Academy of Sciences.

CHAPTER 5
IBRAHIMI MOSQUE

Hebron, Palestine
7:35 PM, May 27th

————

D acio sucked in a shaky breath. From the very beginning, he'd wondered if this assignment was madness. Over the years, he'd stolen many things, but what he'd been asked to steal tonight was incomprehensible. Then again, that had been the appeal—this job was like nothing he'd ever done.

But then the whole mission had gone to hell.

One second, a guard was questioning him, and the next, the man's eyes bulged, and he slumped to the ground.

At first, Dacio wasn't even sure what had happened. It was only when blood burbled from the guard's mouth and his partner pulled a knife from the back of the man's neck that he understood.

He'd just witnessed a murder.

A metallic click drew his eyes back to his companion. After killing the guard in near-total silence, his partner had immediately returned to picking the lock as if nothing had happened. Like some sort of psychopath.

Dacio watched as his partner lifted the silver grate on the strange-looking marble bench, revealing a dark opening. Despite himself, Dacio felt a pull of curiosity so strong, he nearly forgot the corpse next to him. The aperture was about the diameter of a basketball, and its interior was blackened with soot.

This was where his particular skill set came into play.

"Will you fit?" his partner asked.

"Easy," said Dacio. "I have world record for smallest box."

He wasn't lying. In *Guinness World Records*, he held the title in enterology, the art of squeezing into tiny boxes. And that wasn't all he was capable of. As a professional contortionist, he could bend his spine almost in half, escape a straitjacket in less than five seconds, and even twist his right arm a full three hundred sixty degrees. In Paris's Cirque du Soleil, his stage name was Monsieur Elastique.

What few people knew was that the press had given him a second moniker: Babbo Natale Ladro, the Santa Claus Thief. He'd earned that tag after wriggling down a three-story chimney to steal eighty-five thousand dollars' worth of diamonds. All told, across a five-year crime spree that spanned the European continent, he'd stolen almost two million dollars' worth of jewelry.

It was his reputation that had garnered the attention of his current employer. If this job went well, he could retire from the circus. His burglary days would be over, too.

Nervously, he glanced at the dead guard. Right now, success seemed like a big if.

He looked again at the dark opening. A silver candelabra was suspended over the hole by a chain, for reasons Dacio didn't understand. Some religious purpose, he supposed. But whatever the case, it would be his way of getting in.

Behind the cover of the scaffolding, he stripped down to

his underwear. Then, his heart racing, he stepped onto one of the marble petals on top of the plinth. The opening gaped at his feet, pitch black and ominous. He shivered as a cold breeze blew up from the depths.

Taking hold of the candelabra chain, he gave it a sharp tug. When he was convinced it would hold his weight, he allowed himself to hang by one hand with his toes pointed down. As the metal dug into his fingers, he nodded to his partner. *Proceed.*

Slowly, his partner began lowering the candelabra, easing him into the hole. He was in as far as his waist when his partner stopped and fished something out of his pocket.

"You'll need this," he said, handing Dacio a small Ziploc bag containing a lipstick-sized flashlight. Dacio took the bag between his teeth, and his partner went back to lowering the chain.

When the opening reached Dacio's chest, he dropped his left shoulder and dislocated it. This allowed his clavicle to drop, narrowing his torso. Still, it was a tight squeeze, but nothing Babbo Natale Ladro couldn't handle. Soot darkened his shoulders as he slid deeper into the hole.

After a few more links of chain, he was entirely inside, and darkness enveloped him. The passage smelled strongly of candle wax, and it was too narrow to allow a proper breath. He concentrated on staying relaxed.

His partner continued to lower him until the shaft opened into a tunnel about two feet wide—spacious compared to what he'd just passed through. Now Dacio was able to look down. Illuminated by the dim light from above was a dusty floor maybe ten feet below.

With a sinewy twist, he popped his arm back into its socket.

Link by link, the chain inched him closer to the floor. When he was within a few feet, he hopped off and gave the chain a hard yank to let his partner know he'd reached the bottom.

He shivered in the darkness. Usually, he wore tight black clothing on a job, along with gloves and a ski mask. Working practically naked wasn't his standard approach, but he'd had no choice. There had been no way to sneak a thief's outfit through the mosque's security checkpoint, and he would need his clothes clean for the escape.

Sucking in a breath of dusty air, he focused his thoughts. His instructions had been specific.

He extracted the flashlight from the plastic bag and directed the beam around the subterranean chamber. The space was smaller than he'd expected, the size of a cheap hotel room. Against one wall stood three large stone slabs, the tallest of which was about six feet in height, reaching halfway to the ceiling.

He smiled. Exactly what his instructions had said to expect.

He pivoted and shone his light at his feet. As expected, a marble capstone rested toward one side of the floor, covered in dust. It appeared to have been excavated many years ago. Directly next to it was another hole large enough for him to squeeze through. He crouched and directed the beam of the flashlight inside, revealing the raw stone of a natural grotto only a few feet below.

He dropped in.

The ceiling of the grotto was so low, he had to crouch. Motes of dust hung in the air, and a thin layer of grit coated the stone floor. No one had been here in a long time. He flashed his light around the interior of the cave, then breathed out slowly through his nose. Everything was going to plan.

On his hands and knees, Dacio crept forward. The floor sloped up toward one last narrow opening, and he slipped through into an even smaller cave. The dust here was thicker still, the ceiling closer. He wasn't prone to claustrophobia, yet he could feel his heart hammering in his chest. He couldn't escape the feeling that he was doing something sacrilegious.

Still, if this was a sin, it was one that would fill his bank account.

Holding the end of the flashlight between his teeth, he continued crawling forward until a stone on the floor dug sharply into his palm. He picked it up, sat back on his haunches—the ceiling only inches above his head—and directed his flashlight beam at the fragment he'd found.

Dacio smiled broadly. There was no mistaking the pearly sheen. This was no stone. It was a tooth.

His chest unclenched. He was on the right track. He would be out of this place soon.

CHAPTER 6
HARVARD UNIVERSITY

Cambridge, Massachusetts
6:05 PM, May 27th

———

Sara hurried past the Widener Library and into Harvard Yard. Her mind was so filled with fury that she hardly noticed the towering oaks or the regal redbrick buildings. All she could think about was that Dr. Fitzpatrick had given *her* project to Arthur. Arthur! The moron postdoc who didn't know an ancient genome from his own prick.

It was Sara who had made the discovery—a potentially *earth-shattering* discovery. And the credit would go to an idiot who still got chromosome and chromatid mixed up. Arthur, who pronounced the word pseudo with a hard P, so it sounded like pus-way-do. Arthur, who had creeped on literally every woman in the lab.

Worse, Sara was pretty sure this was *exactly* why Dr. Fitzpatrick had given the project away. He wanted Arthur out of his lab. Who wouldn't? The guy was completely useless.

Giving him the lead authorship on a prestigious paper was the fastest way to shuffle him along somewhere else. And now that Dr. Fitzpatrick had learned that Sara produced meaningful work, she would never escape his grip. He would cling to her as tightly as a histone to a strand of DNA.

It took all of Sara's willpower not to scream.

When raindrops began to sprinkle through the leaves, she broke into a jog, her messenger bag bouncing against her hip. The rain would destroy her laptop if her bag got soaked.

She was between the Dudley and Wadsworth houses when thunder growled in the sky and the rain intensified, and her breath was hot in her lungs when she finally ducked into John Harvard's Brewery. She'd managed to keep her laptop dry, and now she was desperate for a beer. Or several.

Ignoring the hostess, she scanned the interior. Proximity to Harvard turned most restaurants into overpriced tourist traps, but John Harvard's managed to retain its identity as a classic New England pub, complete with brick walls and dark wood paneling. Its one unusual feature was a row of stained glass windows that depicted famous figures like Humphrey Bogart and Lyndon B. Johnson.

"Sara! Over here!"

Sara turned and grinned. Sitting under a leering visage of Richard Nixon, a pitcher of beer already in front of her, was her best friend, Amy. Amy was also a graduate student in Dr. Fitzpatrick's lab, and their lab-mates claimed that Sara and Amy were lookalikes, though Sara didn't see it. They both had shoulder-length brown hair—that was it. But apparently, that was enough for some of their lab-mates to jokingly call them "Topher's Twins."

Despite their shared PhD advisor, they rarely worked together. Amy was 100% wet lab, spending her time running assays, making slides, and mixing reagents, while Sara lived in her computer's terminal window. They might never have been more than casual lab-mates if not for the beer. After one trip home, Sara had brought in a growler of Hill Farmstead IPA to a lab meeting. Biology had sparked their friendship, but it was their shared love of good IPAs that had cemented it.

Wiping strands of wet hair from her forehead, Sara sat down across from Amy.

"You never have an umbrella," Amy said with a frown.

"It's just a little water. I grew up—"

"In Vermont. I know, I know. It's the explanation for all your eccentricities. No umbrellas. No sunscreen. Sandals with socks. Plaid shirts. A frankly terrifying knowledge of guns."

"Well, in the Northeast Kingdom, they always say, 'If you don't like the weather, just wait fifteen minutes.'" It was a dumb expression that Sara instantly regretted repeating.

"They say that about literally every part of America. And several parts of Europe."

"Right." Sara reached for the pitcher and began filling an empty pint glass. "What is this?"

"The milk stout. I thought you might be thirsty."

Sara took a long sip, downing half a pint in one go. When she finished, she returned the half-empty glass to the tabletop with an audible smack. The beer hadn't quenched the anger, at least not yet.

"Bad day?" Amy said.

"The worst."

"So it's true? Fitzpatrick really gave the first author position to Arthur?"

"Yup. And I'm supposed to be happy with a co-authorship. Everyone knows the first author is the one who gets the credit."

"That's totally unethical. *You* made the discovery."

"I know." Sara tried to relax by taking another sip of beer. "Unfortunately, there's nothing I can do about it."

"Can't you complain to the dean or something?"

"I already checked the student handbook. Complaints are

supposed to go to an ombudsman."

"Okay, talk to the ombudsman. What is an ombudsman, by the way?"

"No one helpful. Remember Marcia from the Robinette Lab? Her advisor falsified a bunch of data, so she contacted the ombudsman. She said they mostly just tried to convince her not to speak to the press. They *say* they're there to resolve conflicts, but the reality is they just protect the university. Plus, Topher specifically mentioned recommendations. If I want to get a good postdoc fellowship after I graduate, I'll need him to write me a letter and vouch for me as a scientist. The ombudsman can't force him to do that."

Amy scowled into her beer. "So you're screwed. He'll blackball you if you complain."

"Yep. Guess what? The world of science is still an old boys' club."

"Well, then, let's forget all about it. Let's get drunk. We'll do karaoke at Charlie's Kitchen. Then we'll find a hot guy to motorboat your rack."

This was what Sara liked so much about Amy. She was a little wild. They went dancing together almost every weekend. They kissed guys in bars. Amy even got Sara to join Primal Scream at the end of last term. Did Sara really strip down after finals and run around Harvard Yard naked? Yes. Yes, she did!

Still, having a random guy rub his face in her boobs wasn't exactly Sara's idea of fun.

"Do you really think that will make me feel better?"

"No, but I like saying the word *motorboat*," said Amy, grinning. "And *rack*. Anyway, I'm simply suggesting that maybe it's time for you to consider having a social life again." She looked pointedly at Sara's black outfit.

Sara snorted, then went quiet, staring into her beer. She liked hanging out with Amy, but beyond that, her social life was the last thing on her mind right now.

Amy's expression turned serious. "Sara, I know it's been tough losing your mom. But you know she wouldn't want you spending all your time writing code and analyzing data."

Sara touched the tattoo on her wrist. "I know. I just—"

"Plus, I have a crazy idea that might solve your problem with Topher."

Sara looked up, her eyebrows rising. "What is it?"

"First promise me that you'll sing 'Single Ladies' with me."

Sara sighed. Singing Beyoncé would involve more than just holding a mic. Amy would make her do the entire dance routine. Still, her curiosity was piqued. "Fine. One song. But you tell me your idea first."

Amy leaned over her pint, her eyes shining. "You have to promise not to say a word to anyone. Topher would kick me out of the lab if he found out."

"Scout's honor."

Amy leaned in even closer, cupping her hand to whisper, "What if you *scoop* him?"

"What do you mean?"

"You could publish your own work, but under a pseudonym. Or as Arthur would say, a pus-way-do-nim."

Sara tapped her fingertips on the table. "I think Topher would figure out it's me pretty quickly."

"I thought of that. But what if you associated your pen name with someone he'd never speak to?" Amy grinned. "How do you feel about joining the Schröder Lab? You know how much Topher and Walter Schröder loathe each other. Every time one of them publishes something, the other has a public rebuttal on Twitter within hours. Do you remember Walter's plenary talk at the Human Evolution conference? Topher walked out halfway through. They'll never speak to each other about the work. Topher will just assume that Walter got there first. Then he'll break another chair."

Sara set her beer down. "Oh, now *that* is brilliant. And

evil. But in a good way."

Amy's eyes twinkled. "Brilliant and evil. That's me."

Cogs turned in Sara's brain. "I'd have to use a different dataset." This idea was quickly morphing from an insane hypothetical concept into an actual plan. "A group in Denmark just published some genomic sequences of indigenous populations from the Malay Archipelago. They don't have the Rampasasa, but there's a small amount of *Homo floresiensis* ancestry in Malaysia. I didn't tell Topher, but I already ran the neural net on their data as an independent test of my method. If I publish first, before the paper comes out in *Nature*, Topher won't be able to steal my discovery because it'd already be published."

Amy bit her lip. "The only problem is it's going to be expensive. Publication costs are thousands of dollars. You can't even pay your electric bill, and your shoes are held together with duct tape. Don't think I didn't notice. Plus, what if it's rejected? Or—" Her eyes widened. "Or worse, what if Topher is assigned to review it? He could hold it up while Arthur writes your paper. You could be double-scooped."

Sara looked at her beer. Around her, the noise of the bar dimmed as her prefrontal cortex went into overdrive. This was the secret to her success. She'd always been able to hyper-focus, to block out distractions and process information efficiently. To make connections other people didn't see.

An idea came to her. "What if I don't submit it to a journal? What if I just post it as a preprint online? You know—like in bioRxiv. It's fast, free, and there's no review process. It'll be online in twenty-four hours. That should be enough to prevent Topher and Arthur from claiming the discovery as theirs.

"Oooh, now *that's* evil," Amy said with a grin. "In a good way," she added quickly. "Now finish your beer. I wanna sing Beyoncé."

CHAPTER 7
AETER PHARMACEUTICALS

Cambridge, Massachusetts
8:55 PM, June 1st

———

Sameer yanked hard on the parking brake of his Honda Civic before turning off the engine. He sighed, resting his hands on the steering wheel. This was not how he'd planned to spend his Friday night.

Unfortunately, he couldn't exactly complain. Even before he'd accepted the lab tech position at Aeter Pharmaceuticals, the recruiter had explicitly warned him that their employees were expected to work hard. He'd signed on anyway. He'd just never anticipated that "working hard" would mean processing samples at this hour—or that he'd be on call like some sort of emergency room doctor.

What could be so important that the samples had to be processed immediately? It wasn't like they were about to go bad. If there was a reason for this urgency, he wasn't aware of it. They never filled him in on the big picture. He was just a lab tech.

He locked the door with the remote on his keychain as he crossed the empty parking lot. Apart from the brutal schedule, Aeter wasn't a terrible place to work. And he was well compensated for the insane hours—he was paid almost twice the industry average, plus a generous package of stock options. But it wasn't the compensation that convinced him to take the job. At least, not *only* the compensation. It was the connection to Enora Hansen.

Enora Hansen was a legendary figure in scientific circles. A wunderkind, she'd graduated from Harvard at sixteen with a degree in astrophysics. After working briefly at the Los Alamos National Laboratory, she'd done a one-eighty and started a PhD in molecular biology at Berkeley. Even as a mere graduate student, her career had been scintillating, resulting in the publication of a series of ground-breaking papers in both *Science* and *Nature*.

Then—like a firework reaching its zenith—she disappeared in an explosion of acrimony and bad blood. A public fight with her thesis committee led to accusations of plagiarism and sexual harassment. Within six months, she'd quit science altogether and joined a hedge fund in New York.

And that was the last anyone in the scientific community heard from her for more than twenty years, until she suddenly reappeared in Boston with a billion-dollar war chest. Hansen immediately began funneling that money into a wide variety of sometimes-insane projects: space exploration, supersonic jets, nanotechnology, solar-powered cars, a planned human colony on Mars. She established herself as a powerful venture capitalist, purchasing ownership stakes in a number of companies, particularly in the realm of biotech.

Aeter Pharmaceuticals was the first of those companies. Its mission was to develop new drugs, and in doing so, it housed an odd collection of projects, from large-scale CRISPR genomic editing to anti-freeze proteins in Greenland sharks. It also contained an ancient DNA laboratory, which was where

Sameer had worked for the last six months, during which time he'd sequenced over sixty complete archaic genomes. He didn't understand how ancient hominid genomes would help with the development of new drugs, but again, no one told the lab guys anything.

As he reached the glass doors of the main building, he fished his ID from his pocket and swiped it through the card reader. The door unlocked with an electric click, and he crossed into a large atrium with a marble floor.

It was always weird visiting the lab at night, especially when no one was sitting behind the security desk. Most likely, the guard was circulating through the building.

His cell phone buzzed, and a text message flashed on the screen.

> Are you at work?

Sameer groaned. He'd told his mother not to message him because he had to work. Of course she hadn't listened.

> Yes, I'm in the lab.

He'd only just stepped into the elevator when his phone buzzed again.

> You shouldn't work so much. It's not good for your health.

> I know, Mom.

Dots bounced while his mother tapped a reply.

> I was speaking with Nanni. She knows a nice girl you should meet.

Sameer groaned. Not this again. His parents had been born in Bangalore. They'd moved to the United States so his father could get a doctorate in electrical engineering at MIT. While his dad designed computer chips for Intel, his mother raised him and learned English. But they still held to some old traditions, like meddling in their son's love life.

> Thanks, Mom, but I really don't need any help.

More bouncing dots. Sameer looked at the time. 9:02 PM. He was supposed to meet friends for drinks at ten. That left him only fifty-eight minutes to process the samples. He didn't have time to discuss his mother's latest "match."

> She's 23 and has a BA from Mount Holyoke. Her father is a lawyer in DC.

> Mom, this text reads like you're transcribing a marriage advertisement.

Which, basically, was what she was doing. Last time he'd been home, she'd sat him down on the couch and showed him newspaper clippings from the *Times of India*. Literal marriage advertisements.

> I just want you to be happy.

> I am happy.

> If your father was alive, he'd tell you the same. It's time to settle down.

Sameer clenched his jaw. He had his own life, and he didn't need these guilt trips. As the elevator doors opened into a sleek hallway, he thumbed a message.

> Mom, I have stuff to do. I'll talk to you tomorrow. I'm turning off my phone now.

He hated cutting off his mom, but he had to get to work. Enora Hansen had emailed him personally with this request to expedite the new batch of samples. It was cool to get a personal email from a billionaire CEO. It was also more than a little terrifying.

As he stepped into the lab, he spotted a package on his desk—the new samples, presumably. He slipped on a pair of blue nitrile gloves before he opened the box. Inside, packed in bubble wrap and nestled among packets of silica desiccant, was a clear plastic bag. Carefully, he held the bag up to the light. Eight teeth clicked softly inside, and by their dull yellow hue, he could tell they were old. Neanderthal, probably. He had no idea, of course, since no one told him anything.

Holding the bag of teeth, he crossed to the entrance to the cleanroom, placed the bag in a small stainless steel mailbox built into the wall, and flicked on the desktop computer, queueing up a Daft Punk playlist, his favorite work music. To the beat of "Get Lucky," he dressed in a white Tyvek suit, disposable booties, and a fresh pair of nitrile gloves. A hairnet and face mask completed the outfit. This getup made it far less likely that he would contaminate the teeth with his own DNA.

He then used his elbow to flick off the UV light switch. The UV killed bacteria and viruses, and degraded contaminating DNA. Unfortunately, it also degraded the DNA in the samples he needed to isolate. Plus, like a tanning light turned up to max, it could severely burn his skin if left on.

Finally, he entered the cleanroom. On one wall was the other side of the steel letterbox, which acted as a sort of portal between the main lab space and the interior of the cleanroom.

Now humming along with Pharrell, he opened the drawer, picked up the bag of teeth, and crossed to the laminar flow hood. As he placed the teeth on the stainless steel inside, a breeze ruffled the cuffs of his Tyvek suit. The laminar flow hood got its name from the way fans pushed air out to create a positive pressure barrier.

Carefully, he reached into the hood and unrolled a sheet of sterile tinfoil. He withdrew the teeth from the baggie and arranged them in a row on the foil.

He checked the clock and sighed. He should be two martinis into his night, not extracting DNA from chipped molars. And he could use a drink. His work kept him so obsessively focused on cleanliness and precision that when the day ended, he longed for a little chaos. Music that was loud, drinks that were strong. The heat of a stranger standing too close.

But hey, why drink martinis when you can spend your time organizing sterile micro-centrifuge tubes into tiny plastic racks?

He grabbed a Sharpie and labeled the tube's lids, one through eight. Then he did the same for eight small plastic bags.

Now it was time to begin the real work.

Picking up a small Dremel tool, he attached a felt polishing bit and began to clean the teeth. This would also help cut down DNA contamination. When the teeth were clean, he placed seven of them into their plastic bags but left the eighth one on a fresh piece of tinfoil. He replaced the Dremel tool's felt bit with a clean cutting blade and sliced the root from the crown. Using a dentist's drill, he slowly drilled into the exposed root.

Two hundred milligrams of powder on the tinfoil was all he needed.

He opened the micro-centrifuge tube labeled #1 and

poured the powdered tooth inside, then popped the lid closed and lifted it. The tube had been pre-filled with lysis buffer, a special cocktail of protein-degrading enzymes and free radical inhibitors. It would finish extracting the DNA while helping prevent any further degradation.

He put the tube in the rack and moved on to tooth #2, tapping his foot to Daft Punk and trying not to think about all the fun he was missing.

Seven teeth later, he was finally done. He carried the tray of tubes across the room and placed it in a thirty-seven-degree incubator. The samples needed to incubate overnight, which meant that for now, at least, he was done.

Back at his desk, he turned his phone back on. It started vibrating immediately, and messages rolled across the screen.

Ok, but you made me cry.

I'm your mother.

You shouldn't hurt my feelings.

I'm only looking out for you.

I just want you to be happy.

Sameer sighed. His mother was nothing if not persistent.

Another message rolled up the screen. Not his mom this time.

Hey sexy. Are you still coming out?

He smiled, his mood brightening. With the ancient teeth forgotten, he texted back.

Just finished work. Where are you?

Machine. It's fabulous. So many hot guys.

Sameer thumbed a reply.

> Behave yourself, Jake. I'll be there in 15.
> Xoxoxo.

He was ready for a little chaos.

CHAPTER 8
HARVARD UNIVERSITY

Cambridge, Massachusetts
11:34 AM, June 4th

———

Topher sipped coffee at his desk as he worked on revising the paper. All things considered, it was coming along nicely. The editor at *Nature* had been receptive to their work. Assuming there were no significant hiccups, they'd have a draft out for review in a week.

His cell phone rang. Unknown caller, but with a 212 area code. New York City, most likely.

"Yes?"

"Hello, may I speak to Dr. Topher Fitzpatrick?"

"Speaking. Who's calling?"

"This is Marcus Byron from *The New York Times*. I'm hoping to ask you a few questions about your recent discovery."

Topher grinned. The day before, he'd asked Harvard's public relations team to reach out to the media in advance of his new publication, and they'd already come through.

"I'd be happy to tell you about our discovery, but understand it's embargoed until we're officially accepted by a journal. While *Nature* has shown interest, you can't discuss or publish any stories yet." He enjoyed taking control of the conversation.

"That shouldn't be a problem."

"Great."

The reporter's voice became more businesslike. "Can you tell me a bit about what you and your team found?"

"I'd be happy to. We're analyzing genetic data from indigenous southeast Asian populations," Topher began. "Under my direction, my team devised a method to identify the bits of DNA in modern humans that may have been introduced by interbreeding with other hominid species, like Neanderthals or Denisovans. We've reconstructed what appears to be the genome of *Homo floresiensis*. It's truly a fantastic scientific breakthrough—"

He could hear the sound of a computer keyboard clicking. "And *Homo floresiensis* are the short-statured ones, right? Can you elaborate on the broader implications of this work, beyond your discovery of their genome sequence?"

"Well, so far, we've only looked at southeast Asian populations, but since modern humans originated in Africa, I expect we'll find all sorts of interesting archaic genomes in those populations as well."

"Like *Australopithecus*?"

"Perhaps. *Australopithecus* went extinct a bit more than two million years ago, though, and we're still running demographic simulations to determine the limits of how far back we can go. It depends on a large number of factors: population size, recombination rate, geneflow, time of introgression, and so on."

"Gotcha. What about mating with modern humans? Will you be able to tell if they produced viable offspring?"

Topher rolled his eyes. You never could quite predict what

angle the press would take with your work. "Since we were able to extract the genome from modern humans, we know there must have been interbreeding. Now what's really interesting are the genes for short stature—"

"I have another question," said Byron, interrupting. Topher didn't like how the reporter was leading the conversation. Topher was the one with the PhD and the faculty position at Harvard. At best, this guy had a master's in journalism. Unfortunately, he couldn't push back much against a reporter for the *Times*.

"All right." He took a long sip of coffee.

"Can you explain how your work is different from what is described in Walter Schröder's new manuscript?"

Topher nearly spat coffee on his laptop. "I...I'm not sure what you're talking about."

"When I was prepping for this interview, I noticed his lab had just uploaded a preprint to bioRxiv."

Topher placed one hand on this desk to steady himself. A horrible feeling of dread had descended over him. "When was this?"

More sounds of clicking keys. "Uh, looks like last night. It's titled 'A reference-free approach to sequencing archaic genomes,' and the abstract says they were also able to identify an unknown archaic genome in southeast Asian populations."

Topher frantically typed the title into Google. *A reference-free...*bollocks, what was the rest of it? If he had been scooped, *Nature* would pull the plug on his paper. He'd have to publish it somewhere else—if it even *could* be published now.

"It sounds like something I should look into," Topher said quickly. His throat felt tight, the same feeling he used to get when the dolts shot spitballs at his head in primary school.

"Of course. And obviously, I'm not an expert in human evolution like yourself," Byron said, "but conceptually, I thought it seemed pretty similar."

"Can I get back to you after I've taken a look at it?" Topher had to work hard to keep the panic out of his voice.

"Certainly, Professor. In fact, I'm planning to come by Monday morning to interview you and your team. How about we discuss it then?"

"Uh. Yes, yes. That'll be fine."

Topher couldn't get off the phone fast enough. He needed to read this preprint immediately.

CHAPTER 9
HIMALAYAS

———

The abbot pulled his robe tighter, but at nearly eighteen thousand feet, the wind cut through the thin fabric like a knife. Above him stood a pair of cairns, each nearly as tall as a man. They perched on the ridge line, exactly where they'd been built nearly a thousand years ago, alone and isolated. The only evidence of human visitors since then were a few strings of tattered prayer flags strung between the piled rocks.

He looked down the mountainside. The novice monks were still climbing up the snowfield. He waited impatiently, doing his best to keep the gusts from blowing the robe from his shoulders.

At last, the first novice reached him. The young monk stopped just below him, palms together, eyes cast down. A gesture of respect.

"You are slow," said the abbot.

"Bante, I do not have your stamina."

The abbot smiled. "It will come in time. Catch your breath, then you can begin."

The novice stood for only a moment longer before straightening and crossing to the closest cairn. Moving methodically, he began pulling it down. In time, he was joined by five of his brothers.

The abbot watched silently. Worrying. The wind was picking up, and shadows were beginning to creep over the snow field. In a few hours, it would be dark. They needed to hurry.

When the cairn had been torn down and all the stones scattered over the snow, he joined the novices in their labors. He crouched at what had been the very center of the pile and began to dig with his bare hands, tearing at the rough gravel. His fingers bled, but he ignored the pain.

He uncovered a bit of fabric but didn't slow. He continued to dig until he'd exposed a large bundle wrapped in saffron-colored cloth and tied tightly with cords. Gently, he touched it. Still frozen solid. That was good.

"Lift it carefully," he said, standing.

The monks carried the heavy bundle reverently down the mountainside. The snow was slippery, but they moved easily, following their tracks from earlier. After an hour, they'd reached their camp. It was nothing more than an old baku tent. Black and humped, it looked like a giant tortoise shell.

They placed the bundle in the center of the tent, and the old abbot untied the cords. As he peeled back the cloth, a face with dark hair and frozen skin leered at him.

"Michê!" exclaimed one of the monks, jumping back.

"This is not a monster. He is your brother."

The abbot traced his fingers over the back of the frozen body until he found a knife's hilt.

"This blade has helped keep him at bay, but now he is needed again," he said to the novices before he pulled it out.

Then, without hesitating, he drew the blade along his own wrist. He held his arm over the body, and the novices watched as his blood dripped into the ancient knife wound.

After a few minutes, a novice helped him bandage his arm.

He touched a finger to the body's forehead. "He is very cold. Let us warm him." The wind had picked up, buffeting the woven yak-hair fabric of the tent. One of the novices lit a small butter lamp, and as its flame guttered, they clustered around the body. Quietly, they recited a simple mantra. "Hum, hum, hum…"

The abbot studied the flickering flame. The sound of the wind quieted, and he forgot how cold it was. He no longer *saw* the flame.

"Hum, hum, hum…"

He was empty but for a single bright ember burning in his core. His mind cleared. No thoughts intruded.

"Hum, hum, hum…"

This was g-tummo, the meditation of inner fire. The interior of the tent warmed as the monks chanted. Steam rose from their robes, and a thin trickle of water began to seep from underneath the frozen body.

"Hum, hum, hum…"

The candle sputtered out, but no one noticed. Their voices mixed with the cold mountain wind.

"Hum, hum, hum…"

Hours passed. Then a gasping breath cut through the mantra.

The tent fell silent as the body opened its eyes.

The abbot smiled serenely. "I'm sorry to wake you, brother, but I need your help. There's a girl you need to kill."

CHAPTER 10
AETER PHARMACEUTICALS

Cambridge, Massachusetts
10:52 AM, June 6th

———

Even sitting in her sumptuous office with its panoramic view of the Charles River, Enora Hansen was worried. Twenty minutes ago, she'd gotten a call from her son's group home. That was never good news. Mike was thirteen, and she loved him more than anything, but he had severe autism and needed constant supervision.

She'd been in a meeting with investors, so the call had gone to voicemail. Vera, Mike's primary caregiver, hadn't explained what the call was about—just said to call back ASAP. Now Enora picked up her cell phone and returned the call.

"Ms. Hansen?"

"Vera, is that you?" Vera was only twenty-three, but she was no-nonsense, and like Enora, she was a single mom. "I saw that you called."

"Yes, I was hoping to speak to you privately."

Enora felt a twinge in the pit of her stomach. "Is everything okay?"

"Your boy is fine. He's doing a sudoku." The twinge in Enora's stomach disappeared in an instant. Mike loved sudokus, and if he was working on one, that meant he wasn't hurt or upset.

"So what did you want to talk about?"

Vera replied in a hushed voice. "Ms. Hansen, there was another fire."

And just like that, the twinge was back. While it wasn't unusual for people with autism to have obsessive interests, they were typically innocuous: dinosaurs, train schedules, Pokémon trivia, weather patterns. Mike, unfortunately, was obsessed with fire.

Which was why the group home had him on probation. The director had been clear: he would get kicked out if there was another incident. Enora dreaded having to find a new home for her boy. It had been hard enough getting him into this one.

"What happened?"

"He burned some paper towels in the sink."

"I see."

"But he didn't set off the fire alarm."

Enora breathed a sigh of relief. That meant there was a chance no one else knew about the fire.

"Did you tell anyone about this?"

"I didn't say nothin'. You said I should call if anything happened."

"That was very wise of you." Enora leaned back in her chair. Distant sunlight sparkled on the Charles River, and white sails dotted the water. A flock of geese flew into the sky. Everything was going to be okay. "Do you have a Venmo account? I'll send you some money. Does five hundred—"

"Ms. Hansen," Vera interrupted.

"Yes?"

"*My* son, he's been having a hard time at school. The older boys bully him."

Enora frowned. She didn't like where this conversation was going. "Boys can be cruel—"

If Vera heard her, she didn't acknowledge it. "So I was hoping you might be able to get him into Saint Joseph's."

That was unexpected. Enora stalled for time. "I—I don't know…"

"This home is hard to get into, isn't it? But you were able to get Mike in. You must know a lot of important people."

That much was true. Enora had had to pull some serious strings to enroll Mike. The director had made such a big deal of his obsession with fires.

"Vera, this isn't the same…"

Vera spoke in a sharp whisper. "We're both just trying to help our boys, that's all. I don't want my boy getting bullied, and you don't want Mike getting expelled when the director sees the photos on my phone. Right? We both want our kids to be safe. Thanks for taking care of this, Ms. Hansen."

Before Enora could answer, Vera hung up.

Enora swore. She'd never imagined that Vera would have the nerve to blackmail her. And she knew this was no bluff. If she didn't come through, Vera wouldn't hesitate to show the director the pictures. Mike would be expelled, and the news would spread like wildfire through Boston's autism community. She'd never be able to get her son into another group home. And he needed the socialization. His psychologist had been very clear that the most important thing for him was being with other young people, practicing social interactions.

In short, Vera had her over a barrel.

Enora sighed and picked up her phone to call Saint Joseph's. She'd get this sorted out right now, and then she'd get right back to work. It was crucial that she made progress quickly. Her boy needed her.

CHAPTER 11
LONDON, UNITED KINGDOM

5:15 PM, June 7th

———

The black Rolls-Royce Phantom glided through central London traffic like a shark swimming through a school of fish. Inside were two occupants. The first, wearing a black tuxedo, was the chauffeur. The second was crisply dressed in a bespoke Henry Poole & Co. suit and a burgundy silk cravat. He held a cell phone to his ear, the light of the screen illuminating a narrow face with a large nose and a short goatee.

"Hello, Doctor Schröder?" he said.

"Yes," the man on the other end answered in a German accent.

"My name is Frank Gammon. I wanted to congratulate you on your publication in bioRxiv."

"Which publication?"

"The one titled, 'A reference-free approach to sequencing archaic genomes.'"

There was a long pause. "I'm sorry, but I have no idea

what you're talking about."

Frank frowned, his goatee twitching ever so slightly. "Well, sir, I believe this publication has put you in considerable danger. I need you to go home, lock the doors, and do not allow anyone in. I will call you when I arrive."

"Who are you? What are you talking about?"

"Doctor Schröder, I understand why you are suspicious. I realize what I ask of you is quite extraordinary. To help prove my good faith, I have deposited one hundred thousand euros into your personal bank account. Please check your balance, then call me back."

Frank hung up. He hoped that Walter Schröder would call him back. If he didn't do exactly as instructed, he'd be dead within hours.

"How much longer until we reach the airport?" he asked the chauffeur.

"About fifteen minutes."

They were just pulling up to the main terminal of London City Airport when Frank's phone buzzed. It was not a return call from Professor Schröder. Not yet.

The caller skipped pleasantries. "Frank, have you seen the publication?"

"The one in bioRxiv? Yes."

"It's extraordinary," said the voice on the phone. "The ramifications are—"

"Something we should discuss in person."

The line was quiet for a moment before the caller spoke again. "At the very least, we must warn them. Actaeon will have read it, too."

"I just spoke to Doctor Schröder. I'm at the airport, and I'll be in Leipzig in four hours."

There was a pause on the line.

"Bloody hell," said the voice quietly.

Frank frowned. "What's the problem?"

"There's a fire. It's on Channel 4."

Frank poked at a panel on the seat in front of him, and a TV screen flickered to life. Black smoke poured from a glass-walled building while a newscaster spoke dispassionately. "There appear to be mass casualties at Max Planck Institute in Leipzig…"

"Do you think it's connected?" said the voice.

Frank didn't answer. Hanging up, he quickly redialed Professor Schröder. The line rang and rang…and then went to voicemail.

CHAPTER 12
HOTEL SOLERT

Cambridge, Massachusetts
11:32 PM, June 7th

———

aksheesh, that's what he wants, the monk thought.

The bellman had carried his bags from the hotel lobby to his room. He should be paid for the service. How much was the right amount?

"Are you here for a conference?" asked the bellman, making conversation as the monk fumbled in his pockets.

The monk had no idea what the man had said—he didn't speak the language. He frowned at his cash. The money here was confusing, with all the paper bills the same color. He finally pulled out a ten-dollar bill.

The man took it with a smile. "Thank you, sir. Just call the front desk should you need anything else."

The monk nodded and closed the door to his room. He had been traveling for nearly seventy hours, first over washed-out roads, then on trains, and lastly, he'd spent a full twenty-four hours in airports and on airplanes. They'd sent a second monk with him to help him navigate, but he had departed once they'd arrived in the city. They didn't want anyone else involved in what was going to happen next. Now he was on his own.

The monk knew he should sleep, but instead, he crossed to the window to peer through the glass. It was night, but the street below was well lit. The headlights of cars shone brightly, illuminating pedestrians walking quickly along the sidewalks. A distant shout sounded as a group of young people stumbled out of a restaurant.

This world was so different from the one he knew, full of lights and noise. A constant rush of sensation. It made his head hurt.

Instinctively, he lowered himself to the carpet. Crossing his legs and closing his eyes, he drew in a breath, then exhaled slowly.

"Om mani padme hum...om mani padme hum..." he whispered.

When he felt centered, he went to his bag, withdrew a small brass statue of Buddha, and placed it next to the TV. It had been his mother's once, and he'd only recently recovered it. Years ago, after he gave up soldiering and became a monk, he'd cast off all his worldly possessions, the Buddha statue included. He'd carried it to the top of a ridge with a view of the monastery, and after praying and meditating, he'd buried it under a stone.

The abbot had allowed him to dig it up before the mission.

He jumped at the sound of a knock on his door. When he opened it, the bellman was smiling at him. He held out a large cardboard box.

"I should have called, but I thought you'd still be awake. You have a package. They said to deliver it to you immediately."

Again the words were meaningless, but the monk took the box, closed the door, and placed the box on his bed. Inside he found a black plastic case packed in Styrofoam and locked with a padlock. He unlocked it with a key from his pocket and opened the lid.

He stared at the case's contents for a long time. Then he carefully closed the lid and placed the case in the corner of the room.

He paused again to look at the statue of Buddha.

The parting words of the abbot rang in his mind. *You will remain devoted and committed. You will continue to serve your brothers. You will protect the monastery with your life.*

Almost imperceptibly, he shook his head. His eyes glistened with tears as he turned the statue around to face the wall.

CHAPTER 13
HARVARD UNIVERSITY

Cambridge, Massachusetts
6:38 AM, June 8th

———

Sara hurried across the manicured lawn in front of Harvard's Museum of Natural History. Built between 1859 and 1913, the museum was one of the world's preeminent natural history museums, on par with the Field Museum in Chicago, the California Academy of Sciences in San Francisco, and even London's exquisite Natural History Museum. Its public exhibits included an extensive display of rocks and minerals, hundreds of taxidermied animals, and a world-renowned collection of blown-glass flowers. Hundreds of thousands of people visited every year.

But out of sight, deep in its labyrinthine basement, was where its true contribution to the scientific community lay. There, submerged in formaldehyde, stuffed with cotton, and pinned to cardboard or pressed between sheets of acid-free archival paper, were over twenty-one million scientific specimens. Many of these were holotypes, the original plants and animals from which a new species was first described. A collection of near incalculable worth.

Sara swiped her ID and slipped in through a side entrance. She worked in the labs behind the main building, but she enjoyed cutting through the museum, especially early in the morning before it opened to the general public, when she had the galleries to herself.

She was passing through a new exhibit on turtle evolution when her cell phone rang. It was Amy.

"Hey, Amy."

"Sara? Have you seen the news?" Amy sounded upset.

Sara stopped walking. "What news?"

"There was a fire at the Max Planck in Leipzig." Amy's voice cracked. "Walter Schröder and everyone in his lab are dead."

The world around Sara seemed to sag. She sat down on a bench. "Oh, my God."

She could now hear Amy crying. "It's all over the news. Flames and smoke billowing from the building, police, fire trucks, and ambulances everywhere. And I just read a report on Twitter that says there may have been a mass shooting, too. I'm not sure anyone knows yet exactly what happened."

Sara imagined being trapped in a burning building during a mass shooting. The smoke, the heat of the fire, the gunshots, the screams of terror, the overwhelming sense of panic—

Except, of course, if Sara ever found herself in such a nightmare, she wouldn't panic. She knew herself too well. She'd simply dissociate and analyze everything. She'd still be working on a solution even as she burned to death.

"Sara? Are you still there?"

"I'm here," said Sara. "I'm in the museum. I'll be in the lab in five."

"Oh, I'm still at home. I'll be in in an hour. Will you be okay until then?"

"Yeah, I'm okay. It's just so—" Sara paused, trying and

failing to think of the right word to describe her emotional state. She didn't want to say she couldn't feel anything. "It's so weird to know that they're all dead."

"You know what, I'm going to get dressed right now and come on in," Amy said. "You shouldn't be alone."

As Amy hung up, Sara drew in a deep breath. Her friend was being overprotective, but she understood why. Amy had been worrying about her ever since Sara lost her mom to breast cancer three months ago. Sara had taken a leave of absence in February when her mom first entered hospice care, and she'd kept her mom company, slept in her bed, stayed with her every day and night until the very end, one short month later.

She touched the tattoo on her wrist. But she hadn't *really* been there, had she? Not emotionally, anyway. Her mind simply wouldn't let her. It was always trying to find a solution. Even when there was nothing that could be done.

Sara rose to her feet. The museum would be opening in a few minutes. The best thing to do right now was to get to her office, analyze some data, and try to put the news about the Schröder Lab out of her mind.

She pushed through the exit in the back of the mammalogy exhibit and crossed into the stairwell that led to the labs. This section of the building had once been a 1960s architectural monstrosity, but two years ago, it had been torn down and rebuilt. Now windows wrapped the space in a glass exoskeleton that made it look like a giant insect.

Dr. Fitzpatrick's lab was on the fifth floor, and Sara was slightly winded when she reached it. The floor was entirely open, with glass-walled offices along one side, giving her the feeling that she was a fish in an aquarium, or as Amy liked to say in a faux-ominous voice, "It's a human-sized cage."

She dropped her laptop bag next to her desk and turned to look out across the space. At 6:30 AM, it was empty. Light poured in through the east-facing windows, sparkling off rows of glassware and scientific instruments that formed a state-of-the-art wet lab: tissue culture hoods, incubators, PCR machines, and microscopes. Even with the ubiquity of genomic data, publishing in a high-profile journal almost always required follow-up functional assays. As Arthur had said in their meeting, "Correlation is not causation." You had to show that the genetic changes actually caused a real physical difference in the organism. In some cases, they even used live animals to validate their results.

Sara went over to Amy's bench, where a small brown mouse sat in a plastic cage. It looked up at her with black eyes as it scratched itself. Totally adorable, and almost certainly not long for this world. Mice only went in one direction, from the breeding facility to Dr. Fitzpatrick's lab. Never back again.

To her surprise, she suddenly turned and practically ran back to her desk. There was simply too much death to process this morning. Her mom, the Schröder Lab. The little mouse was just one too many.

She felt silly. It was just a mouse. *This* was what got her emotional?

She opened her laptop and loaded up her terminal application. She entered her password to log into Odyssey, Harvard's high-performance computer cluster, and her cursor blinked, ready for her to enter a command. Already she could feel herself relaxing once more, the familiarity of the Linux environment soothing and calming her. She was escaping into a flow state, where the intense mental focus required to analyze data forced her to block out all distractions.

Within moments, she'd pushed the horror and sadness away and let code fill her mind.

CHAPTER 14
HARVARD UNIVERSITY

Cambridge, Massachusetts
8:31 AM, June 8th

———

Marcus Byron sat on a bench and looked out over the green lawn of Harvard Yard. The ancient quad was virtually empty. Two weeks ago, the undergrads had finished their finals, deserting the place, and for whatever reason, the tourists hadn't shown up yet. That left him alone between the trunks of hundred-year-old oak trees, the bronze statue of the university's founder, John Harvard, and the sense of atmosphere that could only be found in one of the world's most respected institutions.

Not that he gave a crap about any of that.

He took a sip from his large Dunkin' Donuts coffee, grimaced, then put it down. He'd gotten it "regular," the Massachusetts shorthand for "extra cream and sugar," and while there was something comforting about ordering in the local jargon, the coffee was far too sweet for his taste.

It was strange to be in Cambridge. He'd spent his teenage years living around the corner in a small apartment on Holden Street. In fact, his mum still lived there, though he hadn't told her he was in town. He felt guilty about that, but she would have wanted him to stay an extra night and visit his cousins, all the while constantly reminding him he should settle down and have a family. The work trip would have turned into a big production. It was easier to just get a hotel downtown, do the interview, then take the train back to New York.

He reached into his pocket, pulled out his reporter's notebook, and read through the questions he'd outlined the night before. Obviously, Dr. Fitzpatrick's finding was extraordinary. A new way to investigate human origins. Marcus had even been thinking about a headline for the article he was going to write: "Harvard lab discovers 'fossil' genomes hidden within our own." There was a good chance it would make the front page. He just needed to clarify the extent of the discovery. Had they run their analysis on any other populations? How far back in time could they go? Would it work on different species?

And then there was the matter of the preprint on bioRxiv. It was obviously relevant to his article on its own, but what made it particularly notable was that it had been sent to him as an anonymous tip. That added a whole new level of delicious scientific intrigue. He couldn't wait to ask the professor about it.

He checked his watch. His meeting was still more than an hour off. He could kill time on the bench drinking the terrible coffee, or he could try to talk with some of Fitzpatrick's lab members first. Get a firsthand account of the discovery. Maybe even work out what was going on with the competing manuscript.

Yes. That was what he should do.

He stood up and took one final slug of the too-sweet coffee

before dropping it still half-full into a bin. Then he started toward Oxford Street.

As he walked, he remembered the first time he'd ever stepped foot in the yard. The fall of 1998. A month after his dad had died in the Nairobi embassy bombing. The second worst year of his life.

He pushed those horrible memories out of his mind, but it was hard to be here and not recall something about those long-ago days. When he found himself passing in front of Widener Library, an imposing edifice with massive marble columns each nearly six feet in diameter, he remembered sneaking past the security guard as a teenager and wandering around inside, soaking up the atmosphere.

He tried to think only of his interview, but his mind insisted on drifting to the strange history of Harvard University. The off-limits library, the network of underground tunnels connecting many of the buildings, the secret societies that had included among their members presidents like Theodore Roosevelt. The campus was ancient, built between Puritan cow paths back when some of Harvard's scientists were alchemists trying to turn lead to gold.

Of course, Marcus had never actually attended the university himself. Despite being a good student, he'd never even considered it. His mum barely had enough money to pay rent. So when he graduated high school, he took a different path. Thirsting for adventure, for his lost childhood, and knowing he needed to travel, he applied to join the Peace Corps. They didn't usually accept volunteers without bachelor's degrees, but by some stroke of luck, they'd taken him, and he ended up teaching English in Myanmar for two years.

Ultimately, the contacts he made in the Peace Corps enabled him to start working as a freelance journalist, which led to more adventure than he'd ever dreamed of. Ten amazing years of it.

Until the day it all went to hell in Aleppo.

He closed his eyes and shook his head as if the physical action would remove the memory of Syria from his mind.

When he looked up, he found that he was standing in front of Harvard's Museum of Natural History. Fitzpatrick's email had said his offices were in the new laboratory building just behind the main museum. Marcus felt his excitement beginning to build.

He would use this interview to tell an amazing story, one that wasn't usually associated with the venerated Harvard University. It was the story of a brilliant scientist who'd been scooped at the last possible minute.

CHAPTER 15
SANTORINI

Cyclades Islands, Greece
3:48 PM, June 8th

———

With a glass of wine in his hand, Alexi rested his elbows on the rail of *Krateros II*, his AMELS 188 luxury yacht. From his perch on the sky deck, three stories above the water, he had a panoramic view of the Aegean Sea. To the west was the island of Therasia. Small and dry, it was hardly more than a rock. To the east, the cliffs of Santorini curved round in a protective embrace. The Meltemi winds had died the day before, and the sea was glassy smooth. It was the beginning of a perfect afternoon.

He swirled the wine before taking a long sip.

For nearly forty-five years, Alexi had made the Aegean his home. He loved all the islands, but Santorini was his favorite. The lagoon provided a sheltered harbor, and the two towns on the island were relatively quiet, not crawling with tourists.

Which was ironic given that Santorini's history was anything but tranquil. Nearly four thousand years earlier, it had been a single island named Thera, home to a large settlement of Minoans. Then, in a volcanic eruption at least one hundred times larger than the blast that destroyed Mount St. Helens, it had been annihilated. The Minoan settlement was buried in two hundred feet of pumice and ash.

The effects had rippled around the ancient world. Tsunamis battered Crete's coastline, and the resulting volcanic winter caused famines as far away as China. But it was the destruction of Thera—the island literally sinking into the sea, taking the lost Minoan settlement with it—that was most famous. Many believed it was what inspired Plato's tale of Atlantis.

Alexi looked out over the ocean, now blissfully still. Only the intermittent toll of a buoy gong marred the tranquility. It rang again now, and he scowled. God, he hated that sound.

"Kostas, you think I can hit that buoy?" he said in Greek.

Kostas was a tall, dark-haired twenty-year-old. Wearing only a black Speedo, he lounged on a deck chair and poked idly at a cell phone. "I am certain of it," he said without looking up.

Alexi squinted at the buoy, gauging the distance. "Come. Look. Tell me what you think."

Kostas sighed in annoyance, but he put his phone down and joined Alexi by the rail. "Oh, that's quite far, Alexi. At least fifty meters."

"It's nothing. Watch."

Handing Kostas his wine glass, Alexi stepped back from the rail. He wore only a pair of blue board shorts, and he rolled his shoulders, stretching the thick muscles of his back, then flexed his toes on the wooden deck, testing their purchase. Finally, he reached for the javelin that lay on a nearby lounge chair.

It was about a foot taller than him with a steel tip. A thin loop of leather was tied round the center. Alexi balanced the butt of javelin on his toe and spun the shaft, tightening the leather strap. He slipped his first and middle fingers through the loop, and then, in a series of practiced moves, he lifted the spear to his shoulder and took three long strides across the deck. As he finished the third stride, he twisted, torquing his body, and whipped his right arm forward. His fingers pressed hard on the leather, transferring the force directly into the shaft.

The javelin rocketed over the sea. Spinning through the air, the steel tip flashed in the midday sun. It reached the apex of its flight, then descended like an eagle diving for a fish. It landed with a tinny *thunk*.

Alexi had struck the buoy dead center.

"What did I say?" he said, grinning.

Kostas nodded, impressed, and handed Alexi back his wine glass. "Very nice."

Alexi was just taking a celebratory sip of his wine when the younger man's cell phone rang.

"It's for you," said Kostas, passing the phone to Alexi.

"Hello?" he said, putting the phone to his ear.

There was a pause, then a man spoke, his voice slightly muffled. "Alexi, we have a problem. There has been a discovery—" Another pause. "Our secret may not be safe."

"Hold on." Alexi covered the microphone at the bottom of the phone. "Kostas, can you give me a moment?"

Kostas shrugged and began to cross to the ship's cabin. "Sure. I need more wine, anyway."

Alexi put the phone back to his ear. "I'm sorry. You were saying?"

The man spoke quietly as he explained the situation. When he was finished, Alexi rested against the railing, digesting what he'd been told. In front of him, the Mediterranean sparkled in the sun.

At last, he responded. "You should have told me about this earlier. Sending a hound was a mistake. That much is clear."

"I had to act quickly. If they'd learned—"

"I understand," said Alexi, interrupting. "I will go to London. I will see that nothing is revealed."

He hung up and looked out over the water. A motorboat whizzed past, and the whine of its engine cut through the air like a klaxon. Alexi wished he still had his javelin.

Grimacing, he followed Kostas into the cabin. He found the young man stretched out on one of the leather settees, a fresh glass of wine in his hand.

"Kostas, how would you like to travel with me to London?"

Kostas grinned. "Could we go to Ministry of Sound?"

Inwardly, Alexi groaned. The pounding bass and flashing lights of the famous London club were not remotely his idea of fun. But just as Kostas indulged his interests—hunting, mixed martial arts, and javelin throwing—so, too, did he have to indulge Kostas's obsession with dubstep.

"Of course."

He sat next to Kostas and put his arm around the man's shoulders. Thin yet strong. He remembered when he'd had shoulders like those—when he'd had the world at his feet. That was so long ago, but it seemed like yesterday.

Kostas leaned against him. Alexi exhaled sharply as Kostas's tongue began to explore the shell of his ear. Gently, he pushed Kostas away.

"Not now."

Alexi loved Kostas deeply, but it was his duty to train him, to teach him how to be a man. And that included learning patience and restraint.

CHAPTER 16
HARVARD UNIVERSITY

Cambridge, Massachusetts
11:55 AM, June 8th

———

Sara jumped when she felt a tap on her shoulder. She pulled off her headphones and found Amy standing behind her. "What's up?"

"Wanna get lunch?"

"It's lunchtime already? I thought you were going to stop by when you came in."

"I did, but you looked really focused." Amy paused, her face clouding. "How are you doing?"

It took Sara a second to realize she was asking about the Schröder Lab. "Better. You?"

"Processing, I guess. It just doesn't seem real..." Amy trailed off, and an awkward silence followed. It was broken by the noise of Sara's stomach growling. "It sounds like you're ready to eat," Amy said. "Pinocchio's Pizza all right with you? Some of the postdocs are going, I thought we could tag along."

"Sure. Pizza's fine." Sara closed her laptop and stood. There were people here now, though she'd been so focused on her work, she hadn't noticed. She spotted Arthur among them, sitting at an empty lab bench, his laptop open. Several other postdocs stood by the door to the hallway, talking to a man she didn't recognize.

No—she *did* recognize him. It was Marcus Byron from *The New York Times*. She'd tipped him off about the preprint she'd submitted, which meant he was here to talk to Topher, which meant…Topher was going to go ballistic when he found out they'd been scooped.

Definitely not a bad time to go for lunch.

While Amy grabbed her purse, Sara waited at the end of the bench. The bench was one of six large black countertops that extended from the wall of windows into the main part of the lab space. Underneath the benches were built-in storage cabinets, and each bench top was divided by a row of shelves filled with reagent bottles, boxes of blue nitrile gloves, plastic containers of disposable pipette tips, and laboratory notebooks. Between each of the benches was a long bay with enough room for four work stations.

Amy's station was close to the entrance of the bay. It was immaculately clean with no clutter. The mouse cage that had been there earlier was gone. In its place stood a large Styrofoam cooler.

"What are you working on?" Sara asked. To Sara, the wet-lab side of science was in many ways a black box. She'd taken an introductory class in molecular biology, but her actual hands-on laboratory experience consisted of basically one lab where she'd grown bacteria on a petri dish after swabbing the inside of her mouth. What Amy did was magic, as far as she was concerned.

"Prepping tissue for histological sections."

"Is that what the mouse I saw this morning was for?"

"Yes. We mutated a gene associated with unusually dark

human pigmentation. I'm working on making frozen sections of the skin so we can get some microscopy of the hair follicles and melanocytes."

It took Sara a moment to process the significance of that statement. "Does that mean you had to skin the mouse?"

The shadow of a guilty look passed over Amy's face. "Unfortunately, yes."

Sara nodded at the cooler. "And you're keeping the sections in there?"

"Temporarily." Amy pushed the cooler toward Sara. Inside, an opaque liquid bubbled and steamed. "This is dry ice mixed with 95% ethanol. It's negative seventy-two degrees Celsius—super cold. I use it for flash-freezing samples." She pointed to some square-shaped plastic containers floating on the surface of the icy slurry. "You can't see because they're frozen, but there are little pieces of mouse skin in the center of each of those cubes. When we come back from lunch, I'll move them to the minus eighty-degree freezer—"

Amy was cut off by three incredibly loud explosions in rapid succession. *Bang! Bang! Bang!* Sara spun toward the noise even as one of the lab's windows shattered behind her. Across the room, a man in a ski mask held a rifle. And it was pointed in her direction.

She practically dove to the floor. Next to her, Amy stood frozen in terror.

"Amy, get down—" she started, but too late.

Bang! Bang! Bang! Another three-round burst.

Amy collapsed.

This isn't happening.

But it was. Someone was screaming. And all around her, the remains of the window sparkled like diamonds. The smell of burned gunpowder filled the room. Sara scrambled around the opposite side of the lab bench.

Her heart was beating a mile a minute.

This is a mass shooting.

There were more gunshots. The screaming stopped, and the lab went silent. Her stomach clenching, Sara realized that everyone must be either hiding or dead. Then she heard the footsteps, pausing at each bay between the benches. Moving inexorably closer to her.

Sara pressed herself against the cabinets beneath the bench. The shooter had nearly reached the bay with Amy's station. In moments, he'd reach the bay she was hiding in.

But even as shock tried to set in, her brain kicked into action. There had to be something she could do. Devise a plan. Think analytically.

What do I know about mass shootings?

She remembered the school shooting mantra: "Run, hide, fight." If she ran, she'd be shot. She didn't have anything to fight with. That left hiding.

She heard shoes crunch on glass. The shooter was close now. If he came around the end of the lab bench, he'd see her. And then he'd kill her. She was certain of it.

She needed to hide. But where?

A few feet away from her was an alcove under the bench where you could push in a chair. It wasn't great, but it was all she had. Keeping her head down, she crawled across the broken glass and slipped inside.

The hiding place was even worse than she'd thought. She'd expected the alcove to be a sort of dead-end nook she could hide in. In reality, it was an open tunnel that led under the bench to the other side. Anyone could see her if they got close enough. She was almost as exposed now as she had been before.

Even worse, from here, she could see Amy. Her best friend was lying motionless, a pool of blood growing around her.

Suddenly, Amy's body twitched. She made a wet, gasping noise. Sara felt a surge of hope.

She's still alive.

Then a pair of black boots stepped into view. Amy gasped again, her diaphragm spasming.

The black muzzle of a rifle appeared above her. He was so close. If he crouched, he'd be looking right at Sara.

The barrel moved toward Amy. Sara watched with detached fascination, unable to tear her eyes away from what was about to happen.

The shape of the rifle jogged an old memory. Back in Vermont, her brother had an extensive collection of guns. The last time she'd been home, he'd mixed margaritas, and they'd gone out back to shoot a few rounds in the woods behind his house.

Why am I thinking about this? But she couldn't put the memory out of her head. The adrenaline had sent her mind in a crazy direction.

"Bullets and booze go together like boobies and beer," he'd said.

He'd grinned wickedly when Sara glared at him.

Now she studied the weapon and realized it *was* familiar. A large triangular sight followed a tapered hand guard. It looked exactly like her bro's Bushmaster XM-15 semi-automatic rifle.

So I've shot the weapon that's going to be used to kill me.

A useless fact. One last irony.

The shooter used the muzzle to flip Amy's right arm over. He grunted something in a language she didn't understand. Then the barrel of the gun disappeared.

Sara tensed as she waited for the shot that was sure to come. But instead of a report and a spray of blood, she heard a shout. Something was driven into the side of the lab bench, and glass bottles shattered. The shooter grunted in pain, and the rifle fell to the floor. A moment later, he followed, rolling across the floor while grappling with another man.

An instant later, the shooter was on his back, the second man straddling him. The man on top slammed his fist into the shooter's masked face with a smacking crack, like a baseball bat hitting a wet tennis ball.

But the shooter was wiry. Twisting under his assailant, he clawed for the rifle. He was punched a second time, just as hard, but didn't stop stretching his hand toward the Bushmaster. And with a sharp twinge of terror, Sara realized that he was going to get it.

There was no time for analysis now. Acting purely on instinct, she scrabbled from her hiding spot under the bench.

Now she could see the second man's face. It was Marcus Byron, the reporter. Both men seemed to pause at the sight of her unexpected appearance. She couldn't see the shooter's face behind the black ski mask, but his eyes seemed to pierce her very soul.

Then his fingers wrapped around the grip of the Bushmaster's lower receiver.

Run.

That was what she should be doing. She *knew* that was what she should be doing. But even as she rose to her feet, she hesitated. The reporter had saved her. She couldn't just leave him.

Her hand brushed against the cooler on the bench.

"Watch out, Marcus!" she shouted, lifting the cooler.

The reporter dodged back. The shooter began to raise the rifle. And Sara flung the cooler at his head.

Again, everything seemed to move in slow motion, a moment captured in time, the cooler frozen in midair, the rifle rising. Then time restarted, and the shooter screamed as a negative-seventy-four-degree slurry washed over his face.

The Bushmaster fell to the floor as the shooter clawed at his head, and Sara lunged for it. She grabbed the gun and aimed it at the shooter.

"Don't move!"

The shooter had managed to wrench his mask off, and the skin of his face was purplish-gray where it had frozen. His eyes were bright with pain. Still, he began to push himself up from the floor.

"I said *don't move*."

The shooter ignored her as he rose to his knees.

"I *will* shoot you."

The shooter lunged, and Sara's finger jerked against the trigger. She fired five rounds into his chest.

The man collapsed at her feet.

"Oh, my God," she breathed, stepping back, ears ringing. Her body shook with adrenaline. She felt sick.

The reporter caught her by the elbow. "Are you hurt?"

"No," Sara murmured, still trying to process everything that had just happened. She'd killed a man. A deranged gunman. Her best friend lay in a pool of blood.

Amy.

Lowering the rifle, she began to kneel at her friend's side.

The reporter held her back. "She's not going to make it."

"She's breathing."

"Agonal breaths. Death reflex."

Sara's stomach lurched. He was right. She knew it. The gasping breaths were only an involuntary brainstem response.

Amy was dead.

CHAPTER 17
MOUNT AUBURN HOSPITAL

Cambridge, Massachusetts
3:31 PM, June 8th

———

Marcus tried to get comfortable on the floor of the cell, but the unyielding concrete, combined with the noise of the other prisoners, made it nearly impossible to sleep. Even now, on the far side of the room, a man moaned softly, calling for his mother.

There was a noise outside in the hall, and Marcus closed his eyes and pretended to doze. Though the sounds were muffled, he could hear the footsteps as ten, twenty, maybe as many as fifty men passed the cell door. They didn't speak or cry out, and apart from their footsteps, they were quiet as ghosts. He kept his eyes closed even after they passed.

When he finally opened his eyes, it was silent. Even the crying man had quieted. The cell was flat and gray in the gloom. Had the men even passed the door? He couldn't be sure.

He was just drifting off when he heard a second noise. Not

outside the door this time. The sound came from beneath the floor, muffled coughing and gurgling.

The sound of fifty men being hanged in the basement.

"Are you all right?" said a voice.

Snapping out of the nightmare, Marcus opened his eyes. The harsh light of an ER waiting room seared his retinas as he squinted up from the chair where he'd fallen asleep.

A nurse hovered over him, arms crossed. "You were moaning. I thought you said you weren't injured."

Marcus realized the nurse wasn't going to leave until he said something. "I fell asleep. Had a bad dream."

"It's not uncommon to have panic attacks after what you experienced. There's a counselor you could speak to—"

Marcus shook his head quickly. "I'm fine, really."

He didn't need another shrink poking about in his skull. It hadn't helped before, and he doubted it would now.

There was a commotion behind the nurse, and they both turned to look. A young woman was nearly shouting at a police officer just in front of the nurses' station. And not just any young woman, Marcus realized—*the* young woman. Brown hair, blue eyes. The woman who'd saved his life. Killed the shooter.

As he watched her argue with the officer, more of the waking world intruded, filling his consciousness: the antiseptic smell, the slightly dingy chairs, the buzzing sound of his cell phone. Only now did his brain start to put the pieces back together. After the shooting, he'd been put in an ambulance and taken straight to Mount Auburn Hospital. They'd said it was standard procedure after these sorts of events. Of course, once he'd arrived and they'd determined he wasn't seriously injured, they'd just sat him in the ER waiting room, where he must have fallen asleep.

His phone buzzed again.

The nurse was still looking at the woman as he pulled it

from his pocket. Twenty-two text messages. The newest one read:

> Where are you? I need you covering the shooting at Harvard.

That was from his boss, Barb Palizzi.

He typed back a response:

> At Mt. Auburn Hospital.

He was going to add that he'd been present at the shooting but stopped himself. That would make him an eyewitness. Barb would send someone to interview him. Probably that new reporter with the slicked-back hair. The guy was ambitious, a total kiss-ass. Marcus was *not* going to let "pompadour" scoop this story.

He made up his mind. The interviews and his firsthand account could come later. Right now, he should talk to the young woman who'd saved him. Get her on the record.

She continued to argue with the police officer, a bit calmer now, but still upset. If he helped her, maybe she'd talk to him.

He stood slowly, testing his legs. A little shaky, but stable enough. The adrenaline had worn off. He drew in a long breath. He was alive. Everything was going to be okay.

The nurse held out a hand. "Sir, I think you should—"

"I'm fine," he said, brushing her off. Then he walked over to the woman who'd saved his life.

The police officer was leaning over her, using his authority to his fullest advantage. Marcus cut in right away. "Is everything okay here?" he said.

"He wants to interview me," the woman replied. She looked up at him, and he could see exhaustion etched in her eyes. He knew that look. She needed a hug and a stiff drink, not a police officer's questions.

He turned to the officer. "Can this wait until later?"

The officer was a large man with cropped hair and thick lips. Early fifties, he guessed. Marcus wouldn't have been surprised to learn they'd stood together in line for coffee that morning. Quintessential Boston cop.

"You're the reporter who arrived with her," the officer said, his eyes narrowing slightly.

Marcus also recognized that expression. The one that said he was a suspect.

"What's your name and badge number, sir?" he asked quickly. Massachusetts law was clear: police officers had to identify themselves. This showed the cop that Marcus knew his rights.

"Lachance, one-eight-seven-four. I'll need to speak to you as well, sir."

Marcus's chest tightened as his adrenal gland released a fresh dose of adrenaline. For a moment, he could almost hear the distant sound of choking. How many men had been hanged in that basement room?

"First and last name?" said the officer, now turned to face Marcus directly. The man's lips were pressed tight; he wasn't going to budge.

"I don't have to tell you that."

"Sir, this is—"

The radio clipped to the officer's breast pocket squawked. "We have a report of an additional shooting suspect. Sara Morin, five-two, one-twenty, brown and blue."

Marcus knew that name, a grad student on Dr. Fitzpatrick's team. She was on the list of names he had planned to interview before—

The officer grabbed the woman's wrist and jerked her arm behind her.

"Ow!" she cried out, instinctively twisting in the officer's grasp.

"Wait," said Marcus. "Her? She's not a suspect. She saved my life."

At that moment, a doctor in bloodstained scrubs burst through a set of double doors, eyes wild with fear. "Help," he gasped, stumbling.

He made it only a few steps before collapsing. It was then that Marcus noticed the handle of a scalpel protruding from the side of the doctor's neck.

Before anyone could react, a second figure burst through the doors behind the doctor. Black hair, piercing eyes. Marcus recognized him instantly.

The shooter from the lab.

And his eyes were locked on Sara.

CHAPTER 18
MOUNT AUBURN HOSPITAL

Cambridge, Massachusetts
3:42 PM, June 8th

———

Sara stared in disbelief as the shooter barreled toward her. How was he not dead? She had shot him point-blank in the chest. Five times. You don't survive that. Yet here he was, his eyes boring into her, bright and fierce. He was alive. And he wanted to kill her.

The police officer released her as he reached for his service weapon. She stumbled backward until a strong hand grabbed her wrist. The reporter again. He started to say something, but his words were drowned out by the sound of the officer discharging his Glock at the charging assailant.

This time, Sara didn't hesitate. She ran, sprinting toward the exit, only glancing behind her as she slammed through the door. The police officer was down. The shooter was crouched next to him. In seconds, he would be armed again.

She burst outside into the late afternoon sun, her eyes searching for a place to hide.

"This way!" shouted the reporter, who had appeared at her side. Together, they raced across the asphalt toward the hospital parking garage.

Behind them were more gunshots, and a bullet whined above Sara's head. The garage's entrance loomed, dark, cavernous, and safe. Sara put everything she had into reaching the protection of its shadowy entrance.

She passed across the threshold at a dead sprint, following the reporter toward a ramp to the upper levels. She wanted to shout at him that they'd be cornered, but she didn't want to alert the shooter to their location, so she just ran after him, her lungs burning.

The ramp twisted back on itself, and they raced another fifty feet before the reporter pointed to a pickup truck.

"Quick," he said, his chest heaving. "We can hide in the back."

They climbed up and lay down flat. Lying next to her on the corrugated plastic of the pickup bed, the reporter held a finger to his lips.

Sara heard the assailant's pounding footsteps coming closer. Her lungs ached for air, but she fought the desire to suck in breaths. Her cell phone was a heavy lump in her pocket, and she considered dialing 911, but that, too, would make noise. Besides, there was no doubt that they'd already been called. So she merely lay still, trying to be as quiet as possible. The realization that this was the end of her life was impossible to ignore.

She suddenly pictured Amy, the blood on her lips, the horrible bubbling breaths. When her mom had been sick, Sara had at least been able to hold her hand until the very end. How was she ever going to tell Amy's parents that their daughter had died alone?

The growl of an engine broke the silence, then more gunshots echoed off the concrete. The reporter squeezed firmly on Sara's wrist, telling her by his grip alone not to move.

A brief period of quiet followed, then the clear sound of footsteps sprinting past them.

She turned to the reporter. *I'm going to look,* she mouthed silently while pointing in the direction the footsteps had gone.

He nodded.

Very slowly, so as not to make any sound, she peeked over the edge of the truck bed.

Almost directly next to the pickup, in between the two lines of parked cars on either side of the concrete ramp, was a blue Toyota Camry. Its windshield was pockmarked with bullet holes. The driver was slumped over the steering wheel, unmoving. She'd been trying to get out of the garage. She didn't make it.

Past the car, at the top of the ramp, was the shooter. His back was to her as he walked slowly, making his way upward to the next level.

Fear clutched at Sara's heart. At the end of the level, the ramp doubled back again, and when the shooter turned the corner and started up the opposite side, he'd have a full view down into the truck bed.

"We can't stay here," she whispered.

"Should we run?"

"No. It's too far. He'll shoot us long before we could escape."

Her brain raced through possibilities. Could they crawl under a car? Create a diversion? Fight the shooter?

Then she had it. The shot-up Camry. Its engine was still running. If they could slip into it quietly, while the shooter was at the top of the ramp…

She peeked over the edge of the truck bed again. The shooter was coming to the end of the ramp. In seconds, he'd come back around and be in position to see them.

"Follow me," she whispered as loudly as she dared.

Moving as quickly and quietly as she could, she slipped over the side of the truck and landed silently on the concrete. An instant later, the reporter was crouched behind her. She caught his eye and pointed at the Camry directly in front of them. He nodded in understanding.

Sucking in a deep breath, she ran to the car. But as she opened the driver's-side door, the first crack in her plan revealed itself. The driver was still in the driver's seat. She'd imagined jumping into an empty seat and gunning the Camry down the ramp and out the exit before the shooter had a chance to line up a shot. Instead, she found herself trying to pull the body of a young woman out of the driver's seat.

And the woman wasn't dead.

"Mmmpphhh …" the woman groaned, eyes staring wildly. Then she flailed and flopped forward onto the steering wheel.

The horn blared like a klaxon.

"He sees us!" shouted the reporter from the back seat.

There was no time. Sara threw herself into the driver's lap and slammed her foot on the accelerator.

This was where the second crack in her plan revealed itself. Instead of going forward, the car lurched backward up the ramp. The woman had apparently just finished backing out when she'd been shot. The car was in reverse.

Instinctively, Sara looked in the rearview mirror. The shooter stood at the top of the ramp, silhouetted against the late afternoon sun. He raised the officer's stolen Glock—

"Get down!" she shouted, ducking her head and jerking the steering wheel. The Camry swerved, the shooter fired, and the rear window exploded in a spray of glass.

Sara needed to get the car going forward. She started to release the accelerator and move her foot toward the brake. But then she hesitated, her mind working. If she stopped the car long enough to put it into drive, the shooter would get a clear shot.

She ducked at the sound of another gunshot. This time, one of the passenger windows shattered.

"Go forward!" shouted the reporter.

The driver moaned, twisting under her.

Sara was going to die.

She glanced at the rearview mirror again. The shooter now stood directly behind them. Sunlight reflected off the Glock as he sighted down the barrel. He was so close, there was no way he was going to miss this time.

That's the solution, she realized.

She jammed her foot as hard as she could against the accelerator.

Beneath her, the injured woman screamed in pain.

Sara looked into the rearview mirror once more. The shooter didn't even try to dodge. He fired once more—another hole appeared in the windshield—before the car struck him, sending him sprawling on the concrete.

Sara jammed her foot on the brake and slammed the car into drive. An instant later, they were flying down the ramp toward the exit. She looked in the rearview. The shooter was already moving, climbing to his knees.

She pressed the accelerator as far as it would go.

They careened around the curving ramp of the parking garage, metal shrieking as they scraped against the concrete wall. The boom gate at the exit was down, but they crashed right through it, snapping the wood like a matchstick.

Sara somehow directed the car toward the main hospital entrance.

The injured driver struggled for freedom.

"Almost there," Sara said. She hadn't saved Amy, but she could save this woman.

She hopped the curb before bringing the Camry to a screeching stop. She threw herself into the passenger seat and screamed at the driver, "You need to get out!"

The driver didn't move. She looked dazed.

"She's in shock," said the reporter. He pushed open his door and came around to the driver's door.

Sara looked back at the parking garage. There was no sign of the shooter. Then she looked toward the hospital entrance. A security guard was crouched just inside the door, eyes wide.

"For fuck's sake, help us!"

A moment later, the guard was helping the reporter pull the driver from the car.

Sara looked back again at the parking garage. The shooter was racing out of the entrance on foot. His shirt was drenched in blood, and there was no sign of the gun. He spotted the Camry and came at them at a dead sprint.

"He's coming!" she shouted.

With the driver out of the car, the reporter jumped into the driver's seat. Tires squealing, he tore out of the parking lot and began flying down Mount Auburn Street. For the briefest of moments, Sara thought they were free, but the reporter was shouting something about the passenger door.

Sara spun—and was shocked at what she saw. The passenger door was partly open, and the shooter was clinging to the bottom of the door frame with one hand, his body bouncing along the pavement beside them.

Even as she stared in disbelief, his free hand reached for her.

She started to lift her foot to stamp on his fingers, then stopped. What if he grabbed her ankle? He seemed impossibly strong.

Instead, she grabbed the door handle and slammed the door shut with all her strength.

There was a bump, and then she saw the shooter's body rolling in the street behind them.

CHAPTER 19
LONDON, UNITED KINGDOM

8:45 PM, June 8th

———

F rank cupped the crystal snifter in his palm and swirled it gently. The trick with Cognac was to allow the warmth of your hand to release the liquor's bouquet. Bringing the glass to his nose, he inhaled the aroma. Floral, with the faintest aroma of vanilla. It was an 1811 Sazerac de Forge & Fils from his cellar, one of his few remaining bottles and virtually impossible to obtain. He took a long sip, savoring the flavor of the ancient liquor. Perfection.

He looked out the tall window at his side and studied London's skyline. Beyond the Oxo Tower, he could see the elongated pyramid of the Shard. A mere one hundred years ago, one could have seen the full breadth of the Thames from this window—the water had been closer then. But the combination of scientific progress and brilliant twentieth-century engineering had rerouted the river a few blocks away. Now all he could see were the dark shapes of buildings.

Behind him, reflected in the window's glass, a TV flickered.

"Breaking news," said the announcer. "There has been a mass shooting at Harvard University's Museum of Natural History."

Frank put down his snifter and turned to face the screen. The feed showed a young reporter standing on the lawn in front of the museum. Sirens screamed amid the flashing lights of ambulances and police vehicles.

"The shooting occurred in one of the labs associated with the Natural History Museum. There appear to be multiple people injured. No word on casualties."

Frank was already reaching for his phone when it began buzzing.

"Hi, Frank—"

"Call London City Airport and ready the Falcon 7X. I'll be there in an hour."

CHAPTER 20
AETER PHARMACEUTICALS

Cambridge, Massachusetts
3:48 PM, June 8th

———

Will I be going to hell for bribing a priest? Enora wondered. Then she decided that if she was going to hell, so, too, was the priest.

The important thing was that she'd gotten Vera's son into Saint Joseph's. The little bugger would be starting next term. It hadn't been cheap, either. A fifty grand donation to the school's general fund plus another thirty-five grand annually for tuition—a steep price to pay for Vera's silence.

Enora looked out her office window. The Charles River sparkled in the distance, dotted as always by the sails of a few small sailboats. She wished she were out there herself. She loved the water, the sound of the waves, the gentle rocking motion. She had her own boat, a 1965 Riva Ariston she'd had shipped all the way from Italy. She kept it up at her home in Gloucester. Whenever her boy visited, he always insisted she take him for a ride.

"Motorboat. Motorboat. Motorboat." He'd repeat his request for hours until she gave in and took him out. Rain or shine, he didn't care.

Thinking about Mike made her want to talk to him, so she unlocked her cell phone and started a video chat. He picked up instantly. If there was one thing her boy loved as much as the boat, it was answering the phone.

"Hi, kiddo. How's your day?"

He didn't respond. Answering the phone he could do; having a conversation, not so much.

"Did you work on any sudoku?"

He ignored her. Enora didn't mind; her love for him was unconditional. And it wasn't as though he entirely lacked talent. He could recite the lyrics to any Beatles song, he was an expert at sudoku, and if a meteor strike ever sent society lurching back to the dark ages, he could start a fire with little more than a magnifying glass and a wad of toilet paper. He was brilliant in his own way.

"I talked to Vera today."

This time Mike looked at the screen. "Unsafe," he repeated in his monotone voice.

"Do you remember what you did that wasn't okay?"

He stared mutely at the screen.

"I know you remember."

"Fire is unsafe," he finally said.

The group home had been amazing in this respect. They'd gotten him to acknowledge when he'd misbehaved. That was real progress.

"That's right," said Enora soothingly. "If you're upset, you can do a puzzle or listen to music with Vera."

Her son's expression began to darken, and she sensed he might have an outburst.

"Do you want me to sing a Beatles song?" she said quickly.

He didn't respond, but she began to sing "Ob-La-Di, Ob-La-Da" anyway. After a minute, he joined in, a bit tunelessly.

When she finished singing, for the briefest of instants, he smiled. Enora felt her heart break.

"I'll visit you tomorrow, okay?"

"Okay," Mike repeated.

Enora hung up and leaned back in her chair, her heart feeling a mix of emotions. She loved her son with every fiber of her being, and she was so incredibly proud of the progress he'd been making, but at the same time, she was terrified for him. She had no family, his dad was a one-night stand, and she wasn't getting any younger. Last month, she'd turned fifty-six. Kiddo was only thirteen. When he was thirty-three, she'd be in her late seventies. And when he was in his fifties, she'd be in her late nineties—if she was even alive.

This was her greatest fear, leaving him alone to fend for himself.

At that moment, she wanted more than anything to hug him and tell him she loved him. She calmed herself by remembering that she'd see him after work tomorrow. She would sing him as many Beatles songs as he liked.

Her office door flew open.

"Ms. Hansen?" Her secretary was frantic. "Have you seen the news?"

"What news?" Enora imagined a crash in the stock market, or one of her investors backing out.

"There's been a mass shooting at Harvard, in the Fitz-patrick Lab."

Enora's stomach clenched. "Did they kill—"

"No. She's alive."

"Have you told Paul?"

"Of course. First thing I did."

CHAPTER 21

The Humvee's engine roared as Marcus pressed the accelerator to the floor. Outside, Aleppo's bombed-out apartment blocks whizzed by in a dusty blur. He glanced at the sky. Was that a helicopter? He didn't have time to process the visual input before the shock wave hit, launching the truck six feet into the air.

The Humvee landed with a crash that—

"Stop! Please stop the car."

The voice was high, almost feminine. He glanced at his passenger. Blue eyes, brown shoulder-length hair. Why was there a woman in the truck?

"Where is Doug?" he said.

"I don't know who Doug is," the woman shouted, "and you're driving like a maniac."

Marcus blinked. There'd been no bomb. He hadn't crashed. The environment had changed. Aleppo's broken buildings had been replaced by huge maple trees and stately Victorian mansions.

He released the accelerator. The car slowed. He shook his head as the dusty street morphed to smooth asphalt. It had been a vision, a waking dream. Another of his PTSD episodes.

"I'm sorry," he said softly. He brought the Camry to a stop on the side of the road.

The young woman stared at him, her eyes wide. "You were going nearly seventy. You almost hit a bus."

He recognized her now. The woman who'd saved his life. Twice now, arguably. Her name…it had come over the police radio. It took a moment for him to remember.

"Sara, right?"

She nodded.

"I was trying to escape." That was true-ish.

He leaned back in his seat and looked in the rearview mirror. There was no sign of the shooter. Still, he gripped the steering wheel to hide his shaking hands.

"Well, we're safe now," Sara said, sounding mollified. "Do you think we should call the police?"

"Definitely."

As she dialed 911 on her cell phone, Marcus tried to gather himself. Breathing in slowly, working to dampen the flow of adrenaline. Next to him, Sara talked to the dispatcher. She explained their situation, gave their location. Finally, she pulled the phone from her ear.

"The police are on their way," she said quietly.

She seemed strangely composed for someone who'd just been chased by a mass shooter. Twice. Her hair was disheveled, and there was a scratch on her forehead.

"Are you injured?" he asked.

"No. I'm fine. It's just—" Suddenly, her whole body shook uncontrollably, and she looked away, out the window. "Oh, Amy. Poor Amy."

He remembered. At the lab. Sara had shouted that name. The dead woman on the floor.

"She was a friend of yours?" he asked.

Sara turned back to him, her eyes shining. "She has the cutest puppy. A little pug. Charlie." She made a sort of cry-laugh sound. "She named him after Charles Darwin." She started to cry again. "Who's going to look after Charlie?"

"She might be okay," Marcus said. "Doctors these days are practically miracle workers."

Sara shook her head vigorously. "No. No. You saw her. Amy was agonal breathing—she's dead."

Marcus knew she was right. He wasn't sure why he had said that. He just wanted to make her feel better. He felt a sudden urge to reach across the center console and give her a hug, but of course, he hardly knew her. So instead, he just watched awkwardly as Sara wiped tears from her face.

"I'm sorry," she said at last. "I don't usually cry. I mean, I never cry—" She drew in another choking breath.

"I'm Marcus. Marcus Byron," he said as gently as he could. Perhaps talking would help keep her distracted.

Sara looked at him, brightening slightly. "Actually, I know who you are."

"You do?"

She hesitated for a moment, almost as if she were afraid. "Topher—Dr. Fitzpatrick— mentioned you might be coming."

"Yes. I was supposed to interview him. And you too, actually. I work for *The New York Times*."

He looked at her more closely now. Chestnut hair and eyes the color of the sea. Pretty. By the way her eyes studied him, he could tell she was fiercely intelligent, too.

"You threw liquid nitrogen on his head," he said suddenly.

A half-smile. "Technically, it was dry ice mixed with ethanol. But yeah, super cold."

"And then you shot him." Marcus's hands tightened on the steering wheel.

"That's what I don't understand," said Sara. "I shot him five times in the chest. I think that police officer in the hospital shot him, too. And I hit him with the car. But he didn't die."

"He was probably wearing body armor. These wackos can buy it online. Stuff's totally unregulated."

"That wouldn't help him with the frozen ethanol."

Marcus frowned. She had a point. "Would the ski mask have protected him?"

"That ethanol mixed with dry ice was minus seventy-two degrees Celsius," she said, remembering what Amy had told her. "Plus, I saw his face when he pulled off the mask. His skin was partially frozen. It didn't look like that anymore in the hospital."

Marcus pursed his lips. It didn't make any sense. But before he could think on it further, his cell phone buzzed in his pocket. Barb.

"I'm sorry, it's my boss. I have to take this."

"Wait," said Sara. "There's one other thing I don't understand. The way he looked at me. He wanted to kill *me*. Me, specifically."

Marcus put down his phone. He could put off Barb for a few more minutes. "What makes you think that?"

"He stared right at me like he knew who I was."

"You're certain of this?" He didn't want to second-guess her, but a look wasn't a lot to go on.

"Not completely. But he showed up at the hospital, didn't he? Ran right at us. And he chased us into the garage when he could have been killing more people in the hospital. Why would he do that?"

"I'm not sure," said Marcus.

Was it possible that this had been more than just a random mass murder? Now that he thought about it, he did remember the gunman looking directly at Sara.

"Let's say he *was* trying to kill you specifically," Marcus said. "As a reporter, the first thing I'd do is talk to your relatives, ex-boyfriends, coworkers. Killers almost always know their victims."

Sara shook her head quickly. "Apart from my brother in

Vermont, I have no family. My ex lives in Seattle, and my coworkers were all in the lab with me…"

She trailed off. Marcus didn't need to read her mind to know that she was revisiting the laboratory shooting, seeing again the death of her best friend. How many others had died in that lab today? He realized he had no idea.

"Do you teach?" he asked. "Could he be one of your students?"

Again, Sara shook her head. "I'm fully funded by an NSF graduate student fellowship. I just do research."

"But you take classes, right? Is it possible he knows you from a course you were in together?"

"I would have recognized him. Graduate-level classes are small. I've never seen him before today."

"But he knows what *you* look like," said Marcus, racking his brain. "He might have seen you online. Are you on social media?"

Sara shook her head. "Avoid it like the plague." Then her eyes widened. "Topher has pictures of all his graduate students posted on the laboratory website."

"Okay, so he knows your face. He knows you work for Dr. Fitzpatrick." Marcus frowned.

"That doesn't explain why he'd want to kill me," said Sara, echoing his thoughts.

"Yeah, I'm having trouble working out a motive, too. Honestly, it's still possible he was just a nutjob high on bath salts or something like that. That would explain the weird looks."

"Maybe," said Sara. "But it's strange…" Her mouth dropped open. "Walter Schröder's lab. You heard about that in the news?"

"I did, and I thought about that," Marcus said. "My story has some connection to their lab. But it's on a separate continent. And that was a fire, not a shooting."

"I heard it might be a fire *and* a shooting."

"Those are just wild rumors. I expect it's a terrible coincidence."

Sara paused, her face clouding.

"What?" Marcus asked.

When she looked at him again, her lips were thin with worry. "This is off the record, okay?"

"Okay..." said Marcus slowly. His journalistic instincts kicked in. "But I want right of first refusal if it turns into a story." Barb would kill him if another newspaper beat him to the punch on this.

"Sure. You can have first dibs on the story." Sara leaned forward. "So, you know how you got a tip about a new paper that was just published on bioRxiv?"

Marcus was taken aback. "How do you know about that tip?"

"Because I'm the one who sent it to you."

Marcus stared at her. She wasn't making any sense.

Sara's eyes glinted excitedly. "And...I wrote the paper. I discovered the *Floresiensis* genome, but Fitzpatrick wouldn't give me credit. He was going to have me co-author it with a postdoc."

Now *this* was a story. Marcus leaned forward. "But it was published by the Schröder Lab."

"So it says. But they had nothing to do with it."

Marcus was impressed. "You used a pseudonym, just like Isaac Newton and George Starkey."

"Isaac Newton? That isn't a pseudonym."

"Yes, but he used one. He published some papers under the name *Jehovah Sanctus Unus* when he was dabbling in the dark arts of alchemy. And George Starkey, one of Harvard's own, called himself *Philalethes* because science was basically witchcraft back then. And then there's William Gosset, who invented the T-test. When he worked for the Guinness Brewery in Ireland, they blocked him from sharing trade secrets even when those 'secrets' had nothing to do with beer.

So he published as *Student*. Just Student. Didn't even bother with a last name. There's a rich history of fake names in science. Sounds like you've joined the greats."

He realized he'd been rambling, but Sara didn't seem to mind. "How do you know all this?" she asked.

"I'm kind of a history buff," said Marcus, grinning. "Also, I grew up a few blocks from here, so I know a lot about Harvard. But here's what I don't understand: why wouldn't Dr. Fitzpatrick give you credit for your work?"

Even as the words left his mouth, Marcus felt bad for asking. It was a stupid question. He'd talked to the man. Even over the phone, Fitzpatrick had reeked of arrogance.

"Because he's in charge. He can do what he wants. He gave lead authorship to this dumbass postdoc who had nothing to do with my research."

"Jesus. If my boss tried to give one of my stories to one of my colleagues, I'd quit on the spot."

Sara shook her head. "It's not so easy to do that in academia. Your advisor makes or breaks your career."

Tires screeched outside, and Marcus turned, expecting to see a police car arriving, but instead, a black van pulled up next to them. An instant later, three men had surrounded the Camry, while a fourth jerked open the driver's door. He pointed a Glock in Marcus's face.

"Marcus Byron and Sara Morin, you'll need to come with us."

CHAPTER 22
BEAUPORT HOUSE

Gloucester, Massachusetts
8:42 PM, June 8th

———

E nora sat at her rosewood desk in Beauport House, a massive, rambling mansion on the shores of Gloucester Harbor about forty-five minutes north of the city. The house had fifty-six rooms all told, but Enora's favorite was the library—a small, circular room inside a stone tower, with curved shelves of books wrapping around her like the arms of a lover.

Enora had first visited Beauport House as an undergraduate at MIT. She'd immediately fallen in love with the building. Built in 1908 by the famous antiquarian Henry Davis Sleeper, it was simultaneously brilliant, whimsical, and mysterious. To Enora, it felt like a physical representation of her mind. A place where she could naturally be herself.

Classified as a National Historic Landmark, the mansion normally operated as a museum. Fortunately, there are few things money can't buy, and much as it had with Saint

Joseph's and with Mike's group home, it had done the trick here as well. A very large donation into the appropriate fund had ensured Enora would be allowed to rent the building indefinitely.

Lights flashed on the drive as a van pulled up. That would be Paul, head of security. Enora watched out the window as her men led a man and woman out of the back of the vehicle, blindfolded and cuffed. When the woman stumbled, falling to her knees on the gravel driveway, Enora swore under her breath. She'd specifically told them not to hurt the woman. Sara Morin was brilliant, and Enora needed her help.

The man struggled free for a moment, but Enora didn't feel the same discomfort when one of her men immediately tackled him. Marcus Byron shouldn't even be here. As a reporter...well, he could make things much worse for them all. But he couldn't be left behind, either. There was no way of knowing how much Sara had told him.

While the captives were led toward the house, Enora made her way downstairs. She'd directed her men to bring Sara and Marcus to the octagon room, and she wanted to be there in advance.

She had just taken a seat in an armchair next to the fireplace when Paul and his security detail led Sara and Marcus in.

"You can remove their blindfolds," Enora said gently.

Paul jerked off the blindfolds, and the captives blinked at the light. Then Sara's eyes narrowed in recognition. "Enora Hansen?"

Enora nodded. "It's a pleasure to meet you, Ms. Morin. I—"

She was interrupted by Marcus, who lunged at Paul, driving his shoulder into the older man's chest. He knocked Paul to the ground but could do little more. He was still handcuffed, and the other two security guards easily dragged him to his feet.

Marcus was struggling in their grasp, blood dripping from his nose, when Sara said, "Marcus, I don't think they're our enemies."

Marcus stopped struggling and turned his gaze on Enora. "Are you connected with the shooting at Harvard?"

"No," Enora said. She was about to say more when she noticed the cell phone clutched in his fist. "Paul," she snapped, "whose phone is he holding?"

"The hell if I know. His, maybe?"

"You didn't confiscate his phone?" Enora's voice rose. "Do you realize it is trivially easy to track a cell signal? That's how I found them."

Paul slapped the phone from Marcus's hand and crushed it beneath his foot. Marcus tried to lunge at him again, but the two other men held him tight.

It was time to dial down the conflict. "My name is Enora Hansen. I'm the CEO of Aeter Pharmaceuticals."

"Then you care about publicity," Marcus said. "If you don't release us at once, I'm going to write the most heinous article—"

Enora cut him off. "You, sir, will shut up and listen. In addition to Aeter Pharmaceuticals, I also have significant equity stakes in a large number of international corporations, including a twenty-three percent stake in *The New York Times*. I will see that any story you write about this incident is buried, that you are immediately fired, and that you never find work in another reputable media outlet again."

She enjoyed watching Marcus's mouth hang open, then slowly shut as he wisely decided to table whatever retort he'd been planning.

"As I was saying," Enora continued, softening her voice as she turned her gaze back to Sara, "it's a pleasure to finally make your acquaintance, Ms. Morin. I am very sorry about the methods of my men, but it was crucial that we meet expeditiously."

"What do you want from us?" Sara asked. She was polite, but Enora could sense steel behind her words.

She looked to her head of security. "Paul, please uncuff Mr. Byron and Ms. Morin."

Paul looked warily at Marcus as he unlocked the handcuffs, but for once, the man didn't try to fight him.

When both guests were freed, Enora handed each of them a document and a pen.

"What is this?" Marcus asked.

"A non-disclosure agreement. If you want to hear what I have to say, you will need to sign it."

Marcus scanned the page. "This is excessive. Monetary damages in excess of a hundred million dollars?"

"Secrecy is of utmost importance."

"Just a minute ago, you threatened to destroy my career."

"One can't be too careful."

Next to him, Sara signed the document. Marcus stared at her, aghast. "You signed? Do you realize—"

"I'd like to hear what Enora has to say. She knew where to find us. I want to know what's going on and why some crazy guy is trying to kill me."

Marcus hesitated. His brow furrowed and his jaw worked as he tried to decide what to do.

"You're only signing away your rights to what I tell you today," Enora offered. "Anything you learn on your own will still be fair game. You're a smart guy; I'm sure you'll be able to find another source."

Always play to a man's ego. That was the secret to ninety percent of Enora's success. But she began to sense Marcus wasn't as susceptible to flattery as most men.

Fortunately, Sara cut in. "Marcus, I'm sure it's going to be really interesting. Enora is absolutely brilliant."

Marcus looked at Sara, then back to Enora. Finally, he barked a crisp "Fuck it" and scribbled his name on the NDA.

Enora smiled as she gestured to a pair of chairs facing her.

"Excellent. Now, make yourselves comfortable. Would either of you like some tea?"

Both Marcus and Sara shook their heads.

"Well, then," Enora said, crossing her legs and leaning back in her chair. "I imagine you have many questions."

"Why did you abduct us?" Marcus demanded. His voice was firm, but Enora discerned a certain wariness, a slight waver in its timbre. Her threat to ruin his career appeared to have had the desired effect.

She sighed. "In hindsight, I should have handled things differently. As soon I heard about the shooting, I sent my security team to protect you, but when they found you'd escaped on your own—well, I couldn't risk you communicating with anyone before I had a chance to speak with you first."

"You know why that man wanted to kill me," Sara said suddenly.

Enora leaned forward in her chair. Sara was as perceptive as she'd suspected. "I'm not one hundred percent sure, but I think it has to do with the paper you published."

"Which paper?"

"You know the one."

For just a second, Sara caught Marcus's eye. Enora knew what that meant. *She already told him about the paper in bioRxiv.*

"How did you know I was the one who published it? I used a pen name."

"On the first point, the human genome holds many secrets of great value," said Enora. "And on the second, *bioRxiv* logs every user's IP address."

Sara's eyes widened. "You hacked bioRxiv?"

Enora laughed. "No. I just paid the developer of their website to send me a copy of their server's access-log file."

Sara swore under her breath. "I should have used a VPN."

"Don't feel too bad," said Enora. "I already had a pretty good idea it was you. I've been collaborating with the

Schröder Lab on another project. They're not working on anything like the paper you submitted to bioRxiv. And I was already following your work. From a distance."

"You were interested in *my* research? Why? Archaic humans weren't exactly paragons of health. Neanderthals were predisposed to cancer and gastrointestinal, liver, and immune-related diseases. Our ancestors wouldn't be a very good source for drug targets."

Enora smiled. She'd been right about Sara: the young woman was absolutely whip-smart. "I'm not working on a run-of-the-mill drug discovery. My work is much more significant. It carries implications fundamental to our very existence."

"All right, so tell us about them," said Marcus, cutting in.

"Even with the signed NDA, I'm afraid I can't disclose any more specifics as to why Sara's work is relevant to my interests."

"You said you'd answer our questions."

"I didn't say I'd answer *all* of them. However, I have a proposition." Enora pulled a flash drive from her pocket and held it up. "There are eight genome sequences on this flash drive. Sara, if you can tell me why they're unusual, I will tell you what I'm working on."

Sara took the drive from her. "You want me to analyze data for you?"

"Yes."

"Why?"

"To be honest? I don't think you'll believe what I have to say until you look at these genomes for yourself. But I'll tell you this much: it will fundamentally change our understanding of biology."

Before Sara could respond, gunshots sounded outside the mansion, and the guards at the front of the house began to shout.

Enora swore. Marcus's phone had been tracked.

"Paul," she said, "you and your men help guard the front. We'll slip out the back."

Paul's expression was grim as he and his two associates ran from the room.

"This way," said Enora, turning to Marcus and Sara. She pulled a brass handle on one of the room's paneled walls. The wall slid aside, revealing a dim pantry, and she ushered them inside.

More gunshots sounded, and Enora felt a surge of adrenaline. This was the first time her life had ever been at risk. She'd survived corporate takeovers, her son's autistic meltdowns, and childbirth, yet none of those experiences had gotten her heart pumping the way the gunshots did. Right now, a wrong decision could mean her death.

She led Sara and Marcus through a series of unlit rooms, passing antique sideboards, hundred-year-old stained glass windows, and irreplaceable Ming dynasty vases. She raised a finger to her lips to indicate they shouldn't speak when they reached one of the mansion's many exits.

This was the most dangerous part. The gunshots had come from the front of the house near the main entrance. This door opened along a wall by the driveway. Assuming the attackers were still out front, they should be out of sight.

Should be.

Enora took a deep breath and slowly pushed the door open. The grounds were dark. She listened for her men, but all she heard was the murmur of waves in Gloucester Harbor and the distant hooting of a barred owl.

Enora grimaced. If her security detail were alive, she'd expect to hear shouts. Gunshots. Something.

They needed to hurry.

"Follow me," she whispered.

They slipped outside and began to slowly creep toward the drive where the van was parked. Enora squinted into the gloom.

Then something moved near the rhododendrons.

"Run!"

The darkness was punctuated by muzzle flashes and gunshots. The last thing Enora felt before her life ended was the impact of a nine-millimeter bullet punching through her sternum and ripping her aorta in half.

CHAPTER 23
BEAUPORT HOUSE

Gloucester, Massachusetts
9:05 PM, June 8th

———

Sara crouched under the branches of an old yew. Pine needles dug into her palms. Twigs caught at her hair. Warm blood trickled down her cheek. She ignored all of it. If she was going to survive, she needed to remain perfectly still.

She concentrated on slowing her breaths. Trying to keep a tight grip on the fear and rage coursing through her. Fear because a gunman was out there in the darkness hunting her, and rage because she'd just seen one of the most brilliant scientists of her generation murdered.

She'd read every one of Enora Hansen's papers on the genomic signals of natural selection. They were seminal works, and the sheer ingenuity, insight, and breadth of knowledge displayed within them had completely blown Sara away. The woman had been without equal.

That was why Sara hadn't hesitated to sign the NDA. If

Enora Hansen said she was working on something ground-breaking, Sara believed her without reservation.

But Hansen was now dead.

Sara wanted to scream with anger at the loss of a such a magnificent mind. Instead, she breathed in slowly, silently, steadying her nerves.

She was lucky to be alive. Hansen had been only a short distance in front of her when the shooting started. The only reason Sara hadn't been gunned down was that Hansen had shouted "Run!" That single word had given her and Marcus just enough time to sprint away. Unfortunately, she'd lost sight of Marcus. She hoped he'd found a good hiding spot.

As she crouched, she spotted a figure moving across an open patch of lawn. A man, by the shape of him. Light glinted off the barrel of a gun.

The gunman was slowly making his way in her direction. For just an instant, light from the mansion's windows caught his profile, and Sara nearly gasped as she recognized the face of the shooter. Yet somehow, she wasn't entirely surprised. There weren't many people who could single-handedly eliminate an entire security detail. At least, that's what Sara assumed had happened. The mansion was deathly quiet.

The shooter paused when he reached a large magnolia. He used the barrel of the gun to brush the branches aside and survey the interior. Apparently satisfied that no one was hiding inside, he moved to the next one. Closer to Sara.

Terror clutched at Sara's heart. She was only four shrubs away.

She tried to formulate a plan. Should she scream for help? Try to conceal herself in the pine needles at her feet? Find a stick to use as a weapon? She was just about to make a break for it when the shooter paused, turning to look at a car passing on the road.

As he watched the headlights, a shadow moved behind him. *Marcus!* He sprinted away from a bush even closer to the shooter than Sara was. Unfortunately, the shooter saw him and fired his weapon just as Marcus dove behind a stone wall.

Had Marcus been hit? Sara hadn't heard a shout.

She watched helplessly as the shooter stalked toward the wall. Suddenly, he stopped and again studied the road. What was he up to?

Then Sara heard it: the unmistakable sound of tires crunching on gravel. An SUV was coming up the drive.

The shooter held the gun loosely at his hip, turning his gaze back and forth between the SUV and Marcus's hiding spot. He seemed unsure whether there was time to kill Marcus before the vehicle arrived. And then it was too late. The SUV rolled to a halt, and its engine turned off. Seconds passed in silence before the door opened.

Sara wanted to shout, to warn the driver that there was a violent murderer waiting to kill him, but she stayed quiet. Shouting would only reveal her location, and she'd end up dead, too. Her heart was in her throat as she watched the shooter raise his gun.

She realized suddenly that she could make a break for it when he fired. The shooter's attention would be focused on the driver, and the gunshot would cover up the sound of her escape. She hoped that Marcus was thinking the same thing. If he was still alive.

Her muscles tensed as the driver stepped from the vehicle. He said something to the shooter, only to be interrupted by gunshots. The reports pierced the darkness like thunderclaps.

Sara seized the opportunity. She leaped from the shadows under the yew, sprinted twenty feet, and dove into the magnolia the shooter had already searched. It was the one place he was unlikely to search again.

She paused a moment, steadying her breath, then cautiously peered from under the leaves.

The shooter's gun remained trained on the driver of the SUV. And yet, the driver hadn't fallen. He stood next to the door of the SUV, exactly where she'd last seen him. The shooter must have missed.

Then, a sudden movement. The driver raised a gun of his own. There was a sizzling pop. Not a proper gunshot. Even so, the shooter staggered, clutching at his chest.

More sizzling.

The shooter collapsed and lay motionless.

The night was completely silent.

The driver crossed to the shooter. He knelt by the body for a long moment, then stood and walked toward the stone wall where Marcus was hiding.

"You there," he said. He had a British accent and was looking directly at Marcus's hiding spot. "Get up."

Sara felt overcome with relief when Marcus stood, uninjured.

"Who are you?" the man asked.

"Marcus Byron."

"Is Sara Morin still alive?"

Marcus hesitated.

The driver spoke again. "I'm not going to hurt her."

"I don't know if she's alive. We got separated."

As the man turned to face the mansion, a new sound filled the night air: the distant wail of a police siren.

"Sara Morin," the man said, projecting his voice. "This is not the end of your ordeal. That man who was hunting you, he's just the beginning. You are the target of a very powerful organization that will stop at nothing to kill you. I understand why you want to stay hidden, but the police won't be able to protect you. I can offer refuge."

Sara remained crouched within the branches of the magnolia. She'd need more than a posh British accent to convince her not to trust the police.

The sound of the sirens grew louder.

"We haven't much time," the man continued. "I cannot remain until the authorities arrive."

Sara looked to the body of the shooter, who lay unmoving on the grass by the SUV. She didn't know how, but she felt certain the driver had killed him. This man, whoever he was, had probably saved her life. But still, she stayed hidden. All she wanted right now was to reach the safety of a police car.

Then Marcus spoke. "Sara, do you remember the police officer at Mount Auburn? He wanted to arrest you. You were a suspect. I'm not sure what's going on, but I think this guy's right. The police aren't safe."

Sara looked between the driver and Marcus. Did she trust the driver? Definitely not. But she *did* trust Marcus. If he thought the police were unsafe…

"All right," she said, stepping from the magnolia.

As she approached, she got a better look at the driver. He was in his fifties, maybe, with reddish-brown hair and a neatly trimmed goatee. A gray herringbone suit and a plum-colored cravat lent him a slightly anachronistic appearance.

The man gestured to his SUV. "Get in. We can talk some-place quieter."

Sirens now pierced the still air, but Sara hesitated. Her eyes were fixated on the shooter lying dead in the grass. What had happened here? She'd seen that man survive all sorts of injuries that should have killed him. And now this man in the gray suit had pulled the exact same stunt. He had been shot at, too, yet he seemed completely unharmed.

Could the two men be on the same side? Was this a trick?

"Why aren't you dead?" she asked, taking a step back. "He shot you. I know he didn't miss. But you're still standing."

"A perfectly reasonable question," said the driver. He unbuttoned a few buttons on his suit coat. Underneath was a heavy black vest. He rapped it with a knuckle. "Body armor. Made from ultra-high-molecular-weight polyethylene. Brilliant stuff."

That, at least, made sense. "All right," Sara said. "I'll come with you."

"I'm going, too," Marcus said.

"Fair enough." The Brit jerked his head in the direction of the SUV. "You get in first, then. It's unlocked."

Marcus opened the door and climbed into the back seat. Sara hurried in after him, and the Brit shut the door behind her.

Marcus looked at her forehead. "You're bleeding."

She touched her brow. "It's nothing. I scratched myself while I was hiding."

Police lights flickered on the trees, and the driver still hadn't gotten in the car.

Sara looked around. "Where's the guy who saved us?"

Behind them, the SUV's trunk opened. The driver stood there with the shooter's body slung over his shoulder in a fireman's carry. "Sorry for the delay, but he's a bit heavier than I thought."

He tossed the body into the back of the vehicle and slammed the door shut. An instant later, he was in the driver's seat.

"Shall we be on our way?" Before they could respond, he started the engine.

"Wait," Sara heard herself say. "Why are you bringing a dead body?"

"Not dead. Incapacitated. I used a stun gun."

Now the strange buzzing sounds made sense.

"Won't he wake up?" Marcus asked.

"Doubt it." The driver held up a syringe. "I also dosed him with five hundred milligrams of ketamine."

Sara expected them to immediately drive off, but instead, the driver began to fumble in the glove compartment. Behind them, the first police car pulled into the drive.

"Sorry, bit of a cock-up. Wires were tangled," said the Brit as he plugged a device into a USB port. An instant later, a blue and red light began to strobe on the dash. He pressed the gas, wheeled the SUV around, and accelerated straight at the oncoming cruiser.

"Watch out!" shouted Marcus and Sara simultaneously.

The driver jerked the steering wheel hard, and they veered right, narrowly missing the police car.

"Terribly sorry," the Brit shouted jovially as they drove down the drive. "I always get a bit flummoxed driving in the States."

CHAPTER 24
BEAUPORT HOUSE

Gloucester, Massachusetts
9:12 PM, June 8th

———

Paul gripped the railing of the steps by the front door, but he nearly fell as his palm slipped on the wrought iron. His hand was slick with blood. His own. He stumbled down the steps toward his boss's body, wheezing with each step. Something wasn't right with his left lung. Every breath made a wet, sucking sound. He'd taken a round in the chest. It hurt like hell.

By the time he reached Enora, he knew she was dead, but he knelt anyway and pressed two fingers to her neck. Just as he'd suspected, no pulse.

Police sirens wailed on the road as he reached into his pocket for his cell phone. There was a protocol for this—especially this. Enora had been adamant that it be followed precisely. The line rang once before it was picked up.

"This is Paul Russo," he wheezed. "Enora is dead."

"Where? How?" The voice on the line was direct, professional.

"Beauport House. Gunshot."

"I will send a team right away."

"Too many…" The world spun, and Paul nearly passed out. "Too many police. I'll transport her to Niles Beach. Have the team meet me there."

"How long?"

"Ten minutes, max."

Drawing in a ragged breath, he lifted Enora's body into his arms. Her arms flopped awkwardly. He stood slowly, grunting in pain. Behind him, police lights flashed against the side of the mansion.

He carried Enora away from the house, toward the sea. He coughed again and nearly choked as blood filled his mouth. By the time he'd reached the jetty, his vision was swimming badly.

"You there! Stop!" a voice shouted from the house. A police officer.

Paul ignored the command. Drawing on the last of his strength, he pushed forward until he reached the boat.

Enora had spent a small fortune on a 1965 Riva Ariston speedboat. Built of varnished mahogany, it looked like it could have been driven on Lake Cuomo by Dean Martin. Tonight, it would function only as an aquatic hearse.

With a grunt, Paul dropped Enora's body on the leather lounge in the stern. He untied the dock lines, then practically fell into the driver's seat. He coughed again, his blood spraying the windshield.

The police officer, still shouting, was nearly to the end of the jetty when Paul got the engine started. Gripping the steering wheel, he pushed the throttle all the way forward. The boat leaped like a quarter horse out of the gate.

A gunshot sounded behind him, and Paul distinctly heard

the whine of a bullet as it passed over his head. Then he was racing over the dark water of Gloucester Harbor.

He steered toward the white sand of Niles Beach. It was close by, less than a quarter of a mile. He kept the throttle maxed out, and the Riva Ariston tore toward the sand.

Enora had been very clear. In the event of her death, time was the most crucial factor.

The boat slammed into the beach at nearly forty miles an hour. Paul was launched through the windshield and hit the ground hard.

Pain shattered his consciousness, and his world went dark.

———

A finger peeled back Paul's eyelid, and a blinding light seemed to pierce his very soul.

"Paul Russo?" asked a distant voice.

"Mghmmm…"

A sharp odor filled his sinuses like someone had poured battery acid up his nose. Groaning, he opened his eyes. Everything hurt.

A man was crouched next to him. He wore a white lab coat, and in his fingers, he held a broken capsule of smelling salts.

"Paul Russo?" he said firmly. "What time was Enora shot?"

Slowly, the world came into focus. Paul wasn't on the beach anymore. He lay on hard metal. It moved beneath him, and a cold wind buffeted him. The air was filled with the deep roar of an engine. When he blinked, he saw the lights of Boston on the horizon. If his chest didn't feel like a three-hundred-pound gorilla was sitting on it, he would have sighed with relief. The team had found him.

"Helicopter?" he asked.

"What. Time. Was. She. Shot?" the man said slowly.

"Nine—" Paul coughed, and the pain was nearly unbearable. "Nine-oh-five."

"Yes, yes," said the man impatiently.

Paul saw then that Enora's body lay next to his own. A woman, also dressed in a lab coat, was crouched beside her with a long IV needle in her hand. She inserted the needle into Enora's neck.

"What happened to the gunman?" asked the man who'd woken him.

"I can't breathe—"

The man leaned in close and pressed his thumb into the gunshot wound in Paul's chest.

Paul screamed.

"What happened to the gunman?" the man asked again.

Paul stared, confused. He had followed the protocol. He had risked everything to save Enora. Why was this man hurting him?

Next to him, the woman spoke into a headset. "Arterial oxygen rising. Cerebral temperature has stabilized."

"What happened to the gunman?" the man asked a third time. He dug his thumb deeper into the wound, and pure agony seared Paul's consciousness.

"I don't know—"

"It is crucial that you tell me everything."

Paul's mind moved slowly, turned to mush by blood loss and pain.

The woman working on Enora looked to Paul's interrogator. "Are you done with him? I need help with the polyvinylpyrrolidone infusion."

The man lifted his hand from Paul's chest, and the pain subsided.

"Help," said Paul. "I can't breathe."

The man slid his arms under Paul, levering him up. Through the helicopter's open door, Paul could clearly see

Boston's skyline. The blocky outline of the Prudential Center loomed closer now. Just in front of it would be Mass General Hospital.

He was going to make it. Against all odds, he was going to survive this night.

Then the man pushed him out. The world lurched, wind roared in his ears, and Paul fell toward the sea.

He opened his mouth, but there wasn't enough air left in his lungs to scream.

CHAPTER 25
ROUTE 128

Beverly, Massachusetts
9:26 PM, June 8th

———

Marcus drew in a deep breath and tried not to think about the fact that only minutes earlier, he'd been nearly murdered. Now, sitting next to Sara in the back of the SUV, the world around him seemed almost like a dream. They'd merged onto Route 128, and as the road moved gently under them, he was tempted to feel like he was finally safe.

But he wasn't. Not yet. They still knew nothing about the driver. It was time to do something about that.

"Who are you?" Marcus asked.

The driver glanced at him in the rearview mirror. "My name is Frank."

Marcus found Frank's posh, clipped tones irritating. When he'd been stationed in Syria, he'd worked out of the *Times*'s London office with a group of Oxbridge graduates, all of whom would take two-hour lunch breaks and come back to the office half drunk, endlessly reminisce about their boarding school days, and drop references to the holidays they had planned in Corsica. Then they'd slur their way through meetings until announcing they'd eaten a bad oyster and had to leave early for the train. And despite their complete ineptitude, no one seemed to care. It was as if their cut-glass accents insulated them from any consequences.

"Frank, do you always wear body armor?"

"Only when necessary."

That wasn't particularly illuminating. "How did you find us?"

"GPS signal."

"From my cell phone?"

"Yes."

Marcus sensed Frank was trying to avoid his questions, so he employed a classic reporter trick. He cut in sharply, trying to catch Frank off guard.

"How are we supposed to know you're not a crazy psychopath?"

Frank's affect remained irritatingly calm. "Perfectly understand your concern, sir. But may I remind you, I saved your life. A psychopath would have allowed you to perish."

"Then why have you abducted us?"

Again, Frank was totally relaxed. He answered in the voice of a man who was used to people serving him. "You had the option to stay behind."

Marcus was getting nowhere. He decided to get straight to the point. "Why do you think we can't trust the police? And what is this organization that you say will kill us?"

"Unfortunately, I can't answer those questions—not until we're someplace more secure."

"We're not safe now?" Marcus said, but Sara cut in before Frank could answer.

"*Why* do they want to kill me?"

"For the same reason they killed everyone in the Schröder

Laboratory. You've discovered something they want kept secret."

A look of horror appeared on Sara's face. "So it *was* connected. Did—did they die because of me?"

Frank's voice softened. "There was no way you could have known. I, on the other hand—" He paused, his voice catching. "I should have sent people directly to the lab to protect them."

Marcus wanted to ask who Frank and his "people" were, but Sara leaned forward in her seat, her eyes fierce. "Why is the genome of *Homo floresiensis* worth killing over?"

Frank laughed suddenly. "It's not your marvelous genome sequence they care about; it's the method." He spoke more firmly. "Now, if you could both be quiet, I would greatly appreciate it. I need my wits about me. Driving in the States is simply ghastly. Everything backward…"

After that, they drove in silence for a while. Then Frank turned off the highway at exit 21.

"This isn't the way to Boston," Marcus said.

Frank's plummy accent returned in full force. "I told you I would protect you. Boston is dangerous."

They passed in silence by a desolate commercial strip until Frank slowed and turned down a tree-lined drive. When they broke from the trees, a sign ahead of them read "Beverly Regional Airport." Beyond the sign was a three-story tower and a large expanse of asphalt.

Frank guided the SUV through an open gate and pulled right up beside the streamlined side of a business jet. "You're not safe anywhere in the States," he said, turning to look at them from the driver's seat. "Not now that the police have found the bodies at Beauport. They are easily bribed. If you were to spend any time in jail…well, I doubt you'd be leaving alive."

"But…where are we going, then?" Sara asked.

"London."

She frowned. "Don't I need my passport for that?"

Frank shook his head. "I'll be taking you into London *discreetly*. You are, after all, suspects in the murder of Enora Hansen." He looked at his watch. "I will be taking off in two minutes. If you want to come with me, consider this your invitation. If not, you can try your luck with the local authorities. But Ms. Morin, I am particularly hoping that you will choose to join me. I have some DNA sequences I need your help analyzing."

Marcus shook his head. More DNA? Whatever Sara had discovered, it was big.

With that, Frank stepped out of the SUV and began to walk toward the plane. A moment later, Sara followed him.

Marcus sighed. Then he, too, started across the tarmac. This was a terrible idea, but he wasn't about to leave Sara alone.

CHAPTER 26
MINISTRY OF SOUND

London, United Kingdom
3:05 AM, June 9th

———

T hump. Thump. Thump.

Even seated in a VIP booth in the back of the upper level of the club, Alexi felt his entire body vibrate with every beat. He sighed and took a long sip of Crown Royal 18. He couldn't think of many places he detested more than this. Goa and Ibiza, maybe?

And to think it had cost him nearly five thousand pounds to reserve the booth. The Deadmau5 show had been sold out for months. He'd had to pull more than a few strings to get them in.

Thump. Thump. Thump.

Kostas insisted the throbbing bass induced a trancelike experience, but all Alexi felt was a pounding headache.

Where was Kostas? Alexi stood, scanning the crowd below. A hallucinatory mix of flashing lights and synthetic fog swirled above a mass of churning bodies. Kostas was down there somewhere, no doubt having an amazing time.

But Kostas wasn't down there, for at that moment, the young man slid up behind him and wrapped his arms around Alexi's chest.

"Isn't this fantastic?" he said, kissing Alexi's neck. "You should have been there when he hit the drop of 'Ghosts 'n' Stuff.' It was filthy good."

"Yes, it was great," Alexi lied.

"Alexi, honey. You need to relax." Kostas nuzzled him again before opening one of his hands. In his palm were two small yellow pills. "Take one of these," he whispered in Alexi's ear. "It'll make you feel *amazing*."

Even as Kostas's other hand slid toward the waist of Alexi's pants, Alexi was pulling away. He held up his tumbler of whisky. "I'm fine with this for now."

"But—"

"I said I'm fine."

"Suit yourself," said Kostas, stalking off.

Thump. Thump. Thump.

The beat was unrelenting.

Alexi returned to the leather booth. What he wouldn't do right now to be on his yacht, enjoying the solitude, the quiet lapping of the waves and the briny scent of the sea. Throw a line in the water and fish for tuna. Now *that* was the life.

His cell phone buzzed in his pocket. He hated the device nearly as much as the pounding bass of the club. It was constantly interrupting him. Even on mute, the buzz set his teeth on edge.

He fished it out and grimaced when he saw the name *Karl* glowing on the screen. He rejected the call and replied with a quick text message.

Too loud to talk, what's going on?

> Just checking if you need anything else for the meeting.

A hound was the last thing Alexi needed. Look how much trouble they'd already caused. Karl should have told him what he was planning sooner. Hounds were a blunt instrument, whereas he could be a scalpel.

> I'm all set. The Russians are letting me borrow some men.

> Fantastic.

> How's Kostas?

Alexi sighed before tapping back,

> Indefatigable.

CHAPTER 27
LONDON, UNITED KINGDOM

12:21 PM, June 9th

———

From the plush leather seat of a Rolls-Royce Phantom, Sara watched a heavy rain lash London's streets. She decided this was the perfect metaphor for her mental state. Her brain was a whirlwind of competing horrors: the escape from Mount Auburn, the attack at Beauport, the death of Enora Hansen. And, of course, there was Amy. That was what hurt most.

She wanted to cry, to scream, to completely lose it. If what Frank had said was true—that the deaths at the Schröder Lab and at Harvard were connected—then it all was her fault. The paper she'd published had set these events in motion. People had died because of her.

Yet as she watched London fly past, she willed herself to keep it together. Whatever happened, she was going to need her wits about her. The sadness could come later.

Next to her, Marcus said, "I recognize this neighborhood. We're near Covent Garden." At Sara's questioning look, he added, "I worked out of the *Times*'s international office when I was stationed in Syria. It's only a few blocks away."

"Shouldn't Frank be taking us someplace more discreet?" Sara whispered. "There are, like, a gazillion people in London."

Frank was sitting in the front, next to the chauffeur. Marcus leaned forward to speak to him. "Where are you taking us?"

"You'll see in a moment. We're just arriving."

The car turned a corner and slowed as they approached a large building. To Sara, it looked like a church, with a large cupola atop an imposing marble facade, but Marcus quickly disabused her of that idea.

"You've got to be kidding. Freemasons' Hall?" he exclaimed.

Frank didn't answer.

The chauffeur pulled to a stop and turned off the engine. Frank stepped out into the pelting rain, expanded a large black umbrella, and came around to open Sara's door. "Please follow me," he said.

"Are you a Freemason?" Marcus asked.

"No."

"But you're taking us inside Freemasons' Hall."

Frank nodded. "I am."

The man was being as uninformative as ever.

Together, they hurried across a small expanse of flagstone, passed between thick marble columns, and approached a set of massive doors. Inscribed on the threshold was a large pentagram. Sara looked questioningly at Marcus, who merely shook his head. He didn't know what to make of it, either.

One of the doors cracked open, spilling light into the driving rain.

Marcus stopped. "Why don't you tell us what's happening before we go in that door?"

Frank looked at him squarely, his face giving nothing

away. "All will be revealed in due course." Marcus began to speak again, but Frank interrupted. "I promise no harm will come to you."

Sara took a final look at the rain-soaked streets. She wished she could fly home to Boston and hole up in her office with her laptop and a hot mug of coffee. She sensed that if she crossed this threshold, everything was going to change. There would be no turning back.

And there was another reason to walk through that door. It was the same thing that kept her up at night writing code until her eyes watered and her laptop screen blurred out of focus, the unquenchable thirst that motivates and drives all scientists: curiosity.

With a nod at Frank, she stepped over the threshold.

CHAPTER 28
FREEMASONS' HALL

London, United Kingdom
12:24 PM, June 9th

———

For the first time in his life, Marcus wished he'd taken the time to visit Freemasons' Hall when he'd worked in London. It hit some of his prime historical interests: classics, occult, and weird history. But he'd always considered the Freemasons to be a bit of a joke, a bunch of old white men wearing fezzes, driving around in mini cars in the St. Patrick's Day parade.

Okay, maybe that was the Shriners, but in his mind, they were practically the same.

Frank led them into a large atrium, empty and still. On the floor, blue and gold tiles were arranged in the shape of a massive eight-pointed star. Twenty feet above, brass chandeliers hung from a coffered ceiling. Shadows gathered in the corners of the room.

"This way," said Frank.

He took them up a grand marble staircase, and Marcus

racked his brain trying to remember everything he knew about Freemasonry. It was an ancient organization, originating from guilds of stonemasons in the twelfth and thirteenth centuries, then evolving into a powerful institution in the centuries that followed. All over London, you could see their square-and-compass symbol inscribed on the walls of buildings, or even in the stones of the streets.

But despite the ubiquity of their emblem, the beliefs of the Freemasons remained enigmatic. Publicly, they espoused a doctrine of charity and brotherly love. Pretty run-of-the-mill stuff. And yet, perhaps it was precisely that—the triteness of their principles—that attracted all the conspiracy theories. Well…that and the obsession with passwords and secret handshakes. In any case, Marcus knew the Freemasons had been accused of all sorts of diabolical connections: working with the mob, operating as an arm of the Illuminati, or simply being Satanists bent on destroying society.

Up until about five minutes ago, Marcus would never have seriously entertained any such preposterous ideas. The Freemasons were just a weird charitable organization, even considering wacky offshoots like the Independent Order of Odd Fellows. But now…

He had to wonder if he should have given more credence to the conspiracy theories.

At the top of the stairs, a robed figure stepped from behind a door, his face hidden behind a large cowl, and spoke to Frank. "They are waiting for you in the Grand Temple."

Marcus knew enough about Freemasons to know who this man was: the Lodge Tyler, the master mason tasked with guarding the door.

Frank nodded without speaking.

The Tyler led them down an equally grand marble hall. At the end of the hall stood a pair of imposing bronze doors, each at least ten feet high. They were carved in relief with a variety of scenes. In one panel, a group of men carried what looked like the Ark of the Covenant; in another, they held a menorah. Other panels depicted men driving oxen and moving blocks of stone. It took Marcus a moment to work out what the panels showed: the construction of the Temple of Solomon, the first temple of the Israelites.

"Did you bring the extra vestments?" Frank asked the Tyler.

The hooded man nodded, and from under his robe, he withdrew three folded robes.

Frank took the robes and turned to Marcus and Sara. "Put these on," he said. "Keep your faces covered."

Marcus unfolded the thick cotton garment, slipped it over his head, and pulled the hood forward. He found that he could easily conceal his face while still being able to see through a narrow slit in the fabric. The robe was identical to the one worn by their mysterious escort, and so was Sara's.

Frank's robe, however, marked him as someone of importance. He had gold embroidery at the cuffs and along the edge of the hood. A large red cross adorned his right breast, with a rose at its center. And though his robe had a hood, he left his head uncovered.

He spoke to them again in a hushed voice. "Only the highest levels of our order were invited to this meeting. I am making an exception for you two, but I insist that you do not speak of what you see or hear. While inside, do not talk to anyone. And do *not* remove your hoods."

Then he turned and pushed open the massive bronze doors.

Marcus followed him into a truly massive room. It was dimly lit, cathedral-like, and at least three stories high. A low stage stood at the far end with an enormous pipe organ behind it. But what was most surprising was that the room was full of people, all of them dressed in the same white robes that he and Sara now wore. Frank was the only person here who was unhooded, and as he pushed the doors fully open, the robed figures all turned toward him.

"Thank you all for meeting at such short notice," said Frank, striding forward.

A hand grabbed Marcus's wrist, and the hooded Tyler quietly led him and Sara to a pair of unoccupied seats. As he sat, Marcus surveyed the interior of the temple. It was exceptionally opulent, with gilding everywhere, from the legs of the chairs to the organ pipes. Even the moldings near the ceiling gleamed with gold.

And then there was the ceiling itself. Several stories above their heads, it was painted with giant frescos.

No, thought Marcus, squinting. *Not frescos—tiled mosaics.*

He was able to identify St. George and the dragon, Helios on a golden chariot, the Star of David, Jacob's ladder, and the All-Seeing Eye. Recessed into the center of the ceiling was an indigo sky with a star emblazoned in gold leaf.

It was then that Marcus's mind made another connection. The rose cross on Frank's robe—he now remembered what it was. It was the symbol of the Rosicrucians, a secretive brotherhood of scientists and alchemists.

Frank hadn't been lying about one thing. Technically, he *wasn't* a Freemason.

CHAPTER 29
FREEMASONS' HALL

London, United Kingdom
12:32 PM, June 9th

———

Sara listened quietly as Frank's voice filled the vast room. "A great deal has happened in the last week that I must address."

He stood on a low stage in front of the gleaming pipe organ. Flanking him were four gilt chairs, each occupied by a hooded figure. Like Frank, their robes were embroidered with golden thread, and each had a different insignia elaborately stitched on their breast: a black cross, a red cross, a red cross with a red sword below it, and a black shield with a white letter Sara couldn't identify.

"The hounds of Actaeon roam amongst us once again," Frank continued.

The hooded figure with the red cross on his chest rose from his seat.

Marcus whispered in Sara's ear. "The red cross was worn by the Knights Templar."

The Templar held a large spear in one hand, but it appeared to be ornamental. Its blade was highly polished and inlaid with gold. He pulled back his cowl, revealing silver hair and a weathered face.

"That cannot be," he said in a gravelly voice. "The last of the hounds were slain a millennium ago."

"I would not lie about something this serious," said Frank. "I was attacked by a hound last night."

The audience began whispering to each other.

"You lie," said the Templar, pointing a finger at Frank's chest. "Actaeon would have released the hounds years ago if they still had any."

Sara's mind was racing. What was this about hounds? They hadn't seen any hounds. Was that some kind of code for the shooter?

"I understand your reticence to believe this terrible news, but I can prove it to you," Frank said.

The murmur in the room grew louder.

Frank raised his hands until the crowd quieted. "I anticipated that there would be skeptics among us. Just as there should be. Bold claims demand solid evidence." The hint of a smile played on Frank's mouth. He turned to the Tyler. "Can you bring in my guest?"

The Tyler disappeared through a side door and returned a moment later, pushing a large box on casters. Or at least Sara thought it was a box; it was covered in a black cloth. As he positioned the object in front of the stage, the hooded audience watched, completely silent now.

"As I was saying," said Frank, stepping down from the stage. "I encountered a hound when I was in Massachusetts. He attacked me, but I was able to capture him."

With a flourish, Frank pulled off the cloth. A collective gasp rose from the audience. It wasn't a box—it was an iron cage. And inside it crouched a man, his clothing torn and stained with blood.

The shooter.

"This is the man who attacked the Fitzpatrick Lab at Harvard. He killed two graduate students."

Under her robe, Sara's fists were tightly clenched. She'd never forget those eyes. Even so, this was the first time she'd actually gotten a good, long look at him. He was slim with dark hair. Asian, maybe? She couldn't be sure. He wore brown trousers and a faded button-down shirt. His eyes were bright, and he studied the room with a fierce intensity.

Then he turned his gaze on Frank, and he began to shout something in a foreign language. Sara didn't have to understand the words to know there were curses involved.

"This is just some bum you picked off the street," said the Templar. "It proves nothing. If he were a hound—"

"I will *prove* he is one of Actaeon's," said Frank, his voice booming through the hall. "Give me your spear."

For a moment, the old man in the Templar robes hesitated. Then he walked to the edge of the stage and handed Frank the glittering weapon.

"Watch closely," said Frank to the crowd. Then, with the speed of a viper, he lunged toward the cage and plunged the spear directly through the center of the shooter's chest.

The shooter's blood pumped around the edge of the blade, and his eyes bulged in agony. Then Frank jerked out the spear, and the shooter fell to the floor of the cage, his mouth open, gasping like a stranded fish.

The audience erupted in screams.

Distantly, Sara heard Frank shouting, "Quiet! Quiet!"

Frank continued to call for quiet until something that resembled calm fell over the audience. Then he pointed the bloody tip of the spear at the prisoner. "Do not take your eyes off him," he said.

The shooter's body was slumped in the middle of the cage. Blood pooled around him. He stared blankly at the ceiling. Not breathing. Dead.

"Watch closely," Frank insisted.

Sara forced herself to stare at the corpse. She wanted to look away, but somehow, she knew she was about to observe something important.

It began in the eyes. She wasn't sure what it was, only that there had been a change. Then it became more apparent: a slight twitching. The slow resumption of saccadic eye movements.

"Do you see it?" she whispered to Marcus.

"Yes," he whispered back.

When the shooter finally drew in a shaky breath, the noise was echoed by the audience.

The Templar spoke, the fear in his voice palpable. "*Where* did he come from?"

"Actaeon sent him to murder a graduate student," Frank replied. He looked at the Tyler. "Take him away."

Sara's mind was racing. What had she just seen? Some sort of magic trick? There was no body armor involved this time. The man had received a brutal stab wound to the chest. He'd lost so much blood. He'd stopped breathing for what had to be a full minute. And yet here he was, his diaphragm filling his lungs with air. Alive.

The Tyler had just begun to move the cage when the prisoner lunged. Thrusting one of his arms through the bars, he wrapped his fingers around the Tyler's throat. The Tyler's eyes widened, and he emitted a short, gurgling cry.

Even as fresh screams erupted from the audience, Frank leaped forward, his spear flashing. He brought it down in a single brutal slice, severing the man's hand from his forearm.

CHAPTER 30
FREEMASONS' HALL

London, United Kingdom
12:44 PM, June 9th

———

Marcus watched the blood pump from the stump of the prisoner's arm. What had he just seen? Frank had stabbed the shooter through the chest with a spear, and the man had bled out and died. There was no question in Marcus's mind about that. In his time in Syria, he'd seen plenty of dead men—and this man had been very, very dead.

But then, he had miraculously recovered.

It didn't make sense.

Even as he tried to wrap his head around it, he saw blood coagulating on the end of the prisoner's arm. It was *literally healing before his eyes.*

God, he was going to need a stiff drink when this was all over.

"Would you like to watch his arm heal?" Frank said. "It will only take a few minutes."

"No," said the Templar. "We've seen enough. Take him away."

While the prisoner writhed on the floor of the cage, the Tyler approached once more—much more cautiously this time. He threw the black cloth over the iron bars and kept his arms extended as he wheeled the cage from the room.

"Do you believe me now?" asked Frank, his eyes searching the audience.

He was answered with a soft murmur of agreement.

Marcus couldn't believe it. These people had just seen a man come back from the dead, and they all simply… accepted it. The reporter in him wanted to stand up and start asking questions, but Frank had specifically told him not to speak.

"Where did he come from?" asked the old Templar.

"I caught him in Massachusetts."

"No, I mean where originally? We believed the last of the hounds died in Sarmada."

Sarmada. Marcus knew that name. It was a town in Syria, near Aleppo.

"Apparently not," said Frank.

"So if Actaeon has had hounds all along, why haven't they used them?"

"My theory is that they were keeping them in reserve."

"For what? And why release them now? What has changed?"

Frank's eyes flashed. "Everything."

To Marcus's shock, Frank turned away from the Templar and pointed his gaze directly at Sara. "Ms. Morin," he shouted. "Please remove your hood."

Next to him, Sara stiffened. Frank had insisted they not remove their hoods. What was this about?

Marcus squeezed her hand reassuringly. She squeezed back, then lifted both hands to remove her hood. As it fell back, revealing her face, the audience gasped.

The Templar barked with barely masked anger. "You brought an *uninitiated* to this meeting?"

Frank remained calm as ever. "I had no choice. We need Ms. Morin to help us. It was crucial for her to see firsthand what we are up against."

"You know our rules. We explicitly do not allow outsiders. If we are exposed—"

"Ms. Morin will not expose us," said Frank. He had not taken his eyes off Sara this entire time, and now he addressed her directly. "Ms. Morin, you agree not to speak of what you have seen here?"

"Yes," said Sara.

The Templar was still enraged. "What are your qualifications, Ms. Morin?"

Sara seemed as confused by the question as Marcus was. *Qualifications? For what?*

"I'm a graduate student at Harvard," she said, her voice shaking.

"A graduate student?" The Templar's jaw quivered with rage. "Frank, she doesn't even have a PhD."

"This isn't a matter of certification, Roger. I believe Ms. Morin has played a crucial role in calling the hounds."

Sara bravely spoke up. "Can you two...could you please explain what you're talking about? What are these hounds you keep referring to?"

Marcus leaned forward. Maybe now they'd get some actual explanations.

"The prisoner in the cage," Frank began, "the man who tried to kill you, is what we call a hound. They are trained to kill. Once they are given a quarry, they will not stop until it is dead. And as you have observed, they have unique healing abilities that make them particularly good at their job." He smiled. "Ms. Morin, do you have any hypotheses that might explain what you just saw?"

Sara frowned. "You do realize I'm a computational biologist, right? I write code to analyze genetic data. Population genetics, genome scans, that sort of thing. I don't know the first thing about human physiology."

"What did I say?" said the Templar.

Frank cut him off. "I am fully aware of your talents and qualifications, Ms. Morin. Indulge me."

Marcus studied Sara as she considered Frank's question. With her lips slightly pursed and her brow furrowed, she managed to look simultaneously confused, thoughtful, and scared. Frank waited respectfully, but the Templar glared at her with an expression that suggested he wanted his spear back so he could hurl it at her head.

"Well," Sara said at last, speaking slowly, "some animals do have exceptional healing capacity. For example, flatworms can be cut into pieces, and then, after a few days, an entire individual can grow from each of the fragments. Likewise, starfish can regenerate entire bodies from a single arm. But in vertebrates, this sort of thing is very rare. Salamanders can regrow limbs, but as far as I know, mammals have very limited ability to heal serious wounds. Humans can regenerate their livers—that's about it."

She tilted her head to one side. "But…assuming there is, in fact, a biological explanation for what I just saw—that this is not some sort of trick—I'd guess your prisoner has a mutation that alters the way the body heals wounds. Even so, to survive a cardiac injury like that…" She trailed off.

"You have my word that what you saw was not an illusion," Frank said. "I've spent years researching this kind of tissue regeneration. I call it the Lazarus Factor. The ability to survive injuries that would kill a normal human."

"I still don't understand why he wanted to kill me," Sara said. "For that matter, I don't understand why I'm here. What do you want from me?"

"I want to know where the hound came from, Ms. Morin. I want to understand where all hounds came from. I believe there was a single evolutionary event that produced this extraordinary healing ability."

Sara spoke quietly. Marcus could tell by the furrow in her brow that she was working through the implications. "If I'm following you correctly, you think these hounds are the result of a single mutation of large effect—that they're a human version of Goldschmidt's hopeful monsters?"

"Not exactly," said Frank. "Richard Goldschmidt hypothesized that macroevolutionary change is caused by rare mutations of large effect. I believe the hounds are hybrids."

Sara's eyes widened. "Hybridization? With what?"

"We don't know."

There was a long silence. Sara's brow once again furrowed with thought. Every single hooded figure seemed to be staring at her.

"You think this Lazarus Factor is some sort of hybrid vigor," she said at last. Marcus could hear the skepticism in her voice. "Then…why don't you just sequence his genome? That'll tell you if his genetic code is unusual. A hybrid would have an excess of heterozygous genetic variants—that's what you get if you combine two very different genomes."

Frank smiled broadly. "I thought the same thing, and I've already had a sample of his blood sequenced. However, a single genome sequence won't tell us the original source of the hybridization event."

Sara's eyes widened with understanding. "*That's* what you want from me."

Now Frank's smile became a full-on grin. "Elaborate, Ms. Morin."

"You want me to look through modern populations and identify the most likely population where this hybridization event occurred. Much like what I did with the Rampasasa and *Homo floresiensis*."

"Exactly," said Frank.

"Well," said Sara, matching his grin. "I think that is something I can help you with."

CHAPTER 31
OFFICE OF THE CHIEF MEDICAL EXAMINER

Boston, Massachusetts
7:48 AM, June 9th

———

ervously, Luis touched his jacket. Through the cloth, he could feel the syringe and blood collection vial stashed in his breast pocket.

"*Mierda*," he muttered quietly. "I am an idiot for doing this."

Of course, that wasn't actually true. He was smart, intelligent, the second in his family to graduate from college, and the first to earn a higher degree. Made the dean's list every semester. Then grad school. A Master's in forensic science had landed him a job at Boston's Office of the Chief Medical Examiner. And that wasn't even the best bit. In six months, he'd be starting his first year at the Boston University School of Medicine—on a full scholarship. Four years after that, he'd be a medical doctor.

Luis was *not* an idiot.

Which was why he'd initially refused the offer. Not only

was two hundred fifty thousand dollars too good to be true, it wasn't worth the risk. What they had asked him to do was clearly illegal—evidence tampering at the very least. If he were caught, he could kiss that med school scholarship goodbye.

Definitely not worth it.

But they'd been insistent…and ultimately convincing. Especially after they showed him copies of his colleagues' paystubs. It was robbery what his boss was doing, paying him almost thirty percent less than everyone else. Literally *stealing* from him.

That was what had changed his mind. It was only fair— no, it was *honorable*—to take back what was rightfully his.

Luis tapped his ID badge on the electronic lock, then glanced at his watch: quarter to eight. Perfecto. The morgue should be empty.

He slipped inside and was heading toward the refrigerators where they kept the bodies when he heard his name.

"Luis?"

Trying not to panic, he slowly turned around. Across the room, by the door to the autopsy suite, stood Dr. Seward, one of the staff forensic pathologists. What was he doing there? "Yes, Doctor?"

"Can you give me a hand moving this patient?" Dr. Seward gestured to a body resting on an examination table behind him.

"Oh. Uh—sure," Luis managed, his voice shaking.

Fortunately, Dr. Seward didn't seem to notice. "These mass shootings are a goddamn fucking shit show. Been working all night."

Seward was famous for cursing at the staff, throwing charts, and generally being impossible to work with. Everyone in the office professed to hate him, though if Luis was entirely honest with himself, he found something deeply compelling about the way Dr. Seward could take over any situation by sheer force of personality. Trouble was, he was the last person Luis wanted to run into this morning. If Dr. Seward figured out what Luis was up to, he'd never give up until Luis's life was completely ruined.

Deep breaths.

Luis crossed into the autopsy suite, and Dr. Seward kept talking as he zipped up the body bag. "Ten fucking bodies in one day," he muttered. "Two from Harvard, two from Mount Auburn, and five from Gloucester. Of course half the fucking staff is on vacation and I get stuck with this mess."

Luis couldn't help himself. "Actually, I think that's nine bodies."

Dr. Seward looked at him, one eyebrow raised. "No, it's ten. There's an unidentified DB. Came in early this morning. Some guy they fished out the bay."

Together, they moved the body onto a cadaver gurney. Luis was afraid Seward would ask him why he was in early, so he desperately tried to come up with some small talk instead.

"Have they found the billionaire lady yet?" he blurted out.

"No, but there's blood spatter that might be hers. I'm waiting to hear back from the state police crime lab. They're supposed to be sending someone over to collect the samples, but they're slow as shit."

"But nothing from the suspect?"

"Just what Mount Auburn sent us. Apparently, the suspect woke up when they were doing blood work, went completely ballistic."

"Wait. He what?"

"He woke up. They thought he was dead. No one even bothered to check for a pulse. Stupid fuckers let him murder a doc and a cop."

They'd pushed the gurney to the row of morgue refrigerators, and now, with a practiced move, they transferred the body from the gurney to the refrigerator. Dr. Seward picked up the tray of postmortem samples, and together, they crossed to the specimen refrigerator on the opposite side of the room. Luis tried to think of something else to say, but his mind was blank.

As Seward opened the door to the fridge, he groaned out loud. It wasn't hard to see why. The normally tidy fridge was a mess of vials, sample bags, and specimen containers.

This gave Luis an idea. "Dr. Seward," he said, trying not to sound too eager, "why don't I straighten this up for you? Sounds like you've earned a rest. There's coffee in the break room."

Dr. Seward looked like he might give Luis a hug. "I could use a fucking coffee."

"Go for it. I'm happy to get this cleaned up. It's literally my job, after all."

As soon as Dr. Seward was gone, Luis began organizing the samples, moving all the sample bags to the bottom shelves and arranging the specimen containers into neat rows. A bit of *mise en place* before the theft. He knew there was a CCTV that took in the entire morgue space. Still, if he crouched close to the door, it would be impossible for the camera to see what he was doing. And besides, it wasn't likely that anyone would ever review the tapes. He wasn't going to be caught.

Carefully, he slid the syringe from his pocket. In the course of reorganizing the fridge, he'd already located three blood vials from Mount Auburn. Moving quickly, he pushed the needle through the rubber top and drew out one milliliter of blood. He repeated the process on the other two vials, then deposited the combined contents of the syringe into the empty blood collection tube he'd been keeping in his pocket.

He was about to stand up when a fresh wave of panic hit him. What was he going to do with the syringe? He couldn't toss it in the sharps container; the camera would catch that act, and how would he explain it? And putting it back into his pocket wasn't an option. The last thing he wanted was a stick from a used needle.

The solution was easy. He simply tossed it into the back of the fridge. Someone would probably find it six months from now, but it would mean nothing to them, and most importantly, there would be no way to trace it back to Luis. The worst that would happen would be a bullet point in a staff meeting reminding everyone to dispose of sharps properly.

He grinned to himself. He wouldn't even be at that staff meeting. By then, he'd be at med school halfway across the city with a fresh two hundred fifty thousand in his bank account.

CHAPTER 32
FREEMASONS' HALL

London, United Kingdom
12:58 PM, June 9th

―――

"Thank you for agreeing to assist us, Ms. Morin," said Frank with a smile. "Let me invite you to stay at my home. You can work on analyzing the hound's genome, and I will see that no harm comes to you."

Without waiting for Sara to answer, Frank addressed the full audience of robed figures. "The return of the hounds is a terrifying development, but with Ms. Morin's help, we have new tools at our disposal. I am confident we will find and defeat Actaeon." He clapped his hands together. "This meeting is adjourned."

The audience began to file toward the doors. Sara hesitated, unsure whether she and Marcus were supposed to follow. Then she felt a tug on the edge of her robe.

"This way," whispered a hooded figure. Sara recognized the voice of the Tyler.

The man shepherded them out a side entrance into an antechamber, where he had them remove their robes. "You need to move quickly. We can't have anyone seeing you," he said.

He then hurried them through a series of empty corridors and pushed open a door to the outside. Though it was after ten in the morning, the light was dim, the rain having been replaced with a stygian fog. Classic London weather.

Frank strode up to them with his umbrella. "Follow me," he said curtly.

Sara and Marcus started after him. They'd only gone a few yards before Marcus spoke. "I figured out who you are."

A thrill of excitement shot through Sara. Was she finally going to get some answers?

"Really?" said Frank without turning round.

"Yes. The rose cross on your robes, that's the symbol of the Rosicrucians. You're not a Freemason."

What the hell are Rosicrucians? Sara wished she still had her cell phone to google it.

"But what I don't understand," Marcus continued, "is why there was a Knight Templar at your meeting. Isn't that a different order from the Rosicrucians?"

"We fight the same fight," Frank said. "We have the same enemy." He spoke with a finality that indicated the discussion was over.

Marcus ignored him. "And that would be Actaeon?"

Frank picked up his walking speed. Clearly, he didn't want to discuss this subject.

"If I remember correctly," Marcus said, "in Greek mythology, Actaeon was a hunter."

"You have an impressive memory," said Frank. His tone reminded Sara of Topher when someone answered a question at a lab meeting a little too easily.

"I've always been interested in history," said Marcus, acting as if he hadn't noticed Frank's tone. Sara guessed this was a necessary skill for a reporter. He probably caught a lot of attitude when asking tough questions. "So, the man who attacked us in Boston was a hound of Actaeon, and Actaeon is some sort of modern-day hunter?"

Frank didn't answer, and they walked in silence for a few more paces.

"Are you going to answer my questions?" Marcus asked.

"I am sorry," said Frank, "but there are some questions for which I have no answers."

"Or *won't* answer," Marcus grumbled.

They walked between white marble façades as pale as bone. The rain was letting up, but the air was cold and heavy with humidity. Sara wished she was wearing something warmer than a T-shirt. She glanced at Marcus, wondering if he was going to ask anything else, but he appeared to be lost in thought.

She decided she should do the same. There was, after all, a lot of new material to synthesize.

First, Frank had confirmed what she'd only previously suspected: the Harvard shooter could heal from wounds that would kill a normal person. This was something never before seen in mammals.

Second, her enemy had a name now: Actaeon. That was who wanted her dead.

Third, she finally understood the why. Her research. And not her findings, but her method. This Actaeon recognized its potential to uncover a dangerous secret: the hounds' origins.

She was about to ask Frank more about it when he stopped outside of an enormous Neo-classical building. "We're here," he announced.

Marcus looked confused. "But this is Somerset House."

Frank sighed. "I see you *also* know your London landmarks."

Walking quickly, he led them through a grand arched entrance and into an inner courtyard. This place was no house; it was a palace. Three floors of ornate marble blocks and huge decorative columns. The courtyard alone was big enough to fit a football field.

"You live *here*?" Sara asked.

"Some of the time."

"How can you have a home in a museum?" Marcus asked.

"Actually, it's owned by the Somerset House Trust."

"Right, but how—"

Frank cut in. "Did you have this many questions for Enora?"

Marcus crossed his arms. "I'm a reporter. It's my job to ask questions. Where are you taking us?"

"I'm taking you to my private apartment. Not many people know of its location, and I'd prefer to keep it that way."

He pulled a key from his pocket, unlocked a nondescript door, and pushed it open to reveal a wood-paneled antechamber. Elevator doors stood on the opposite wall.

Though Marcus entered the antechamber begrudgingly, Sara couldn't help but feel excited about the prospect of seeing where Frank lived. The man was truly an enigma, and she hoped his home might shed a little light on what kind of a man he was.

Inside the elevator was only one button, which Frank pressed. The elevator ascended, and the doors opened directly onto a magnificent living room. A living room that made clear—as if it hadn't been already—that Frank was shockingly wealthy.

The room was big enough to fit the entirety of Sara's Cambridge apartment. On one wall stretched a long row of windows each at least ten feet tall, and the other walls were adorned with huge gilt paintings. A pair of leather couches faced one another in the center of the space, and a small bar with neatly arranged crystal tumblers stood by the windows.

The overall effect was masculine and austere, but not as revealing of Frank's inner nature as Sara had hoped.

They all jumped—even Frank—when a man rose from one of the couches.

"You're late," he said in a thick accent.

Frank replied with a voice contorted with fury. "Alexi, if you do not leave at once—"

"You will shoot me with your stun gun? You thought I wouldn't find out about that, didn't you? But of course I did. I keep close tabs on my men. What do you call them again? Hounds?"

Panic coursed through Sara's veins. Was this Actaeon?

Alexi started toward Frank, and Frank reached a hand toward his jacket pocket.

"I wouldn't do that, if I were you," Alexi growled.

Sara took a step backward toward the lift, only to feel the hard muzzle of a gun press into her lower back. Apparently, another man had been hiding next to the elevator. She looked over at Marcus and Frank, and saw that two more men were holding them at gunpoint as well. A third man, younger, stood nearby.

Alexi turned his gaze on Sara. "You must be the Ms. Morin we've all heard so much about."

Sara's fists clenched involuntarily. Alexi's tone reminded her of the St. Johnsbury Academy students she'd known in rural Vermont. The prep school kids were always polite, nice even, yet there was a constant undercurrent of superiority in the way they spoke to her. They assumed they were smarter than her simply because their parents could afford to send them to a fancy school.

She studied the man before her. He was short and stocky, with broad shoulders and the faint paunch of a man in his early forties. He had a large nose and curly brown hair, but it was his eyes that demanded her attention. They were heterochromatic: one blue, the other brown. Together, they held an expression that was equal parts disdain and fury.

"Can someone tell us what the hell is going on?" said Marcus.

Alexi shifted his unsettling eyes to Marcus. "Talk out of turn again, and you're dead."

The man holding Marcus pushed him to his knees and pressed a gun into the back of his head.

Alexi turned back to Frank, and his voice took on an almost friendly tone. "I have to give you credit, Frank. You're indefatigable, but your attempts to thwart us will never succeed."

"No matter what you do to me, we will never stop fighting you," Frank spat. "It is our moral imperative to prevent the horror you wish to unleash."

"Horror?" Alexi's full lips cracked into a smile. "Nothing is further from the truth. Our goal is purity, perfection, beauty. Look out there," he said, gesturing to the row of windows behind him. "Is the world not sinful? Unclean? I only wish to tidy up the mess *you've* made."

"Mess?" Frank was furious. "I have brought only progress, like Prometheus—"

Alexi interrupted, his rage matching Frank's. "And like Prometheus, you brought only ruin! This progress you seek leads to corruption and the desecration of the natural order— a world sullied by man's excess."

"Man is *part* of—"

Alexi held up his hand. "Enough. I am here for the girl and the data. I have one. Now hand over the other."

Tight with rage, Frank didn't answer.

"Kostas, search him," said Alexi. The young man who'd been watching with amusement now stepped forward and patted Frank down. It took him only a few seconds to find the flash drive in Frank's breast pocket.

"Is this it?" Kostas said holding it up.

"Yes, but—" Frank began, only to be interrupted by Alexi.

"Shoot him."

The guard behind Frank fired his gun. Sara's ears rang as Frank fell to the floor, blood pumping from a wound in the center of his chest.

CHAPTER 33
AETER PHARMACEUTICALS

Cambridge, Massachusetts
8:11 AM, June 9th

———

After Enora Hansen's murder, Sameer had assumed that he'd be looking for a new job. Usually, the death of the CEO heralded the end of the company, even a well-funded one like Aeter Pharmaceuticals. So he was more than a little surprised when his boss, Dr. Mulligan, called to tell him that he'd been transferred to a new project and given a promotion to Laboratory Technician III.

Now, instead of processing ancient bone and tooth samples, his job was to isolate and purify white blood cells. Sameer didn't understand why someone in the Greenland shark blood anti-freeze group couldn't do the work, but he wasn't about to complain. It was better than being laid off.

Unfortunately, the hours were just as bad as before. It was seven AM, and he was already in the lab. Worse, he was still a bit drunk from last night's revelries. It had been Jake's twenty-third birthday, and there had been more than one dirty martini. Four, if he recalled correctly.

In the ancient DNA lab, he'd worked primarily on his own, but in the new lab, he shared the space with two other techs, Meagan and Patrick. Meagan was fresh out of college, a quiet woman whose life, as best Sameer could tell, revolved around drinking herbal tea, listening to audiobooks, and posting pictures of her cat on Instagram. Patrick, on the other hand, never shut up. He spewed a constant stream of inane commentary, including announcing every morning whether he'd gotten laid the night before, and repeatedly cornering Sameer to explain his theory about how dinosaurs might actually exist deep in the Congo. "Not a T-Rex, obviously," he would say. "But definitely velociraptors."

A normal man would be laughed out of the lab, but Patrick wasn't normal. Six foot six with broad shoulders, he was built like a Greek god. People listened to him because, well, with a physique like his, who wouldn't? His father was apparently a big-shot real estate developer, and he'd grown up in some fancy mansion out in Lexington. He was the perfect example of someone who'd been born on third base and thought he'd hit a triple.

This morning, as Sameer walked in, Patrick was striding across the lab in the direction of his lab bench. Meagan was also in early, but her face was pinched, and she looked like she was about to cry. Something was up.

"Are you all right?" said Sameer, crossing to her.

From the opposite side of the lab, Patrick nearly shouted, "She's fine."

Sameer ignored Patrick's outburst. "What's the matter, Meagan? You look upset."

"It's nothing," said Meagan, quickly wiping her eyes. She was a terrible liar.

Sameer sat on an empty stool next to her. "It doesn't look

like nothing." He lowered his voice. "Was Patrick bothering you?"

Meagan shook her head, but Sameer sensed, based on how her eyebrows had moved when he'd mentioned Patrick, that he'd hit on the truth.

"Look," he said gently, "if you want to talk to me about it, I promise to keep whatever you say in confidence, okay?"

"You know whispering is rude?" said Patrick loudly.

Sameer was about to tell him to shove it when Meagan jumped up.

"I have some mice in the animal facility I need to check on," she said quickly, then hurried from the lab in the direction of the elevators.

Sameer thought about running after her but decided against it. She probably just needed some time alone. Honestly, the poor girl had had a rough time in this lab already. The worst of it was when she'd accidentally played one of her audiobooks, a very spicy romance novel, over the lab's wireless speaker system. He hadn't been there to hear it himself, but apparently, the phrase "he sank into her glistening sex" had played at full volume before Meagan managed to hit pause. There had been a big to-do with Dr. Mulligan, culminating in a verbal warning from HR. And of course, Patrick would never let her live it down.

Sameer turned to his lab bench. Seated in a small bucket of ice was a single vial of blood, labeled with only a barcode sticker. He may have left the ancient DNA behind, but some things hadn't changed: he still didn't know where his samples came from.

There were times he missed academia. The professors were pompous and lacking in the most basic social skills, but at least they told him what he was working on. Here, every day was a new set of anonymous specimens. If he ever did discover something groundbreaking, he wouldn't have any way of knowing it.

With a resigned sigh, he got to work.

First, he pushed the needle of a syringe through the blood sample's rubber cap. After withdrawing a small amount of blood, he deposited it in a sterile vial. Carefully, he mixed in an equal amount of buffered heparin solution. It was important to dilute the blood to reduce its viscosity, and the heparin prevented coagulation.

With the blood and buffer mixture resting on ice, he got a sterile centrifuge tube from one of the drawers on his bench. To this tube, he added three milliliters of a special density-gradient media known as Ficoll solution. Ficoll was the crucial ingredient in the purification of white blood cells. If you spun a blood-and-Ficoll solution at a high enough speed, the red blood cells would pass into the Ficoll, while the white blood cells and plasma would remain on top. The trick was adding the blood without mixing it with the Ficoll.

Sameer rested his elbows on the edge of the lab bench as he carefully pipetted the blood and buffer solution on top of the Ficoll. It required a steady hand.

When he was done, he leaned back and studied his work. The contents of the centrifuge tube looked a bit like a Dark and Stormy cocktail, though in this case, the storm clouds were literally bloodred.

With the centrifuge tube filled, he weighed it on a digital scale. Then he weighed a second centrifuge tube and carefully filled it with water until the weights matched.

If he'd needed to centrifuge at high speed, he would have had to get the weights identical. Unbalanced samples could cause centrifuge rotors to break off and go flying around the lab like tops—tops that weighed twenty pounds and obliterated everything they touched. Fortunately, Ficoll purification was done at low speed. Off by three-tenths of a gram was close enough.

He walked over to the centrifuge and slid the tubes into

wells on opposite sides of the rotor. He was adjusting the speed settings when he felt a tap on his shoulder.

"I saw you talking to Meagan," said Patrick.

Sameer twisted away. "Can't you see I'm working?"

Patrick pressed the button on the centrifuge, and the motor started up. "There, now you're not working."

Sameer stiffened. "Dude. Don't mess with my samples."

"What did Meagan say to you?" Patrick was leaning over him, using his physical size as an implicit threat.

Sameer wanted to lie, to tell him that Meagan had told him everything and that he could go to hell, but he decided against it. Whatever their issue was, it wasn't any of his business.

"She didn't say anything," he said. "I was just trying to cheer her up."

"You should stay away from her. She's crazy."

Sameer felt his jaw tighten. That was exactly the sort of phrase that men like Patrick used to dismiss women.

"I'll make up my own mind about that," he replied, but Patrick was already walking back to his desk. The guy was such a prick.

Just then, Dr. Mulligan poked his head into the lab. "How's everything going?"

Sameer wanted to reply that Patrick had upset Meagan, but he simply said, "All good."

"How about the new blood sample?"

"It's in the centrifuge now."

"Excellent. Let me know the results. I have a good feeling about this one."

As he waited for the centrifuge to finish spinning, he checked Facebook on his phone. He got wrapped up in replying to a post and was startled when the centrifuge's timer buzzed. He opened the lid, retrieved the sample, and held it up to the light. It had separated into four parts. The red blood cells had settled to the bottom, leaving a clear layer of

Ficoll between them and the plasma at the top. Along the upper surface of the Ficoll was a very thin, almost imperceptible, beige-colored layer. That was what he was after, the buffy coat: the mononucleated white blood cells.

White blood cells were the most interesting component of blood. They included all the cells of the immune system: monocytes, neutrophils, eosinophils, basophils, even the T helper cells that were famously targeted by HIV. He thought of Jake. Now that he was in a serious relationship, he didn't have to worry nearly as much about contracting that particular virus.

He returned to his bench, gently placed the centrifuge tube in a wire rack, and used a pipette to extract the layer of plasma, which he saved in a small vial. When he was within about half a centimeter of the Ficoll layer, he got a fresh vial. Then, taking care not to disturb the Ficoll, he removed the last of the plasma and the thin buff-colored layer of white blood cells.

Putting everything back on ice, he leaned back in his chair and exhaled. He was done.

He looked around, only to find that the lab was now empty. Meagan still hadn't returned from the mouse colony, and Patrick had disappeared—probably a piss break.

At that moment, Patrick's phone buzzed on his bench. A text message. Then it buzzed again. And again.

Despite himself, Sameer let curiosity get the better of him. What were all these texts about?

He crossed to Patrick's bench, and as he looked at Patrick's phone, another text came in.

You are disgusting.

It was from Meagan.

Sameer looked at the door. Still no sign of Patrick or Meagan. He picked up the phone and tapped the screen. He expected a password prompt, but instead, it opened. Was Patrick really that casual with his cell phone security? Apparently, he was.

Sameer scrolled back through the messages. Meagan seemed to be really upset about something. Then he saw why: a text from Patrick to Meagan. It included a photo, slightly out of focus and shot in a dark room.

Despite the poor photo quality, there was no question what it was. A dick pic. Patrick's dick.

Below the photo, the text read,

> Cum sit on my glistening sex.

No wonder Meagan was so upset. Patrick was parroting the line from the romance novel to sexually harass her. He probably thought he could get away with it because Meagan had already been warned by HR.

Sameer wished he could give Meagan a hug and tell her everything would be okay. But the feeling of empathy was accompanied by hot rage. He wanted to beat the shit out of Patrick. Of course, he couldn't do that. He'd lose that particular fight—badly—and he'd be fired.

He looked back at the phone in his hand. Maybe there was *something* he could do.

Before he could decide it was a bad idea, he copied the dick pic into a new message, typed in Dr. Mulligan's cell phone number, and hit send.

HR was about to get very busy.

CHAPTER 34

Marcus came to upside down, the nylon strap of the seatbelt cutting sharply into his neck. He moaned, and while he could feel his vocal cords vibrate, the only thing he could actually hear was a high-pitched ringing sound. Slowly, the world slid into focus. Through the shattered windshield, red liquid dripped from the crushed front end of the Humvee. At first, he thought it was blood. Then he smelled the diesel fuel.

The world shifted, and the red liquid became actual blood. Blood that was slowly bubbling up from Frank's chest. Marcus's ears still rang from the gunshot. And from another noise. The younger man—Kostas—was screaming incoherently.

"Shut up, Kostas," Alexi growled.

Kostas continued to scream, his hands pressed to his face, his eyes peeking through his fingers at Frank's bloody body. Whoever this Kostas guy was, he was apparently not accustomed to seeing a man gunned down right in front of him.

Alexi nodded to Frank's former guard, who wrapped one big, meaty hand around Kostas's mouth. The young man's eyes bulged, but his screaming stopped.

Marcus felt for the kid. He, too, couldn't help but stare at

Frank's body. Blood stained his cravat, and his eyes stared blankly at the ceiling. Frank was clearly dead.

Marcus's stomach clenched as epinephrine flooded his circulatory system. Then his back arched, and he dry-heaved.

"Never seen a man die before?" said Alexi with contempt.

Marcus fought his gag reflex. The worst part of the panic attacks was how they activated his acute stress response.

"What should I do about him?" asked the guard behind him, and Marcus felt the cold barrel of a gun against the back of his head.

"Kill—"

"Wait!" shouted Sara.

Alexi held up a hand. "This had better be important."

The subtext was clear. No one told him what to do.

"You need my help, right?" said Sara. "Well, I need *his* help."

Alexi shook his head. "You and I both know perfectly well that's a lie."

Marcus keenly felt the gun's icy barrel pushing against his scalp, and a dissociation settled over him. He knew the end was imminent, yet he wasn't scared. In fact, he was surprised to discover that his primary concern was how much he hoped he didn't shit himself when he died. He didn't want Sara to see that.

"How about this, then?" Sara said. "If you kill him, I won't help you."

"I very much doubt that," said Alexi. He started to lower his hand, then hesitated. "But you do make an excellent point. Marcus will prove useful as leverage. He can live for now."

Marcus felt the barrel of the gun leave his skull. His legs felt like jelly, his body shook with every breath, but there was a silver lining. He hadn't shit himself.

CHAPTER 35
AETER PHARMACEUTICALS

Cambridge, Massachusetts
8:41 AM, June 9th

———

The Aeter laboratory building was like an iceberg. It was an ordinary two-story office building above ground, but its innocuous appearance belied the numerous basements and sub-basements hidden below. Sameer worked three stories below street level. While everything down here was kept brightly lit, the cooler air and lack of windows were a persistent reminder that he was subterranean.

He walked down the main hallway carrying the ice bucket that contained the three fractions of the blood sample he was working on: the red blood cells, the plasma, and the white blood cells. With his free hand, he swiped his ID through a card reader by a door labeled *Gnotobiotic Mouse Facility*. The lock buzzed, and he pushed his way into an antechamber—essentially a changing room.

He put on the familiar outfit: white Tyvek suit and booties, hairnet, face shield, a pair of clean nitrile gloves. When he was done, he placed the three blood fractions in a wire rack and sprayed the outside of each tube with 70% ethanol to sterilize them. Then, tucking them under an arm, he entered a small room about the size of a telephone booth.

He hummed the *Doctor Who* theme song under his breath as the HEPA-filtered air blew on him from all angles. Totally sci-fi.

Now freed of any dust or contamination, he stepped from the air shower, through a second door, and into a larger room. Two of the walls contained floor-to-ceiling wire shelving. Against the third stood a laminar flow hood just like the ones in the DNA lab where he used to work. The only chink in the armor of sterility was the faint ammonia scent of mouse urine.

Sameer crossed to a Plexiglas container the size of a shoe-box. Inside was a thin layer of sterile corn-cob bedding, a small water bottle, and a food dish. The lid was connected to a separate HEPA filtration system, ensuring that even the air inside was completely sterile. Curled up under a pile of shredded filter paper were three white lab mice.

He shook his head as he smiled behind his mask. It was hard to believe these little guys were the reason he had to go through so much trouble to stay completely sterile. But it was crucial. They were SCID mice—Severe Combined Immune Deficiency. Essentially, the mice were born with no immune systems. This meant the entire colony could be wiped out by a single viral or bacterial infection. Anyone who worked with them had to practice extreme sterile technique.

But they were necessary for this study. A normal mouse, one with a functioning immune system, would reject human blood cells.

Sameer carried the mouse cage to the laminar flow hood. Next to the hood stood a spray bottle full of 70% ethanol, and he used it to disinfect the outside of the cage and the three blood fractions a second time just to be safe. Lastly, he sprayed his hands. Even through the gloves, he could feel a cooling sensation as the alcohol evaporated.

He placed the sterilized mouse cage and blood fractions inside the laminar hood. Then, sitting on the stool in front, he scanned the interior of the hood, double-checking that everything was ready for the next steps of the protocol. There were stainless steel biopsy punches, ketamine and xylazine solutions, electric hair clippers, a small bottle of Nair, and an assortment of sterilized forceps, scissors, and syringes.

With everything ready, he sat back and drew in a deep breath. The next few steps would require his full attention. Any screwup could result in the loss of the samples—and worse, his job.

He began by anesthetizing each mouse with ketamine and xylazine. When the mice were asleep, he shaved the fur off their backs with the electric hair clippers. This required a gentle touch, as the mouse skin was very delicate. Once the mice were shaved, he applied the Nair solution to remove any remaining hair. The entire process took about ten minutes, leaving him fifteen minutes before the anesthetic began to wear off.

The next step was to use the biopsy punch to create a wound in each of the mice. He did this by gently pinching the skin on the mice's backs and pulling up. He could then press the punch through the skin, creating a pair of circular holes, much as if he had folded a piece of paper in half, poked a hole through it with a pencil, then unfolded it.

With the three mice punched and sleeping on the floor of the hood, he began the final step of the procedure. Using a small syringe fitted with a thirty-gauge needle, he sucked up 0.25 milliliters of the red blood cell solution and injected it into the first mouse's tail vein.

The ability to do this well was the closest he got to having job security. Anesthetizing and shaving mice could be taught in a day or two, but tail vein injections were something of an art. He doubted that anyone in the Greenland shark group had ever done one.

He put the mouse back into the cage, then injected each of the other two mice. The second mouse received the white blood cell solution, and the third was injected with the plasma solution.

As he was putting the last mouse into the cage, he frowned. Had he made a mistake? He could have sworn he'd punched all three mice and had done all three injections. Yet of the two mice already in the cage, only one had the pair of puncture wounds on its back.

The other was entirely healed.

CHAPTER 36
SOMERSET HOUSE

London, United Kingdom
1:43 PM, June 9th

———

A lexi led Sara and Marcus down a hallway into what looked like an old library. Floor-to-ceiling mahogany bookshelves lined three of the walls, and against the fourth stood an antique desk under a large window.

"Sit," Alexi said, pointing to a heavy oak table in the center of the room.

Sara found herself moving toward it. Everything Alexi said was a command. He spoke with the voice of a man who expected to be obeyed. Sara wondered if he had a military background.

As Sara seated herself, Alexi turned to Marcus. "You looked like you were about to piss yourself back there."

Marcus's skin was pale, and his hands were shaking. "I have PTSD," he said quietly. "From when I was in Syria."

Unexpectedly, Alexi's expression softened. "You were a soldier?"

"No. Journalist. I was a war correspondent for *The New York Times*."

"Not anymore?"

"After Assad's forces released me from prison, I was reassigned."

Sara sensed that Marcus was embarrassed. He didn't want to talk about this.

"War is fear, savagery, terror," said Alexi firmly. "Tests a man's character."

Marcus didn't answer, but Sara sensed he was retreating into himself. If they were going to get out of this alive, she needed him present.

"Leave him alone," she said. "PTSD is nothing to be ashamed of."

"You're right," said Alexi sardonically. "It's best not to get sidetracked with the lives of cowards."

He looked to the guard standing by the door, then shifted his eyes to Marcus. Almost imperceptibly, he nodded.

The guard leveled his gun at Marcus's chest.

"On your knees, coward," Alexi said.

Sara could only watch as Marcus did as he was told.

"What are you doing?" Sara demanded. But even she could hear the fear in her voice.

"You ask what I am doing, Ms. Morin? I am asking you nicely for assistance with some data I'd like analyzed."

Sara met Marcus's eye. He didn't speak, but his expression said, *Do what the man says.*

"Okay. I'll help you," she said quietly.

"Good. Do not forget that your friend here is my leverage, and remember what happened to Frank. If you don't do exactly what I ask, he dies. Notify the authorities, he dies. Omit anything, he dies. Lie to me, he dies. Understood?"

Sara swallowed. "Understood."

Alexi nodded to the guard again, and with a sudden strike, the man slammed the butt of his gun into Marcus's temple.

Marcus collapsed.

"What the hell!" Sara shouted. "I said I'd help you!"

"Consider that an additional reminder that I'm in charge. And now that we won't have any more interruptions, shall we begin working on the data?"

Alexi handed her the flash drive he'd taken from Frank, then set a laptop in front of her. When he took Marcus's empty chair beside her, she had to fight the urge to shy away. This man was clearly a psychopath, and she was now alone in a room with only him and his guards.

"What, exactly, would you like help with?" she asked as calmly as she could.

"Begin by telling me what I've got on this drive."

Sara navigated to the contents of the flash drive. There were two files:

```
9801980351_R1_001.fastq.gz
9801980351_R2_001.fastq.gz
```

"These look like compressed fastq files."

"English please," said Alexi in a voice that made it clear he hated admitting that he didn't know what she was talking about.

"It looks like data from a high-throughput DNA sequencer. Probably an Illumina machine."

"Looks like?" Alexi echoed.

Sara closed her eyes for a moment. The man was an ass. A psychopathic ass.

"Gimme a sec," she said, forcing herself to remain composed. "I'll take a look at the contents of one of the files."

She opened a terminal window and typed a command:

```
gunzip -c 9801980351_R1_001.fastq.gz | head
```

The first ten lines of the file spooled down the screen.

"Yeah," she said. "This is definitely output from an Illumina sequencer."

"What did it sequence?"

"I can't tell just by looking. But Frank said he'd sequenced the genome of the hound he captured."

"And what was he going to have you do with it?"

Sara thought quickly. Either Alexi didn't know what Frank had been up to or he was testing her. She could lie. But if he discovered she was being untruthful—she thought of Frank shot through the heart just a few rooms away—he'd do the same to Marcus. She couldn't risk that.

She wouldn't lie. Still...she didn't have to volunteer *everything* she knew.

"He wants to know where the hound came from. Demographically."

"You can work that out from this genome sequence?"

"Yes."

"How long will it take?"

"It depends on whether I have access to high-performance computation."

"Money is not an object here."

"Okay. Best case...I'm guessing the fastest I could get this analyzed is in about a day."

Alexi frowned. "That's a long time."

"You have more than sixty gigabytes of data here. File I/O is a limiting factor." She was pretty sure Alexi had no idea that file I/O simply meant how long it took a computer to read the data off the hard drive, and she didn't care. If he wanted clarification, he could ask for it. "Also, unless you happen to have a server lying around, I'm going to need access to a cloud computing platform. Amazon Web Services, Google Cloud, Rackspace. Something like that."

Alexi's frown deepened. "That would require internet access."

"If you expect me to run the analysis on just this laptop, it'll take at least a week. Probably longer."

Alexi studied her with narrowed eyes, as if determining her veracity. Finally, he stood. "I am going to talk to my tech guy. You are going to stay here."

As soon as the door closed behind Alexi, Sara got up from her chair. "I'm just checking on my friend," she said to the guard, holding up her hands.

She kneeled beside Marcus. A thin trickle of blood ran down the side of his forehead. As she was checking his pulse, he moaned, and his eyelids flickered open. He stared at her, pupils unfocused.

"Marcus, can you hear me?"

He groaned. "What happened?"

"The guard hit you with his gun."

"Are you okay?"

"I'm fine," she said.

"What does he want with you?"

"He wants me to analyze Frank's data."

"And I'm collateral to make sure that happens."

Sara nodded. "You guessed it." Her emotions finally boiled over, and tears filled her eyes. "I'm so sorry you got dragged into this," she said, her voice cracking. "They killed Amy. They killed Enora Hansen. They killed Frank. And I think they're going to kill you."

"It's okay," said Marcus. "I've been in worse situations."

"The PTSD," said Sara, understanding.

"Yeah. I was captured in Syria. I spent nine months in the Saydnaya military prison. I saw—" Marcus paused, clearly remembering something horrific. "I saw terrible things. It really messed me up."

Sara swallowed. "Which is why you're now working for the Science section."

"My shrink said I needed something more intellectual and less stressful." Marcus laughed. "I thought the worst of it would be interviewing a bunch of arrogant, egghead PhDs."

"Well, I guess being shot at and abducted *is* worse than talking to Topher," Sara said. Then she smiled. "But only slightly."

CHAPTER 37
SOMERSET HOUSE

London, United Kingdom
10:03 PM, June 9th

———

Marcus drew in a deep breath, then another. He desperately needed to steady his nerves.

He was seated against a wall, his hands tied tightly behind his back. His head ached, and there was a hard welt on the side of his head where he'd been pistol-whipped. But it wasn't pain that had him nearly hyperventilating. Being imprisoned had raised the cortisol in his blood to nearly intolerable levels, and he sensed the ever-present threat of a panic attack bubbling in his subconscious. So he kept inhaling, one breath after another, focusing all his energy on remaining calm.

Sara sat at the table in the center of the room, typing away on a laptop. A single guard remained stationed behind her. But they'd been joined by one other. Seated on the floor next to Marcus was the young man named Kostas. He had stopped screaming, but only because he'd been gagged. Duct tape was now wrapped around his mouth like a silver muzzle.

"Kostas," Alexi had explained when he deposited the young man here, speaking as though this should be perfectly obvious, "shouldn't do so much molly."

Before leaving, he'd instructed the guard that even Kostas wasn't allowed to leave until he had pulled himself together. He also insisted the guard watch carefully to see that Sara didn't email, IM, or do anything else to try to get help. So the guard stood behind her, his eyes fixed on the screen as Sara typed away.

She'd been at it for nearly seven hours now.

Marcus looked around the room. Thick Persian carpets covered the floor, and on the few spaces on the walls that weren't covered by shelves, he could see hand-painted wallpaper depicting peacocks and pheasants. Someone had arranged a row of orchids along the window ledge. Pretty standard rich-person decor.

But the contents of the shelves were not standard. In addition to books, they held an extensive collection of scientific curiosities and ephemera. One shelf was completely devoted to vintage microscopes and surgical instruments. Another held a display of dark and light morphs of peppered moths, stag beetles of various sizes, and a collection of butterflies with shiny blue wings.

Even the books weren't your usual fare. There were copies of Darwin's *The Voyage of the Beagle* and *On The Origin of Species*, Hooke's *Micrographia*, Newton's *Philosophiæ Naturalis Principia Mathematica*, and even a framed copy of Mendel's *Versuche über Pflanzenhybriden*. Frank, it was clear, had been a great historian of science, with a keen interest in biology.

But what interested Marcus most was the magnificent antique desk situated in front of the windows. It was a secretary desk with a cylindrical top to protect the writing surface, and nearly every inch of exposed wood was inlaid with intricate marquetry panels and gold leaf. As best as Marcus could tell from his seat on the floor, each panel depicted a different god in the Greek pantheon: Athena with her owl, Zeus holding a thunderbolt, Hephaestus at his forge, Poseidon with his trident. The largest panel was a diptych of classical images. In one, Prometheus brought fire to mankind, and in the other, Prometheus was chained to a rock while an eagle ate his liver.

Frank, Marcus remembered, had compared himself to Prometheus. Was this desk somehow related?

"I need to use the restroom," Sara said.

The guard hesitated for a moment. "All right," he said at last in a thick east London accent.

Kostas grunted through his gag.

The guard rolled his eyes. "Sure. You can come, too."

As Sara and Kostas stood, the guard tucked Sara's laptop under his arm. He looked at Marcus. "Need the loo?"

"No," said Marcus as casually as he could.

"Stay here."

The guard unlocked the door to the hallway, and he, Sara, and Kostas headed out. Marcus heard the door lock behind them.

He stood. His legs were pins and needles, but he managed to stagger forward. His hands were still tied. He would need to do something about that. Fortunately, twelve hours of sitting had given him ample time to devise a plan.

He staggered to the shelf with the surgical implements. He had to contort himself, but he managed to pick up an ancient scalpel-like blade even with his hands tied behind his back. Luckily, the thing was still razor sharp, and he was able to cut through the paracord with ease.

His hands free, he crossed to the desk. He pulled at the lid, but it was locked. There appeared to be no keyhole.

"Crap," he muttered.

Maybe there was a hidden button or lever? He felt under

the edge of the desk but found nothing. Just polished mahogany...and some symbols he hadn't seen from across the room. Four triangles outlined in brass.

Marcus smiled. He knew exactly what those symbols represented. They were the four primary alchemical elements: Fire, Air, Water, and Earth.

He touched the triangle that represented water. The marquetry was flush with the rest of the wood, but he was able to depress it about an eighth of an inch. It was definitely some sort of button. But the desk didn't open.

He scanned the intricate panels, looking from Zeus to Poseidon. Poseidon was the god of the sea. *Water.* He ran his fingers over the image of Poseidon. When he touched the head of the trident, it depressed with a soft click.

Now we're getting somewhere.

He quickly investigated the rest of the panels. He found buttons hidden in Zeus's lightning bolt, Hephaestus's anvil, and Demeter's cornucopia. Another minute of experimentation revealed that the triangular buttons had to be pressed before the corresponding marquetry button could be activated. And when he'd pressed all eight buttons in the right order, he heard a turning of gears.

The cover of the desk rolled open.

Marcus wanted to shout with excitement, but of course, that could draw attention. Instead, he desperately searched the interior.

The back of the desk held a row of shelves and drawers, while the writing area in front was littered with a mess of papers, Post-it notes, pens and pencils, and—he sucked in an involuntary gasp—a handgun. A Browning Hi-Power semi-automatic, by the look of it.

He was reaching for it when he instinctively stopped moving. The shape, the gestalt of the object, triggered something deep in his subconscious. The thing was so out of place that his brain didn't at first compute what it was. In fact, if he hadn't spent years working in war zones, he might not have recognized it at all.

Resting on a shelf at the back of the desk was a fragmentation grenade. It was behind glass, but a thin black string was attached to the pin and led through a hole into the innards of the desk. Marcus guessed that it was attached to a counterweight so that if he'd tried to break the desk open, it would have set off the grenade.

Frank had definitely been keeping something important in the desk. But what was it?

He was just leaning in to inspect it more closely when he heard Sara's voice in the hallway. He grabbed the Browning and tried to close the desk. The lid didn't budge. He heard the guard's key in the door and knew he was out of time. All he could do was hide the gun behind his back as he spun toward the door.

Sara entered first, followed by Kostas and the guard. Marcus twisted his features into what he hoped was a casual expression.

"So you see," Sara was saying to the guard, "I should have some preliminary results in the next hour or two."

The guard shut the door and then locked it. Immediately, Marcus leveled the Browning at the man's chest. "Say a word, and you're dead."

The guard saw the gun and froze. He started to open his mouth, but Marcus racked the Browning's slide. The guard's mouth closed.

Marcus gestured with the gun. "You and Kostas. Both of you lie down with your hands on top of your heads."

"Marcus, what are you doing?" said Sara.

"Saving us."

"If I just finish analyzing—"

"When you're done, they'll kill us both." He looked at her meaningfully. "Trust me."

Kostas and the guard lay down on the floor. The guard glared, but he didn't say a word. Marcus was relieved. He wouldn't hesitate to shoot the man, but if he did, the sound of the gunshot would alert everyone in Frank's apartment. A Browning had a thirteen-round magazine, and he doubted that would be enough to win a gunfight with Alexi and his bodyguards.

Then he remembered the guard was also armed.

"Take his gun," he said to Sara.

Sara knelt by the guard and drew a Glock from his waistband. She stood, and Marcus saw that she held the gun with her finger alongside the barrel.

"You've handled a gun before?"

Sara nodded.

"Okay, don't let them move. There's something important in here."

He turned back to the desk. What was he looking for? What was so important to Frank that he'd hidden it in this weird desk, and booby-trapped to boot?

"Marcus, what are you doing?"

"Just a sec—"

He heard a grunt and turned just in time to see the guard scissor his legs into Sara's. She stumbled and fell awkwardly against the shelves, sending an antique microscope crashing to the floor. As Kostas scrambled away, the guard lunged for Sara's gun.

Marcus fired the Browning twice. The first bullet hit the guard in the stomach. The second took his jaw clean off.

CHAPTER 38
SOMERSET HOUSE

London, United Kingdom
10:19 PM, June 9th

———

T he guard writhed at Sara's feet, desperately pressing the remains of his jaw to his face as if he could somehow reattach it. Kostas scrabbled away frantically, screaming through the gag.

From the hallway came a muffled shout that sounded like "Kostas?"

A sharp spike of adrenaline sent Sara's heart racing, but there wasn't time to panic. They needed a plan.

"Marcus?"

Marcus had turned away again. He appeared to be inspecting the interior of the desk.

"Marcus, what are you doing?"

"There's something important in here."

Someone was banging on the door.

"Marcus!" she shouted. "What's. The. Plan?"

Marcus spun around, his eyes wild. Shit, was he having another episode? Sara couldn't be sure.

"Marcus, are you here with me?"

"We need more time," he said. "Can you help me barricade the door?" He gestured toward the oak table.

Okay, that was a good idea. Sara ran to one end, and together, they pushed the heavy table against the door.

"Good," he said, stepping back. "That should hold them off a bit."

"I have an idea," Sara said. "I can access Twitter from the laptop. I'll post a message telling people I'm in trouble and to call the police. What's the name of this place again, Somerville house?"

"Somerset House. But don't post anything yet."

"Why?"

Marcus was once again staring at the desk. "Look at this first."

What the hell was he doing? They needed to get out of here. Escape through one of the windows, maybe? As soon as Alexi and his men broke through the door, they would almost certainly kill both her and Marcus. Or Marcus, at least. Yet Marcus was focused on an antique desk?

"This desk is important," Marcus repeated. He showed Sara the symbols. "It has something to do with alchemy."

"Wait," said Sara. "Is…is that a hand grenade?"

Marcus seemed unconcerned. "I think it's just there to prevent people from breaking the desk open. If it was going to explode, it already would have."

"That's not actually making me feel very okay."

Alexi's voice boomed from the hallway. "Open this door at once!"

Sara could feel her panic rising. Kostas had gotten his gag off and was now screaming to Alexi in Greek, and Alexi was banging on the door. They needed to escape—*now*. Yet she couldn't leave without Marcus, and he was obsessed with the desk, grabbing papers and tossing them aside.

Suddenly, he straightened up in excitement. In his hand was an oblong-shaped piece of steel covered in alchemical symbols.

"What is that?" Sara asked.

"I don't know."

"Whatever it is, it's all you're gonna get out of that desk. We're out of time," she said. Kostas was already starting to push the table away from the door.

"The window," Marcus said.

Together, they ran to the window. Marcus unlatched it and pushed it open.

"You first," he said.

"Why?"

"I'll be right behind you. Just go."

Kostas was moving the table back, and the door was starting to scrape open. Alexi bellowed something in Greek.

Sara leaped up on the sill and climbed out onto the roof. There was a narrow terrace there, with a low marble balustrade to separate her from a four-story drop to the courtyard below.

She turned and gestured for Marcus, but he wasn't at the window. He had gone back inside the room. She was about to shout for him when he reappeared once more.

As he climbed onto the sill, the door opened enough for a guard to squeeze through. He raised a gun.

Hardly thinking, Sara leaned past Marcus and fired the Glock. Once, twice, three times.

The man at the door fell back.

Then Marcus was next to her, pulling her away. He pushed the laptop into her arms. That's what he'd gone back for.

But not only that. Clutched in his fist was the grenade. Ripping out the pin, he tossed it through the open window.

"Cover your ears!" he shouted.

Dropping the Glock, she clamped her hands to her ears. Together, they crouched. "One, two, three, four—"

The grenade detonated, shattering glass and sending dust and smoke bursting from the room. Someone screamed. Probably Kostas.

They ran, sprinting along the narrow terrace, which continued all the way along the edge of the roof. Sara saw now that Somerset House consisted of three wings, each a half a block long, forming a rough horseshoe shape. They'd been in one leg of the horseshoe, and across the courtyard from them, the opposite wing was wrapped in scaffolding.

Below them flashed the lights of emergency vehicles. The gunshots must not have gone unnoticed, and the emergency personnel had certainly heard the explosion. But whatever their plan, they wouldn't arrive in time to help—and Sara didn't know if she could trust them, anyway. She and Marcus had to get out of this mess on their own.

Sara's breath was hot in her lungs by the time they reached the wing that formed the top of the horseshoe. As they came around the corner, she looked back and saw a man emerging from the window. He held a rifle in one hand.

"We need to get down," she gasped.

"We have to get to the scaffolding," Marcus said. "We'll have cover there."

He threw himself into a higher gear, and Sara sprinted after him. As they neared the scaffolding, a gunshot echoed over the courtyard, and marble dust sprayed up from the edge of the balustrade just a few feet ahead of them.

Marcus was the first to reach the scaffolding. It was wrapped in plastic, and he had to pause to tear a hole in it. More gunshots sounded, and bullets whizzed over their heads. Sara remembered her brother explaining that the sound of bullets was due to supersonic shock waves—literally miniature sonic booms.

Suddenly, Marcus stumbled, grunting with pain.

"Are you all right?" Sara cried.

Marcus didn't answer. He finished ripping the hole in the plastic and dove through. Sara was right behind him.

It was dark inside the scaffolding, and it took a few seconds for Sara's eyes to adjust. When they did, she saw Marcus leaning against a metal support. Blood had soaked his shirt.

"You're shot!" she said.

"Yeah. Got hit in the shoulder."

The man with the rifle hadn't given up, and it sounded like he was no longer alone. Several bullets pierced the plastic around Sara and Marcus, creating a constellation of holes not far from where they stood. Additional gunshots sounded like they were coming from the courtyard below. That must be the London police engaging Alexi's men.

"We have to keep moving," Sara said.

Marcus grunted, straightening in obvious pain.

They were still standing on the terrace. From here, the scaffolding rose over their heads, farther up the side of the building, as well as down into the courtyard. Below were the police, who might not be trustworthy. Which meant...

"We need to go up," she said.

Marcus didn't complain as they climbed, despite his injury. A few minutes later, they reached the roof of the wing, crossed over it, and came down again through more scaffolding on the opposite side. There were no emergency vehicles over here, and no one saw the two figures who ran from the site of yet another shooting.

They took cover in an alley across from a Starbucks. A light rain was falling. Marcus panted heavily, and blood dripped from his fingertips.

"You need to go to the hospital."

Marcus shook his head, mumbling something that sounded like, "I'll be okay."

"Fine. But we have to go *some*where."

On the other side of the building, they could still hear the police sirens interrupted by the occasional gunshot. At least Alexi and his men seemed to be occupied.

Marcus nodded to the laptop under her arm. "Ridecarz," he gasped.

Of course. Sara flipped open the laptop even as the rain intensified. Connecting through the Starbucks Wi-Fi network, she navigated to ridecarz.com and logged in.

"Do you know somewhere we can go?" she asked. "Somewhere safe?"

"An old friend. Spitalfields..." Marcus drew in a shaky breath. "Green Terrace Apartments."

Sara entered the address and hit submit. A moment later, text appeared on the screen:

YOUR DRIVER WILL ARRIVE IN THREE MINUTES.

Marcus leaned against her, his eyes closed.

"Stay with me, Marcus," she whispered as she watched the car-shaped icon on the map move toward their location.

CHAPTER 39
GREEN TERRACE APARTMENTS

Spitalfields, London
11:09 PM, June 9th

———

Mercedes sat in her leather Omega gaming chair wearing a bathrobe, her favorite furry slippers, and a pair of pink headphones. The screen of a large flat-panel monitor illuminated her face. It was nearly midnight, and she was already three hours deep into an all-night gaming session.

She was playing *Leader of Gods*—so named because if you were any good, you felt like an actual god. The game was simple but became complex through emergent gameplay. You used your mouse to direct your character across the screen in a top-down perspective, loaded up with guns and special abilities, and killed your opponents.

She took a sip from a can of Red Bull before navigating her character—Nyxobas—into the bushes near the bottom of her monitor. She enjoyed playing Nyxobas best. The character was supposed to be some sort of all-powerful demon, but she didn't care about the specifics of the lore. She liked Nyxobas because he excelled at ganking: sneaking up on and killing other players' characters.

She pressed P and clicked the left mouse button to ping her location, then typed in chat, *Ganking mid, need CC follow up.*

On the mini-map, she could see Ruadan, a bruiser character with a nasty stun, begin moving toward her position.

"Good, someone's not a complete noob," she muttered to herself.

As she waited for Ruadan's arrival, she lucked out. A bear-shaped character named Bartholomew entered her area battling a group of computer-controlled peons. In *Leader of Gods*, you needed to kill peons to grow stronger, but doing so was risky. It left you exposed and easy prey for a stealthy assassin like Nyxobas.

Mercedes pressed Q to activate Nyxobas's soul-siphoning ability, then with a click of her mouse, she directed the character to charge forward. As soon as Nyxobas left the safety of the bush, Bartholomew began to retreat, but it was too late. In addition to draining health, soul-siphon also caused a slowing effect. Nyxobas quickly gained ground.

That was when Ruadan appeared in a flanking position.

Well played, Mercedes thought.

Ruadan cast his death-coils spell, freezing the bear in place. It was over now. Mercedes tapped E, activating Nyxobas's blade of darkness. Not that she needed it—Bartholomew couldn't move or attack—but she liked its animation. With a single stroke of her deadly blade, his health dropped to zero.

"Hell, yeah!" Mercedes shouted into her empty apartment.

She was directing Nyxobas back into the safety of the bushes when her intercom buzzed.

Who the heck would be at her door at this ungodly hour? The most likely answer: her ex. He had a bad habit of ringing her up when he was steaming drunk. He might have grown up in South Kensington, but he had no manners.

At that moment, a computerized voice intoned "DEATH IS COMING" in her headphones.

"Bloody hell!" she screamed, looking back at her screen.

Already, the image on her monitor was shimmering and losing focus. In the few seconds she'd been distracted, the opposing team's Black Monk had cast his Tears of the Damned spell on Nyxobas. She wouldn't be able to see anything on screen for an entire eight fucking seconds. Where the fuck was Ruadan? She needed him. The bruiser could peel for her, fight off the Black Monk who was surely preparing to attack.

"Bollocks, bollocks, bollocks!" she shouted as she mashed buttons on her keyboard. She was going to die because her numpty ex-boyfriend was trying to get buzzed in at midnight, hoping she might shag him. Like *that* was ever going to happen again.

The button-mashing did no good. She couldn't see the scene, but she could see Nyxobas's health bar and could only watch in agony as it dwindled to zero.

She leaped from her seat, cursing loudly. This late in the match, her character would stay dead for more than a minute. She was basically out for the duration.

The intercom buzzed again. Blind with rage, she answered it.

"Stop pushing the buzzer, you bloody gormless arsehole!"

Static hissed for a few seconds before a female voice answered her. "Hello? Is this Mercedes?"

A woman's voice. She sounded American. Definitely not her ex.

Shame washed over Mercedes as she realized she'd just cursed out a stranger. Quietly, she said, "Yes, this is she."

"I'm with Marcus Byron. He's badly hurt. Can you let us in?"

CHAPTER 40
GREEN TERRACE APARTMENTS

Spitalfields, London
11:16 PM, June 9th

————

Sara wasn't sure what to expect after being called a "bloody gormless arsehole," but it wasn't this. The door to the apartment was opened by a tiny woman dressed in furry yellow slippers and a pink bathrobe. So this was Marcus's friend Mercedes.

The tiny woman's eyes went immediately to Marcus's blood-soaked shirt. "Oh, my God, Markie! What happened?"

"I got shot," Marcus mumbled.

"Is it okay if we come in?" Sara asked.

"Yes, of course." Mercedes opened the door wider. "I can call an ambulance—"

"No!" Sara interjected. "We can't have anyone knowing we're here." She stepped into the apartment, half-dragging Marcus with her.

"What happened? Is he going to be all right?"

"That depends," Sara said. "Do you have anything we can use to stop the bleeding? A first aid kit, maybe?"

"I—maybe." Mercedes rushed from the room, and Sara was left alone to maneuver Marcus onto the couch. She felt bad about bossing Marcus's friend around, but under the circumstances, it had to be done. She could apologize later.

Mercedes returned with her arms full. "I don't have a first aid kit, but I have all this." She dumped her supplies on the coffee table. A roll of athlete's tape, a bottle of hydrogen peroxide, a vial of ibuprofen, a towel, and a small pair of scissors.

"These were a good idea," said Sara, picking up the scissors. She turned to Marcus. "I'm going to cut off your shirt, okay?"

Marcus nodded, his eyes glazed.

Sara didn't know what she was doing, but she knew that the wound needed to be cleaned. Marcus was wearing a polo shirt, and Sara carefully cut through it, then peeled the fabric back slowly. The cloth near the shoulder was saturated with coagulated blood, and Marcus grimaced when she tugged at it.

"Mercedes, do you have tweezers? Also, we need sterile gauze."

"I'm pretty sure I have tweezers, but I already looked for gauze and didn't find any."

Sara paused to think. "Do you have menstrual pads?"

"Yes. Great idea." She darted off again.

"Also, grab a needle and thread!" Sara shouted after her. She grabbed the bottle of hydrogen peroxide and turned back to Marcus. "This is going to hurt."

Marcus met her gaze. "Do it."

Sara poured the hydrogen peroxide liberally onto his wound. Marcus sucked in a sharp breath, his blue eyes fixed on her. As the peroxide bubbled, Sara tugged at the shirt again. This time, she was able to remove the remaining fabric from his shoulder. She'd expected to find a single puncture wound, but instead, he had several deep lacerations, almost as if he'd been mauled by an animal.

Mercedes reappeared and handed Sara a sanitary pad. Her gaze must have fallen on the wound because she gasped. "What else can I do?"

"Just stand by in case we need something else."

As Sara began to dab at the wound, Mercedes said, "You know what Markie's nickname was here at the *Times*?"

"Markie?"

"No, that's *my* nickname for him. In the office, he was 'Girly-boy' on account of his long eyelashes."

Sara realized that joking must be Mercedes's way of handling stress. The woman was trying to be lighthearted, but the tension in her voice was unmistakable.

Marcus groaned. "You know, this *really* hurts."

"Right," said Sara. "Mercedes, can you give him some of that ibuprofen?"

Mercedes grabbed the bottle and opened it.

"I don't think you were hit by a bullet," Sara said to Marcus.

"Yeah?" he said. "I'm gonna have to beg to differ."

"No, I mean, I think this wound was caused by bullet fragments." Sara's brother used to say that "close only counts in horseshoes, hand grenades, and 5.56 NATO" while explaining how powerful his Bushmaster was. According to him, the ammo was so powerful that simply getting hit by bullet fragments was often enough to kill you.

"Is that good?" Mercedes asked as she gave Marcus four ibuprofen tablets.

"It may be the only reason he's not dead. If he'd taken a direct hit at this location, the bullet could have severed his brachial artery. He'd have bled out in minutes."

"Oh, my God," said Mercedes.

"Can I have those tweezers now?"

Mercedes handed over the tweezers. Sara cleaned them with peroxide and a fresh pad, then leaned in close to inspect the wound.

"I'm looking for bits of shrapnel," she said as she gently teased apart the edges of the largest laceration. Sure enough, a bit of metal glinted inside.

"Do you have to do that?" Marcus grunted.

"Girly-boy," said Mercedes, "stop whinging."

Marcus grimaced.

Sara removed three pieces of bullet and a small chunk of stone—probably a bit of marble balustrade. When she was satisfied that there were no more foreign objects in Marcus's shoulder, she asked Mercedes for the needle and thread.

"This is going to hurt again," Sara said to Marcus.

He gritted his teeth. "Everything you're doing hurts. Just do it."

Sara wished she had time to watch a YouTube video on suturing. She was certain her technique left a lot to be desired. She had to enlist Mercedes's help in holding the lacerations shut, and her handiwork looked like crap, but in the end, she managed to stitch everything shut. When she was done, she pressed a clean pad to Marcus's shoulder and taped it in place.

Finally, she sat back on her heels. "You're going to be okay, Markie," she said quietly.

─────

While Marcus rested and Mercedes filled an electric kettle, Sara took in the apartment, not that there was much of it to see. A short hallway had only two doors, which she assumed led to a bedroom and bathroom, and just off the living room was a small kitchen and dining area. It didn't look like anyone did much dining here, however, for the table was covered with computer equipment: an ultra-wide LCD monitor, a custom PC that blinked with LEDs, and a black gaming keyboard and mouse.

Mercedes handed her a cup of tea. "You're Sara Morin, aren't you?"

"How did you know that?"

"You and Marcus are all over the news."

"Wait, what?"

Mercedes nodded. "It's the biggest story coming out of the States right now. A massive manhunt is underway in Massachusetts for you two. They say you're both wanted in connection with the murders at Harvard, some fancy estate, and a hospital."

"They think *we* did all that?"

"I'm not sure exactly *what* they think. Most of the big news sites are describing you as 'persons of interest,' but with stuff like this, conspiracy theories abound. On Reddit, they say you're collaborating with the Illuminati."

Sara laughed. "That's not as far off as it sounds."

Mercedes raised an eyebrow. "Is now when you're going to tell me what's going on with you two?"

Sara hesitated. The truth was, she didn't know Mercedes at all. And worse, the one thing she did know was that Mercedes worked for *The New York Times*. That meant she had the means and motive to get their story before reporters.

But Marcus had said she was a friend. Thus far, she'd acted like one. And Sara could use a friend right now.

She took a sip of her tea and made a decision.

"It's a long story."

For the next twenty minutes, she recounted as many of the details of the past few days as she could remember. When she mentioned Frank, Mercedes's eyes widened slightly, but at no point did she interrupt. Mercedes waited until Sara's story was complete before asking a question.

"How much do you know about this Frank?"

Sara shrugged. "Just what I've told you. He's extremely wealthy and some kind of leader of a secret society. And now he's dead."

"I think I might know who he was."

"Who?"

Mercedes sat down at her computer and typed the name "François Gammon" into the browser. She navigated to the image results and pulled up a blurry picture of a man standing on a beach. "Is this him?" she asked.

Sara squinted. The picture was taken from a distance, and his face wasn't clear. He was the right height and build, but that was about all she could say for sure.

"Maybe," she said. "Surely there must be better pictures?"

Mercedes shook her head. "François Gammon is—or was—extraordinarily secretive. This is one of the only pictures of him anywhere on the web."

"And what makes you think he's Frank?"

"François Gammon is one of the richest men in the world. He's a huge benefactor of science here in the UK. And also, there's the name." Mercedes shrugged. "Frank, Francois…"

Sara was skeptical. "That's not really a lot to go on."

"I know. But there's something else. François Gammon gives an enormous amount of money to universities. Have you heard of King's College London?"

"Yeah. One of our lab's collaborators works there." A fact that now seemed strangely distant, like Sara was talking about another life.

"The Gammon Foundation accounts for almost their entire endowment. And King's College is literally right across the street from Somerset House."

"How do you know all this?" Sara asked.

"Last year for work, I put together an infographic showing the different sources of funding in the UK."

"You do data-vis for the *Times*?"

"Amongst my many duties," said Mercedes with a smile.

"And this is your workspace?"

Mercedes laughed. "Hell, no, that's all at the office. This is my gaming rig. In fact, I was in the middle of a game when you—"

A heavy thud sounded from the living room. Sara and Mercedes both leaped up and ran to check on Marcus.

They found him lying on the floor, flat on his back.

"I fell," he said, looking up at them groggily.

"I'm so sorry," said Mercedes. "We should have pulled out the couch. I didn't think—"

"It's okay. I didn't hit my shoulder," Marcus said, sitting up. "But I could really use something to drink."

"What do you want?" said Mercedes. "I have tea, orange juice, milk, water—"

"Water."

As Mercedes hurried back into the kitchen, Marcus looked up at Sara. "Thanks for saving my life."

"You would have done the same for me. In fact, you already did."

Marcus didn't answer—he just stared at her. There was something sad, almost forlorn about his expression.

This man has some serious demons.

Mercedes reappeared with a large glass of water. As Marcus took a long sip, Mercedes began removing pillows from the couch. Sara helped shift Marcus out of the way, and together, she and Mercedes arranged the pull-out bed.

"If you've finished that water, you need to go to sleep," Sara said to Marcus. "You've lost a lot of blood. You'll feel better after you get some rest."

She and Mercedes helped Marcus into the bed. He looked

exhausted, his skin pale. He shivered, and when she touched his cheek, it was clammy.

"He's freezing," she whispered.

"I'll get some blankets," Mercedes said.

As she disappeared down the hall, Sara climbed into the bed next to Marcus and pulled the covers over them both. He didn't speak, but the intensity of his shivering lessened.

CHAPTER 41
PRESIDENTIAL SUITE, LANESBOROUGH HOTEL

London, United Kingdom
8:30 AM, June 10th

———

Alexi studied himself in the gilt mirror of the hotel suite's master bathroom. Blood streaked his bare torso, and his eyes were ringed with deep circles. He looked like shit.

He felt even worse. Kostas was dead. Alexi had seen the body. His heart ached. Kostas had been his *eromenos*—his best friend, his lover—and Alexi had failed in his duty to protect him.

He should have anticipated this. If there was one thing he prided himself on, it was tactics and strategy. He'd known the location of Frank's apartment for years but had waited to act until he could use that knowledge to inflict the most damage.

He'd planned everything meticulously, taking care to disable Frank's security system, stationing his guards by the elevator. He'd had the element of surprise. He'd neutralized

Frank. Captured the girl alive. It had unfolded exactly as he'd designed it.

But he'd misjudged the reporter. The man had appeared weak. Impotent. Broken. Alexi had dismissed him as a threat. He'd even allowed himself to feel pity for the man.

He would not make that mistake again.

He palpated a blood-streaked patch of skin under his right collarbone. Then he reached into his leather Dopp kit and withdrew an antique straight razor with an ivory handle. He opened the blade with a flick of his wrist and slid the edge of it along his thumbnail. Even with no pressure applied, the blade dug in. Alexi nodded. It was sharp enough.

He drew the point of the blade along the skin beneath his collarbone. Blood beaded under the steel. He breathed out sharply as he pressed his thumb and forefinger into the incision. Closing his eyes, he worked by touch alone.

With a grimace, he plucked the bullet from the incision and dropped it into the empty basin with a clink.

He needed a new strategy now. It was crucial that their great secret not be revealed. But the reporter and the girl had gone to ground while he'd been tied up all night putting out fires. It had taken time—and money—to pay off law enforcement and quash the story in the newspapers.

Now he was back to his primary task: eliminating the threat. He just needed to find them. The girl would give him what he needed.

And then he would kill them both.

His eyes returned to the mirror, and he smiled as the incision knitted itself together.

CHAPTER 42
GREEN TERRACE APARTMENTS

Spitalfields, London
8:32 AM, June 10th

———

Sara lay awake in semi-darkness. Across the room, below the TV, LEDs on the cable box blinked the time: 8:32 AM. She knew she should sleep, but her mind raced with questions. What was going on in London? Had Alexi and his men been caught? How much danger were they in?

Next to her, Marcus stirred, reminding her that she was not alone. His breaths were regular. When she gently touched his cheek, he felt warm. She closed her eyes, relieved. He was no longer about to die from blood loss.

Taking care not to wake him, she slipped out of bed. She stood for a moment in the middle of the room and stretched. London's skyline glimmered faintly through the windows, and she suddenly felt terribly alone.

Lights flickered in the kitchen, and like a moth, she was drawn to them. She found Mercedes seated in front of her computer, headphones over her ears, her eyes glued to the screen.

When Sara tapped her on her shoulder, Mercedes yelped.

"Sorry," said Sara as Mercedes pulled off her headphones. "I didn't mean to scare you."

Mercedes laughed. "No worries. I'm just not used to having other people around."

Sara looked at the computer screen. "You've been playing all night?"

Mercedes nodded, looking sheepish. "On Friday nights, I stream on Twitch. My viewers would be disappointed if I weren't online."

"What's the name of your stream?"

Mercedes mumbled something that sounded like "sulpap."

"Sulpap?"

"What? No. It's an acronym. SKLK," said Mercedes.

It took Sara a moment to digest what Mercedes had just said.

"*You're* Skulk?" she replied.

"Yes," said Mercedes looking away.

"But—you're internet famous. Even *I've* heard of you."

She didn't mention that the reason for this was that her ex had been obsessed with video games and was always watching Twitch streams on his laptop. It was no wonder that he had zero publications eight years into his PhD.

It was also no wonder that she'd broken up with him.

Mercedes didn't meet Sara's eyes. "I try to keep it quiet. If work found out…"

"I don't understand. Why would they care?"

"They wouldn't, except my contract says I'm not allowed to have a second job."

Sara laughed. "Streaming on Twitch is hardly a job."

Mercedes continued to avoid eye contact. "I made more

than double my income at the *Times* from streaming last year."

"You what?"

"I made almost four hundred thousand pounds."

"Oh, my God! That's amazing!"

"Shh …" said Mercedes, putting a finger to her lips.

"There's no one here."

"If you shout, you might wake up Markie."

"Oh, right. Well, your secret is safe with me."

"Thanks," said Mercedes. She looked back at her computer screen. "I really should get back to it."

Sara noticed the laptop she'd taken from Somerset House at the end of the table. She flipped it open, but the screen didn't come on. "Crap."

"What's the matter?" Mercedes asked.

"It's dead. I didn't think to take the power cord."

"You can borrow my laptop, if you like." Mercedes pointed to a silver MacBook.

"You don't mind?"

"The password is X41822N. All caps."

Sara closed Alexi's laptop and opened Mercedes's. This time, she was greeted by the gentle glow of an LCD screen. She rolled her shoulders, then pulled two flash drives from her pocket, one from Frank, the other from Enora Hansen. They looked innocuous, but she knew that hidden somewhere in the nonvolatile memory of these devices were fantastic secrets. Secrets men had killed and died for.

She cracked her knuckles. *Good thing I'm not a man.*

CHAPTER 43
THE PRESIDENTIAL SUITE, LANESBOROUGH HOTEL

London, United Kingdom
8:51 AM, June 10th

———

Alexi was tracing his fingers along his abdomen, checking that he hadn't missed any pieces of shrapnel, when his cell phone rang. Tightening a towel around his waist, he returned to the main room of the suite. One of his men stood by the door.

"I will need some privacy," said Alexi. As the man stepped into the adjoining room, Alexi put the phone to his ear.

"I thought you had everything under control," said the voice on the other end of the line.

"There was an unexpected development."

Alexi looked out the window. The Lanesborough Hotel was in central London, next to Hyde Park. In the distance, he could see the roof of Buckingham Palace, and closer by, just across the street, was the gray stone of Wellington Arch. Built in 1926, the arch celebrated the British triumphs in the Napoleonic Wars. From here, Alexi could clearly see the bronze quadriga on top—a massive statue of Nike, the goddess of victory, driving the chariot of war.

If only things were as simple as charging forth to smite one's enemies.

The voice on the other end of the line berated him. Alexi listened quietly for a while before he interjected. "The thing is, they've disappeared."

"Then you need to find them."

"I'm working on it."

"Do you need another hound?"

"No," said Alexi emphatically. "I have this under control."

"If you don't get this wrapped up, the consequences will be—"

"I *know* the consequences. I will find the girl and the reporter, and I will kill them."

CHAPTER 44
GREEN TERRACE
APARTMENTS, SPITALFIELDS

London, United Kingdom
9:48 AM, June 11th

———

"Hit him!"

The shout woke Marcus. He groaned and squeezed his eyes tighter, trying to will a few more hours of sleep. He'd almost succeeded when the voice shouted again.

"Hit the bloody bastard!"

This time, he opened his eyes. Daylight poured into the room, and he blinked at it as he sat up slowly. He rubbed his face with open palms and tried to wrest back some consciousness.

Gradually, his memories solidified. Their escape from Somerset House. His injury. Mercedes's apartment.

"Get 'em!"

He recognized the voice now. Mercedes.

"Activate your Dooooom-hammer!"

Of course she was playing video games.

Marcus stood unsteadily and walked to the door of the kitchen. Two women sat in front of a computer screen, and Marcus was surprised to find that it was Sara, not Mercedes, who manned the keyboard.

Mercedes yelled again. "Now. Hit him now!"

"Is all this screaming really necessary?" Marcus said.

The women spun, speaking in unison. "You're awake!"

Marcus's head throbbed. "Honestly, not much choice in that department."

"Mercedes is teaching me to play *Leader of Gods*," Sara said.

Mercedes grinned. "She's actually pretty good for a noob. Decent reflexes."

"And this is why you were screaming?"

Mercedes's grin turned guilty. "I mean...she *was* just about to kill their healer."

"Well, if you want *me* to heal up, you might want to tone down the yelling a bit."

Mercedes and Sara exchanged a look.

"What?" said Marcus.

"Have you considered a shower?" Sara offered. Her eyes said it was something to do with his appearance.

Marcus looked down. He was wearing only underwear. A thin film of dried blood encrusted his chest. He looked like an extra from a zombie movie. A shower was an excellent idea.

"Where's the bathroom?"

"First door on the right." Mercedes pointed down a short hallway.

Inside the bathroom, he studied himself in the mirror as he waited for the shower to warm up. God, he was a wreck. Half-naked, hair a matted mess, a makeshift bandage on his shoulder. He grimaced as he realized he would have to remove it before he got in the shower.

He peeled back the tape that held the bandage in place. His shoulder was the color of an eggplant and caked with clotted blood. On the plus side, the lacerations didn't appear to be infected. Mentally, he thanked Sara for stitching them up. She had saved his life. He was certain of it.

He removed his boxers and stepped into the shower. For a few minutes, he simply let the water wash over him. The pounding in his head slowly abated.

"Everything okay in there?" Sara called through the door.

"Yes," Marcus answered. He picked up a bar of soap and began scrubbing off the dried blood.

When he finally turned off the water, he felt like a new man. The steam and spray had restored some of his missing humanity. As he was drying himself, a soft knock came at the door.

"I have some clothes for you," Mercedes said.

He cracked the door wide enough for her to pass in a bundle: clean socks, underwear, a pair of blue jeans, and a T-shirt featuring a pixelated image of Donkey Kong. He dressed gingerly, careful not to tug on the stitches in his injured shoulder.

The women were waiting for him in the kitchen.

"How are you feeling?" Sara asked. She looked worried.

"Could be worse. You did really good work on my shoulder."

She smiled. "Thanks."

"Did you get enough sleep?" asked Mercedes.

"Yeah, but my head feels like shit."

Sara nodded. "You lost a lot of blood."

Marcus felt his stomach grumble. "Would it be possible to get something to eat? I haven't eaten in—" He paused. Was the plane the last time he had eaten? He couldn't remember.

"About forty-eight hours," said Sara, glancing at a clock above the doorway.

"What would you like?" Mercedes asked. "I could do eggs and soldiers."

"That would be fantastic."

As Mercedes began getting food from the fridge, Marcus sat down at the kitchen table. Sara brought him a hot cup of tea.

"A lot's happened since you fell asleep," she said, taking the seat across from him.

Marcus could see from her expression it wasn't good news. "How bad is it?"

"We're the targets of a massive manhunt in the US. We're 'persons of interest' in the shootings at both Harvard and Beauport."

"Crap."

"Do you think we should go to the police?"

Marcus shook his head. "They're never going to believe us. I mean, would you? Our story is that we were abducted by the now-murdered head of a secret society and that the Harvard shooter was some sort of super soldier. Besides, I suspect Frank was right about the authorities being compromised."

"So what do you think we should do?"

Marcus considered the possibilities. "Has there been any indication in the news that we're in London?"

"Not that I've heard."

"What are they saying about Somerset House?"

"They're describing it as a potential terrorist incident."

"Any suspects?"

"No. And no mention of us at all."

That was good news. "All right, as long as our pictures aren't splashed all over *The Sun*, I guess we're safe here for a little while." He paused. "How visible is the story in the States?"

"Front page," said Mercedes, who was putting bread in the toaster. "And I wouldn't be so sure about *The Sun*. You're big news here, too. You're going to need a disguise." She turned and held up a Tesco bag. "Which is why I bought hair dye this morning." Her eyes twinkled mischievously. "I think you'll look good as a blond."

Marcus shook his head. "No way. Not going to happen."

"Come on, Markie!"

"Do you have a hat?"

"You're no fun," said Mercedes with a sigh. "But yes, I have a hat you can wear."

Sara cut in. "Hiding out is one thing, but we can't stay here forever. Alexi is going to come for us."

Marcus took a sip of his tea. "I agree. We need some sort of leverage. Something we can hold over him if he finds us."

Sara frowned. "What if we threatened to publish the genome sequence Frank gave us? The one from the hound. Do you think that would be enough?"

"Maybe…"

"I could get the *Times* to write a story about it, if needed," said Mercedes, scooping eggs from a pot of boiling water. "Better yet, *you* could write the story, and I could just drop it into SCOOP."

"Scoop?" asked Sara.

"That's the name of the *Times*'s content management system. I can put a story in the queue there so it's ready to publish at any time."

Sara looked to Marcus. "What do you think?"

"I think it's a good idea. But first, I need to understand what it is the genome contains. I can't write a story about it without even knowing what's important about it."

Mercedes began buttering slices of toast, and Marcus's stomach suddenly felt very empty. "That smells delicious, by the way."

"Maillard reaction," said Sara.

"What?"

"It's what happens to amino acids and sugars when they're cooked. Why toasted bread tastes good." Sara blushed. "Sorry, can't help the science talk sometimes."

"I had no idea there was a term for that," said Marcus, impressed.

"Well, now you know. And as for Frank's genome, I already have an analysis running. Mercedes hooked me up with some computing resources."

"She's using my gaming rig," Mercedes explained.

"I should have results by tomorrow morning," Sara added.

"Wow. That's quick."

"Markie," said Mercedes, "you've been asleep for more than twenty-four hours."

"Oh. I didn't realize."

Mercedes set his breakfast in front of him, and for a moment, he forgot all about Frank's genome. He tore into the food with a primal hunger, hardly even chewing between bites.

CHAPTER 45
PRIMORSKY DISTRICT

St. Petersburg, Russia
12:05 PM, June 11th

———

I f Yevgeny had opened his window shades, he would
have seen an overcast sky, the beige concrete of the apartment block across the street, and the steel-gray water of
the Baltic Sea in the distance. But Yevgeny never opened his
shades. He liked his bedroom dark. Like a cave. It meant less
glare on his computer screen and an easier time getting into a
flow state.

He clicked open a terminal window and typed `whoami` on
the command line. An instant later, a line of text appeared on
the screen:

```
magomed
```

The username was short for Magomed Ibragimov, the best
Russian lightweight mixed martial arts fighter. Yevgeny liked
to imagine he was the computer version of Magomed, his

fingers tapping the keyboard as quickly as Magomed's right hand jabbed his opponents. And just like Magomed, he could destroy people.

He typed a command into the terminal:

```
ssh magomed@130.24.11.5
```

His screen filled with new text.

```
Ubuntu 16.04.5 LTS (GNU/Linux 4.4.0-83-generic x86_64)
 * Documentation: https://help.ubuntu.com
 * Managment: https://landscape.canonical.com
 * Support: https://ubuntu.com/advantage
```

Yevgeny laughed. It always amused him when the tech company IT guys decided to customize the Linux login screen. None of their programmers actually gave a crap whether it was the default login or the company logo converted to text, but it sure made it easy for hackers like him to confirm they'd found the right server.

He entered more commands to log into RideCarz's primary database. He'd have thought a company worth nearly fifty billion dollars would use a bespoke database, but this was simple MySQL.

"*Raz pljúnut'*," he said under his breath as he entered a select statement:

```
SELECT *
FROM rides
WHERE
date BETWEEN
UNIX_TIMESTAMP('2018/06/10 04:00:00')
```

```
AND
UNIX_TIMESTAMP('2018/06/10 06:00:00');
```

This returned almost two thousand rows of unique rides. Way too much data. He would need to add more filters to the search. Something specific about the location, maybe.

```
SELECT *
FROM rides
WHERE
date BETWEEN
UNIX_TIMESTAMP('2018/06/10 04:00:00')
AND
UNIX_TIMESTAMP('2018/06/10 06:00:00')
AND pickup_address LIKE '%Strand%';
```

Now the results were limited to fifty. This was more workable, though still quite a few more hits than he'd prefer. As he scanned through the list, he immediately saw why. The Strand was one of London's longer and busier roads. He needed to narrow the results further.

Pulling up Google Maps, he searched for Somerset House. It was located at Strand, London WC2R 1LA, UK. He tried that as the pickup address.

The resulting table was empty.

"*Der'mo,*" he muttered under his breath.

He rubbed the faint stubble under his chin. Nearly two weeks' worth. Facial hair wasn't a strength of his.

The results made sense when he thought about it. They wouldn't have called a car to meet them right in front. From what he'd seen on TV, the place had been crawling with police.

He turned back to the map. They would have stayed off the main road—used a side road, most likely. Just to the east of Somerset House was Surrey Street. He replaced

"Strand" with "Surrey" in the select statement and hit enter.

"Ypa!"

There was only one result that matched that time and place.

The drop-off location for that ride was someplace called Green Terrace Apartments in Spitalfields.

Yevgeny smiled.

CHAPTER 46
AETER PHARMACEUTICALS

Cambridge, Massachusetts
7:04 AM, June 11th

———

S ameer hurried along the corridor toward room B418. He shivered, wishing he'd had time to throw on a hoodie. The bright LED lights did nothing to warm the cool basement air.

Don't be late, the email had said. *We need the cells at exactly seven AM.*

So of *course* this would be the day when he'd forgotten to plug his phone in. It was dead by morning, and if Jake hadn't stopped to say goodbye on his way to the gym, Sameer would still be asleep. He'd somehow managed to get to the lab by a quarter 'til, but that hadn't left him enough time to thaw and prep the cells.

In a way, though, he didn't feel too bad about it. Ever since his discovery of the regenerative leukocytes, he'd been pulling twelve-hour days culturing the cells and performing experiments. Yes, he'd overslept. But that was because they literally weren't giving him enough time to sleep.

That said, the work was exciting. He sensed he was on the edge of a tremendous discovery, something with the potential to save millions of lives. The white blood cells were incredibly potent. He'd discovered that a mouse injected with only a few thousand cells could heal deep wounds and even repair internal organs. There was no question that the pharmaceutical implications of his work were enormous.

That wasn't to say the cells were perfect. The healing ability wasn't permanent. After a mouse had healed a few wounds, it seemed to revert back to normal. Sameer was currently structuring an experiment to test if the mice's autoimmune responses were causing this fall-off in activity.

But at the moment, his only job was to deliver these cells. The hall ended at a set of double doors: room B418. As Sameer was deciding whether to knock, one of the doors swung open, and a severe-looking man in a winter parka looked him up and down. An Aeter Pharmaceuticals ID badge pinned to his jacket read "Dr. Gallagher."

"Hi. I—I'm here with the cells." He held up the ice bucket. "Leukocytes cultured in RMPI 1640 and bovine calf serum. Washed and resuspended in PBS. About a billion cells, give or take."

"You're late," the man said curtly.

"I had trouble finding the room." Sameer wasn't about to admit that he'd overslept.

"Follow me," said the man.

Sameer followed him into room B418—and immediately shivered. It was freezing cold in here, like walking outside in Boston in the middle of January.

The whole room must be a giant refrigerator.

Lots of lab supplies needed to be kept cold. Petri dishes with growth media needed to be refrigerated, low–flash point chemicals like benzene and acetone could explode if they got too warm, and some experiments needed to be done entirely in the cold. Sameer had heard horror stories of lab techs working on protein purification forced to spend entire days in nearly freezing rooms processing samples.

As they crossed the lab, they passed an enormous circular structure the size of an above-ground swimming pool. The air had a slightly fishy smell.

"Are you part of the Greenland shark group?" Sameer asked.

Dr. Gallagher didn't answer. He walked to a second set of doors, but instead of opening them, he handed Sameer a packet containing a disposable gown, face mask, and gloves. "Put these on," he said.

Sameer didn't understand why he needed to be dressed in sterile attire to deliver cells, but he was used to not knowing why he did things. Plus, they might keep him a bit warmer. He pulled the gown over his head, put on the gloves—taking care to touch only the cuffs—and donned the face mask.

"This way," said the doctor. He pushed the doors open.

The room on the other side was just as cold as the lab. It was outfitted as a full surgical suite, complete with IV stands and instrument racks. A bright light had been set up over a long steel table. And on that table, shrouded by a green drape, was the unmistakable form of a human body.

"What's the status of the patient?" asked Dr. Gallagher, his voice all business.

"Stable. I have cryoprotectant flowing through the cardiopulmonary bypass at one point nine liters per minute," said a blonde woman seated next to a large medical device that whirred rhythmically.

"What's the temp?"

"Negative three."

"Rate?"

"Increasing one degree every five minutes." The seated doctor looked at Sameer. "Is this the guy with the cells?"

"Yes."

"Cutting it close…"

"Increase the rate to a degree every two minutes," Dr. Gallagher said. "When we reach ten degrees, begin the washout procedure. Sameer, this is Dr. Mesle. She'll fill you in."

Sameer crossed to Dr. Mesle. From this new position, he could see an LCD screen playing a video feed of the patient's chest cavity. He grimaced. It was spread open like a butterflied shrimp. Various tubes led inside. Silver instruments protruded. The heart itself was covered in black sutures. It did not beat.

"What's the volume?" she said curtly.

"The what?" Something about Dr. Mesle's tone put him on edge.

"Tell me the volume of the resuspension." She inclined her head toward the ice bucket.

"Five milliliters, plus or minus."

"All right. Load them into this." She handed him a ten-milliliter syringe.

Sameer did as she asked, carefully sucking up the cells.

"Increase the flow to two point two," said Dr. Gallagher. "Add ten thousand units of heparin."

Dr. Mesle poked at the buttons on the machine. Sameer had decided it must be a cardiopulmonary bypass unit, an artificial pump used for heart surgeries. That would explain why the patient's heart wasn't beating.

"Blood parameters?" Dr. Gallagher asked.

"Temp twenty-two, pH seven point three, partial pressure oxygen sixty-five."

"Great. Let's increase whole blood perfusion until oxygen is at seventy-five."

Dr. Mesle twisted a knob on the instrument. "Seventy, seventy-one, seventy-two," she said, reading a screen on the device. "Okay, we're at seventy-five."

"Hold at seventy-five," said Dr. Gallagher. He sounded agitated. "Temperature?"

"Thirty-three."

"Add the cells."

Dr. Mesle held out her hand, and Sameer passed over the syringe. She injected its contents into a rubber port. So the cells were going into—

Holy shit.

"Five milliliters of cells are inline!"

For a long moment, the room was dead silent except for the rhythmic pumping of the cardiopulmonary bypass unit. Everyone seemed to be holding their breath.

"I'm going to remove the aortic cross-clamp," said Dr. Gallagher.

Dr. Mesle watched the large LCD screen as Dr. Gallagher unclipped a pair of forceps from the surgical wound.

"We have flow through the native coronary arteries. Fuck, I'm seeing a significant bleed in the aorta," said Dr Gallagher.

Sameer winced. Blood was now filling the patient's chest cavity.

"Should I abort?" said Dr. Mesle.

Dr. Gallagher held up a hand. "Wait. I'll apply vascular sealant."

He leaned over the patient, then froze.

"What is it?" asked Dr. Mesle.

"Are you seeing this?" On the screen, Dr. Gallagher pointed with a gloved finger. They all watched in silence as the heart began to slowly beat.

"Just amazing, just amazing," said Dr. Mesle in a hushed voice.

Sameer stared. Completely awed. No question now: those twelve-hour days had been one hundred percent worth it.

CHAPTER 47
GREEN TERRACE APARTMENTS, SPITALFIELDS

London, United Kingdom
12:03 PM, June 11th

———

Marcus felt a lot better after eating, but as he stood from the kitchen table, his vision narrowed and the room shifted sharply to the right. He fell awkwardly against the wall.

"Oh, shit," said Sara, spinning around.

He began to slide down the wall, and she had to pull his arm over her shoulder to keep him from collapsing completely. Vertigo nearly overwhelmed him, and he sucked in deep breaths.

"What's wrong with him?" Mercedes asked, though she seemed to be speaking from a great distance.

"His blood pressure is low because he lost so much blood. He needs liquids, ideally a sports drink of some sort."

Marcus heard the fridge open, then Mercedes again. "Is this okay? Lucozade is like the British version of Gatorade."

"Perfect," said Sara. She pushed the bottle into his hand. "Drink this."

Marcus took a long slug. It was very sweet and tasted strongly of artificial orange flavoring. "You actually like this stuff?" he said after swallowing.

"Not really," said Mercedes. "My ex used to drink it when he was hung over."

Marcus took another long sip. His head felt like it was stuffed with cotton balls. "Any idea how long I'm going to feel like garbage?"

"If you keep drinking liquids," Sara said, "your blood pressure should re-equilibrate pretty quickly. But it'll probably be at least a month before your body regenerates all the blood cells you lost. I think you can expect some shortness of breath for at least a week."

"How do you know all this?" Marcus asked. "I thought you did mostly computer stuff."

"I was briefly premed as an undergrad. I remember a few things."

Mercedes cut in. "I hate to do this, especially right now, but there's a staff meeting at one that I really shouldn't miss. Will you two be okay here on your own?"

"Of course," said Marcus. "I'm sorry we're imposing."

"It's not a problem," she said. "Besides, this is going to make a great story someday. Promise I get a byline?"

"Promise."

Mercedes left the room, calling over her shoulder, "I'll be back after work. There's plenty of food in the fridge. Help yourself to whatever you need."

Marcus took another sip of the Lucozade. It was gross, but he had to admit that it did make him feel better. With Sara's help, he sat down at the kitchen table again.

"You look exhausted," he said to her. Her hair was disheveled, and there were dark bags under her eyes. "Have you gotten any rest at all?"

"I slept some." Sara looked a little guilty. "But not a lot. I needed to finish analyzing the hound's genome. I lost all my progress back at…"

She trailed off, and Marcus could tell she was thinking of their bloody escape from Somerset House—when she'd had to shoot one of Alexi's guards.

"We did what we had to," he said as firmly as he could. "Alexi would have killed us as soon as you'd finished your analysis. You saw what he did to Frank."

"I know. It's just, there's been so much death…"

Marcus quickly changed the subject. "So, what have you found out about the hound's genome?"

Sara brightened slightly. "Nothing yet. It doesn't come in a little at a time; I won't have anything until the entire analysis is finished running. But soon."

"What about the silver box from Frank's desk?"

"That's your project, so I've been saving it until you woke up. Stay here, I'll go get it."

She returned a moment later with the box. It was about the size of a paperback book, with a row of six circular dials on the top.

"Looks sort of like a jewelry box," Sara said.

Marcus gently fiddled with one of the dials. It turned with a soft click. Around its edges were the numbers from 1 to 9. Then he traced his fingers along the sides of the box. He found a button on one edge, but when he pushed it, nothing happened.

"I think this is a combination lock."

"I think so, too," said Sara. "Unfortunately, six dials means there are five hundred thirty-one thousand four hundred forty-one possibilities. Not exactly something we can brute-force."

"That would be a bad idea. Remember how the desk was rigged with a hand grenade?"

Sara's eyes crinkled with amusement. "I meant brute-force

in the sense of trying all possible combinations. But yeah, I agree trying to physically break it open wouldn't be wise, either. We don't know what's inside it."

"At this point, I'm going to assume the worst."

Sara pointed at a particular spot on the lid of the box. "Did you see this pattern?"

Marcus peered closer. The silver surface was inscribed with a series of triangles.

"The alchemical elements. Just like the ones on the desk," he said under his breath. "It's either a puzzle or a clue."

"I agree. Now look at the bottom."

Marcus turned the box over. A strange curling design was embossed into the metal.

"It's the cross-section of a seashell," Sara said. "A nautilus."

"Weird." Marcus flipped the box back over, looking again at the six dials and the pattern of alchemical symbols.

"So we have to discover a combination," he said, thinking out loud.

"And our clues are the triangles and a nautilus shell."

"Not a lot to go on."

"I read the nautilus Wikipedia entry while you were asleep," Sara said. She looked sheepish. "Sorry, I didn't *entirely* wait for you. Anyway, they're a type of cephalopod. Look kind of like a squid with a shell. There are only three species alive today, though they have an extensive fossil record. In fact, the nautilus is a famous example of a living fossil."

"I don't really see how a nautilus shell is a clue to a combination lock. What if it's something simple like a word?" Marcus asked.

"But the dials are numerical."

"We could substitute the letters with numbers. You know, like A is one, B is two, et cetera."

"N is fourteen, A is 1, T is twenty...that's not going to

work. The dials only go up to nine. And I don't think Frank would have done something so easy," Sara said. "That'd be like setting his email password to PASSWORD."

"You're not supposed to set your email password to PASS-WORD?" Marcus asked.

He let Sara stare at him for a good ten-count before he cracked a smile.

"Sorry, couldn't resist. But it's nice to know that you believe I'd actually use PASSWORD as a password."

Sara's face turned bright red, and Marcus felt guilty for embarrassing her.

"What if the code is related to the one needed to open the desk?" he said.

"What do you mean?" asked Sara, frowning.

Marcus quickly described the Greek mythological marquetry, the alchemical symbols, and the hidden buttons.

"So you had to know about alchemy and classical history to unlock the desk? That's *really* impressive."

He looked her in the eye. "You know, I'm confident in my abilities. You don't need to worry about my ego—"

"Sorry! I'm just so used to working with fragile academic personalities. If I told Topher that I thought he might use PASSWORD as a password, he'd be super-pissed."

"It's fine. I was teasing you. Us reporter types are pretty chill."

Sara flashed a relieved smile, then turned back to the box. "I don't think this one has to do with classical mythology."

Marcus studied the dials on the box. "So not letters, something to do with numbers...or maybe it's a date? That would fit into six digits. I'm going to look up famous scientists' birthdays." Marcus opened the laptop and found a website with a list. "Einstein was born March 14, 1879, Galileo February 15, 1564, Stephen Hawking January 8, 1942...there's a lot here. We need to narrow it down."

"Hmm, I think we need a biologist," said Sara, peering

over his shoulder closely enough that her hair brushed his cheek. " How about Charles Darwin? He was born February 12, 1809. Try zero, two, one, two, zero, nine."

He tried the code in the lock, but nothing happened.

"What about British format, One, two, zero, two, zero, nine?" said Marcus, but that didn't work either.

They tried a few more, Rosalind Franklin, Gregor Mendel, even Richard Dawkins, but the puzzle box remained locked.

Sara shook her head. "I don't think this is it. It doesn't fit with the numerical theory."

"So, something more science-y?"

"Yeah…something any scientist would know that has to do with numbers…" She trailed off.

Marcus tried to remember what scientific numbers he'd learned as an undergrad. "What about that avocado number? I had to memorize it for chemistry."

"Avogadro's number?" She shook her head and spoke in the monotone voice of someone dredging up an ancient memory. "Six point oh two two times ten to the twenty-third. That's not it. But I think you're on to something—a scientific constant would make a ton of sense." Suddenly, Sara's eyes flashed. "What if it's a *series* of numbers?"

"What do you mean?"

"Fibonacci! The Fibonacci sequence begins with zero, one, one, two, three, five. Fibonacci's sequence is seen in flower petal arrangements, the twists of DNA molecules, *and* the shape of nautilus shells!"

Marcus picked up the box and began spinning the dials. He looked at Sara. "You might want to stand back in case it explodes."

Sara didn't move.

"As you wish."

Marcus set all six dials, then exhaled slowly before pressing the button on the side of the box.

With a click, it opened.

Marcus peered inside. No explosive device presented itself, just a piece of paper covered in dense writing.

"What does it say?" asked Sara excitedly.

Marcus began reading out loud:

Dear Sir or Madam,

If you are reading this, I am most likely dead or otherwise incapacitated. Please understand that you are on the brink of one of the most important scientific discoveries in the history of mankind. If you are one of my order, you will know what to do with this information. If you are not, I beg you to consider carefully the effects of making this discovery public. There are those who would do anything to acquire this information for themselves. As such, you are almost certainly in grave danger.

Yours,
François Gammon

Sara breathed out. "So Mercedes was right. Frank was François."

CHAPTER 48
SPITALFIELDS DISTRICT

London, United Kingdom
12:51 PM, June 11th

———

A man tapped on the window of Alexi's black Audi A8. He was dressed in a Nehru jacket and held a sign written in English but with lettering reminiscent of Nagari script. "Best vindaloo on Bricklane!" he shouted through the glass.

The sign read "Trimurti," which Alexi decided must be the name of a restaurant. He shook his head at the man, but the man shouted, "Free parking!"

Alexi scowled. *Why did GPS send me down Bricklane?*

Although it was technically a street, Bricklane was heavily pedestrianized—and, he now remembered, full of Indian restaurants. *Aggressively advertising* restaurants.

Finally, the man stepped aside, and Alexi pressed his foot to the accelerator. He swore in Greek: "*Amathés!*" Now he was going to be late. He should have never driven this way.

In the back seat, his two bodyguards stared fixedly out the windows. Very sensible. They knew what he could be like when he was upset.

At the end of the block, he cut left and out of the crowd. Green Terrace Apartments was only a block away. Before he left the hotel, he'd done some research and found a connection. One of Marcus Byron's former coworkers, a woman named Mercedes Bailey, lived in the building. He was now certain that he'd found where his two fugitives were holed up.

He guided the Audi into a parking space at the end of the block.

"Wait here," he said to his bodyguards. "I'll call if I need you."

He went around to the boot, retrieved a black duffle bag, and hoisted it over his shoulder. Then he headed down the block.

Green Terrace Apartments was an ordinary three-story brick building. But what was important to Alexi was that the building just across the street was the exact same height. Without even glancing at Green Terrace Apartments, he stepped into the lobby of the building opposite. The lobby was empty other than a single security guard lounging at a desk, looking at his phone. Alexi strode confidently past, as if he belonged here, and pressed the button to call the elevator. In the reflection of the stainless steel doors, he saw the security guard lift his head to look at him, then turn back to his phone.

Act like you own the place, Alexi thought. *Works every time.*

He took the elevator to the top floor, then walked down a long hallway to a door labeled "Roof Access." He climbed a single flight of stairs, opened the door at the top, and stepped outside.

He pushed the door shut, then knelt and opened his duffel

bag. He removed a door wedge with an adjustable foot and slid it under the door.

Now that he was certain no one would be bothering him, he crossed to the edge of the roof.

In only a few more minutes, he'd have his revenge.

CHAPTER 49
GREEN TERRACE
APARTMENTS, SPITALFIELDS

London, United Kingdom
12:56 PM, June 11th

———

Marcus squinted at the page. *Where is the discovery?*

"There's more written on the other side," Sara said.

"Oh!" Marcus turned the page over. Again, he read aloud:

No longer mourn for me when I am dead
Then you shall hear the surly sullen bell
Give warning to the world that I am fled
From this vile world, with vilest worms to dwell:

Nay, if you read this line, remember not
The hand that writ it; for I love you so
That I in your sweet thoughts would be forgot—

1MhqdvTcYqDtGgtQ5h6Z7Kn5op9uQeyarB
42.876888 | 1.834011

"I think it's some kind of riddle," said Sara.

Marcus nodded in agreement. "An easy one, for a change. That pair of numbers looks like GPS coordinates."

Sara grabbed Mercedes's laptop. "I'll google them."

He set the paper in front of her and peered over her shoulder as she typed. A map of the coordinates appeared on the screen, showing a road, a bit of blue that appeared to be a stream or river, and three words: *Château de Montségur*.

Marcus blew out a long breath as the magnitude of what this meant washed over him. Frank had been right: this was a monumental discovery—and they were in grave danger.

"Sara, this is not good. I think we should consider going to the authorities after all."

"What?" Sara looked at him like he'd just asked her to set herself on fire. "What are you talking about?

"Do you know where Château de Montségur is?" said Marcus.

"Based on the name, I'd guess it's somewhere in France."

"Southern France. Close to the border of Spain."

"How do you know this? And why is it important?"

"I visited the château on vacation with my parents when I was fifteen. It's quite famous. A ruined castle on a hilltop with cliffs all around it. In the early thirteenth century, it was the seat of the Cathar religion. Do know about the Cathars?"

Sara shook her head.

"Well, they were Gnostics. They believed there were two gods, a good one and a bad one. Or to put it another way, in their view, Satan was not just a fallen angel, but also a god."

"Okay. Are you going to tell me why this means we need to turn ourselves in?"

"I'm getting there. The Catholics considered the Cathars heretics, so in 1243, they sent a force of ten thousand men to exterminate them. They laid siege to Château de Montségur for nearly nine months before they succeeded in taking it. And when they did, all the Cathars were burned to death. But here's the crazy bit: they voluntarily climbed onto the pyre themselves."

Sara's eyes widened. "Why would they do that?"

"There are a couple of possibilities. One is that, according to the Cathar religion, human souls are the spirits of angels imprisoned in human bodies. So by immolating themselves, they merely hastened their ascent to heaven."

"That's crazy."

"Yeah. The Cathars did not mess around. The second reason is that the Cathars volunteered to be burned alive so that they wouldn't be tortured. You see, there's a legend that says they kept a great treasure hidden at Montségur. The theory is that they may have been afraid of revealing its location."

Sara's curiosity was clearly piqued. "What was this treasure?"

"No one knows. It's believed that a few Cathars escaped the siege and buried it in the forest nearby, though it's never been found. It might have been money, jewels, or religious relics." Marcus paused, almost embarrassed to mention this last bit. "One theory posits that they were hiding the Holy Grail."

Sara laughed. "Let me guess: this is what you believe."

"Well…it *would* help explain Frank's secret society. And although the Rosicrucians aren't associated with the grail, the Knights Templar are—supposedly, it's their job to protect it. In addition, drinking from the grail is said to heal all wounds. We've seen a man survive injuries that should have killed him, right?"

"Are you suggesting they've used the grail? Because in that case, the grail would already have been found—by Alexi. He's the one who sent the hound."

Marcus pursed his lips. He hadn't thought of that. "I don't know, Sara. I just—I'm really starting to feel like we're in over our heads. We're illegally in the UK. We have no money. We have no idea what's going on. Alexi's out to kill us, and now we're potentially getting mixed up in some ancient battle over the Holy Grail. I can't see a way to get out of this mess without help from the authorities."

Sara frowned. "Let me think for a second."

She closed her eyes. Marcus watched her as she sat still in her chair, her face illuminated by the soft glow of the computer screen. She looked relaxed, almost serene, but beneath the quiet exterior, he knew her brain was working like crazy. She stayed like that for a full minute, maybe two.

And then she opened her eyes again. Marcus expected her to speak, but instead, she opened a fresh Word document and began to type.

WHAT WE KNOW FOR CERTAIN:

- When I discovered a way to identify ancient genomes within contemporary populations, they (Alexi / Actaeon) sent a "hound" to kill me
- Hounds are men that can heal from serious injuries
- Frank (and Alexi) wanted to learn which human population the hounds came from
- Frank had a hidden note that speaks of Montségur and an important scientific discovery (possibly the Holy Grail?!)
- Enora also had genome sequences that she said I needed to analyze

She turned to Marcus. "Did I miss anything?"

"I don't think so." Marcus read through the text once more. "It seems contradictory, though. Frank has apparently gone to great lengths to keep some scientific discovery from the public, yet he also wanted you to do genomic analysis that —I think—would have helped illuminate that discovery."

"Yeah," said Sara. "I'm still confused about Frank's motivations. And Frank and Alexi were enemies, yet both of them wanted me to discover where the hounds came from."

"Except that the hounds seem to be on Alexi's side. He referred to them as 'my men.' So shouldn't he already know where they came from?"

Sara paused. "He knows they exist. Frank did, too. But apparently, neither one actually understands their biology."

"That's where the genomic component comes in."

Sara nodded in agreement. "Wanting to understand the hounds' origins seems like the most parsimonious explanation."

"Parsimonious?" Marcus echoed. He knew the meaning of the word, but no one ever used it, at least not in casual speech.

"It means simplest—" Sara's eyes narrowed as Marcus cracked a grin. "Damn it, Marcus, I'm trying to think."

"Sorry, I couldn't help myself. But I just thought of something else. Instead of using the genome to discover the hounds' origins, wouldn't it be more useful to use it to find the precise genetic basis for the regeneration ability? I mean, the history is interesting, but it's the ability itself that's truly valuable."

Sara shook her head. "It's a good idea, but it's not nearly as easy as you make it sound. Take any two humans, and their genomes will be, on average, ninety-nine point nine percent identical. So you just find the point one percent that's different, and that's what's important, right? The problem is, the human genome is more than three *billion* base pairs long. So that tiny point one percent of differences works out to about three *million* differences between any two human genomes. How do we figure out which of them are responsible for this particular ability?"

"I guess it was a dumb idea," said Marcus.

"No, I think you're on to something." Sara's eyes flashed. "One hound genome wouldn't be enough, but if I had a whole *group* of hound genomes, then maybe I could narrow it down. It would certainly make the exercise a lot easier."

Marcus put it together. "*That's* why Frank wanted you to learn where the hound came from." He grinned. "I'd even go so far as to say it's…the most parsimonious solution."

Sara punched him in the shoulder.

Marcus laughed. "I deserved that."

"Yes, you did."

"So…what do we do now?"

Sara looked again at Frank's note. "I think if we go to these coordinates, we'll learn something really important. I think we should see what's there."

"But how? We have no money and no passports. And don't forget we're wanted by the police."

Sara pointed to the strange list of characters just above the GPS coordinates. "How much do you want to bet that code is a Bitcoin address?"

CHAPTER 50
SPITALFIELDS DISTRICT

London, United Kingdom
1:06 PM, June 11th

———

Alexi lay prone on the asphalt roof, his eyes pressed to a pair of 8x30 Steiner binoculars. Beads of sweat trickled down the back of his neck, and every breath filled his nose with the hydrocarbon-rich stench of warm tar. Even with London's bog-standard cloudy weather, midday in June was still miserably hot.

But he hardly noticed the physical discomfort. He was completely focused on his task. He methodically scanned the windows of Green Terrace Apartments, searching for any sign of Sara or Marcus.

Unfortunately, he hadn't observed so much as a single person.

This shouldn't have been surprising. While the Spitalfields neighborhood had once been a slum teeming with people, now the Old Market had been converted to a posh outdoor mall, and the tenements had been replaced with luxury condos. Its new residents, mostly young urban professionals, hurried to the Tube every morning, with Starbucks venti lattes clutched tightly in their hands. The neighborhood was virtually empty by 9 AM.

Usually, for a job like this, Alexi would have subcontracted to an expert. But he was one of the few people who'd seen both Sara and Marcus in person. He would be the best at making the ID.

Though if he was being honest, that wasn't the real reason. Marcus had bested him. He had killed Kostas.

Alexi smiled at the black SRS-A1 Covert sniper rifle that rested next to him.

He never subcontracted vengeance.

Looking again into the binoculars, he scanned the windows once more. Where were they? This had to be the place. Marcus's colleague lived here, apartment 18. Which one was that?

Alexi was about to have his men check when a flicker of movement caught his eye. Was it a pet? He'd already identified two feline residents of Green Terrace Apartments. This most likely was another, but—

He inhaled sharply as a man's face came into view.

Marcus Byron.

Alexi set down the binoculars and deftly fitted the butt of the SRS-A1 to his shoulder. The Covert was perfect for this job. A smaller version of the Desert Tech Stealth Recon Scout sniper rifle, the SRS-A1 stretched a mere twenty-seven inches from muzzle to butt pad. It was about the size of a tennis racket, which made it easy to conceal in a duffle bag. It was even affordable, at just over three thousand US dollars—or it would have been if large-caliber rifles were legal in the UK. Since they weren't, Alexi had been forced to purchase this one at almost triple the list price from a connection in the Russian mob.

The rifle was fitted with a KAHLES K624I scope, and Alexi

carefully centered the reticule on the back of Marcus's head. The reporter turned, and Alexi could see the movement of his lips. He was talking to someone out of view. Sara, presumably.

Alexi considered the best approach. The major negative of the SRS-A1 Covert was that it was bolt action. This meant that after the first shot, he would have to break shooting position to run the bolt—to discharge the empty bullet casing from the chamber. That would give Sara plenty of time to run or hide.

Then again, did he even want to kill her? He'd *said* that he'd kill her, but she could still be useful to him. She presumably still had Frank's flash drive with the genome data. And without the interference of the reporter, he could force her to decode it for him.

Keeping the reticule trained on Marcus, he formulated a plan. With one phone call, his two bodyguards, still waiting in the car on the street, could be in the apartment in less than three minutes. He'd shoot a round into Marcus's skull, then send his men up to collect Sara.

The skin of his neck was sweating against the rifle's rubberized cheekpiece. His index finger rested against the trigger. He blew out a long breath.

This was the shot.

Aiming at Marcus's head, he slowly tightened his finger on the trigger.

At that moment, Sara finally came into view, speaking to Marcus. She didn't matter. But her sudden appearance did cause Alexi to shift his reticule ever so slightly. It landed on a laptop sitting on a table between them.

Alexi gasped and nearly dropped the rifle. The image on the screen…it wasn't possible. There could be only one reason why they would be looking at a map of Château de Montségur.

Alexi set down the SRS-A1.

His vengeance would have to wait.

CHAPTER 51
GREEN TERRACE APARTMENTS

London, United Kingdom
1:09 PM, June 11th

———

S ara slowly read aloud the string of characters, and Marcus typed them into www.blockchain.info's search bar. As she read them a second time so he could double-check that he hadn't made a typo, she took the opportunity to study him. He looked much healthier than he had when he first woke up: his skin less pale, his eyes brighter. And though the T-shirt Mercedes had given him was too small, she had to admit he filled it out rather nicely.

Could he really be on to something with this Holy Grail theory? she wondered. It didn't make any sort of scientific sense, and yet she'd seen things in the last forty-eight hours that shouldn't have been possible. At least, not by any of the biological and physical laws she'd been taught.

"Okay," said Marcus. "Ready?" The mouse pointer hovered over the submit button.

"Ready."

Marcus clicked the button, and a new page loaded.

Sara blew out a low whistle. "Five hundred bitcoin."

"Wow," said Marcus. "What are we going to do with the money?"

"Nothing," said Sara. "We can't access it."

"What do you mean? This was your idea. You said this was our way to get to the Château de Montségur."

"I forgot we'd need a seed phrase to open the wallet."

"Seed phrase? Like a password?"

"Yes, but in this case, a random string of words. Not, you know, P, A, S, S, W…"

Marcus rolled his eyes. "I'm never going to live that down, am I?"

"Nope," said Sara, grinning.

"Frank gave us the Bitcoin address, didn't he? I'm sure he wouldn't do that without also giving us the password thing. What about the poem? Could that be it?"

Sara nodded. "Good point. That poem has to be important. Frank wouldn't have included it if it weren't. But it's too long. Seed phrases are only like ten or twelve words."

Marcus read the first line of the poem aloud. "'No longer mourn for me when I am dead.' I'm pretty sure that's Shakespeare."

"Google it."

"Right," he said, and quickly typed the first line into Google. "Sonnet 71. A love poem about a dead guy. An appropriate choice, given the circumstances."

Sara tried not to think of Frank, Enora, Amy, and all the people she'd seen killed in the last two days.

"It's odd that the poem is truncated," Marcus said.

"What do you mean?"

"A Shakespearean sonnet is always three quatrains of four lines followed by a couplet," said Marcus, sounding mildly professorial. "Frank's paper has only one quatrain and three additional lines, and there's no couplet. It's been cut in half."

Sara stared at the poem. Why was it included? And why was it truncated? At this point, she had to assume Frank did everything for a reason.

"How do these passwords—er, seed phrases work, exactly?" Marcus asked.

"They're just a random set of words that give you access to the bitcoin wallet. They can be anything."

"Anything at all? Even archaic words like 'writ'?" He pointed to the word in the second-to-last line.

The beginnings of a thought flickered in the back of Sara's brain. "Probably not. I would guess they come from some sort of word list. But I'm not sure."

"Google it, right?" said Marcus, his fingers flying over the keyboard. A second later, he'd pulled up the relevant Wikipedia page. He read aloud, "Bitcoin seed phrase words must come from a corpus called BIP39 that contains two thousand forty-eight unique words."

Sara studied the text of the sonnet. Again, she felt that flickering deep within her mind. "Can you double-check how long seed phrases are supposed to be?"

Marcus pulled up another Wikipedia page. "You were right. Twelve words."

Sara smiled. "How much do you want to bet that there are only twelve valid words found in that sonnet fragment?"

Marcus matched her smile. "Would five hundred bitcoin be too much to wager?"

"Who said all the money was yours?" Sara snatched up the paper like she planned to steal it.

"All right, we'll share it," said Marcus, laughing.

Sara laid the paper back on the table, and together, they compared the words of the sonnet to the BIP39 word list. They circled each word that was on the list and crossed out the ones that weren't. When they were done, Marcus read the circled words aloud.

"Long When Then Give World That World Remember Hand Love That Sweet."

"Exactly twelve words!" Sara exclaimed.

Marcus entered the words into blockchain.info's recovery page.

An instant later, they were logged in.

CHAPTER 52
SPITALFIELDS DISTRICT

London, United Kingdom
1:11 PM, June 11th

———

Alexi continued to watch Sara and Marcus through his binoculars. He couldn't kill them now. If they'd found what he thought they had, then he needed them alive.

They were working on the laptop, but the reporter's head blocked Alexi's view of the screen, so he couldn't see what they were doing. After a while, Marcus shut the laptop and stood. He and Sara talked for a moment, then she disappeared into another room. When she returned, she was wearing a pair of sunglasses and a red beret. She handed Marcus a baseball cap.

Disguises. They were going out.

He dialed his men in the car below.

"I have a pair of targets leaving the building. A man, six-two, and a woman, five-three. She's wearing sunglasses and a red beret."

"What would you like us to do sir?"

"One of you, tail them on foot."

Stuffing the rifle and binoculars into the duffle bag, he hurried back to the door. Two minutes later, he was sprinting past the security guard, who barely looked up from his phone as Alexi burst onto the street. The Audi was waiting for him at the curb. He jerked open the passenger door and jumped in.

"I've got your man on speaker," the driver said.

"Do you have visual?" Alexi said.

"Yes, sir, right here," said a voice over the car's speaker.

"Where are they?"

"Bricklane and Fournier Street."

"Still on foot?"

"Yes."

Alexi turned to the driver. "Take us to Whitechapel Road. Let's avoid Bricklane this time."

They drove toward Whitechapel along back streets. A few minutes later, the bodyguard tailing Marcus and Sara spoke again.

"They've stopped at an ATM near Whitechapel."

"Keep following them. And don't let them see you."

CHAPTER 53
TRAIN À GRANDE VITESSE

Central France
9:35 AM, June 12th

———

The French countryside rushed past at one hundred and eighty-six miles per hour, a green blur broken only by the intermittent flash of cottage roofs. They were on the TGV train between Paris and Montpellier, and for the first time since leaving Mercedes's apartment, Sara felt like she could relax.

She certainly hadn't relaxed during a tense afternoon traveling around London, withdrawing cash from various Bitcoin ATMs. Or during the sketchy meeting in a café in Bethnal Green where they'd purchased a pair of counterfeit Italian passports from an old connection of Marcus's. But the most stressful bit was the border security in St Pancras. Fortunately, it had been after midnight when they'd arrived, and the French agent had hardly looked at the passports as they went through customs. One of the perks of being an EU citizen, Marcus had explained later, was that customs was mostly a formality. Even so, Sara had been practically hyperventilating by the time they finally got to their seats on the train.

Now, an hour outside of Paris, she felt like the worst was over. Marcus appeared to feel the same, as he'd fallen asleep in his seat. But try as she might, Sara couldn't manage to drift off. Instead, she found herself reaching into the bag at her feet and retrieving the new laptop they'd purchased at the Apple store in Covent Garden.

She flipped it open, connected it to the train Wi-Fi, and navigated to nytimes.com. She was relieved to see that she and Marcus were no longer on the front page. Then she opened a terminal window and typed a command:

```
ssh ubuntu@192.0.2.0
```

A moment later, she was logged into the remote server she'd set up before leaving Mercedes's apartment. She'd migrated her analysis to bithost.io, one of the few cloud computing platforms that accepted bitcoin.

She typed `tmux a -t GATK` to bring up the session she started before they'd left.

The analysis was complete.

She smiled, making a silent fist pump. Then her fingers flew over the keyboard as she began to summarize the results.

CHAPTER 54
TRAIN À GRANDE VITESSE

Central France
10:13 AM, June 12th

————

Sara knew she should let Marcus sleep. He'd lost a ton of blood, and more than anything, his body needed rest as it worked to replace his red blood cells. But she had to tell him about what she'd discovered. It was too important. So, as gently as she could, she nudged him until he began to stir.

"What's up?" he said groggily.

"I finished the analysis of the hound genome."

Marcus rubbed a hand over his face, perking up immediately. "What did you find?"

"Let me show you." She turned her screen so Marcus could see it. "Frank only gave me short-read data. Do you know what that is?"

"Do I look like know what it is?" Marcus was fully awake now, his eyes bright with excitement.

"Um, maybe?"

"Sara," said Marcus with a grin, "I have absolutely no idea what you're talking about. Honestly, you can just assume I don't know anything when it comes to science."

Sara sighed. "How, again, did you become a science reporter for *The New York Times* ?"

Marcus shrugged, and his smile faded. Only then did she remember that he'd said he'd been assigned to the Science section because of PTSD.

"Well, anyway," she said quickly, desperate to move past the awkwardness, "short-read data is the raw output of a high throughput DNA sequencer. It's currently impossible to sequence an entire genome at once, so what we do now is sequence millions of fragments of DNA. In this case, Frank gave us a text file containing four hundred million fragments of the hound's genome. So I had to assemble all those pieces into a new genome. The easiest way to do that is to align them to one that's already been sequenced."

Marcus stared blankly at her.

"It's like..." Sara struggled to think of an analogy. Something historical that Marcus would understand intuitively. "Imagine that you had a new and an old dictionary, but the old dictionary was so ancient, it was only scraps of paper. How would you put it back together?"

Marcus thought for a moment. "Well, I guess I could compare each of the scraps to the new dictionary."

"Exactly. You use the new dictionary as a reference. This is how I can create a new human genome from little bits of DNA. I simply find where each piece matches to the full-length human genome."

"Fascinating," said Marcus. Then he paused. "But what if the new dictionary is a different edition?"

"What do you mean?" said Sara, trying not to smile. This was precisely the line of reasoning she had hoped Marcus would follow.

"Well, every few years, companies like Merriam-Webster

release a new version. They add new words like 'instagram' or 'bingable,' and they remove some, too. Do you know the meaning of 'frutescent'?"

Sara shook her head.

"It means shrubby. But don't try looking it up in Merriam-Webster. They deleted it!"

"This is actually the same problem I have with reconstructing the genome," Sara said. "Just as dictionaries have changed over time, the human genome has, too. This makes the short-read alignment process a challenging computational problem. There are all these differences between individuals that the algorithm needs to account for."

"You're talking about mutations now, right?"

Sara arched an eyebrow. "I thought you said you didn't know anything about science."

Marcus grinned. "I don't. But I'm not a *complete* idiot."

"Good to know." She smiled back at him. She was beginning to find flirting with Marcus was more fun than it had any right to be. It was nice to talk with someone who wasn't constantly judging her. With him, she could just be herself.

"Okay, so now I understand what you *did*," said Marcus. "But what did you find out?"

"Hang on, I'm not there yet. The alignment is only the first step. Remember how Frank theorized that the hound might be a hybrid?"

Marcus nodded.

Sara frowned, trying to think of how best to explain. "Do you understand how sex works?"

"I'm familiar with the concept," said Marcus, grinning broadly. Too broadly.

Sara felt the blood rush to her face. "No, I mean the genetics of sex. Gametes and chromosomes. Not like *actual* sex. Not penises or—" *Oh, God, what am I saying?*

Marcus held up a hand. "I got it. Just explain the science."

Sara felt like her cheeks might melt off, but she plowed

forward. "So, your genome is a combination of your mother's and father's DNA. You're fifty percent of each of your parents."

"Yep. I got my mom's eyes and my dad's hair."

"Right. Well, when it comes to genetic variation, it's a bit different. The majority of your parent's genomes are actually the same—they're both humans, after all. But when I do the short-read alignment, I can also check for the parts of the genome where the parents were different from one another. We call these single nucleotide polymorphisms, SNPs."

"Okay…?" said Marcus, obviously not following.

"What I mean is, SNPs are the parts of the genome where your mother and father had different DNA. Typically, this is about point one percent of the genome."

"Got it." Marcus looked at her expectantly. "But in the hound's genome?"

"The hound is variable at point one four three one percent of his genome. It's a little high but still well within the normal genetic variation I'd expect to see in a modern human."

Marcus looked at her blankly. "What does that mean? I mean, why is this important?"

"It's important because this result shows conclusively that the hound is *not* a hybrid. If one of his parents wasn't a modern human, I'd have found a *lot* more SNPs."

"So much for Frank's theory then."

"Yeah."

"So how on earth did that guy survive being stabbed in the heart?"

Sara sat back in her seat. "I have absolutely no idea."

CHAPTER 55
TRAIN À GRANDE VITESSE

Central France
10:24 AM, June 12th

———

zzz...bzzz...

     The old Brit grimaced. A phone call was the last thing he needed right now, but he had no choice but to answer it. Only Alexi had the number for this particular mobile. As quietly as he could, he leaned forward, withdrew the phone from the cleft between the seats, and texted a message back.

> Can't talk now. Recording.

A moment later, his phone buzzed in response:

> Did you get a seat near them?

> Yes, directly behind.

He looked up, double-checking that Sara and Marcus hadn't left their seats.

> Have they said where the treasure is?

> No.

Alexi was easily his least favorite employer, constantly micromanaging and demanding overtime. Worse, his boss seemed to be absolutely terrified of Alexi, which meant the Greek basically ran the show. The only decent thing about Alexi was that he paid nearly as well as a Saudi prince. And at this very moment, he didn't give a toss about money. Not after he had been forced to forfeit a pair of Man U vs. Liverpool tickets to sit on the train with a bunch of French frogs. He could literally smell the cheese—

Another text came in.

> What are they talking about?

> Science mumbo-jumbo.

> WHAT ARE THEY TALKING ABOUT?

It took nearly all of his self-control to keep himself from throwing the phone across the rail car.

> Do I look like a bloody scientist?

As he waited for the reply, he second-guessed his decision to use the word bloody. Fortunately, Alexi didn't seem offended.

> Send me the recording as soon as they get off the train.

He didn't bother replying, but he did swipe over to the voice-recorder app to make sure it was still running before he slid it back between the seats.

CHAPTER 56
CHÂTEAU DE MONTSÉGUR

Commune in the Ariège department, France
3:13 PM, June 12th

———

The ruins of Château de Montségur gleamed white in the hot Mediterranean sun. Not that Marcus was looking at the castle. His gaze was fixed on the dirt at his feet as he leaned forward, his hands on his knees, and sucked in deep breaths.

"Are you all right?" Sara asked. She stood a few feet up the trail, and Marcus could tell she was worried about him.

"Yes," he said between gasps.

"It's because of the blood loss, you know. You don't have as many erythrocytes as normal. That's why exercise makes you hypoxic."

Marcus had no idea what erythrocytes were or what hypoxic meant, but he didn't bother asking. He was simply focusing on not passing out. "Maybe you should go on ahead."

"No," said Sara firmly. "We need to stay close. Whatever

this treasure is, we should find it together." She held out her hand. "At least let me carry the backpack."

Marcus straightened unsteadily, then passed over his bag. Before heading to the château, they'd visited a camping store in Montpellier, where they'd purchased the backpack, a folding shovel, and a small GPS unit. They would use the GPS to find the precise location in Frank's note, and they got the shovel just in case they needed to dig when they arrived.

Marcus really hoped that wouldn't be necessary.

Sara slung the backpack over her shoulder and turned back up the slope. "It's not much farther," she said optimistically, but Marcus could see they still had at least a quarter of a mile before they reached the ruined castle.

Drawing in a deep breath, he plodded after her.

———

It was nearly five PM when they reach the summit. Marcus immediately collapsed onto his back in the grass. It was a few minutes before he felt well enough to sit up, and even then, he felt light-headed.

Still, even in his current state, he could appreciate the beauty of the Château de Montségur. The walls were enormous, at least thirty feet high. Nothing remained of the roof or battlements, but he knew the castle would have been virtually impregnable in its heyday. The ancient stones glowed in the late afternoon light, and beyond them was an unobstructed view of the French countryside.

"You ready?" said Sara, holding up the GPS unit.

He nodded and stood—slowly.

Sara pointed toward the northwest portion of the ruin. "According to the GPS, the treasure is that way. I'm surprised it isn't in the castle."

"I'm not. Remember what I said before? The Cathars are believed to have hidden the treasure somewhere beyond the walls. Besides, the original castle was destroyed after the siege." He gestured to the walls. "This is actually the remains of a seventeenth-century structure."

Together, they walked along a path that skirted the castle. When the pin on the screen of the GPS indicated the treasure was less than fifty yards away, Marcus could sense Sara's excitement. They were so close to answers now.

"All right," said Sara, looking at the GPS unit. "It should be just over there." She pointed, and Marcus followed her finger. They stood on a steep slope that led to a cliff edge. The ground was nearly bare, with just grass, small bushes, and a few limestone boulders. And where Sara was pointing was in midair—right off the edge of the cliff.

"Are you sure you entered the coordinates correctly?" he asked.

"Yes," said Sara. Though she sounded less than certain. "It must be below, I guess."

They carefully made their way down the slope to the cliff edge. As they neared the precipice, Marcus realized the drop was at least two hundred feet. A slip would lead to certain death. He really wished his legs felt steadier.

Sara walked right to the edge. "According to the GPS, we're here," she said. She peered over. "Do you think it could be on the cliff face itself?"

Marcus shook his head. "I hope not. We didn't bring any rope."

"I'm not seeing anything, anyway."

Marcus sat down on a boulder to catch his breath. Sara looked over at him, and then her brow furrowed.

"What?" he said.

"Can you move your right foot?"

"Um…sure?" Marcus moved his foot away.

Sara's eyes flashed. "I found it."

"Huh?"

"Look at the rock you're sitting on."

Marcus looked down. Some sort of symbol was carved into the stone, just where his right foot had been resting. His heart raced with excitement.

Kneeling beside the boulder, he traced a finger over the symbol. "This is definitely it," he said. "It's shaped like a dove. To the Cathars, the dove represented the holy spirit."

"Should we dig?"

Marcus nodded. "Let's do it."

Sara pulled the shovel from the bag. Marcus wanted to offer to help, but he knew he wasn't physically up to it at the moment, and another bout of dizziness might send him toppling off the cliff. He crouched as he watched, the sun warm on his back.

"There's something here," said Sara breathlessly.

Marcus peered into the hole she'd made. Sure enough, she'd uncovered a rectangular outline, maybe four by six inches.

She brushed off some dirt, then frowned. "This is made of plastic."

Plastic? That definitely wasn't from the Cathar era.

A minute later, Sara had unearthed a modern Tupperware container. Without digging it out, she removed the lid.

"Whoa…" she whispered.

It was full of electronics. A battery pack, a tangle of wires, and a cell phone. Marcus wasn't sure what to make of it. At that moment, the phone's screen flickered to life and it sent a text.

Warning, box discovered.

Then it made sense. It wasn't a treasure, but rather a signaling mechanism. He was turning to Sara when a voice cut in from above.

"What'd you dig up?"

CHAPTER 57
CHÂTEAU DE MONTSÉGUR

Commune in the Ariège department, France
5:23 PM, June 12th

———

Marcus's blood froze. As he turned, his eyes confirmed what his ears had already told him. Alexi stood on the slope above them, flanked by a pair of guards.

He knew he should be terrified, but instead of fear, his primary emotion was of disappointment. Now he'd never learn the truth of the Cathar treasure. What was it that Frank had gone to such great lengths to keep hidden? Who had just been texted? Instead, Alexi would take the box and then murder them. At this point, his death was inescapable.

Still, maybe he could give Sara a fighting chance.

"How did you find us?" asked Marcus, stalling.

"Vengeance is a powerful motivator," Alexi said. His voice was ice. "Kostas is dead. *You* killed him."

"It was self-defense. Your men would have gunned us down," Marcus countered.

"An eye for an eye," Alexi said. He started down the slope, and his men spread out to flank them.

This was the moment.

"Run, Sara!" he shouted, lunging up the slope toward Alexi.

He hit the Greek solidly, sending them both tumbling against the rocky hillside. They struggled, grappling, but already, Marcus was gasping for breath. He was no match for this man, not in his current condition.

In seconds, Alexi had him pinned. He grabbed Marcus's wrist and twisted his arm behind his back. Marcus was jerked to his feet, and he screamed as the stitches in his shoulder tore out.

"*Ma ti chalvás eísai esý!*" said Alexi, then shoved Marcus toward the cliff edge—hard.

Marcus staggered forward, stumbling. His vestibular system fought to regain his balance, but it was futile. He fell and began rolling down the steep slope towards the edge. For an instant, his fingers wrapped around a clump of grass, but the grass tore free without slowing his descent.

As he tumbled head over heels, he caught a glimpse of one of Alexi's men holding Sara. Beside him, Alexi's lips spread into a broad smile.

Then Marcus was over the side, and there was nothing but air between him and a field of boulders two hundred feet below.

CHAPTER 58
CHÂTEAU DE MONTSÉGUR

Commune in the Ariège department, France
4:23 PM, June 12th

———

Sara felt like she was living a nightmare. Marcus had just fallen to his death. Murdered. She wanted to scream, but a guard's hand was clamped over her lips.

She was forced to watch in silence as Alexi collected the Cathar treasure and handed it to a guard. Then he stalked toward her, his expression predatory.

"Show her," he growled.

Wrapping his free arm around her waist, the guard lifted her bodily into the air and walked her forward until they were right at the cliff's edge.

Alexi pointed at the rocks below. "See what vengeance looks like?"

Sara tried to look away, but Alexi grabbed her by the hair and forced her head forward so that she had no choice but to look down.

Crumpled on the rocks two hundred feet below was Marcus's broken body. Unmoving. Already, blood was pooling beneath him.

"No…" she heard herself moan.

Alexi snorted. "I didn't realize you *liked* him."

The guard twisted her around to face Alexi, and she saw that the Greek had drawn a dagger from his jacket. He pointed it at her stomach.

"I have a few questions for you before we end this, okay? Scream, and it'll end more painfully. Understood?"

Sara nodded.

The guard removed his hand from her mouth.

"Bastard," she said.

Alexi laughed sharply. Then he pressed the blade right up against the soft flesh just below her ribs. "You're feisty. But you'll die as easily any other."

Sara knew he meant what he said. He was going to kill her. Her mind raced. There had to be a way to stop him.

"I've analyzed your hound's DNA," she said. "I know what makes them heal so easily. Marcus wrote an article about it, and if you kill me, it'll be on the front page of *The New York Times* tomorrow."

Of course, none of this was true. But Alexi didn't know that.

Alexi laughed. "If you knew all that, you wouldn't be *here*. Still, you've discovered far more than you ever should."

Sara knew that whatever she said next would decide her fate. Her bluff had failed. What else did she have? Something valuable that only she knew…

"Enora Hansen. Do you know who she is?"

The pressure of the blade relaxed slightly.

Sara dug her hand into her pocket. Her fingers wrapped around Enora's flash drive. She held it up so Alexi could see it.

"She gave me this. It contains eight genomes. She said

they will fundamentally change our understanding of biology."

Alexi shrugged. "I don't care about stolen pharmaceutical secrets."

"This isn't about drugs. She said to me, 'I don't think you'll believe what I have to say until you look at these genomes.' I think what this drive contains has to do with my method of inferring ancient genomes."

Alexi's eyes narrowed. "What are the eight genomes?"

"I don't know yet. I haven't exactly had a lot of time to look."

Alexi's blade remained pressed to her stomach. She needed more leverage.

She had an idea.

With a smile, she tossed the flash drive over the side of the cliff. It spun, glinting in the late afternoon sun, then disappeared from sight.

Alexi frowned. "That was foolish."

"Was it?" said Sara, meeting his gaze. "Now the only way you'll know what was on that drive is if you let me live long enough to analyze the cloud backup I made of it."

CHAPTER 59

---

he guards never spoke to the prisoners when they entered the cells. They didn't have to. The rules were simple: prostrate yourself, don't move, don't talk. Otherwise, you will be punished. Marcus followed the rules. He pressed his head to the floor. He closed his eyes. He wasn't religious, but he prayed fervently: Please not me. Please not me.

The guards spoke only to the shawish—the leader of the prisoners.

"Five names."

The cell was silent as the shawish replied. "Omar, Rifat, Nizar…"

Marcus squeezed his eyes more tightly, pushed his forehead so hard against the concrete that white flashes ghosted across his retinas.

"Kadar."

Marcus held his breath. One name left. The cell was completely silent. No one dared to move.

"Maarrcus."

The shawish spoke with a thick Arabic accent, but there was no question as to whom he was referring to. Even so, Marcus pretended not to hear.

This can't be happening. This can't be happening. This can't be happening.

He continued to prostrate himself until the guards jerked him up. Before he was even on his feet, one of them punched him hard in the ribs. He cried out.

They dragged him from the cell and into the hallway beyond. He knew what was coming, and yet a strange excitement filled him… almost like happiness. For the first time in weeks, he was out of the cell. He smelled fresh air. Through a window, he could see the sky, the sun.

Then the guards yelled at him to pull his shirt over his head. He did as ordered, the fabric forming a gauzy blindfold. The guards shouted again, and he and the four other prisoners walked single file down the hallway.

They were led into a small cell. Dark. No windows. Told to line up in a row. A guard kicked Marcus, and he fell to his knees.

He crouched and looked down. They'd hurt him less if he was submissive.

Another shout: "Look up!"

A guard stood before them. A big man with a thick mustache. His eyes blazed. In one hand was a long piece of rubber. What had once been a tire tread. He slapped it against the floor, and it cracked like a gunshot.

The guards shouted for them to prostrate themselves, but it was hardly necessary. They were cowering already. Marcus pressed his face to the dusty concrete.

Crack!

The first man in the line of crouching prisoners screamed as the heavy whip struck his back. Marcus's jaw clenched, and his hands balled into fists.

Crack!

Another scream.

Crack!

The room filled with the sound of pain.

Crack!

Marcus's shoulders tensed—he was next.

Crack!

Agony shattered his consciousness. Even with his eyes pinched shut, the world became incandescent.

———

Marcus woke with his entire body throbbing with pain. He remembered the beating, the whip, the blood, the screams.

And yet he wasn't on the floor of the cell. Concrete wasn't digging into his cheek. His tongue didn't crave water like a dry sponge. Instead, a soft cotton sheet covered him, and the air smelled of fresh pine, juniper, and rosemary.

Where am I?

He opened his eyes. He was lying on a bed in a room he didn't recognize. Through a window framed by white curtains was a craggy mountain with what appeared to be some sort of castle at its peak. It looked familiar, but try as he might, he couldn't recall its name.

He now realized the beating had been a dream, even though the pain in his muscles remained all too real. *Everything* hurt. Worse, when he tried to sit, nothing responded. For an instant, he wondered if he was paralyzed, but then he saw the ropes that bound him to the bed.

It sank in quickly. He was a prisoner again.

His heart began to race. He started to hyperventilate. Frantically, he scanned the room. A wooden dresser. A bookcase. A telescope by the window. Nothing that would help. Nothing he could use to free himself.

The door of the room creaked open. Panic welled within

him.. The face of the guard from his dream flashed in his mind's eye.

But when the door fully opened, it was an older man. Long nose, a pair of bushy white eyebrows.

He held Marcus's gaze for a long moment before he spoke. "Who the hell are you?"

CHAPTER 60
AMELS 188 LUXURY YACHT

Mediterranean Sea
5:03 PM, June 13th

———

A lexi was speaking, but Sara wasn't listening. Instead, she was frantically trying to work out where she was. The room was small, barely large enough for a double bed, a tiny bedside table, and a little table next to the window with two chairs. She knew she was on a boat—that much was clear based on the room's sway and the view out the window, an endless vista of shimmering blue water.

But where am I, exactly?

"Sara," growled Alexi.

"Yes?"

"Do you understand the terms?"

Crap. What has he been saying?

Alexi's eyes narrowed. "You have a day to analyze Enora's dataset. After that…" He drew a finger across his throat. "*Tha se skotóso.*"

"Okay."

It wasn't a very good response, considering the threat, but while part of Sara's mind realized her life was in danger, the main part was still working feverishly to devise an escape plan.

After they'd hiked down to the bottom of the hill, Alexi's men had blindfolded her before stuffing her in the back of an SUV. When they'd let her out again, the salty air had told her she was by the sea. Based on where they'd captured her, her best guess was that they'd taken her somewhere on the French Riviera.

But then they'd led her onto an airplane, and she'd made a crucial mistake. Exhaustion, combined with the sensory deprivation of the blindfold, had finally caught up with her, and she'd fallen asleep. She had no idea how long the flight had been.

She'd woken for the landing. Still blindfolded, she'd stepped straight from the plane to the boat. That suggested she'd been on some type of amphibious seaplane. What sort of distance could a seaplane travel? She'd google it, but of course, they'd taken her phone.

"Sara," said Alexi, "meet Karl."

He gestured to a man standing in the corner of the room. Karl was tall, with a protruding Adam's apple and a large forehead. Dressed in a black turtleneck and gray slacks, he wouldn't have looked out of place in a physics department, except for the Glock 19 at his hip.

"Karl," Alexi continued, "is my tech guy. He'll be looking after you."

Karl flashed a toothy grin and said, in a thick German accent, "Sudo, don't screw with me."

Sara couldn't help herself. She knew they were planning to kill her, but the joke was so unexpected, she laughed. Had Karl really just made a computer science joke?

Alexi glared. "Why are you laughing?"

Karl answered for her. "Is funny. 'Sudo' means she must do exactly vat I say."

Alexi shook his head, his expression one of annoyance and disgust. Sara was beginning to realize that while Alexi was in charge, he wasn't the one who understood the science. This elicited a new question: how had he found out about her work?

"Remember," Alexi said to Karl, "that Kostas was the last one to guard her, and he ended up dead."

Alexi left, and Karl's expression turned serious. No more joking, apparently.

He pointed to a laptop resting on the table. "Use zis laptop. I watch. No funny business." He patted the Glock on his hip for emphasis.

Sara sat down at the table. Thankfully, the laptop was a Mac, so she'd be able to work in the built-in Unix environment without any additional setup. She'd expected Karl to stand behind her as the guard in Frank's apartment had, but instead, he took the seat next to her, close enough that she could smell his cologne.

"Vat are you going to do?" he asked.

"I'm planning on logging into a remote server I have running. Is that okay?" She didn't want him to think she was trying to communicate with someone.

"*Ja*," said Karl, nodding.

She opened a fresh terminal window and logged into the server. With a few keystrokes, she navigated to the folder that contained Enora's dataset.

"Vat are ze files?" asked Karl.

Sara hadn't expected him to question her about her work. "These are the genomes Enora gave me."

"Vat are zey?"

"Based on the file names, I think it's short-read data."

"You are not sure?"

The guy was persistent. "I haven't even looked at the files yet."

Sara typed a few commands, and the contents of one of the files appeared on the screen.

```
@SN7001204_0527_AHJLJYBCXX_R_PEdi_L5727_37_5:2:2212:7473:32288/1
AGCAGGTCACATAGCGATAGCAGGATAAAGAGAGTGAGGGGGAAGGTGCCACACTCTTTTAAACAACCAGA
TTTCA
+
DCDDDIIIIIIIIHIIHIHHHHIIHHHIIFHHFHIHEEEHHH]]]]]]]]]]XB@BECD@@AC@BBBBBBB
BBBBB
@SN7001204_0530_BHJMM3BCXX_R_PEdi_L5727_37_8:2:2210:12995:10115/1
CCCCATCAGAACTTGCTTCCAAATATTCCCTTTGTGGGGCTGGGGACGCCCACTGGGCTGGGGGTGCTACA
CTGGC
+
<D@<<FHHHHIIEHHCCCEHCH1CGHHHH?GHEHIHHHHH?GHCHGCDHGC@EEHI?
CHGDGHHEHHHIHIFHHCF
@D00829_0040_AHHL73BCXY_R_PEdi_L5829_D8608_F3442:1:1101:9183:21174/1
AACATCAGAGCCCCTGGAGGAAAGGGCACAGGCTTGAAGGCTGCTGCTCCAGGACTGTCCTCCTGGCTGGC
TTCCT
+
BDDCDIHIIIIHEIHIIGIIIIRTT\]]
[]dddd`ddd^dddadd^BBBBBBBBBBBBBBBBBBBBBBBBBBBBBBBBBBB
```

Karl frowned as he studied the characters. "Okay," he said after a few seconds. "Ze second line starts with AGCAGG. Zat's DNA?"

"Yes."

"What is rest of zis gobbledygook?" He pointed at the other lines on the screen.

Between his Unix joke and his interest in her work, Sara decided that she kind of liked Karl, even if his cologne was a little strong. She hoped this wasn't early-onset Stockholm Syndrome.

"This data is in FASTQ format," she said. "It's the standard output from a high throughput DNA sequencer." She pointed at the screen. "This first line, the one that starts with the 'at' symbol, is the unique label for that particular sequence. The plus is a delimiter. Then this fourth line, with the alphanumeric characters, is the information about DNA quality. The higher the number, the better quality the DNA is."

"I do not see numbers," said Karl, frowning.

"Each character is associated with a number."

"Like ASCII character codes?"

"Exactly!"

"*Geil*!" said Karl excitedly. Then he pointed at the end of the fourth line. "What are all ze B's?"

"That *is* strange. B's typically represents DNA that should be discarded. With today's tech, it's pretty uncommon to see sequences of this low quality."

"Low quality? You said data vas important." Karl's tone suggested that he thought she might be lying.

Sara rubbed her forehead, thinking furiously. She didn't usually have to explain her thought process as she did an analysis. Part of her wanted to remind Karl that she only had twelve hours to get Alexi results, and to politely ask him to shut up. But his apparently genuine interest in her work suggested he *could* be an ally. It made sense to answer his questions, at least a little bit longer.

"If we assume that whoever Enora paid to generate the data didn't screw up, then the B's *could* indicate that the sample was low quality to begin with. But that seems unlikely. Enora has a ton of funding. Unless—" She looked up, her eyes shining with excitement. "Ancient DNA tends to be highly degraded."

"*Alter*! So zis is Neanderthal DNA?"

"Let's not jump to conclusions. I'd have to do more work to see if it's Neanderthal." Sara squinted at the laptop screen again. "This is also odd. The sequences are shorter than I'm used to seeing—" She ran her finger along the string of characters as she silently counted them. "Looks to be about seventy base pairs long. Most of the data I work with are one hundred and fifty base pairs at least."

"Maybe is less expensive?"

"Like I said, Enora had oodles of funding, so that can't be it." Sara sat back as things clicked into place. "If Enora *knew* this was ancient DNA, then it would make sense not to bother with sequencing one hundred fifty base pair–long reads because half of the data wouldn't be usable."

"Because ancient DNA is broken into tiny pieces?"

"Exactly. It's super degraded." Sara closed her eyes as she tried to put everything in context. "Karl, are you familiar with my work?"

"*Ja*. I vas one who found your paper on bioRxiv."

Sara sucked in a short breath. If Karl was the one who'd first told Alexi about her paper, then he was the one who'd set everything in motion—the fire in the Schröder Lab, the attack at Harvard. Amy, Frank, Enora, and Marcus—they were all dead because of him. Any sense of Stockholm Syndrome left her in an instant, and it took all her self-control not to go for his gun.

"So... so..." Sara stammered, trying to keep her composure. "You understand that I worked out a way to sift out the bits of ancient genomes from modern sequences? I'm guessing these ancient DNA sequences might be related to that work."

"Vat is so interesting about ancient DNA?" asked Karl. But even through his thick German accent, Sara sensed a slight hesitation in the way he spoke. He was holding back, testing her, maybe. No question he knew more than he was letting on.

Sara looked him dead in the eyes. "I don't know, but I intend to find out."

CHAPTER 61
FARMHOUSE IN MONTSÉGUR

Commune in the Ariège department, France
4:35 PM, June 13th

————

arcus twisted violently in his bonds, trying to escape, even as the old man stalked toward him. "What's going on? Why am I restrained?" he demanded.

The man ignored him. He stared at Marcus with an expression that appeared to consist primarily of anger. Only when he reached the foot of the bed did he finally speak, asking again, "Who the hell are you?"

To Marcus's surprise, the man had a posh British accent. Whoever he was, he wasn't French. Was that important? Marcus had no idea. Still, he needed to make a decision. Cooperate or stay silent? There didn't seem to be much point in the latter.

"I'm Marcus."

The old man reached into his shirt pocket and produced a

piece of paper. "Where did you get this?" he asked, holding it up aggressively.

It took Marcus a moment to recognize Frank's note, the one he and Sara had found in the booby-trapped desk. The man seemed to know something about it, but what, exactly? Did he know about Frank? The Cathar treasure? The Bitcoin account? Marcus decided it was best to reveal as little information as possible. "I found it in a desk."

"Where?"

"In an apartment."

"You robbed this apartment?"

"No. I was imprisoned there after the owner was murdered."

This didn't seem to be the answer the man was expecting. He turned to the window and stood silently for at least thirty seconds. There was something about his expression that was familiar. Then Marcus realized he'd seen Sara make that exact face when she was thinking hard.

When the old man finally spoke, his voice had lost its imperative edge. "Frank is dead?"

So he knows Frank. "Yes."

"How?"

Marcus decided there was no point in holding back. If this man was one of Alexi's, if he was part of Actaeon, he'd already know this. Marcus explained that he'd seen Frank shot to death. The man listened without interrupting. Only when Marcus was finished did he speak.

"And you are completely sure of this?"

"I saw it happen."

The man's eyes narrowed, his bushy eyebrows knitting together. "So you don't know what you're dealing with?"

"I know what exactly what I'm dealing with," Marcus said. "Frank was a Rosicrucian. He was murdered. I was almost murdered myself. My friend—" He paused. He remembered the train ride, renting a car in Montpellier, and then after that, his mind was blank. Nothing there. Like the news feed of his life had been severed. What had happened? It hit him like a punch in the gut. Where was Sara?

"Where is my friend?"

"Who?"

The old man leaned over the bed, his eyes boring into Marcus. Still angry, but curious, too. Marcus stared back, not breaking eye contact. He couldn't be sure that this wasn't some sort of ruse. This man could be working for Alexi, simply pumping him for information. It was time to play a little hardball.

"It's your turn to answer a question," Marcus said. "Where am I?"

"You can't figure it out?" The man gestured to the window. "Surely you recognize that vista."

"It looks familiar," Marcus began, then it hit him. "It's the Château de Montségur! I was here once before—in high school."

"I found you at the bottom of the mountain," said the old man. "You should be more careful near cliffs."

"How did you even know I was there?"

"You dug something up that sent me a signal, so I went to take a look. I helped you once I found you."

Marcus closed his eyes, trying to recall. He didn't remember digging or finding anything. But now, more memories had returned, and he could almost remember climbing the hillside. Sara had been with him—he was sure of that much. They'd been looking for the treasure, that's right. And...

He strained, squeezing his eyes tightly shut. He remembered being angry, and...a fight?

It hit him. Alexi had been there. Which meant—

He opened his eyes. "I think he tried to push me off the cliff."

But he didn't succeed...right? He obviously didn't, or

Marcus wouldn't be here. But then... He shook his head. *Why do I feel like I remember falling?*

One of the man's eyebrows twitched. "Who?"

"Who are you?" Marcus retorted. It was a stupid response, but he was tired of being kept in the dark.

"Tell me who pushed you," said the old man, with emphasis.

As much as Marcus wanted to argue, he was the man's prisoner. Literally tied to the bed. If he wanted to be released, he'd need to answer the question. The trick was to not provide too much information.

"His name is Alexi."

The man sucked in a sharp breath, and for an instant, his gaze moved to the window again. Marcus was surprised to see a flicker of fear wash over his features.

"Alexander was *here*?"

———

To say Marcus was frustrated was a significant understatement. As soon as he'd mentioned Alexi, his captor had clammed up. He'd just stood there, staring out the window, for at least ten minutes. Thinking, apparently.

Of course, Marcus had tried to get the old man to talk, badgering him with questions.

"Why am I tied to this bed?"

Silence.

"How did you find me?"

No answer.

"How long have I been here?"

Marcus had a moment of intuition then.

"What do you know about Alexi?"

Still no answer.

"At least tell me who you are."

More silence.

"Why don't you release me? I'm not going to hurt you."

The man spoke sharply. "If you don't pipe down, I *will* gag you."

Marcus lay still on the bed—which wasn't that difficult, considering he was lashed to it. The curtains rustled in the window. He could hear the hum of insects. A bird flitted through the pale blue sky.

Interrogation wasn't working. He needed a different approach. Something gentler.

"My friend Sara, I think Alexi may have kidnapped her."

This time the man responded. "Who?"

"Her name is Sara Morin—"

His captor spun round, eyes blazing. "You were with Sara?"

"You know her?"

"No, but I've read her paper."

This was it, Marcus realized, the opening he'd been looking for. He spoke slowly. "She and I are working together. We're looking for the treasure described in the letter."

The old man studied him with narrowed eyes. Marcus sensed he knew something. At last, he spoke. "And you believe Alexi has her?"

"Yes."

Again, the man stared at him for a long moment, his expression inscrutable. "Then we'd best find her," he said at last.

"How? Alexi and his men will be long gone. We'll never find them."

"I know a way."

CHAPTER 62
AETER PHARMACEUTICALS

Cambridge, Massachusetts
10:05 AM, June 13th

———

She was pretty weak, but Enora should have felt a lot worse, considering she'd been dead for nearly three days before they revived her.

It definitely helped that she had the best doctors money could buy. Dr. Gallagher had been taking excellent care of her. He was still checking her vitals every hour or two.

In regard to the fatigue, her working hypothesis was that her mitochondria hadn't fully healed, but honestly, she had no idea.

As she made a note to have Dr. Mulligan's lab look into it, the phone on her desk rang. Since she'd been keeping her recovery very quiet, it could only be three people: Dr. Gallagher, Dr. Mesle, or the young technician who'd purified the cells that'd saved her life.

She lifted the phone to her ear.

"Dr. Hansen?" He sounded nervous.

"Who's this?"

"Sameer."

"I've been meaning to check in. What's going on?"

There was a long pause. That didn't bode well. "I have bad news. I'm running out of cells."

"What do you mean?"

Sameer's voice grew smaller. "I've tried everything. I've activated with both PHA and lipopolysaccharide, I supplemented the media with interleukin-2, but nothing seems to work. They're not proliferating at all."

"Well, I can't say I'm surprised," said Enora gently. "White blood cells are notoriously difficult to culture."

She'd expected Sameer to sound relieved, but instead, he continued with a voice tinged with fear. "That's not all. The inoculated mice, the ones I injected with the white blood cells? They no longer heal like they used to. I tried taking a biopsy punch. It scabbed over, but it didn't fully heal—not like before, anyway."

Shit. This *was* bad news. Enora rubbed her forehead as she worked through the implications.

"Have *you* noticed any changes?" Sameer asked.

A good question. "Just a sec." Enora put the phone down and rummaged in her desk for a safety pin. She dragged the sharp tip across the inside of her forearm, wincing as blood beaded on her skin. Pain receptors were definitely working.

"All right," she said, picking up the phone. "I just cut myself, and…" She double-checked her arm. "I'm still bleeding."

"You, uh…" Sameer stammered. "Are you sure you're okay?"

"I'm fine," said Enora firmly. Keeping the phone to her ear, she rested her elbows on her desk and closed her eyes. "How many more cells do you have?"

"I have one tube of a billion cells left frozen in liquid nitrogen. Do you want me to try to culture them?"

"No, keep them frozen. Let me think for a bit."

"Will do. I'm sorry for the bad news, Dr. Hansen."

Enora wanted to scream, to throw the phone across the room, but somehow, she forced herself to remain calm. "You did the right thing. I'll call you in a few minutes."

She hung up and leaned back in her chair. Despite the complication, she found it hard to stay upset for long. The simple reality that she was alive and breathing was a constant damper on any negative thoughts.

Her plan *had* worked. She'd pumped millions into legitimately outlandish projects: cutting-edge cryogenics, ancient genome sequencing, and Greenland shark biology. And then, of course there'd been all the quiet under-the-table work: the corporate espionage, the blackmail, the theft of antiquities, even a murder. But in the end, she'd done what no human had ever done.

She'd beaten death.

Sameer's laboratory troubles were only a temporary setback. They'd find a way to culture the white blood cells, she was certain of it. Then, when she revealed this discovery to the world, a Nobel Prize would be too small. They'd place her among the pantheon of the greatest scientists to ever live: Aristotle, Galileo, Isaac Newton, Charles Darwin...

Again, she was interrupted by the ringing of her phone.

"Hello, Sameer?"

A brief hesitation. "No, this is Dr. Gallagher. There's been a development. Marcus has appeared in France."

"Where?"

"He just checked into a hotel in Montpellier."

Enora swore. "What the hell is he thinking? Actaeon will get him." She paused as a new thought occurred to her. "Is Sara with him?"

"Just Marcus."

Enora sucked in a short breath. Marcus wasn't dumb. If he

was turning himself in, that could only mean that he wanted Actaeon to know where he was. Which meant—

She swore again. Actaeon must have Sara.

"How soon can I get there?"

"Ten hours."

"Get the plane ready. I'm leaving now."

Enora began to stand, then paused to pick up the phone once more. Quickly, she dialed the Mulligan Lab.

Sameer answered. "Hello?"

"Sameer, I need those cells ASAP. Does your lab have a portable liquid nitrogen dewar?"

"Yes—"

"Good. Get the cells in it, and meet me out front in five minutes."

CHAPTER 63
AMELS 188 LUXURY YACHT

Mediterranean Sea
4:48 PM, June 14th

———

The sun outside was slowly dipping toward an azure horizon, but Sara was unaware, her eyes fixed on the glowing laptop screen. She'd been at it for almost twenty-four hours now, shepherding Enora's genomes through her analysis pipeline. Even as her eyes burned with fatigue, she felt a thrill of excitement. As soon as the current analysis was completed, she'd have some preliminary results, and hopefully answers.

Over the course of the last couple of hours, she'd worked to align Enora's eight genomes to the human reference genome. Although she had nearly six gigabases of raw sequence, eighty percent had been fungal and bacterial contamination. That left a patchy final product with, on average, less than two archaic fragments at any part of the human reference genome. This had made it tricky to identify the genomic positions that varied from the reference.

She checked the running analysis again and inhaled sharply when she saw its status. *Complete.*

Quickly, she pulled the data into an interactive session. A few more keystrokes, and she'd visualized the results.

Her tired eyes widened. "Whoa—"

"Vat is it?" said Karl.

Focused as she was, Sara had forgotten about him, but of course, he was still sitting next to her.

She pointed at a scatterplot on the screen. "You see these points?"

"*Ja.*"

"This is a PCA plot of the genetic dataset."

"A vat?"

"PCA—Principal Components Analysis. It's a method for simplifying multi-dimensional data."

"English?"

Sara sighed. Putting complicated genomic analysis into layman's terms was never easy.

"Enora supplied eight individual genomes. Each genome has a bit more than two million genetic variants that differ from the reference genome. So if you want to compare individuals, that works out to sixty-four unique comparisons. However, I want to compare each variant, so multiply sixty-four by two point five million."

Karl's eyes widened. "I see…"

"And that's not all the samples I analyzed. I also included reference samples. I incorporated the Simons Genome Diversity Project dataset as well as chimpanzee, Neanderthal, and Denisovan genomes.

"Why chimpanzee?"

"If Enora's samples represent an entirely new lineage of archaic humans, including chimp will help separate them from Neanderthal and Denisovan."

Karl still appeared confused. "Vat is zis…Simons Genome dataset?"

"It's a collection of more than two hundred sixty complete genomes from one hundred twenty-seven populations of modern humans," Sara said. "It's important to include it because if Enora's samples are modern human, then the Simons Genome diversity samples will help us determine which population they came from."

Karl rubbed his chin. *"Ich verstehe."* Then to Sara: "I see."

"Good," said Sara, pushing forward. "So once I added all these additional genomes to the analysis, that works out to about twenty thousand comparisons at more than two million genomic positions."

"A computer can calculate zat pretty easily."

"Yeah. The main issue is that you can't visualize it. There are too many comparisons. That's why I ran a PCA."

"I still don't understand PCA," said Karl.

"Do you know what an American football looks like?"

"Ja."

"Close your eyes. Can you envision a three-dimensional arrangement of points in the shape of a football?"

Next to her, Karl shut his eyes. *"Ja."*

"Great. Now, how do you make a football two-dimensional?"

"Deflate it?"

Sara couldn't help herself. "That would be Tom Brady's approach."

"Tom Brady?"

"It was a joke—not really important here. Anyway, imagine you have a really long, thin needle. Take that needle and push from one pointy end of the football-shaped cloud of points to the other."

"All right," said Karl. "I have needle in American football."

It took all of Sara's willpower not to make another joke about Tom Brady and the Patriots. "Okay. If you were to measure the distance from every point in the football-shaped cloud of points to the closest part of the needle, you'd get a list of distances, right?"

"I don't understand vy—"

"The idea is that you're trying fit a line—a needle—through the point cloud so that it's as close to as many of them as possible."

"Ahhh…" Karl's face lit up with a genuine gleam of excitement.

"Right? Statistics can be kind of cool when you understand it," said Sara, matching his enthusiasm. "Anyway, that list of numbers is called the first principal component."

Karl frowned. "But you cannot just plot series of distances."

"Exactly!" said Sara. She started to jump up, but her eyes fell on Karl's Glock, and she thought better of it. "So you need to identify a second needle—a second line—and fit that through your football. But this time, the line needs to account for the shape of the points in a way that complements the first component. Basically, you poke a needle through the fattest part of the football."

"And zen you measure ze distance from each point to closest part of ze second needle?"

"Yup, and then you can plot those two sets of distances as the X and Y coordinates in a standard two-dimensional scatterplot. The end result is that genomes that are genetically similar to each other will be plotted close together."

"Zat is vat you have done?"

"Essentially, yes. The big difference is that there are far more than three dimensions with genetic data. Remember how big the dataset is? It's highly multi-dimensional. You have to use a computer to figure out where to put the needles —to fit the principal components."

Karl turned back to Sara's laptop screen. It showed three points in the shape of a triangle, with a fourth slightly blobby-looking point in the center. "Vy only four points on zis plot? Shouldn't zere be hundreds?"

"These three represent the chimp, Neanderthal, and Denisovan samples," Sara said, pointing to the three points at the vertices of the triangle. "And—"

Karl cut in. "And zat one is Enora's sample?"

"Well, not exactly," said Sara. She typed in a few commands, and the plot zoomed in. The blobby point in the center expanded into a rainbow-colored sea of points. "The modern humans group closely together." She pointed to a small group of black dots near the center of the screen. "These represent Enora's samples. Any theories about what they might be?"

Karl's brow furrowed. "Zey are grouped vith modern humans, so I guess zey are not archaic samples."

"Yup. Definitely modern human. If they were a previously undiscovered group of archaic humans, we would have seen them as a separate set of points when I first plotted the PCA results."

Karl pointed at the other points on the screen. "Vat are ze rest of ze samples?"

"I've colored the points based on populations. For example, these points in shades of red are Biaka and Masai individuals from Africa. And these points in blue are Peruvian and Colombian individuals from South America."

"Vat are zese?" asked Karl, pointing to a group of pale yellow points.

"Those are Middle Eastern populations: Jordanian, Iranian, Druze, and Iraqi and Yemenite Jews. It looks to me like the samples Enora gave me were Middle Eastern. It's a little hard to tell, but they seem to fall between the Iraqi and Yemenite Jews. If I had to guess, I'd say these samples are from an ancient Jewish people."

Karl snatched up the laptop and leaped to his feet. "You stay here. I speak to Alexi."

"Wait—why?"

But Karl was already hurrying from the room. There was a click as he locked the door behind him.

What the hell was going on?

Sara stood for the first time in hours. Her brain felt foggy. She pressed her palms to her face. Every part of her just wanted to sleep, but of course, she couldn't do that. Karl had finally left her alone. This was her first real chance to escape.

Pulling her hands from her eyes, she scanned the cabin. Built into one wall was a pair of doors that Sara guessed was a closet. Pulling them open revealed turtlenecks hanging from a rack and gray trousers stacked and folded on a shelf. No question, this was Karl's personal quarters. A small set of drawers contained socks and underwear but nothing that might help her escape. Certainly nothing she could use as a weapon.

She turned and surveyed the room again. Her gaze fell on the bedside table. She opened its single drawer, but it held only a pair of glasses and a tube of lip balm.

"Fuck," she muttered under her breath.

That was when she noticed the picture on top of the bedside table, an old black-and-white photograph in a small silver frame. There was no mistaking one of the men: short, with dark hair and a toothbrush mustache. That was Adolf Hitler leering through the camera at her, clear as day. But it was the man standing next to him that thoroughly perplexed her.

He looked exactly like a slightly younger version of Karl.

CHAPTER 64
PLACE DE LA COMÉDIE

Montpellier, France
3:57 PM, June 14th

———

Marcus stood at the eastern end of the Place de la Comédie in downtown Montpellier. He gazed enviously at the cafés that lined the plaza. The weather was perfect, and they were filled with dining tourists. He knew exactly what'd he'd order: a glass of Minervois, half a baguette, and a big hunk of Bleu des Causses. He wished terribly that Sara were here with him.

Instead, he was here with his former captor, whose name was, disarmingly, Ike.

"Are you ready?" asked Ike.

Marcus turned his attention from the bustling plaza to the gray-haired man standing next to him. It was Ike who had devised the plan to find Sara.

"You realized this is completely insane," Marcus said.

"It's the only way to find Alexander."

In front of them, next to the tourist office, curved the blue glass façade of the Commissariat de Police. At the entrance stood a uniformed police officer. *No*, Marcus reminded himself, *not a "police officer."* A gendarme.

"I could go to prison for years," Marcus said.

Ike touched him on the shoulder, trying to reassure him. "For every action, there is an equal and opposite reaction. If you go to the authorities, Alexander will come for you. I know him. It is his nature."

Marcus knew Ike was right. Alexi hated him for killing Kostas. Alexi *would* come for him as soon as he learned where he was.

The thing was, it wasn't Alexi that Marcus was afraid of—it was prison. Captivity, confinement, isolation. He couldn't handle it again.

He shook his head. "I just can't do it—"

"Gendarme! Police!" shouted Ike, suddenly grabbing Marcus's arm. "*Cet homme est un terroriste!*"

Instinctively Marcus pulled away, but the gendarme was already sprinting toward them.

"*Arrêtez!*" shouted the officer.

Marcus twisted from Ike's grasp, but the officer was there now, his hand tight on Marcus's forearm.

"*Il est recherché pour meurtre aux États-Unis,*" said Ike.

Marcus wished, for the first time ever, that he'd paid more attention in French class.

"*Arrêtez. Ne bougez pas,*" said the gendarme firmly. He wrenched Marcus's arm behind his back and cuffed him.

Marcus lowered his head. There was no turning back from the plan now. He was all in.

"My name is Marcus Byron," he said softly. "I'm not a terrorist, but INTERPOL has a Red Notice out for me. I'm here to turn myself in."

"And I helped him," Ike added.

As the gendarme led them into the police station, Marcus took a final look at the plaza. Why hadn't he insisted on drinking a glass of Minervois first? It would have helped settle his nerves.

CHAPTER 65
AMELS 188 LUXURY YACHT

Mediterranean Sea
5:14 PM, June 14th

———

"What are you doing?"

Sara started, nearly falling over. Karl was behind her. Somehow, he had returned without her hearing him. She rose slowly, trying to pretend she hadn't been searching his room.

"I did not say you could get up."

"I had to pee."

Karl's lips had compressed to a thin line. "Ze bathroom is over zere," he said, pointing at the door on the other side of the bed.

"Yes, I know," said Sara, trying to maintain the charade, although it was obvious to both of them that she hadn't simply been going to the bathroom. "I was just heading back to my chair when I noticed this picture on your bedside table." She held it up so that Karl could see. "Is that really Hitler?"

Karl's eyes widened like he'd just been caught looking at porn. "Ze Führer? *Ja.*"

"Who's the man in the picture with him? He looks like he's related to you."

"Zat is my great-uncle." Karl paused for a moment. "Vilhelm."

"Your great-uncle was a Nazi?"

"*Ach nein*, not a Nazi," said Karl, stiffening. "German administrator."

Sara wanted to explain that being an administrator and a Nazi weren't necessarily mutually exclusive roles, but Karl spoke first. "Alexi vill see you in tventy minutes. Any additional analysis, you do now."

He pressed the laptop into her hands.

"I thought I had until the morning. Alexi said I had twenty-four hours."

"He has changed his mind."

You mean you've changed his mind, Sara might have said if she hadn't suddenly had an idea.

The only question was whether twenty minutes was enough time to test it.

————

Sara's fingers flew over the keyboard. A few more commands, and she'd have the results finalized.

Karl tapped her shoulder. "Ve have to go. Alexi is expecting us."

"One sec—"

Sara clicked shift-enter to run the script, then stood and stuffed the laptop under her arm. Even with the laptop screen closed, the code would run. Hopefully, it would be done by the time they met with Alexi.

She followed Karl through the door and into the hallway. As he walked ahead of her, she studied her surroundings, searching for opportunities to learn where she was and how she might escape.

"Zis vay," said Karl over his shoulder.

There was a row of windows on her left, and through them, she could see a great expanse of water. "Is that the Mediterranean?"

"Ze Aegean." Karl stopped and poked a call button beside an elevator door. "I know you are zinking about escaping. Don't vaste your time. Ve are twenty nautical miles from closest land." With an electronic ding, a door in the wall slid open. "Zis vay."

Sara's heart was desolate as they rode up the elevator. Karl had told her they were in the Aegean, and that was something...but it wasn't much. With no land in sight, her hope of escape was fading rapidly.

With another ding, the door opened onto an opulent lounge. The room had long windows with a view of the sea, plush leather couches, and even a marble bar. At the far end, there were floor-to-ceiling windows and glass doors that led to a deck.

Alexi lounged on one of the couches, a glass of wine in his hand. He appeared relaxed, but he studied Sara with a fierce intensity. "Karl tells me you've made an important discovery."

"Apparently so," said Sara guardedly.

"What have you found?"

"The samples Enora gave me appear to be ancient DNA."

Alexi's expression remained taut. "How do you know this?"

"The DNA sequences are consistent with highly degraded samples." Sara explained how she'd found extensive bacterial contamination and how the DNA sequencer had produced fragments with unusually low-quality DNA.

"So these are Neanderthal samples?"

"No. They appear to be modern human."

Alexi frowned. "You're saying that Enora sequenced degraded modern human samples."

"Yes. Modern humans have existed for thirty to forty thousand years. Of course, if the samples weren't well preserved, it's possible they could only be a few thousand years old. Just because the DNA is degraded doesn't *necessarily* mean that it's old. I set up a historical demography analysis in MSMC—that's short for the Multiple Sequentially Markovian Coalescent—and—"

But Alexi wasn't paying attention to her explanation. "Why would she sequence these samples?"

"I don't know."

"You were supposed to learn why Enora was interested in your research!" Alexi's heterochromatic eyes flashed with anger. "That is the *only* reason I didn't throw you over the edge of the cliff."

Sara took a deep breath. Lab meetings had been stressful in Dr. Fitzpatrick's lab, but a mistake in how she presented her findings there only resulted in a public shaming. Here, an error could lead to her death.

"Here's what I've learned," she said carefully. "I compared each of these sequences to modern populations—"

Alexi interrupted her immediately. "I thought you said the samples were degraded."

"They are, but there's enough data to run a basic demographic analysis. And like I said, I've been working on dating them with MSMC."

That seemed to satisfy the Greek, though he continued to glare at her.

Sara took a deep breath before continuing. "What I know now is the following: the samples appear to be modern humans from Middle Eastern populations, specifically the Jewish diaspora."

Alexi leaned forward. "Do you know which populations?"

Sara shook her head. "There's not enough genetic information. But I did check one other thing. Have you heard of the Cohen Modal Haplotype?"

Alexi shook his head.

"The Cohen Modal Haplotype is a Y-chromosome haplotype—"

"English, please."

"Well," said Sara slowly, "because a man inherits his entire Y-chromosome from his father, we call it a haplotype. The Cohen Modal Haplotype is an unusual Y-chromosome discovered in the late 1990s. It's found in Kohanim populations and in many Jewish people with the surname Cohen."

"Are you saying zere is a special Y-chromosome associated vith Jews?" said Karl eagerly.

With a sickening twist in her stomach, Sara remembered the picture of Hitler on Karl's nightstand and how he'd rushed to talk to Alexi as soon as she'd mentioned the genomes might be associated with Jewish populations. What, exactly, was going on here?

She ignored Karl as Alexi steepled his fingers. It was only Alexi she needed to answer to.

"How familiar are you with your biblical history?" Sara asked. She suddenly wished terribly that Marcus were with her. But he'd never be with her again. Marcus was dead. Broken at the bottom of the cliff—

"I'm familiar," Alexi said sharply.

Sara drew in a deep breath, willing herself to concentrate. "Historically, Kohanim were the priestly class." She tried to remember the Wikipedia entry she'd skimmed fifteen minutes earlier. "And many, if not most, contemporary Jewish people with the last name Cohen are their relatives. They are believed to be descended from a single paternal line that extends all the way back to Aaron."

"Brother of Moses, son of Jacob," said Alexi quietly. He leaned forward, his strange eyes boring into her.

"That—that sounds right," Sara stammered.

Next to Alexi, Karl was nodding. "Zat is also my understanding."

Alexi shook his head, his face transforming into a mask of
rage. "This is exactly why you never trust fanatics. They will
fuck anything if they believe it'll further their cause!"

Sara backed away. She'd seen that look in men before. Like
the time when Dr. Fitzpatrick broke a chair after learning that
Walter Schröder had been accepted into the National
Academy of Sciences. Or when her ex screamed and threw his
Xbox controller across the room when he got fragged playing
Call of Duty. The only reason women were so often called
"emotional" was because men had normalized their rage.

Alexi continued to rant. "I mean, how many wives did
Abraham have? At least three!"

"Alexi?" said Karl, holding up his cell phone. "Alexi! Zere
has been important development."

"What?" Alexi stopped shouting, but his voice said this
had better be really important.

"Zey have found ze reporter."

Sara felt a momentary flicker of hope. Marcus! Was he
alive? But no, of course not. She'd seen him fall off the cliff.
She'd seen his body splayed on the rocks. They hadn't found
Marcus; they'd found his body.

"I don't give a crap about his corpse," Alexi snapped.

"No," said Karl, "it is not like zat. Ike is vith him."

The rage remained on Alexi's face, but now, with it, there
was something else.

Fear.

"Prometheus? Ike the thief?" Alexi asked.

"Is my understanding," said Karl.

Alexi paused for a long moment. Then he eyed Karl
coldly.

"Bring them to me."

CHAPTER 66
TECHNOHULL SEADNA 999 TENDER

Cyclades, Aegean Sea
10:51 PM, June 14th

————

Marcus leaned over the side of the boat and vomited into the sea.

"Are you all right?" asked Ike.

"Yes," said Marcus even as he fought to keep his insides from expelling themselves again.

Ike was having no such trouble himself. Heck, the man hadn't so much as burped. Marcus decided that he hated him deeply, but it was hard to stay mad. After two hours in a holding cell, Marcus and Ike had been released—directly into the custody of Alexi's men.

Ike's plan had worked like a charm.

"Try to focus on the horizon," Ike said.

Marcus looked out over the gray sea. Salty wind wet his face, and above him, the evening sky had cleared. This far from land, there was no light pollution to obscure the stars.

For a moment, he felt better. In fact, he was filled with excitement. He was on his way to rescue Sara.

But then his gut clenched, and he doubled over once more.

———

It must have been nearly one AM when they arrived at the massive luxury yacht. Its windows were aglow with light, making it look like an apartment building floating sideways on the ocean.

Marcus took a long look before crouching down, his back against the side of the tender. The wind had picked up, and an icy spray blew off the tops off the waves. Ike had explained that this was the beginning of the Meltemi winds, a seasonal high-pressure system that drove air out of the Balkans and across the Aegean.

The tender was crewed by a captain and a stony-faced guard. The captain manned the wheel, while the guard watched over Marcus and Ike. Marcus thought the guard's job was pretty pointless, given that they had nowhere to escape to at this juncture. Sure, they could leap over the side, but with no land in sight, they weren't going anywhere unless it was a one-way trip to the depths.

The boat circled the yacht while the driver spoke with someone on the other ship over a handheld VHF. After a lot of rapid-fire Greek, they approached the stern of the larger vessel.

Marcus saw then the reason for the heated conversation. The waves were causing the yacht's stern to surge up and down. If they got too close, the larger vessel could slam down on the tender and send them all into the water.

As the captain approached cautiously, easing the small boat closer and closer to the stern of the super-yacht, the guard shouted in broken English, "You, forward." He waved his Glock at Marcus. Marcus very much doubted the man would be particularly accurate with the gun, given the way the boat was bouncing around in the swell, but he moved forward anyway, with Ike following. He *wanted* to get onto the yacht. Finding Sara was his only objective.

He reached the bow just as the tender neared the stern of the yacht. A broad expanse of teak rose and fell like a massive piston.

"*Álma!*" shouted the guard.

"What?" The wind plus the sound of the yacht's engine made it difficult to hear.

"He wants you to go first," yelled Ike. The older man stood next to him, one hand bracing himself against the rubber side of the tender.

Marcus's stomach clenched, and not only from seasickness. The ocean seethed, and the distance from one ship to the other ranged from three feet to ten, depending on the swell. If he jumped at the wrong moment, he'd end up in the sea—and he doubted they'd stop to fish him out.

The tender heaved toward the yacht. Six feet. Five feet. Three. It was now or never.

Marcus leaped. For an instant, he hung suspended over the boiling waves. He could see he'd timed his jump well— he'd make it to the deck. But he could also see that he hadn't accounted for a sudden upward movement of the superyacht.

The deck flew up like a rocket, and he heard the sick crunch as he landed awkwardly. Pain exploded up his right leg.

Ike landed lightly beside him. "Get up."

"I broke my ankle," said Marcus, clutching his foot.

Something ice-cold pressed against his cheek. The muzzle of a gun.

"*Síko.*"

It wasn't Ike's voice. Marcus looked up to see a guard standing over him.

Marcus didn't have to know the meaning of "*síko*" to understand that the guard was deadly serious. He'd be shot if he didn't move. Tenderly, he pushed himself to his feet. The pain was excruciating, like someone was repeatedly stabbing and twisting a hot knife into his foot. But Ike held out a hand, and somehow, he managed to stand unsteadily on the bobbing deck.

The guard used his gun to gesture toward steps leading up. Gritting his teeth, Marcus forced himself to take a step forward. He'd expected that putting weight on his broken foot would be agonizing, but it wasn't nearly as bad as he'd anticipated. He managed to limp up the steps, again with Ike's help. At the top, he glanced over his shoulder to see that the tender had pulled back and was now attached to a tow line.

The guard led them through an atrium and into an elevator. Even the elevator was opulent, with walls of pale marble and railings that gleamed with polished chrome. Marcus might have been impressed had his attention not been focused on the pain in his foot and the queasiness in his stomach. Just as he was thinking there might be an emergency situation, the doors opened onto a sky deck.

There was more sparkling chrome here, along with sumptuous leather, but the effect was marred by an enormous TV blaring a mixed martial arts fight. Alexi was lounging on a calfskin sofa in a pair of khaki shorts and a white linen shirt. In one hand, he held a glass of wine.

Sara was here, too, sitting awkwardly on one of the couches. He was surprised at just how relieved he was to see her again. But when he smiled at her, she looked back at him with an expression he didn't understand.

"Choke him out!" Alexi shouted at the screen. Then, without taking his eyes off the TV, he spoke to Ike and Marcus. "Welcome to my home."

Ike whispered in Marcus's ear. "Don't be afraid. Alexander

follows the traditional rules of hospitality." Then he spoke to Alexi. "Alexander, I see that you still hold an affection for blood sports."

Alexi grunted. "Magomed has the heart of a molossus. Have you seen him fight? He would have submitted Dioxippus in his prime."

Marcus recognized the Russian fighter now. Magomed Ibragimov, known to his fans as The Falcon, was one of the best lightweight MMA fighters in the world. On screen, Magomed had wrapped a muscular forearm around his opponent's throat.

"Choke him out!" Alexi shouted again.

"This needs to stop," said Ike, walking toward Alexi. "You crossed a line with Frank. There will be war if you don't make peace now."

The man under Magomed twisted, and for a moment, he seemed to break free. But Magomed torqued his body and slammed his right fist into his opponent's temple. The man slumped against the wire wall of the cage.

"He's out! He's out!" screamed Alexi, leaping up from the couch.

Marcus looked to the guard who'd escorted them to the sky deck. He, too, was staring rapturously at the TV screen. This was Marcus's chance to speak to Sara. Quickly, he crossed to her. "Are you okay?" he whispered.

Sara didn't answer. She just stared at him with her beautiful blue eyes.

Marcus was worried. He'd never seen her like this before —speechless. "Alexi didn't hurt you, did he?"

Sara spoke slowly. "I...I saw...you...die."

Of all the things he'd thought she might say to him, this was the least likely. "What are you talking about?"

"You fell off the cliff."

"What cliff?" asked Marcus, thoroughly confused.

"At the top of the hill. At Château de Montségur. He pushed you." Her voice cracked. "You fell to your death."

Marcus shook his head, trying to remember. He could recall climbing up to the castle. His lungs had been burning with fatigue when they'd sat together at the summit. He remembered how excited they'd been. So close to the truth. He knew Alexi had been there, and he had a vague memory of being pushed.

"I...I think I remember Alexi, and maybe I was pushed, but...then it's just blank until I woke up. Ike says he found me at the bottom, that he helped me, but obviously, I didn't die."

"You did," said Sara. She had a fierce look in her eye, an expression that said she was one hundred percent certain. "I looked over the edge. I *saw* you, Marcus. I saw your body lying on the rocks. There was blood everywhere. You were dead." She leaned forward, her blue eyes seeming to pierce his very soul. "Are you one of them, too?"

CHAPTER 67
BELL 429 HELICOPTER

Cyclades, Aegean Sea
1:12 AM, June 15th

———

The wind was blowing at close to forty-five knots, with every gust threatening to send the helicopter weathervaning into the sea. And there'd been a lot of gusts. Bruce's feet ached from constantly adjusting the anti-torque pedals.

He wished for the hundredth time that he hadn't accepted the gig. This job was supposed to be *fun*. He got paid to fly glamorous people to beautiful Greek islands. Trips in high winds in the middle of the night were not part of the job description.

Six months ago, he'd moved to Santorini to work for Luxi-copter, a boutique heli-charter company. It had been a massive step up from mustering cattle as a helicopter cowboy in the Australian Outback. And he'd quickly discovered that "I'm a helicopter pilot"—in his Aussie accent—was literal catnip to uni students on holiday. There'd been a Swiss girl named Astrid with the most incredible pair of—

"There it is!" shouted his companion, pointing at the sea below.

Pushing Astrid's perfect breasts from his mind, Bruce strained his eyes, trying to follow the path of the finger. But it was hard to see through the raindrops that raced over the curved cockpit glass.

"There!" repeated his passenger. And this time, he saw it: a distant glimmer on the horizon.

Fighting the wind, he directed the chopper toward the light. As they approached, he saw that it was the running lights of an enormous super-yacht.

"I'm not going to be able to land on that," he shouted over the howling wind.

"There's a pad."

"Doesn't matter. It's too windy."

"Just get me close."

"Are you sure?"

"I'll double your fee."

Bruce was used to dealing with rich people now, but this passenger was clearly nutters. No one sane wants to fly in the middle of the night in shit weather. He'd even seen her inject something into her arm before they'd left.

Still, with the extra money, he could take a few weeks off. Maybe visit Astrid in Frankfurt.

"Okay, I'll give it a go."

White-knuckling the cyclic, he swung the helicopter toward the yacht's upper deck. The wind was insane, throwing them up and down like a drunk kangaroo. This wasn't going to work. They were going to have to turn back.

Then his passenger wrenched the door open.

"Stop!" Bruce shouted as swirling wind filled the cockpit.

CHAPTER 68
AMELS 188 LUXURY YACHT

Cyclades, Aegean Sea
1:21 AM, June 15th

———

Marcus clamped his hands to his ears, trying to block out the deafening noise of the helicopter. Its searchlight scanned wildly back and forth, intermittently blinding him.

Across the room, Alexi had lost his mind. *"Gamo ti poutana mou!"* he shouted, ripping open the glass doors and charging out onto the deck. He waved his hands wildly at the helicopter as if it were a seagull that had stolen his lunch.

Marcus caught Sara's eye, then looked pointedly to the doors of the elevator. This was their chance to escape. But she shook her head, then twitched her chin in the direction of the guard. He was still watching them closely.

Marcus returned his attention to Alexi. Gesticulating like a maniac, the Greek continued to scream at the chopper. Marcus very much doubted the pilot could hear anything he was saying.

Sara nudged him, then pointed upward. "Look," she said. "I think someone is trying to get out."

Even as wind buffeted the helicopter, a figure could be seen crouching on one of the landing skids. Marcus sucked in a tight breath. What were they thinking? He'd barely made his jump from the tender to the yacht, and this was much farther.

Shouting profanities, Alexi raced across the deck, stopping only when he reached a rack of what appeared to be spears. Even as Marcus processed the strangeness of that, Alexi grabbed one and flung it at the chopper.

The downdraft of the main rotors blew the spear away. Alexi screamed in frustration.

The helicopter was close to the ship now, maybe thirty feet above the deck. The figure on the landing skids appeared to be saying something to the pilot.

Then Alexi reappeared, swinging something above his head like a lasso. Torquing his body, he flung the object at the helicopter. It took a moment for Marcus to realize what it was: not a spear, but a dinghy anchor on a chain.

Everything seemed to move in slow motion. The passenger leaped, the anchor arched toward the hovering chopper, and Alexi raised his arms in triumph.

Then everything snapped back into real time as the anchor and its chain—with a tremendous screech of shearing metal— was sucked into the rear rotor.

CHAPTER 69
BELL 429 HELICOPTER

Cyclades, Aegean Sea
1:23 AM, June 15th

———

Bruce couldn't explain what had happened. One instant, he'd been adjusting the collective, trying to keep level with the yacht, then something had hit the rear rotor.

He jammed his feet against the anti-torque pedals, but they were useless. Still, he somehow managed to steady the helicopter long enough to look down. He'd moved to one side, maybe fifty yards from the yacht, with nothing between him and the sea.

Letting go of the collective, he gripped the stick of the cyclic in panic. He knew he should cut the throttle, but then he'd crash into the ocean.

"You're going to need to jump!" he shouted to his passenger, then saw that she was already gone. "Bugger me—"

A gust caught the main rotors, and the helicopter twisted.

Below him, the ocean loomed black and cold, nearly indistinguishable from the sky above him.

"No," he gasped. "Not like this—"

The helicopter kept spinning. Slowly, the yacht came back into view. Running lights blazing like a landing strip.

He pushed the cyclic forward, and the chopper moved toward the yacht. There was only one option left. He killed the throttle. The last thing he saw before he died was the teak deck of the yacht racing up toward him.

CHAPTER 70

O utside the Humvee, Aleppo's streets flew by in a dusty blur. The sky was the palest of blues. The sun shone brightly. Marcus was excited. It'd taken nearly a month to coordinate an interview with the SDF resistance leader.

The wub-wub sound of a helicopter's rotors had been the only clue that his world was about to be shattered. With tremendous noise, the blast wave of a barrel bomb launched the Humvee ten feet into the air. In an instant, his eardrums ruptured, two ribs were fractured, and his head was slammed into the steering wheel.

He'd awoken upside down, hanging by his seat belt, blood dripping from a deep gash in his forehead. Everything stank of diesel. A noise, unnaturally high, squealed in his ears.

Somehow, he managed to release the belt—and fell onto the inside roof of the Humvee. It was only then that he saw his partner. Doug was hanging in the seat next to him, half his face blown off.

It took far too long for Marcus to realize that Doug was dead. But when he did, the mental anguish hurt more than any of his injuries. It was his fault. He should have heard the whistle of the bomb. Driven faster. Escaped.

"Marcus?" A woman's voice. "Marcus?"

He opened his eyes. Plush carpet pressed into his cheek. Feminine hands gripped his shoulders. He blinked as Sara came into focus. She looked worried.

"Are you all right? You were mumbling."

"I'm okay," he said, crawling to his knees. Everything came back in a flash: the yacht, Alexi, Sara.

He looked up. The doors and windows to the deck were completely blown out. Through these fresh openings, he could see smoke billowing from the stern of the yacht. "The helicopter crashed?"

Sara nodded. "Who's Doug?"

Doug's broken face flashed again in his mind's eye. "My old partner. Amazing photographer. He was killed…in Syria."

She touched him on the shoulder. "You were there, weren't you. When he died?"

Marcus nodded, unable to speak.

"Was this a PTSD flashback?"

"Yes," he said softly.

Before he could protest, she hugged him.

Warmth filled him. He wrapped his arms around her. Her hair was soft against his cheek. She smelled nice, like lavender soap. He hadn't realized how much he'd missed her.

"I was worried about you," he whispered. "I'm so glad you're okay."

Sara held him a moment longer before releasing him. "We can't stay here."

He nodded. The smoke rising from the stern was now so thick, it blotted out the stars. The ship was burning. The howling wind would spread the fire. They needed to get to the tender quickly.

"Are you hurt?" he asked, suddenly realizing he hadn't checked.

"I'm fine. I fell on top of you."

He looked around. Nearby, the guard was dead, a pool of

blood spreading around him. Ike was crouched next to him, the guard's Glock now in his hand.

"Ike, we need to get to the tender. It's—"

Just as he realized it was on the other side of the fire, there was a shout.

"Goddamn it!" screamed Alexi, stepping from the swirling smoke. Soot caked his face like warpaint, and he held a fresh spear in his hand. "They wrecked my boat!"

At that instant, there was a deep groaning, the sound of tearing steel. The ship pitched starboard twenty degrees. Marcus fell to the carpet of the lounge. When he returned to his knees, a second figure stood on the deck.

Marcus stared. It was impossible. He'd seen her die. Shot in the chest three times. And yet, he could see her clearly now. Fully alive.

Enora Hansen aimed a rifle at Alexi.

Alexi's face was a mask of rage. "Was that your helicopter? You piece of—"

"It is a pleasure to finally meet you, Alexi. Or should I call you Alexander?" said Enora coolly. She turned at Ike. "And you must be Ike. Or should I call you Isaac?"

Alexi looked at Ike. It was subtle, the slightest of nods, but Marcus saw it. Agreement.

And then, with a flash of gunmetal, Ike raised the Glock and fired through the now empty window frames. The bullet hit Enora in the throat.

She staggered and barely held on to her rifle. With her free hand, she clutched at her neck. But even as blood gushed between her fingers, she seemed to straighten. Slowly, the flow slowed to a trickle. She lifted her hand from the wound, and though Marcus could see blood, the skin beneath appeared smooth and unblemished.

Enora's eyes flashed with anger. "Fuck, that really hurt."

Ike began to raise the Glock again.

"I wouldn't do that if I were you." Enora had her rifle leveled at his chest now. "Know what this is?"

Ike shook his head.

"Pneu-Dart X-Caliber Long Range Projector. Used for anesthetizing cattle. Fires a 5CC dart. I don't suppose you know how much propofol it takes to sedate a man?"

Neither Alexi nor Ike spoke.

"A dose of propofol at about two milligrams per kilogram of body weight," Enora continued, "will drop an average-sized adult male in less than five seconds. How much do you weigh, Isaac? I'd say a hundred and eighty pounds? I've loaded the dart with nearly two grams of the stuff. Do you think that would be enough to put you down?"

"What do you want?" said Ike through gritted teeth. "We can pay you—"

"Oh, I don't want money. I have plenty already. It's information that I value. I want to know *how*."

Marcus had no idea what Enora was talking about, but Ike seemed to understand.

"You look like you're doing fine," Ike said.

"For now," said Enora. "But I'm running out of cells, and the effect isn't lasting. Tell me how to make it permanent. My son needs me."

Marcus's mind was racing. What was she talking about? And more importantly, how was she still alive?

He looked between Alexi and Ike. Or was it Alexander and Isaac? All he really knew for certain was that the Greek and the Brit were on different sides, and yet they had just conspired to murder Enora Hansen. What were they trying to protect? Hounds? The Cathar treasure? Something else entirely?

And then it all fell into place, and everything made terrifying sense.

He turned to Sara. "Alexi," he said to her. "I know what —*who* he is."

Before he could finish, something streaked into the lounge, and he was thrown backward off his feet. Hot blood filled his mouth.

He looked down and saw a spear quivering in the center of his chest.

CHAPTER 71
AMELS 188 LUXURY YACHT

Cyclades, Aegean Sea
1:34 AM, June 15th

―――――

Sara screamed as Marcus clutched at the spear, trying to pull it out. Instinctively, she started toward him.

"Stop!" barked the older man, the one Marcus called "Ike" and Enora called "Isaac."

"He's going to die," she protested.

"I'm sorry, Sara, but he knows too much." Ike trained the Glock on her. "Unfortunately, so do you."

He was interrupted by the sharp hiss of depressurizing gas, and a metal dart struck the side of his neck. He clawed at it for a moment, and then his eyes widened and his diaphragm began to spasm. He fell to the floor with a thud, his body twitching.

"Okay, then," Enora said. "I think that's more than enough bloodshed—"

But Alexi was already driving a shoulder into her ribs,

slamming her to the deck. Enora twisted, reaching for her dart gun, but Alexi pressed a dagger to her throat.

Then Sara was hurled from the lounge as a massive explosion tore through the yacht. The back of her head slammed into the teak decking, and everything went black.

———

Sara woke to the smell of diesel and a thick wall of smoke billowing from the stern. It didn't take a PhD in thermodynamics to see that the yacht would soon be consumed by the massive fire. There was no sign of Alexi or Ike. The yacht was listing steeply, and the bodies of Marcus and Enora had slid down to wedge themselves against the starboard rail.

Please be alive, she thought as she scrambled toward Marcus's still form. But hope died when she reached his side. The spear still protruded from his ribs. His eyes were closed, his chest still.

Then she pressed her fingers to his neck, and hope rekindled. There was the faintest of pulses.

Only then did she look at Enora's body. The scientist was clearly dead, and there was no need to check for a pulse. The unnatural twist of her neck made that quite obvious.

Sara's stomach clenched. More death.

Her mother's final hours had been so much easier, peaceful and calm. She had been able to drift away dosed up on midazolam. There had been no blood, no gore, no glazed eyes staring into the night sky.

"Get yourself together," Sara said to herself. "This boat is sinking. You'll find a way off it or you'll die, too."

And yet she couldn't stop thinking about what Marcus had said: *I know what*—who *he is*. Those had been his final words. He had figured out something. Something important.

She jumped as Marcus's body took in a sudden gasp. Hope thrilled within her until she realized she recognized the sound. It was the same noise Amy had made, an agonal breath. That meant he was virtually brain-dead.

She pressed her fingers to her forehead, trying to think. Maybe there was still a way to save him. He'd died once already, hadn't he? She was certain of it.

And then there was Enora. Just moments earlier, she had recovered entirely from that gunshot wound. Like the hounds, she had some special way of healing. The Lazarus Factor, as Frank had called it. Tissue regeneration, if she wanted to be perfectly accurate.

This wasn't the first time Sara had seen Enora shot, for that matter. And the first time, there had been no question the woman was dead.

Which means Enora was literally brought back from the dead. Just like Marcus.

The yacht shuddered as something deep within it gave way.

The implications unspooled in Sara's brain. Enora was no hound, but from what she had said, it seemed she had done something to herself to give herself the same healing ability. Had the same thing been done to Marcus? Perhaps by that guy Ike? If so, why? And what?

With Enora, it was probably some complicated pharmaceutical method. But that didn't make sense in Ike's case. Marcus had said Ike had found him at the bottom of the cliff, and that he'd helped him.

Which meant there might be an…easier way. Could that be what Frank had wanted to keep secret? What he'd wanted so much to protect? Was the Cathar treasure actually a method—the *protocol*, for rapid tissue regeneration?

Maybe that was it? Ike knew how to heal people who'd been mortally wounded. He'd used it to save Marcus.

She looked for Ike, but there was no sign of him. Perhaps he'd gone overboard. Or perhaps he was off looking for a way off this burning ship.

If someone was going to save Marcus, it would have to be her.

She turned her gaze to the spear protruding from Marcus's chest. If Marcus had the hounds' healing ability, then the spear would be preventing the wound from closing. If he didn't...

If he didn't, it was already too late.

The boat was listing heavily, but Sara managed to position herself so that she straddled Marcus's body. She grasped the shaft of the spear and pulled, but her fingers slipped on the blood-slick wood.

Below her, Marcus gasped, his back arching. Another agonal breath. There wasn't much time.

She pulled off her shirt and used it to wipe the blood away. This time, when she pulled, the spear came out with a wet, sucking noise. Through the torn fabric of Marcus's shirt, she could see the wound clearly. She stared at it, waiting, willing it to close up. Ten seconds. Twenty.

Enora and the hound had both healed almost instantly.

A minute passed. Nothing was happening. Whatever healing ability Marcus had once had, it wasn't working now.

Then she remembered something Enora had said: *I'm running out of cells, and the effect isn't lasting.*

The woman had literally stormed Alexi's yacht to find out why.

An idea began to coalesce in the back of Sara's mind. When she'd analyzed the DNA of the hound, she had found very moderately increased heterozygosity. She'd assumed it was normal variation. But...what if it wasn't?

She studied Enora's body now. The woman's eyes were glazed with death. Her limbs limp. And her head...Sara gagged, tasting bile. Alexi had nearly severed it. Now it lay twisted at an odd angle in a deep pool of blood.

Blood.

That was it. The increased heterozygosity she'd seen in the

hound genome. If Frank had sequenced the hound's blood, and if the blood was contaminated with a small amount of another's, it would appear that he had more genetic variation than expected.

Quickly, Sara dipped her fingers into Enora's blood, then wiped it on Marcus's wound.

She waited, holding her breath.

Marcus's body spasmed. Another agonal breath.

The wound in his chest still bled.

Frantically, Sara scooped up more of Enora's blood.

CHAPTER 72
AMELS 188 LUXURY YACHT

Cyclades, Aegean Sea
1:58 AM, June 15th

———

Reality slowly filtered into Marcus's consciousness. The hard deck under his back, the acrid smell of burning fuel. And most of all, the intense pain in the center of his chest.

A woman's voice shouted in his ear. "Please wake up!"

He opened his eyes.

Sara knelt over him, her face illuminated by flames.

"Oh, my God," she said, grabbing his shoulders, tears streaming down her cheeks. "Oh, my God. It worked—"

"What?" gasped Marcus. His throat was a desert. Every one of his muscles felt like it had been beaten with a club. "Where am I?"

Sara glanced over her shoulder at the fire. "Can you move?"

"I don't think so," said Marcus, but Sara was already standing, pulling at a white fiberglass box.

"There's a life raft here."

The boat shuddered beneath him. Marcus could feel the heat of the fire against the side of his face. He understood now why she hadn't listened to his response. It was move or die.

Somehow, his muscles barely responding, he managed to push himself up.

Sara was struggling with the fiberglass life raft case. "I can't open it," she said.

"Just throw it in the sea."

"What?"

"They work hydrostatically. Water will start inflation."

He wanted to help, but he could barely sit up. His arms and legs felt like they weighed a hundred pounds each. It took every bit of his willpower just to keep from collapsing back to the deck.

Sara managed to tip the case over the side. He couldn't see it hit the water, but he heard the splash. They wouldn't have much time before the raft drifted away. He pulled himself forward on his hands and knees. Somehow, he was going to have to climb over the railing.

"You first," he gasped.

Sara stared, aghast. "No, you can barely move. I'll be right after you."

Before he could protest, she grabbed him, reaching under his armpits and lifting him up so that his back rested against the teak rail. If he could have struggled against her, he would have, but his muscles were like rubber bands.

"What is wrong with me?" he said.

"You were dead," Sara replied matter-of-factly, as if that explained everything.

He looked over the side. Below him, the yellow life raft bobbed. All they had to do was get on board, and they'd be safe.

Sara lifted him higher, her face only inches from his.

Flames glittered in her blue eyes.

He kissed her.

His arms and legs might be next to useless, but his lips worked just fine.

After an instant of hesitation, her fingers twined in his hair, and she kissed him back.

This was why he'd agreed to Ike's plan. Why he'd risked imprisonment and Alexi's wrath. *Sara*. She was the perfect combination: brilliant and beautiful.

Suddenly, she stopped kissing him. He thought she was angry, but then her eyes sparkled with a mischievous smile.

"Try to swim, okay?"

She pushed him over the side.

Marcus flopped ungracefully into the sea. For a long moment he drifted, submerged. Above him, through the waves, he could see the outline of the yacht silhouetted by flames. Then he tried to kick, to get to the surface, but the nerves in his legs refused to listen to his brain. He was going to drown.

A splash from above was followed by a shimmering stream of bubbles. Sara was diving toward him. She grabbed his arm and pulled him up.

He gasped as his head broke the waves. All he could do was float and try to keep his chest full of air as Sara pulled him along.

"I'm going to climb on board first, then I'll drag you in," she said, breathing hard. He realized they'd reached the raft. "Can you hold on to the side?" She pushed his hand against a bit of nylon netting.

With a grunt, she climbed aboard. Still limp, Marcus watched her. She looked absolutely exhausted, soaking wet, her hair plastered to her face. She was reaching for him when, in a blinding flash of light, the yacht exploded.

Marcus's grip was torn from the raft as the sea twisted into a churning maelstrom.

CHAPTER 73
SURVITEC INFLATABLE
LIFE RAFT

Cyclades, Aegean Sea
4:43 AM, June 15th

————

S ometime near dawn, the Meltemi winds had died. Now the Aegean was becalmed, and only the sound of water lapping against the floor of the life raft disturbed the silence.

Sara lay on her back, feeling the ocean undulate beneath her. Her throat ached, but not from thirst. She'd called Marcus's name for hours after the explosion—after he'd disappeared. Now a desolate rage filled her. They had been so close to escape. She'd been bracing herself to pull him aboard when the yacht detonated. The blast wave had nearly flipped the raft, and then he was gone.

She didn't want to accept it, but she was going to have to. Marcus was dead—permanently, this time. No amount of Enora's blood could save him from the depths of the sea.

She drew in a long, shaky breath, trying not to cry.

He'd been with her from the beginning. He'd helped her

escape in Boston, had fought to free her in London, and had risked everything to come for her on Alexi's yacht. He'd saved her life. And she'd failed him.

It's not fair. She slammed her fist onto the bottom of the life raft. Then she did it again and again, until she was too tired to lift her arm.

She must have fallen asleep, because the next thing she knew, she was waking to sun on her face and the distant sound of a motor. Crawling to her knees, she peered through the bright orange canopy that covered the raft. Above her, an airplane flew across a clear Mediterranean sky.

Frantically, she waved her arms. The plane banked, swinging toward her. It waggled its wings.

Sara dropped back into the raft. They'd seen her. She was going to be rescued.

Though she wasn't sure if it mattered anymore.

————

The roar of the white and blue helicopter was nearly deafening as it hovered over the life raft. There was a splash, and a search-and-rescue diver swam toward her.

"*Ya sas!*" he shouted in Greek. "*Eísai kalá?*"

"English?"

The diver paused, treading water, before speaking. "Injured?"

"I'm okay," said Sara before asking the question she'd been dreading. "Did you find my friend? His name is Marcus."

The diver looked confused. "You get in basket?"

"Marcus? Did you pick up a man named Marcus?" Sara yelled, trying to be heard over the thundering noise of the rotors.

"No Marcus," said the rescue diver, shaking his head.

"You get in basket, okay?" He pointed to a stretcher-like cage swinging down from the helicopter.

Sara nodded, her heart aching. She still hoped that somehow, Marcus had been picked up by some other vessel.

"Can you swim?" the diver asked.

Sara nodded before slipping into the sea. The spray from the downwash was blinding, but with the diver's help, she was able to climb into the cage. The diver signaled to the chopper, and she was hoisted into the air.

Twenty seconds later, she was pulled on board, and a heavy wool blanket was wrapped around her bare shoulders. The hoist operator handed her an aviation headset.

"Who are you?" he asked. His English was better than the diver's.

"Sara Morin."

"You were on the *Krateros*?"

"Yes," said Sara, guessing that must be the name of Alexi's yacht. "Do you know if there are any other survivors? My friend and I got separated."

The officer looked down. "I'm sorry. We search all day. Only you."

CHAPTER 74
SALAMIS NAVAL BASE

Cape Arapis, Greece
6:28 PM, June 15th

———

t was a standard holding cell. A metal door, a narrow cot bolted to the wall, and a single barred window. There was no toilet, but the Greek soldiers had explained that if she needed to pee, all she had to do was shout, and they'd take her to a bathroom down the hall.

They'd locked her up pretty much as soon as she'd arrived. She'd explained that she was a US citizen and wanted to speak with the consulate, but they said nothing would happen until the morning. On the plus side, they'd fed her well: chicken and spinach casserole, fresh bread, salad, even a piece of baklava.

She'd gobbled it down and paced around a bit before simply standing by the window and looking out. The view wasn't much—mostly bland concrete dockyard—but she could see soldiers moving about, and if she stood on her tiptoes, she could make out a tiny sliver of the sea.

It was something to do to pass the time, to keep her mind off what had happened the night before. Or at least try to. It was nearly impossible not to think about the helicopter crash, the yacht exploding, Marcus's death...

With a loud creak, the door opened behind her. She spun around. A man stood in the entrance. A dark silhouette. Not a guard. A gray suit with an ivory silk cravat. A goatee twitched jauntily.

"Hello, Ms. Morin."

She'd already guessed who he was, but the posh accent confirmed it. "Frank?" This was becoming a habit. First the hound. Then Marcus. Then Enora. Now Frank. "You're one of them, too?"

"It's a bit more complicated than that."

"All right," she said slowly, keeping her distance. "What do you want?"

"First, I need to explain a few things. Then, if you'll agree to keep quiet, I will help you get out of here. I'll fly you back to Boston. I'll get the police to drop their investigation. You can go back to working at Harvard. I can make everything the way it was before."

Sara stared. He was offering to help her, to get her home. And yet she found that his words enraged her. He could never take things back to the way they were before. People had *died*. Amy. The entire Schröder lab. Marcus. Especially Marcus.

Frank's voice was silky smooth. "Sara, let me help you."

Something within her snapped. She was tired of being kept in the dark. She took a step toward him. "I think if you came here to speak with me personally, to offer safety and a way out, it's because you need my help. You *need* me to leave with you. So I'm going to ask you some questions. And if you answer them to *my* satisfaction, then I'll consider your offer."

All the convivial benevolence drained from Frank's face.

His eyes turned flinty, his lips thinned. He opened his mouth to speak, but she cut him off.

"You've been able to heal all along? Like the hound?"

"Yes."

Sara had a million questions, but she decided to keep it simple. Start at the beginning and work from there. "Then why were you wearing body armor when you saved me outside of Enora's mansion?"

"Getting shot is exceptionally painful."

"And this is why Alexi shot you?"

Frank nodded. "He was a sadistic fuck, and it was an easy way to incapacitate me."

That Frank was actually answering her questions reinforced Sara's theory that it was she who held the power. "Why did Actaeon send a hound to kill me?"

Frank didn't answer.

"You don't know?"

"They were worried you might reveal something they wanted kept secret."

"The origin of the Lazarus Factor?"

Frank nodded.

"What is Actaeon?"

"Actaeon is a very old organization. Similar to the Rosicrucians, they have the Lazarus Factor. But unlike us, they abused the ability to gain power and influence. They tried to conquer the world. When our order was first founded, we fought Actaeon. Many died, but in the end, we defeated them."

This jogged a memory from the meeting in Freemasons' Hall. "This was why your colleague said that the last hound died centuries ago?"

"Exactly," said Frank. "After Actaeon was defeated, they simply disappeared. No more hounds, no more fighting."

"So if you thought Actaeon wasn't a threat, then why didn't you share the Lazarus Factor with the world? It's an enormous medical breakthrough. Think of how many people could have been saved over the centuries. I thought you were supposed to be like Prometheus giving fire to mankind."

Frank answered slowly, and Sara sensed he was choosing his words carefully. "We worry that governments and corporations will misuse it, much like Actaeon did. If it fell into the wrong hands, the results would be catastrophic. Can you imagine an army consisting entirely of hounds?"

Sara had to admit this made sense. An army of hounds sounded like a terrible idea. But she wasn't about to let Frank off so easily. "So you're not really like Prometheus, then. Instead of giving fire to the people, you withhold it."

Frank laughed, his eyes flashing with mirth. "I'm not sure how familiar you are with the story of Prometheus, but after he stole fire for mankind, the gods exacted revenge. They gave Pandora a box of evils. The myth supports a balanced approach of sharing neither too much nor too little."

Sara was beginning to understand Frank's role better. He and the Rosicrucians had acted as a sort of check on Actaeon. But she still didn't understand the strange journey he had sent her on. Her and Marcus.

"What was the point of the note and the GPS coordinates?" she asked. "Why send us to Ike?"

She had deduced that must have been the purpose of the electronics in the box she and Marcus had dug up. They must have been there solely to send a signal to Ike that someone had found it.

"There was..." Frank paused. "There was a bit of a falling-out between Ike and the rest of the order. I made the box so that in an emergency, he could be found."

"Why all the codes, the hand grenade, the treasure hidden in Montségur?"

"I was trying to reduce the chance that Acteon found him. Imagine that Alexi thought something important was in my desk. Do you think he would have taken the time to work out the code? No, he'd have bashed it open—"

"And blown up the note," said Sara putting it together.

"And, to open the lockbox, you needed to know something about math and science. Alexi wouldn't have figured that out, either."

This made a lot of sense, but it didn't explain the big picture. "Why was Ike so important?"

Frank's expression shaded, and he looked away. "Ike knew how the Lazarus Factor worked."

"I don't understand."

"There was a compound that gave people the Lazarus Factor. Ike stole it from Alexi. Studied it. Used it, too. Eventually, there was none left. We've been trying to work out how to recreate it, but without any luck. But Ike, I think he truly understood it."

"You were hoping I'd figure it out. That I'd find out what Ike already knew."

Frank nodded. "This was why Actaeon was so eager to kill you. They don't want that information to get out."

"Because then anyone could have access to the Lazarus Factor."

"Exactly."

"So all these people died for nothing. Amy, Enora, Marcus." Sara began to laugh—not a happy sound, but more like an ironic cackle. "Because you do realize there was never enough information to reverse-engineer the Lazarus Factor, right? My code can infer only a single ancestral genome. There's no way to tell how it does the wound healing."

"What if you compared it to other human genomes?"

"I'd find thousands of differences. There'd be no way to identify which are responsible for the Lazarus Factor. You never had anything to worry about."

"But Enora figured it out."

For a moment, Sara thought he had a point, but then she

remembered what Enora had said on the yacht. "No, she didn't. She said her approach wasn't lasting. That was why she came to talk to Alexi."

Frank nodded. "At least Alexi is dead."

As if that was any solace. Her friends were all dead.

"So what now?" she asked.

"I can take you home. You'll just need to go along with our cover story to explain why you disappeared for a week: after the shooting, you had a mental break, and you don't remember anything until you were found floating in the Mediterranean."

"No," said Sara quickly. "I can't agree to that."

Frank's eyes narrowed. "You can't?"

"That would ruin my career. No one will hire me if they think I'm mentally unstable."

"I thought your generation was supposed to be more understanding of—"

Sara cut him off. "Your generation is still in charge. They still make the hiring decisions." She thought for a moment. "Could you say I was abducted? Maybe by an obsessed undergraduate?"

Frank grinned. "Absolutely."

CHAPTER 75
HARVARD UNIVERSITY

Cambridge, Massachusetts
11:23 AM, June 18th

———

All things considered, it could have been worse, Topher thought. The blood spatter was painted over, and the broken windows would be replaced by the end of the week. While the shooter had killed two of his graduate students, neither of them was actually crucial to the day-to-day functioning of his lab. Really terrible for them and their families, of course—but for him, everything was going to be fine.

In fact, while he would never admit it out loud, the death of Walter Schröder was turning out to be a wonderful boon. Now he had virtually no competition when it came to studying the genetics of East Asian and Oceanic human populations.

He leaned back in his chair and laced his fingers behind his head. There really was a silver lining to everything.

A knock sounded on his open office door, and he jumped.

It was Sara. He almost started to chastise her for disturbing him when he remembered she'd made an appointment to meet him.

"Dr. Fitzpatrick, are you free to chat now?"

"Yes, yes," he said, smiling.

Sara had returned only a few days before after being picked up floating in the Aegean. Everyone had been surprisingly quiet about her disappearance, HIPAA regulations and all that, but he understood she'd been abducted by some crazy undergrad. Probably turned the poor guy down too many times. Pretty girls like her could be so cruel.

"I was hoping to speak with you about the *Homo floresiensis* publication."

"Oh, right," said Topher. In the chaos after the shooting, he'd entirely forgotten about the discovery. Not that there'd been much to do. "I'm sorry, but I must have forgotten to tell you. We got scooped. The Schröder Lab posted a preprint to bioRxiv, and *Nature* has asked us to resubmit to a lower-tier journal. There's no hurry."

He'd expected her to tear up, or maybe even cry a little, but her expression remained surprisingly stoic. Which was frustrating. He particularly enjoyed this part of the job. Being the source of a woman's emotional distress was always a major turn-on.

Instead, Sara spoke calmly. "Actually, I believe the preprint has been retracted. The authors noted fundamental errors in the research."

"It's been withdrawn?" said Topher, leaning forward. "Are you certain?"

"I just checked this morning," said Sara smoothly.

"Let me call the editor at *Nature*."

"Wait," said Sara quickly. "There's more."

Topher frowned.

"After reading the retraction," she continued, "I took a look at my own work. I think there's also a bug in my code.

Unfortunately, the genome I found appears to be a technical artifact."

"You can't be serious!"

He shook his head. This could have been a *complete* disaster. He'd have had to speak to the editors at *Nature*, explain that there'd been a phenomenal screwup. If the work had been published, he would have had to issue a retraction. It would have hurt his reputation with the premier scientific journal.

It took all his willpower not to leap over his desk and throttle her.

CHAPTER 76
1369 COFFEE HOUSE

Cambridge, Massachusetts
1:03 PM, June 18th

———

S ameer sat at a small table in the back, his laptop open, a tall iced latte ready to drink. He closed his eyes for a moment, enjoying the bustle and hum of the café, the people coming and going, the earthy scent of the coffee, the chatter of the baristas as they took orders. It was so relaxed and friendly, the antithesis of the sterile lab environment.

Opening his eyes, he logged into LinkedIn and took a long sip of his latte. Since he'd been laid off two days earlier, he really should be trying to cut his expenses, but the drink was an indulgence.

The entire layoff experience had been legitimately traumatizing. Aeter Pharmaceuticals had dissolved overnight, and no one seemed to know why. They'd simply been hustled into one of the big conference rooms and told to pack up their desks. No explanation given. Now his stock options were worthless, and he was living on the three grand he had in his savings account.

He sighed and took another sip of the latte. He needed to begin filling out unemployment paperwork, but he wasn't ready for the finality of that. Instead, he scanned job postings on LinkedIn, searching for new lab tech positions.

Lab Associate, Animal Husbandry.
In charge of maintaining a large mouse colony —

Boring. He moved to the next one.

Protein Purification Technician.
Primary responsibilities include running an E. coli bioreactor —

Sameer nearly gagged on the latte. Taking that job would be like signing up for a daily bath of human waste.

Lab Manager, Harvard University.
The laboratory of Topher Fitzpatrick is looking to hire an experienced technician to manage their extensive collection of DNA samples. Tasks will include DNA extraction, purifi-cation, PCR, next-gen library construction, laboratory maintenance, training and mentoring graduate and under-graduate students. Looking for a detail-oriented and professional —

Sameer cracked his knuckles. This was exactly the type of job he wanted. Simple protocols, minimal responsibilities, and excellent benefits. Plus, everyone knew that working at Harvard meant you could take classes for free.

Of course, it wouldn't nearly pay as well as Aeter had, but

he could one hundred percent live with that. He'd enjoyed spending the last couple of evenings at home with Jake. Turned out that not only was mixing cocktails at home cheaper, but if Jake had more than two, it didn't take much to convince him to dance around the apartment in his underwear.

CHAPTER 77
DAVIS SQUARE

Cambridge, Massachusetts
8:14 PM, June 18th

————

Sara slowly climbed the stairs to her apartment, weighed down by a messenger bag full of groceries. On the way home from the lab, she'd picked up the ingredients for pasta carbonara, along with garlic bread and some salad greens. She'd also impulse-purchased a bottle of wine and a pint of Ben & Jerry's ice cream.

On the third-floor landing, she fished her keys from her pocket and opened the door to her apartment. She stood in the doorway for a moment, enjoying the cool AC and the familiar scent of her place. After everything that had happened, it didn't seem quite real to be home.

Still, it hardly compared to her first night back. She'd landed at Logan Airport at three AM after a thirteen-hour redeye from Greece. The sense of relief she'd felt upon entering her apartment had been simply overwhelming.

She'd just collapsed on the couch and cried. Eventually, she'd pulled herself up, taken a gloriously hot shower, eaten all the emergency chocolate, and finally crawled into her own bed to sleep for what felt like the first time in weeks.

This evening, she managed to hold it together. She crossed to the kitchen and set the oven to four hundred. As she began to fill a pot of water, she found herself brimming with resolve. She'd kept her commitments to Frank. Now it was time to honor the rest of her commitments. The ones she'd made to Amy, to Enora, and especially to Marcus.

With the pot heating on her stove, she sat down with her laptop and opened a terminal window. She was ready to start coding, but as she stared at the blinking cursor, she felt suddenly overwhelmed. There were so many unanswered questions, so many loose ends. It seemed impossible to determine where to begin.

She closed her eyes and thought for a long moment. What she needed to do, she decided, was to clearly specify the question. She got a pen and notebook from her bag, flipped to a blank page, and began to write.

What I don't know:

- *How (biologically) do hounds heal themselves?*
- *Where do Enora's ancient genomes fit into the picture?*

She ran her finger under the first line: *How (biologically) do hounds heal themselves?*

She had a theory about this now. The increased heterozygosity she'd observed in the blood was due to contamination. She'd been able to save Marcus because she'd mixed Enora's blood with his. It was most likely this contaminating blood that provided the healing properties...which meant that if she could infer the sequence of the contaminating genome, she might be able to learn something. In theory, she could phase haplotypes and extract the new sequence, but there wasn't enough of the contaminating DNA.

She swore under her breath. Try as she might, she couldn't see a clear path forward. But even as she faltered, an idea came to her: maybe there was a different way to think about the problem. If she first defined a baseline of understanding, then maybe she could think of a way to push beyond it.

Picking up the pen again, she began to write.

What I know for certain:

- *There are people who can heal from wounds that should kill them*
- *"Contamination" in their blood can revive people who are dead (e.g., Marcus & Enora)*
- *They appear to have otherwise normal human genomes (hounds are not hybrids)*
- *Enora's genomes are from modern humans from the Middle East (likely Jewish priestly ancestry)*
- *My genomic artifacts method is important to all of this...*

Sara was studying the list when she realized the soothing bubbling in the background was the pasta water boiling. She hopped up and dumped in the noodles, then put the garlic bread into the oven.

Sitting down again, she looked over the bullet points. There were so many directions she could go. She could check if there were any unusual DNA insertions or deletions, try mapping ancestry to individual regions of Enora's genomes, or simply research wound healing more thoroughly. Any of these approaches might provide a critical insight.

She rubbed her face. It was just so hard to decide where to begin.

Start with a tractable problem.

That was what Topher was always saying in lab meetings. When spoken with his usual undisguised condescension, it was the last thing she wanted to hear, but right now, it was good advice.

She jumped as her doorbell rang, klaxon-like in her quiet apartment. She wasn't expecting anyone.

Do Jehovah's Witnesses come by at night? she wondered for a moment. *No, it's probably a delivery guy who inadvertently pressed the button for the wrong apartment. Best to just ignore it.*

The bell rang again.

Then a third time.

Crap. She was going to have to answer it.

She left her apartment and hurried downstairs, one half of her brain thinking about how to analyze the data, the other half preparing to tell any potential Jehovah's Witnesses that she firmly believed in evolution.

She pulled open the door to the building. It was dark out, later than she'd realized, and a man stood on the steps. He was dressed in dark jeans with a hoodie pulled over his head. Not a Jehovah's Witness. Must be a delivery driver.

"I didn't order—" But before she could finish, he'd pushed past her and into the building.

Instantly, a hot rush of adrenaline sent her flight-or-fight response into overdrive. Was Frank wrong about Actaeon? Was this another hound sent to kill her? She spun, and before the man could turn to face her, she pushed him hard in the back. He stumbled, then fell awkwardly. His head smacked against the stairs with an audible thunk.

Sara didn't hesitate.

"Help!" she shouted. "Help!"

For what seemed like ages, but was probably only seconds, she was alone with the stranger in darkness. Then her neighbor's door popped open, and light flooded into the hall. They both stared at the man at the bottom of the stairs, his face still hidden under the hoodie.

"What the hell—" Sara began, but then the intruder spoke.

"Sara, it's me."

CHAPTER 78
DAVIS SQUARE

Cambridge, Massachusetts
8:22 PM, June 18th

———

Marcus had expected Sara to be surprised to see him, but he hadn't anticipated being pushed headfirst into a flight of stairs. But now, as she looked at him, her expression was pretty much everything he'd hoped for: first confusion, then dawning recognition, and last, pure excitement.

"*Marcus?*"

Okay, maybe a little anger, too.

"You know this man?" asked a beefy guy standing next to Sara. Marcus guessed this was a neighbor.

Sara ignored him. "How did you? I saw you—"

Marcus grinned even as he rubbed his forehead. "Maybe we can talk somewhere more private. It's a long story."

Sara stared at him like he was some sort of alien creature.

"I can call the police," the neighbor said.

"No," said Sara quickly. "That won't be necessary."

"Are you sure?"

"I didn't recognize him in the dark—he's a friend."

Her neighbor's expression suggested that it wouldn't take more than a hint for him to haul Marcus onto the street.

Fortunately, Sara spoke again. "Marcus, why don't you come up?"

As he stood, Sara slipped past him and started up the stairs. Feeling a little woozy, he followed along behind.

As they neared the third floor, Marcus noticed an acrid smell. "Is something burning?"

He didn't get a chance to finish as Sara swore loudly, then raced through an open apartment door. He hurried after her into total chaos. A thick haze filled the air, and water bubbled and steamed all over a stovetop. Sara jerked open the oven door, and a dense cloud of smoke poured out. Almost instantly, the smoke alarm went off.

Sara swore louder.

"I got the alarm," Marcus shouted over the beeping.

The smoke alarm was on the ceiling, out of reach. He grabbed a notebook off the kitchen table and used it to fan the air under it. Sara ran around opening windows. After what seemed like ages, the alarm stopped.

From behind him, he heard Sara's voice. "It's really you?"

He turned around. Sara looked exactly as he remembered: brown hair, blue eyes, the usual intense expression. The only difference now was that she was awkwardly holding two pieces of charred garlic bread.

Marcus grinned. "It's really me."

"I thought you were dead—" Her voice cracked. Tears shone in her eyes. Marcus had to resist giving her a hug.

"Fortunately, you were wrong." He pointed at the burned bread. "You can put those down if you like. I don't think they're edible."

"Right," said Sara, placing the bread on the countertop. Then she looked him over again. "But how did you survive?

You were in the water when the yacht blew up. You couldn't swim."

"Honestly, it was pure luck. After the explosion, I somehow ended up on the surface. And remember Alexi's rack of spears? It popped up next to me. I was able to climb onto it."

"But you were in the middle of the ocean. Miles out to sea. The Greek navy said there were no survivors."

"A Syrian refugee boat found me in the morning. They took me to Rhodes."

"Okay...but how did you get *here*?"

Now that was a good question. Marcus pulled a piece of paper from his pocket. "Recognize this?"

Sara's expression said that she didn't. Grinning like an idiot, Marcus began to read from it. "No longer mourn for me when I am dead, then you shall hear the surly sullen bell—"

Sara's eyes flashed. "You have Frank's note!"

"Yup. It's been in my pocket ever since that day on the cliff. A little worse for wear thanks to a dip in the ocean, but still legible." He handed Sara the tattered piece of paper. "Did you know there's exactly one ATM in Rhodes that accepts bitcoin?"

Sara studied the note before looking back at him. "Why didn't you go to the authorities? The US consulate?"

"I didn't want to alert Actaeon."

"Marcus..." Sara laughed. "It would have been fine. Alexi's dead. I spoke to Frank. Yeah, he's alive. Apparently, he also has the Lazarus Factor."

"Wow. So he was part of Actaeon, too?"

"I don't think so. I'm not entirely sure how it all works." Sara gestured to the notebook he was holding. "Before you scared the crap out of me by ringing my doorbell in the middle of the night, I was trying to figure some stuff out. Here, let me show you."

She took the notebook from him, flipped to a page, then handed it back.

Marcus scanned the page, feeling more and more bewildered. "Uh, Sara? Why is my name listed under 'people brought back from the dead'?"

Sara's eyes widened. "You don't remember?"

"Remember what?"

"Do you know why you were unable to swim?"

"I think something hit me on the head."

"Marcus," said Sara slowly. "You're not going to believe this."

Then she proceeded to tell him the most insane story he'd ever heard. When she'd finished, he stared dumbly.

"So you pulled a spear from my chest and smeared blood on the wound, and that healed me?"

"Yes."

What Sara was telling him seemed crazy. But he knew it was possible. He'd seen the hound survive being stabbed in the chest. He'd seen Enora Hansen alive and well. And apparently Frank was alive, too.

"Lift up your shirt," said Sara. "You should have a scar just below your ribs."

Marcus pulled up his shirt. His chest and stomach looked normal. "I don't see anything."

"Let me look," said Sara.

She stepped close. He held his breath as she traced a finger along the skin of his abdomen.

"There," she said. "I think that's it."

He checked the spot. Sure enough, there was a scar just under his sternum so thin and well healed that he hadn't noticed it.

For a long moment, Marcus just stared. Then at last, he spoke. "Does this mean I'm one of *them* now?"

"Maybe? I honestly don't know," said Sara. "But I don't think so. Like I said, you needed Enora's blood to heal. And

Enora said the effects of whatever she did were temporary. So it's probably worn off by now."

There was only one way to check. Before Sara could stop him, he picked up a paring knife from beside the sink, gritted his teeth, and drew it across the meat of his thumb.

Sara stood beside him. Together they watched blood drip onto her countertop. Ten, twenty, thirty seconds. There was no sign of immediate healing.

"I guess I'm normal now," he said.

"You didn't get very much blood from Enora. And you didn't need to cut yourself. I could have told you that you still have a bump on your forehead from when I pushed you into the stairs."

Marcus shook his head, then sat down at Sara's kitchen table. "So what now?"

"Hang on." Sara hurried from the room, and when she returned, she had a box of bandaids. "For your finger," she said. "As for what now...I think we need to tell Frank about you."

"Really?"

"I know," said Sara, joining him at the table. "I don't really trust him, either, but he made things right for me. I'm sure he'll help you when he learns you're alive..." She trailed off and her eyes filled with tears. "It was awful, Marcus. I thought I'd lost you."

He touched her hand gently. "I'm sorry."

"It's okay," she said, looking up. Her eyes glistened, but her expression was fierce. "I'm just glad you're here now."

For a long moment, they looked at one another as if afraid of ever looking away again.

Then Sara suddenly jumped up from her chair. For a split second, Marcus thought something bad had happened, but then he saw that the water on the stove was boiling.

"Noodles are done," she called over her shoulder. "Are you hungry?"

"Downright starving. The meal on the plane was some sort of meat patty with mushroom sauce." Marcus stood. "Would you like any help?"

Sara passed him a chef's knife and a whole head of garlic. "Dice this."

"Sure. How much?"

"Six or seven cloves' worth." She grinned. "I like a lot of garlic."

As Marcus worked on the garlic, Sara filled him in on everything else that had happened: her conversation with Frank, the retraction of her article, her cover story about having been abducted. "There's still a lot I don't under-stand," she explained as she whisked eggs. "Like...why did they try to have me killed? What was so threatening about my research that Actaeon was willing to reveal that they still had hounds?" She paused to look at him. "On Alexi's yacht, right before you...almost died...you said something. You said you knew who Alexi was. Do you remember that?"

This seemed vaguely familiar, but try as he might, Marcus couldn't dredge up the memory. "I recall arriving with Ike. I had to jump from the tender to the stern. I hurt my foot. Then...nothing."

"Gah," said Sara, shaking her head. "You sounded as if you'd worked out something important."

Marcus finished chopping the garlic. As Sara used tongs to move pasta to a sauté pan, he returned to his chair, bringing with him a glass and a bottle of wine.

"Not to state the obvious," he said as he watched Sara cook, "but maybe there was a genome they didn't want you to find."

"I've thought that, too. But here's what doesn't make any sense: let's say I didn't know about Frank and Actaeon, and I uncover this genome. How would I know it confers a miracu-lous wound-healing ability?"

"You were able to deduce that the *Homo floresiensis* genome was associated with height-related genes, right?"

Sara shook her head. "In that case, I had a hypothesis, and I knew to look for height-related genes. But if I simply characterized a new ancient genome, I wouldn't know to look for wound-healing genes. Even if I did a gene pathway analysis on it and discovered an enrichment in wound-healing genes, I still wouldn't know how *well* the wound-healing worked. Without a functional study—knocking out a gene in a mouse, for example—it would be nothing more than an interesting association."

Marcus took a sip of wine as he mulled this over. "I see what you're saying. There's a limit to what information you can extract from the DNA alone."

"Exactly."

"So there must have been some other characteristic of the genome they were afraid you'd uncover. Like its age or something?" Marcus was just spitballing at this point. "I mean, we know the hounds have been around for a long time. Frank said they'd disappeared for centuries."

Sara handed him a plate of pasta and sat down next to him. Marcus took a bite of the pasta. It was absolutely delicious, rich, garlicky, and dusted with fresh Parmesan.

"You like it?" asked Sara hopefully.

"It's amazing. Thank you." Marcus ate a few more bites before continuing with the conversation. "So what do you know about the hound's genome?"

Sara's eyes flashed with excitement. "Modern human. East Asian ancestry, no evidence of hybridization. The only weird thing is a very slight increase in heterozygosity."

Marcus vaguely recalled her telling him this. "Remind me again what that means."

"Remember how Frank thought the hounds might be hybrids? Well, I checked that genetically. A hybrid would have two completely different sets of chromosomes, which would mean many more places for them to differ. More places that differ means more heterozygosity."

"I remember now. You didn't think it was a big deal."

Sara poured them both more wine. "It was only a very slight increase in heterozygosity. I thought it was normal variation. But when you were dying on the yacht, I realized it was real. That was how I figured out that Enora's blood was what I needed to help you heal. The problem is that the contamination is really low, so I can't reconstruct the contaminating genome."

"How about Enora's genomes?" said Marcus.

"They appear to be quite old. Not Neanderthal or anything like that, they're modern human. Middle Eastern ancestry, most likely part of the Jewish diaspora."

"They're part of the Jewish diaspora? How do you know?"

"Some of them have the Cohen Modal Haplotype on the Y-chromosome."

Now this sounded interesting. "What's the Cohen Modal Haplotype?"

"It's a Y-chromosome sequence of DNA only found in some Jewish populations. Alexi went crazy when I told him about it."

Marcus put down his glass. It was all coming together. The tribe of Levi. The Cohanim. The first high priest of the Israelites. This had to be it. The missing piece of the puzzle.

"Do you know who Aaron is?" he asked. He didn't wait for Sara's answer. "He's a figure from the Old Testament, the older brother of Moses. He was the leader of the tribe of Levi, which in turn became the Cohanim, the Jewish priestly class. Enora's samples are from ancient priests." An absolutely crazy idea occurred to him. "Google the Cave of the Patriarchs."

"The what?"

"The Cave of the Patriarchs." Marcus grabbed her laptop

and swung it around, then quickly typed "Cave of the Patri-archs" into Google.

Results filled the screen. A picture of a blocky stone temple. A link to a Wikipedia entry. Information about Abraham and Rebecca.

"Whoa," said Sara leaning over his shoulder. "Look at that." She pointed to a news headline: "Caretaker Murdered in the Cave of the Patriarchs." "This is from three weeks ago."

Marcus's mind was racing a hundred miles an hour as everything finally began to make sense.

"Sara," he said slowly, "the Cave of the Patriarchs is one of the holiest sites in Israel. It holds the tombs of Jacob, Leah, Isaac, Rebecca, Sarah, and Abraham."

"The Biblical figures?"

"Yes." Marcus could barely speak. "Biblical figures who are all related to Aaron."

"I don't understand the connection."

"Sara...they're all thought to have lived for hundreds of years."

"I don't—oh." Sara's eyes widened. "You think that if a person could heal from any wound..."

"Then they could live a really long time," said Marcus, finishing her thought.

"Oh, my God."

"Right? And this would explain why Actaeon tried to have you killed when you published your preprint. When you discovered archaic genomes, you might have accidentally stumbled onto genetic evidence that there are people who are immortal. They shouldn't have called it the Lazarus Factor. In truth, it's the Methuselah Factor."

———

Marcus opened his eyes, startled awake. Soft light filtered through the curtains. Birds chirped outside. Distantly, he heard the rumble of a car engine. But otherwise, it was peaceful. What had roused him?

It certainly wasn't Sara. She was curled up under the covers, sound asleep. He studied her for a long moment. Her head haloed by light brown hair. Her eyes closed. Her breathing even and slow. He smiled. They hadn't exactly gone to bed early.

He tried again to remember what had woken him. Not a dream—he'd been too tired for those. He squinted his eyes, trying to recall. But whatever it had been, it was gone.

His stirring must have woken Sara, for she mumbled something that sounded a lot like "Coffee?"

Not a bad idea.

He kissed her lightly on the cheek, then slipped out of bed and padded into the living room. Her apartment was small, but it was well-appointed, with lots of plants and windows. In the kitchen, a drip coffee maker stood next to the sink along with a tin labeled "Coffee." Sara had everything organized and clearly labeled. No question this was the apartment of a scientist. Before she visited his place, he'd have to do some serious tidying.

Marcus put in a clean filter and fresh grounds, poured some water in the reservoir, then hit the on button. As the coffee perked, he tried again to remember what had woken him. It had been something important. An idea…or some sort of insight.

He rubbed his eyes. He shouldn't have drunk so much wine.

But they'd been celebrating. They'd solved the puzzle. Worked out what Alexi and Frank had wanted kept secret. Why Enora had flown out to the Krateros. There were literally people who lived forever. He felt himself grinning. It was insane. The most important discovery of all time.

And of course, they couldn't tell anyone.

Well, technically, *he* could. Frank hadn't forced *him* to

agree to be quiet. And Enora's NDA was a non-issue now that she was dead. Still, revealing the truth would jeopardize Sara's arrangement, and without rock-solid evidence, no one would believe him, anyway.

He sighed. It was pretty fucking frustrating.

As the coffee maker burbled, he mulled over something Sara had told him. She'd said he'd worked something out, just before Alexi had impaled him. He strained his brain to remember it, but that, too, was gone.

Maybe it'd come to him after he'd had some coffee. And something to eat.

He considered going out and getting bagels, but he didn't want to leave the apartment yet. He went to the fridge, which was as neatly organized as everything else. She had eggs, creamer, cheese, various pieces of produce, a package of fake bacon. He pulled out the bacon, the carton of eggs, and a hunk of cheddar. He'd make breakfast sandwiches.

A cast-iron skillet rested on the stovetop. He gave it a quick rinse, then turned on the burner. While the pan heated, he poured himself a cup of coffee and took a long sip. Absolutely delicious.

He was reaching for the package of bacon when it hit him. The insight that had woken him.

He nearly fell over.

"Sara!" he shouted. "Get up! It's important."

Ten seconds later, Sara burst from the bedroom, wrapped in a blanket. "Marcus? Is everything okay?" Her voice was tinged with panic.

"I'm fine." He pointed to the table. "You need to sit down."

She gave him a look that suggested she thought he might have gone crazy, but she sat. He poured her a cup of coffee.

"Okay," he said breathlessly. "This is going to sound completely insane."

Sara nodded.

"I know who Frank is."

Sara's eyes widened. "You do?"

"Yes. Remember how you said Ike referred to Alexi as Alexander? Well, I was thinking, what if Frank's name was a nickname, too?"

"I thought it's short for François. François Gammon."

"Right. But Gammon is a nickname, too. Gammon is a type of cured pork." Marcus held up the package of bacon. "It's a fancy French word for bacon."

He smiled at Sara.

She looked blankly back at him for a long moment, and then her eyes widened in understanding. "No way. Frank… Bacon. He's Sir Francis Bacon."

Marcus was having a hard time modulating his voice. "We know they can live forever. And get this: Sir Francis Bacon was a Rosicrucian!"

"Oh, my God!" Sara leaped up, nearly spilling her coffee. "That would explain Frank's interest in science. He—Sir Francis Bacon—literally developed the scientific method."

"He was also one of the founding members of the Royal Society…which used to meet at Somerset House."

"Holy shit, Marcus. You've figured it out."

Marcus grinned. "I may not be a scientist, but I am a science reporter."

"What about Alexi?" Sara asked. "On the boat, it was Alexi, not Frank, that you thought you knew something about."

"I still don't remember any of that," Marcus said, but I have a thought. "Google 'Alexander the Great.'"

"You think?"

"Just google him."

Marcus paced as Sara typed in the search. He was already pretty sure this was right, but he wanted Sara to confirm.

"Okay, I've got his Wikipedia up."

"What does it say about his appearance?"

"Stocky, with brown hair—"

"Does it say anything about his eyes?"

Sara scanned the article. Then her hands dropped to her lap, and she just stared at him. "Wikipedia says they were heterochromatic. One was brown, one was blue."

"Which is something I knew—or thought I remembered, anyway. I just wanted to check to be sure."

"Wow. Alexi was Alexander the Great..." Sara said. Then something else occurred to her. She looked up at Marcus once more. "I think I met a Nazi."

"Really?"

"Yeah, but on the plus side, he's dead." She told him about the photo on Karl's bedside table. If he'd had a long life, too, that wasn't a photo of some relative; that was a photo of Karl himself.

"What about Ike?" she said. "Or Isaac. Who was he?"

Marcus thought back over what he knew about Ike. He was British, and he and Frank knew each other—though if both had been alive for centuries, they would have met thousands of people.

Sara thought of the answer first. "Isaac Newton," she said quietly.

For a long moment, they just stared at each other.

"It fits," said Marcus at last. "Isaac Newton was an alchemist. And he was a member of the Royal Society."

Sara shook her head. "I can't believe I met Isaac Newton and Sir Francis Bacon. Oh, I wish you could publish this in *The New York Times*!"

Marcus laughed. "It would never get past my editor. It's the most insane story I've ever heard. We have no proof, most of them are dead, and like you said, there isn't enough genomic evidence."

"And it's not like Frank is ever going to reveal to the world who he is," Sara said. "Their whole thing is secrecy."

"We may not be able to publish this," said Marcus. "But there is one thing we can do."

"What's that?" Sara asked.

He grinned. "I could cook you breakfast, and then we could go back to bed."

Sara flashed him a cheeky smile.

CHAPTER 79
HIMALAYAS

Tibet Autonomous Region
7:13 AM, June 25th

———

It felt like someone was whacking Frank's head with a cricket bat, a hard pounding just above his eyes. At nearly fourteen thousand feet, his body simply didn't have enough red blood cells to keep his brain properly oxygenated. The result was a brutal headache.

On the plus side, the views were spectacular. Above him towered snowcapped peaks, while below, the valley floor was covered in a primordial forest. The air was still. The only movement came from a few distantly circling birds.

He'd arrived late the night before, exhausted from the long climb up the mountainside. Even so, he'd woken at dawn.

Between the altitude sickness and the noise, it was hard not to. The monks were up at first light for morning prayers. For a few minutes, he'd listened to them pray, then wandered outside the main gate to admire the view and try to clear his head.

He was rubbing his temples when a voice interrupted, "Mr. Gammon?"

It was a young monk dressed in simple burgundy-colored robes—a *novice*, if he remembered correctly. "Yes, that's me."

"The abbot is ready for you."

The monk beckoned, and Frank followed him through a small courtyard, passing by the main temple, to the residential quarters. The novice led him inside, then down a short hallway to a small study.

"Wait here," said the novice, gesturing to an ancient sofa.

The novice left, and Frank was alone.

The floor of the study was covered in faded rugs, and the walls, once brightly painted in yellow, red, blue, and green stripes, were now stained with candle soot. The herbal scent of Tibetan incense permeated the air. From a pair of open windows, he could hear the murmuring sounds of monks praying and the faint twitter of birdsong.

After a few minutes, the door to the study opened. Frank stood as the abbot entered. Like the novice, the abbot wore burgundy robes. His hair was cropped short, his skin deeply lined. He looked at Frank, and his expression was soft, almost sad.

"So it's true, then? Alexander and Isaac are dead?"

Frank nodded. "Drowned. Even you and I cannot survive at the bottom of the sea."

The abbot looked down, his lips moving in silent prayer. When he looked up, his eyes were shining with tears. "Alexander was a good man. Honorable. Brave."

"A man like him can never be dissuaded once he sets his mind to a task. That's what made him great." Frank laughed at his joke, then his expression shaded. "They killed his *eromenos*. He would never let that go."

"He was trying to protect us."

"I had it under control."

The abbot crossed to the nearest window and looked out. "So what now? They are still a threat, are they not? They know the truth about what we are. I don't like killing, but what other choice do we have?"

"They won't talk."

"How can you be sure?"

"No one will believe them. They have no proof." Frank shook his head. "You should never have sent a hound. You overreacted."

The abbot idly traced a finger along the windowsill, mulling this over.

"I will keep an eye on them," said Frank. "I promise our secret will remain safe."

Slowly, the abbot turned from the window. "All right. I can live with that." He held out a hand. "A deal, Francis?"

"A deal, Genghis."

They shook, and then the abbot laughed. "Now that's a name I've not heard in a very long time."

Mailing List

Discord

Thank you for reading **The Lazarus Factor**.

You can join my reader group on Discord to talk to me and other readers about the book. Or, if you only want to hear about new releases, you can sign up to my newsletter at nickcrowauthor.com/email-list.

ACKNOWLEDGMENTS

―――

First and foremost, I must thank my wife and fellow author Christine. She's amazing in so many ways and offered extremely helpful comments throughout the process. I also thank David Gatewood for his detailed edits and critiques, Lauren Simpson for proofreading, Rick Gualtieri and Michael Omer for beta-reading early drafts, Nick Sullivan for bringing Sara and Marcus to life in audio, Damonza and Shayne Rutherford for designing the book covers, and JABberwocky Literary Agency for representing this work.

Several friends and colleagues provided valuable technical feedback. They include Dr. Bebo Seward for his unique Md/Ph.D. perspective, Dr. Yuanqing Feng who helped with the SCID mouse scene, Dr. Yoson Park who gave very thoughtful sensitivity suggestions, Detective Sergeant Benjamin Katz for the low down on morgues, Retired Chief Warrant Officer Paul Deaver whose advice significantly improved the helicopter scene, and Perry Wright for help with the cover design.

I would be remiss not to acknowledge the mentors who guided me along my scientific journey. Dr. Sarah Tishkoff took me into her lab and taught me all about human genomics. I owe her an enormous debt of gratitude. I also thank Drs Pytel, Reeder, Glenn, Schneider, Benson, Hokestra, Losos, Mullen, Simison, Kapan, and Tishkoff (yet again!), who helped shepherd and guide me through my bachelor's, Master's, Ph.D., and beyond.

Lastly, I thank all my author friends, particularly those in Author's Corner.

SELECTED REFERENCES

———

Here are a few references loosely grouped. Note that in some (many) cases, I embellished or outright lied about the findings. For example, at the time of publishing, there's no evidence that *Homo sapiens* and *Homo floresiensis* ever interbred.

Genomic Resources:
Mallick, S., Li, H., Lipson, M., Mathieson, I., Gymrek, M., Racimo, F., Zhao, M., Chennagiri, N., Nordenfelt, S., Tandon, A., Skoglund, P., Lazaridis, I., Sankararaman, S., Fu, Q., Rohland, N., Renaud, G., Erlich, Y., Willems, T., Gallo, C., Spence, J. P., ... Reich, D. (2016). The Simons Genome Diversity Project: 300 genomes from 142 diverse populations. Nature, 538(7624), 201–206. https://doi.org/10.1038/nature18964

1000 Genomes Project Consortium, Auton, A., Brooks, L. D., Durbin, R. M., Garrison, E. P., Kang, H. M., Korbel, J. O., Marchini, J. L., McCarthy, S., McVean, G. A., & Abecasis, G. R. (2015). A global reference for human genetic variation. *Nature, 526*(7571), 68–74. https://doi.org/10.1038/nature15393

Saydnaya Prison:
Amnesty International, Human Slaughterhouse: Mass Hangings and Extermination at Saydnaya Prison, Syria, 7 February 2017, available at: https://www.refworld.org/docid/5899bd9a4.html

Archaic Introgression and Ghost Genomes:
Durvasula, A., & Sankararaman, S. (2020). Recovering signals of ghost archaic introgression in African populations. Science advances, 6(7), eaax5097. https://doi.org/10.1126/sciadv.aax5097

***Homo floresiensis* Interbreeding and Genomics:**
Tucci, S., Vohr, S. H., McCoy, R. C., Vernot, B., Robinson, M. R., Barbieri, C., Nelson, B. J., Fu, W., Purnomo, G. A., Sudoyo, H., Eichler, E. E., Barbujani, G., Visscher, P. M., Akey, J. M., & Green, R. E. (2018). Evolutionary history and adaptation of a human pygmy population of Flores Island, Indonesia.

Science (New York, N.Y.), 361(6401), 511–516. https://doi.org/10.1126/science.aar8486

Neanderthal and Denisovan Interbreeding:
Slon, V., Mafessoni, F., Vernot, B., de Filippo, C., Grote, S., Viola, B., Hajdinjak, M., Peyrégne, S., Nagel, S., Brown, S., Douka, K., Higham, T., Kozlikin, M. B., Shunkov, M. V., Derevianko, A. P., Kelso, J., Meyer, M., Prüfer, K., & Pääbo, S. (2018). The genome of the offspring of a Neanderthal mother and a Denisovan father. Nature, 561(7721), 113–116. https://doi.org/10.1038/s41586-018-0455-x

Sequence Contamination:
Jun, G., Flickinger, M., Hetrick, K. N., Romm, J. M., Doheny, K. F., Abecasis, G. R., Boehnke, M., & Kang, H. M. (2012). Detecting and estimating contamination of human DNA samples in sequencing and array-based genotype data. American journal of human genetics, 91(5), 839–848. https://doi.org/10.1016/j.ajhg.2012.09.004

Fiévet, A., Bernard, V., Tenreiro, H., Dehainault, C., Girard, E., Deshaies, V., Hupe, P., Delattre, O., Stern, M. H., Stoppa-Lyonnet, D., Golmard, L., & Houdayer, C. (2019). ART-DeCo: easy tool for detection and characterization of cross-contamination of DNA samples in diagnostic next-generation sequencing analysis. European journal of human genetics: EJHG, 27(5), 792–800. https://doi.org/10.1038/s41431-018-0317-x

Genome Dating (MSMC):
Schiffels, S., & Wang, K. (2020). MSMC and MSMC2: The Multiple Sequentially Markovian Coalescent. Methods in molecular biology (Clifton, N.J.), 2090, 147–166. https://doi.org/10.1007/978-1-0716-0199-0_7

Cohen Modal Haplotype:
Hammer MF, Behar DM, Karafet TM, Mendez FL, Hallmark B, Erez T, Zhivotovsky LA, Rosset S, Skorecki K. Extended Y chromosome haplotypes resolve multiple and unique lineages of the Jewish priesthood. Hum Genet. 2009 Nov;126(5):707-17. doi: 10.1007/s00439-009-0727-5. Epub 2009 Aug 8. PMID: 19669163; PMCID: PMC2771134.

The Genetic Cost of Neanderthal Introgression:
Harris, K., & Nielsen, R. (2016). The Genetic Cost of Neanderthal Introgression. Genetics, 203(2), 881–891. https://doi.org/10.1534/genetics.116.186890

Berens, A. J., Cooper, T. L., & Lachance, J. (2017). The Genomic Health of Ancient Hominins. *Human biology, 89*(1), 7–19. https://doi.org/10.13110/humanbiology.89.1.01